D0445437

MONTANA BRANCH
Santa Monica Public Library

AUG - - 2015

~The~

Nightmare
Dilemma

Tor Teen Books by Mindee Arnett

The Nightmare Affair
The Nightmare Dilemma

The Nightmare Dilemma

MINDEE ARNETT

TOR®
TEEN

A Tom Doherty Associates Book

NEW YORK

This is a work of fiction. All of the characters, organizations, and events portrayed in this novel are either products of the author's imagination or are used fictitiously.

THE NIGHTMARE DILEMMA

Copyright © 2014 by Mindee Arnett

All rights reserved.

A Tor Teen Book
Published by Tom Doherty Associates, LLC
175 Fifth Avenue
New York, NY 10010

www.tor-forge.com

Tor® is a registered trademark of Tom Doherty Associates, LLC.

Library of Congress Cataloging-in-Publication Data

Arnett, Mindee.
    The Nightmare dilemma / Mindee Arnett.—First ed.
        p. cm.
    "A Tom Doherty Associates book."
    ISBN 978-0-7653-3334-6 (hardcover)
    ISBN 978-1-4668-0068-7 (e-book)
    1. Magic—Fiction. 2. Supernatural—Fiction. 3. Dreams—Fiction.
4. Boarding schools—Fiction. 5. Schools—Fiction. 6. Mystery and
detective stories. I. Title.
    PZ7.A7343NK 2014
    [Fic]—dc23

                                                        2013039498

Tor Teen books may be purchased for educational, business, or promotional use. For information on bulk purchases, please contact Macmillan Corporate and Premium Sales Department at 1-800-221-7945, extension 5442, or write specialmarkets@macmillan.com.

First Edition: March 2014

Printed in the United States of America

0 9 8 7 6 5 4 3 2 1

To Betty Garybush, for lighting the way

Acknowledgments

As always, thanks to God and his Son.

Thanks also: to my rock star editor, Whitney Ross, for your love and support of these characters and this story, and for making it better with your magical insight. To the team at Tor Teen for your ongoing support—Lisa Davis, my production editor; Amy Saxon, assistant editor; Seth Lerner, the art director; Jane Liddle, the copy editor; Sally Feller, my publicist; and John Morrone, the proofreader. And a huge standing ovation to Tom Doherty and Kathleen Doherty—you are the best.

This book would not exist without the enthusiasm and support from my agent, Suzie Townsend. Thank you for everything you do, which I know is more than I will ever realize. Same goes for the entire crew of New Leaf Literary and Media who have helped me turn my hobby into a career—Joanna Volpe, Kathleen Ortiz, Pouya Shahbazian, Danielle Barthel, and Jaida Temperly.

To the Usual Suspects of Awesome, my critique partners and beta readers: Amanda Sharritt, Lori M. Lee, Cat York, Sarah Goldberg, Kathy Bradey, Farrah Penn, Mallory Hayes, and Jason Sharritt.

To all the readers, librarians, bloggers, and book enthusiasts for giving stories like this and writers like me purpose.

And finally to my family, who puts up with the long hours and crazy up-and-down days. You make the magic possible.

The
Nightmare
Dilemma

∼ 1 ∼

Where No Nightmare Has Gone Before

The mermaid was lying on the hospital bed, looking distinctly un-mermaidish. And not just because she was in her human form. Britney Shell looked more like a zombie with her skin the color of cigar ash and ghoulish lines of black stitches across her forehead, cheeks, and neck.

I turned to face the only other person in the room, the woman who'd summoned me out of my dorm in the middle of the night to the school's infirmary for a reason I was sure I didn't want to know. Lady Elaine stood near the foot of the bed, her pale, cloudy eyes fixed on Britney. She was an old woman, and tiny, hardly bigger than a kid. But that didn't make her any less intimidating. As a chief advisor to the Magi Senate, her presence at Arkwell Academy meant trouble.

"What happened to her?" I said.

A grimace crossed Lady Elaine's thin face, turning the wrinkles into deep crevices. "We don't know. That's why you're here. To help us find out."

"Me? What can I do?"

"You're a Nightmare."

I frowned. Not because this was an insult or anything. It was true. I am a Nightmare, or at least a half one. My mom's a full Nightmare, but my dad's an ordinary human. Not that you can tell by looking at me. For the most part, Nightmares look like ordinaries, but we're magical beings who feed on human dreams.

"You want me to dream-feed on her?"

"Precisely," Lady Elaine said, clanking her teeth.

I didn't know why I was surprised. There wasn't any other reason a person as important as Lady Elaine would want someone like me here. Britney and I were friends, but given the number of magickind police officers waiting out in the hallway, I didn't think this was a bedside vigil.

I shifted my weight from one foot to the other. "How's that supposed to help? Dream-feeding doesn't heal people, right? I mean, if it does, then calling my kind Nightmares is like false advertisement."

Lady Elaine scowled. "Now's not the time for cheek, Destiny Everhart."

"It's Dusty," I mumbled, looking back at Britney. Guilt made my skin prickle. Lady Elaine was right. Now wasn't the time for smart-ass remarks, but I couldn't help it. Seeing Britney like this freaked me out, an event that never failed to make my mouth run away with me.

Lady Elaine let out an exaggerated sigh. Out of the corner of my eye, I watched her turn and sit down in a chair on the other side of the bed. Like everything else in the room, the chair was the mottled gray color of cinder blocks. Lady Elaine's feet dangled two inches above the ground. "You're here because you might be able to identify Britney's attacker by what you see in her dream."

More confused than ever, I swung toward her. It wasn't the first time I'd been asked to identify a bad guy through someone's dream. A few months ago I discovered I was a dream-seer, that I could see the future in certain dreams. But . . .

"I thought my dream-seer skills only work in Eli's dreams."

Lady Elaine waved a hand at me. "I'm not asking you to predict the future but to read the past."

"Huh?"

She sighed again, clearly at the end of her patience. Not that this was anything new. She crossed one leg over the other, feet swinging. "Whoever attacked Britney did so less than an hour ago. And as far as we can tell, she's been in a constant dream-state ever since. If she saw the person, there's a good chance his image has left a residue on her dream."

"A residue?"

"Yes, a *magical* residue," said Lady Elaine. "She was hit by a powerful curse. One we haven't been able to identify yet. But all magic leaves traces of the person who wielded it, and only a very few magickind would be skilled enough to remove those traces."

I considered the idea, pushing back strands of my curly red hair that had escaped my haphazard ponytail. "So it's kind of like a fingerprint or DNA."

Lady Elaine gave me a blank stare.

I crossed my arms, wishing I'd worn something more substantial than a hoodie, hastily donned over my pink-and-red-striped pajamas. The mid-April rain outside tapped against the windowpane, putting a damp chill in the air. "You know, like forensic science stuff. How ordinary cops figure out who the bad guy is."

Lady Elaine's stare deepened toward incredulity.

I couldn't figure out what her deal was. Most magickind were junkies for ordinary pop culture. "Don't you watch TV?"

She looked taken aback by the question, but recovered quickly. "Not *those* kinds of shows."

I raised an eyebrow, wondering what kinds of shows she *did* watch.

"But I suppose your interpretation is correct," said Lady Elaine. "It is something like magical DNA."

Which made me the scientist in this scenario. What a joke.

Still, I didn't protest as I turned my gaze back to Britney. If she'd been hit by a curse, then it was my fault. I might not have done the actual cursing, but I'd played a big part in making it possible for magickind to use combative spells whenever they wanted. It used to be that such magic was prohibited by The Will, a massive spell designed to keep magickind in line. But I inadvertently helped destroy The Will a couple of months ago. At least I'd been fighting an evil warlock at the time, one with Hitlerish ideas about world domination.

Small comfort now.

And no comfort at all to Britney. She looked miserable, her expression pained even in sleep. Her eyelids quivered as her eyes pulsed back and forth beneath them.

Even though I knew I was responsible, I didn't want to dream-feed on her. What if I messed up? I might miss something important.

I cleared my throat. "Isn't there some other Nightmare better qualified?"

"No," Lady Elaine said, a pointed edge to her voice. "Well, yes, there are certainly others more qualified, but none available tonight. Someone else was supposed to be here, but they've been delayed, Bethany Grey is still imprisoned, and your mother is still out of town. Which leaves only you."

I swallowed hard, my stomach twisting into a knot. The pathetically small number of Nightmares in existence wasn't something I wanted to think about right now. This attack on Britney was just another in a string of magickind-on-magickind violence that had been happening since The Will broke. The same kind of violence responsible for my lack of Nightmare relatives.

Screwing up my courage, I said, "So you want me to figure out who she's dreaming about."

Lady Elaine gave me a tight-lipped smile. "Yes. Just observe and report."

Sounded simple enough, although in my experience nothing to do with magic was ever simple.

I drew a breath. "Okay, but tell me more first. Who found her? Where was she?"

Lady Elaine frowned. "There's no time for details. She might stop dreaming any moment, and the longer we wait the fainter the residue becomes."

"I get it, but her dreams aren't going to be all clear like Eli's. If I've any hope of spotting the person, I need to know more about what to look for."

This sounded mostly true, even to my ears, but secretly I was thinking about how if Eli were here he would demand to know more. Ever since we defeated the evil warlock, Marrow, he'd had his heart set on starting an amateur student detective agency. We'd worked one minor "case" involving a stolen necklace, but this was the first hard-core mystery. He would want to investigate. As always, thoughts of Eli made me feel both flustered and comforted at the same time, a result of our more-than-friends-but-not-really status.

"Fine." Lady Elaine stood up, her heels giving a little click as her feet touched the floor. She marched past me out the door. I heard a murmur of voices, and then she reentered the room, followed by a tall, hairy-looking man in a dark blue policeman's uniform.

Sheriff Brackenberry fixed an irritated look at me. It was the same look he'd given me when I arrived a few minutes ago and Lady Elaine had asked him to wait out in the hall. I couldn't decide if his irritation was strictly for me or just a side effect of being bossed around by a little old lady. Probably both. I smiled sheepishly back at him, trying to win him over. Not only was he the magickind sheriff, he was also head werewolf, which made him only slightly less scary than Lady Elaine.

"We need to hurry this up," said Brackenberry. "Britney here is due to be transferred to Vejovis Hospital as soon as you're done."

The knot in my stomach twisted harder. Her injuries must be pretty bad if they were sending her there. I opened my mouth to tell him no need to bother with the details, but he started speaking before I got the chance.

"She was discovered at approximately eleven forty-five P.M. by Ms. Hardwick in one of the alcoves of the tunnel between the library and Flint Hall," said Brackenberry.

I grimaced at this news. Ms. Hardwick was the school janitor and resident hag. Definitely not the kind of person I wanted to meet inside a dream. Especially one other than Eli's. With any luck, she hadn't been involved, although I wouldn't put it past her.

"There was no apparent sign of a struggle," Brackenberry went on. "But Britney was lying half in, half out of the water, which suggests she might've been trying to flee her attacker. It appears Ms. Hardwick arrived only minutes afterward, but she didn't see anyone else." Brackenberry's tone turned scornful. "Is that enough information for you?"

I gulped. "I think I can make do with it."

"Well, go on then." He shooed at me.

I bit my lip. "Would you, um, mind leaving again?" Dream-feeding was kind of personal, and the last thing I wanted was a male audience.

If I'd been a bowl of ice cream I might have melted on the spot from the hot intensity of his stare. I glanced at Lady Elaine, hoping for some support, but she looked as impatient as the sheriff.

Resigning myself to the inevitable, I walked around to the side of the bed. I was just about to climb onto it and resume the proper Nightmare position, when I remembered a mere touch would do. I closed my eyes and reached my hands toward Britney's forehead.

"What are you doing?" Lady Elaine said.

I looked over my shoulder. "Checking her temperature."

She stomped her foot. "Not like that. This is too important, Dusty. You need to be in the traditional position to get the deepest connection to her dreams."

It was my turn to scowl as I climbed onto the bed. I hadn't dream-fed on anyone besides Eli in a long while. And feeding on a girl, especially one my age, just felt weird. There was nothing sexual about dream-feeding, but the pose was a bit on the lewd side.

I swung one foot over Britney's middle. Then I squatted down onto her chest, doing my best to keep as much weight off her as I could. I wasn't that heavy, but Britney was smaller than me, and I didn't want to hurt her.

As always, the moment I was in place, instinct took over. Britney was dreaming, all right. The stuff of those dreams, the fictus, made something deep inside me burn with a terrible thirst. A thirst for magic.

Closing my eyes, I stretched my hands toward her temple. When my skin touched hers, I felt my consciousness slip from my body and slide down, down, down into the world of Britney's dream.

A swirl of colors—a chaotic mixture of blues, purples, and greens—enveloped me like some kind of living light, warm and pulsating with energy. It lasted a long time before the chaos settled, and I found myself in a dark, damp cave. A single torch hung nearby, its light making the wet walls around it glisten and reflecting in the water from the canal that ran parallel to the walkway I stood on. To my left and right, the canal and walkway disappeared into the blackness of a long tunnel. Across from me, the canal widened into a small, circular pool, one of the many alcoves in Arkwell's tunnel system.

The clarity of my surroundings surprised me. Most dreams, aside from Eli's, were confused, disorienting things, usually in black-and-white, but this place was so real for a moment I thought I'd been transported here in the waking world.

The illusion broke almost at once. The walls began to lean inward, as if the tunnel were being drawn in on itself. The natural orange glow of the torch turned a molten red. And the water began to bubble and spurt in a rapid boil.

A scream rang out even louder than the raging water. I looked down to see Britney's head break the surface of the alcove's pool. I'd never seen her in her natural mermaid form, but I knew her skin should be pale, almost translucent, not the angry red color it was now. Blisters popped up on her skin. She was being cooked alive.

No, this wasn't real. This wasn't even a dream.

It was a nightmare.

My first instinct was to change the dream, manipulate the

setting to somewhere safe and calm, but I resisted. Observe and report, Lady Elaine had said.

It was hard, especially as Britney swam toward the edge of the pool, struggling to pull herself out of the water. I wanted to help her, but I couldn't, not here. Any physical contact with my dream-subject and I would be kicked out.

I closed my eyes, unable to watch any longer. I was about to cover my ears when everything went silent. I opened my eyes again, relieved to see the scene had shifted on its own. The tunnel had given way to a strange, small room with bright, colorful walls. I felt oddly weightless, and as strands of my red hair swam into my vision, I realized I was under water. As soon as I thought it, I became aware of the wetness and a sudden need to breathe.

Britney floated a few feet away from me in her mermaid form, her long tail a strawberry pink color that matched her hair. I focused my imagination on copying her form, and a moment later my body had transformed into a mermaid and my panic subsided.

I looked around at what I guessed was her bedroom. No furniture decorated the place, unless you counted the gigantic sea anemone growing along one side of the room that looked big enough to sleep in. But there was something personal and bedroom-ish about the trinkets set on the floor-to-ceiling shelves built into the coral walls.

Before I could examine the items, an odd, garbled, shrieking sound drew my attention. It seemed to be coming from Britney, who had her back to me. I swam to the left to see around her. Another mermaid floated in a small opening into the room. She had the same strawberry pink-colored hair, and I guessed it was Britney's mother. They were arguing. Loudly. But in mermench.

Even though I couldn't understand them, there was no mistaking the animosity. Fury seemed to emanate from both, but when I cast a sideways glance at Britney, she looked frightened, too.

The scene changed once more, the colors melting and bleeding together before righting again. This time Britney and I stood in the middle of a forest full of dead, deteriorated trees like hundreds of brittle finger bones sticking up from the earth. A stream full of glowing green water ran sluggishly through the trees. Garbage lined its banks. A terrible chemical smell hung in the air, burning my nose. The stench of rotting fish blended in with it. Several animals moved among the trees, all of them looking as sick and listless as the water in the stream. A deer hobbled past me on three legs, scorch marks on its body.

The scene shifted again. We were back in the tunnel, but the water no longer boiled. This time Britney stood beside the alcove's pool in her human form, her hair more blond than pink, her skin fair but not covered in translucent scales. A dark figure stood a few feet down the tunnel across from her, face hidden in shadows.

The residue. I moved toward the figure, eager to see his face and leave this dream behind. But the scene shifted again, back to the underwater bedroom. The change was so abrupt, I fought back dizziness. Pinwheeling my arms through the water, I focused on Britney still caught up in the argument with her mother.

A moment later, we were back in the forest. But as with the tunnel scene, we were no longer alone. Britney was arguing with a guy, one whose face made my heartbeat double and all the air vanish from my lungs. Paul Foster Kirkwood, my ex-boyfriend.

What was he doing in Britney's dream? For a moment, I thought he must be her attacker, until I remembered that Paul was in jail, awaiting trial for his involvement with Marrow's scheme to overthrow the magickind government.

I took a step toward him and realized it wasn't Paul, not exactly, but close, as if Britney had seen the real Paul but her dreaming mind had forgotten the details.

The scene shifted again, back to the tunnel. After that, the changes started happening so quickly, my vision blurred as if I were riding an ultrafast merry-go-round. I tried to close my eyes, but couldn't. I kept catching glimpses of the almost-Paul and Britney's mother, even Britney herself, crying out in pain.

Finally, when I didn't think I could stand it any longer, I reached out with my Nightmare magic and willed the dream to stop its chaotic swirl. At once, everything went still.

The scene before me was the strangest yet. It seemed to be a mash-up of the three scenes, blended into one. I stood in the tunnel again, but the walls were now made up of those spindly, dead trees. The canal water glowed the same sickly green of the stream. It wasn't boiling. In fact it wasn't moving at all, but looked as if it had been frozen in place.

Glancing around, I realized that everything was frozen, including Britney, who hung suspended mid-jump into the pool. A look of terror darkened her features. Behind her, I saw the shadowed figure again, frozen as well, but in an attack position, one arm stretched out in front of him as if he were hurling a knife at Britney's back.

I took a step toward the figure, and pictured a flashlight in my hand. It appeared there at once. I switched it on and shone it at the person. He carried a wand, held out in front of him like a gun. I raised the light to his face and let out an involuntary gasp of alarm. It wasn't Paul, as I'd expected. It wasn't even Britney's mother.

It was Eli Booker.

~ 2 ~

Dream a Little Dream

*D*reams are symbolic, not literal. *Dreams are symbolic, not literal.* I told myself this over and over as I walked back to my dorm room, escorted by a silent, lumbering werewolf policeman. It was a futile attempt to staunch the guilt bubbling up inside me with every step. I hadn't told Lady Elaine about Eli. I just couldn't. It seemed too much like a betrayal. Eli was my . . . friend? Partner?

Soul mate.

No, we weren't even together. But there was definitely something between us. It had been there since the night we defeated Marrow. Since the night he kissed me.

The policeman left me at the bottom of the stairs leading up to Riker Hall. I climbed them slowly, my mind full of the images from Britney's dreams. Seeing Paul in there was almost as troublesome as seeing Eli. I couldn't think of any reason why Britney would dream about Paul. As far as I knew, they'd never met. Paul was a senior, two grades above Britney and me. Sure, everybody knew who he was now because of all the press about his involvement with Marrow. But that didn't seem a strong enough reason for his presence. He was more likely to haunt my nightmares than Britney's.

Still, when I mentioned him, Lady Elaine had dismissed it. Paul was in jail. There was no way it could've been him. Then she pointed out that Britney wasn't a dream-seer, which meant her dream was just a dream and nothing more.

When I emerged into the foyer, I gave a half-hearted wave to Frank and Igor, Riker Hall's resident suits of armor and security guards. Frank bowed his head in my direction. The knights used to ignore my greetings, but lately they seemed to be developing more prominent personalities from the animation effect of magic and electricity. It wasn't surprising, honestly. Since The Will broke, the amount of magic usage on campus had gone up a thousand percent.

I went faster up the three flights of steps to my floor, eager to talk to my roommate. Selene hadn't woken up when the policemen knocked on our door an hour ago to fetch me down to the infirmary, but I would wake her now. I needed her to validate my reasons for not telling Lady Elaine the whole truth of Britney's dream. The idea of Eli being the attacker was absurd. He couldn't even do magic. He was an ordinary, just like my dad and all my old friends at my old ordinary high school. The only reason why he attended Arkwell now was because of the dream-seer stuff.

Feeling better already, I pushed open the door to my dorm and let it swing closed harder than normal. I glanced expectantly at the doorway from the living area into the bedroom, but nothing seemed to be moving in there.

Stifling yet more guilt at the idea of disturbing Selene's sleep, I walked into the bedroom and approached her bed on the far wall, opposite mine. The light from the living area illuminated just enough that I could see Selene's massive poster of a teenaged Bob Dylan hung over the foot of the bed. Even though Dylan was an ordinary, he was Selene's favorite musician. She believed he possessed some diluted strain of siren blood. I doubted it, but Selene insisted no ordinary could be that good without some kind of magic. Me, I thought it was more a matter of opinion.

I stopped and looked down at the bed, my brain slowly processing what my eyes had been telling me for the last thirty seconds. Selene was gone. I touched the mattress, confirming it.

Where was she? It didn't make sense. There was nowhere else for her to be but here. It was a Monday night and well past curfew. I thought back to those few seconds it had taken me to climb out of bed and answer the door when the werewolf policemen had come knocking. Had she been there then? I thought so, but I hadn't actually checked. Come to think of it, it was a little weird that she hadn't woken up, too. She was a light sleeper, normally.

I walked over to my nightstand and picked up my cell phone. As usual, it had taken the liberty of shutting itself off during the night, its surly personality a result of the animation effect. I pressed the on button and waited impatiently for it to boot up.

No messages. No missed calls.

I dialed Selene's number and let it ring until her voice mail picked up. Then I texted her and waited for a response. Fifteen minutes later I was still waiting. I checked the desk and the nightstand to see if she'd left her cell phone but didn't find it. A cursory glance at her shoes lined up neatly on the floor of her closet showed me her black boots were missing. Wherever she was, she'd gone deliberately. Under normal circumstances, I wouldn't have been too worried, but considering what had happened to Britney, I couldn't help feeling a little concerned.

I sat down on my bed and sent Selene another text. It took me the better part of five minutes to type it, as my cell kept shutting off, making obnoxious twittering sounds as it did so. It was supposed to be a smartphone—oh, the irony.

I was just about to hurl the damn thing across the room, when the door into the dorm opened and a disheveled-looking Selene stepped inside. She was indeed wearing her black boots as well as camo jacket and matching camo ball cap and black pants. Her outfit wasn't particularly suspicious—Selene had been rocking the tomboy look for more than a year now—but the telltale wetness on her hair told me she'd been outside.

I just stared at her for a moment. She stared back, her mouth dropping open as if I had taken her by surprise rather than the other way around.

I stood up, narrowing my eyes at her. "Where the hell have you been?"

Right away I knew I'd struck the wrong tone as Selene's surprised expression turned stormy. Never mind that my harsh tone stemmed from fear rather than anger. She put a hand on her narrow waist and flung her black hair over her shoulder. "What's it to you?"

I gaped. "What do you mean? You were gone. You snuck out in the middle of the night. Without me."

Selene's nostrils flared. "It might come as a surprise, Dusty, but my life doesn't end and begin with *you*."

I took an involuntary step back. She might as well have slapped me. Selene never acted like this. Not toward me.

She bit her lip, a stricken expression crossing her face. "I'm sorry. I didn't mean to snap. It's just . . . I didn't think you'd be awake."

I crossed my arms, her apology having little effect on my

tumultuous emotions. Anger and hurt were stubborn that way, quick to come and long to leave.

When I didn't answer, Selene unzipped her coat and flung it over the nearby sofa. "So why are you awake?"

I fought back the automatic instinct to answer her. We were best friends. We shared everything—or so I thought. I opened my mouth to demand she tell me what she'd been doing first, but I closed it at once, certain she would refuse. I didn't think I could handle that kind of rejection right now.

I shook my head. "No reason." I turned and headed back into the bedroom, switching off the light as I went.

Then I lay down and closed my eyes, all the things I'd needed to talk about like caged, restless animals inside of me, pacing back and forth, pawing at the door. It took me a long, long time to finally fall asleep.

The nightmare was my own, the same one I'd been having for weeks now. I stood on the top of a tall stone tower. Wind buffeted my body, ripping my hair from its ponytail. The force of it pushed me backward until my back hit the hard edge of the parapet. Pain arced down my spine. I lurched forward, struggling against the wind as a terrible, all-consuming need drove me forward. Ahead, a stone square block sat dead center of the tower. I had to reach the plinth.

I didn't know why I needed to get there, and I didn't care. The need was too great for thought. My life depended on it. The world depended on it. At first, nothing happened as I moved my arms and legs. It was as if a cruel puppeteer held me back with invisible strings attached to my body.

Then finally, slowly, I began to make forward progress. Each step was like trying to swim through wet concrete. By the end of it, I crawled on my hands and knees. But that was okay. I needed to be on the ground. I needed to read the word etched into the side of the plinth. I pulled myself up to a kneeling position before it. If I could have stood, the plinth would've reached my knees, but now its top was level with my eyes. The wind continued its assault on my body. Tears streamed from my eyes as I forced them open against it.

I stared at the letters, but I couldn't make them out. The impressions were too faint. I stretched my hands toward them. If I tried hard enough, I might be able to read it like Braille. The plinth felt as hard and rough as uncut diamonds beneath my fingers. An idea rose up in my mind: if I could break through that hard surface, then I could read the letters. I began to scratch at it, a frenzy coming over me.

Scratch, scratch, scratch. My nails broke off one by one. My fingertips began to bleed. I balled my hands into fists, scraping away with my knuckles, oblivious to the pain. My skin ripped to shreds, but still I persisted. A part of me, the part of my brain that remained tethered to the waking world, even in dreams, knew that I should stop. That this was madness. Even worse, that it wasn't real.

But I couldn't stop. The part of me that existed only in dreams knew I had to read those letters. That part held sway here.

I would succeed or die trying.

~ 3 ~

The Will Guard

I woke exhausted the next morning, but was glad to be awake. Glad the dream was over. I slapped the wooden lever on the side of the alarm next to my bed, engaging the snooze spell. The alarm clocks at Arkwell were standard-issue and one of the few fully magical instruments on campus. The school administrators didn't want students blaming tardiness on the animation effect. Shame, I could've used such a handy excuse this morning.

Sighing, I rolled onto my back. I raised my hands and squinted at them, my eyes stinging from lack of sleep. I half expected my hands to be covered in sores from a night spent clawing at a stone plinth, but they looked as normal as ever.

I should've been relieved but I wasn't. I felt empty on the inside, my body hollowed out, as the need to know what those letters spelled lingered like the hangover of some powerful drug. I lay there for a couple of minutes, picturing the faint imprint of letters on the plinth. Maybe my waking mind would have better luck discerning them.

When my alarm went off again, I gave up and got out of bed. Typically, Selene was still asleep. As a siren, she didn't need to spend as much time getting ready in the morning. Her alarm would go off in twenty minutes, and she would roll out of bed with her dark hair looking perfect and shiny and her skin aglow. She had to bathe as regularly as anybody, of course, but she didn't have to worry about hair dryers and flatirons, and she hadn't worn makeup regularly since her turn toward tomboyhood. She didn't even wear it to hide the long thin scar running down the side of her face from where she'd been attacked by Marrow's familiar, the black phoenix. Not that she needed to. If anything, the scar gave her a wild, fierce look that only enhanced her beauty.

I gathered my things as quietly as I could then headed for the shower. But when I returned a half hour later, Selene was still in bed. I poked my head through the door. "You getting up?"

Selene rolled over, turning toward the wall. "Sleeping in," she mumbled. She sounded as exhausted as I felt. I supposed it made sense, considering she'd been out half the night. I considered confronting her about it right then, but I already had one tough discussion to accomplish today. Just how I was going to broach the subject with Eli, I didn't know.

I headed down to the cafeteria still trying to figure it out. I approached the table I usually sat at with Selene and Eli, but he wasn't there. I scanned the room for him, but the chaos of people and activity made it difficult to see much.

Mealtimes at Arkwell had become even more interesting since The Will broke. Paper airplanes flew complicated loop-de-loops in between the tables, obeying the magical commands of their makers as they delivered notes or dive-bombed unsuspecting victims. A girl across the way was manipulating the water in her goblet to make it flow upward in an inverted waterfall. The boy sitting behind her juggled a half-dozen glowing magical orbs that changed color every time he touched them.

Two tables over, a crystal goblet half full of some white liquid drew my attention as it hovered above the heads of several unsuspecting students. I watched it tip sideways right over Nick Jacobi. Milk—at least I hoped it was milk and not some dangerous potion—splashed downward. Nick raised his hand a split second before the liquid hit him, freezing it with a spell. Everyone at the table applauded his quick thinking. Nick started laughing at the boy across from him who had been controlling the goblet.

No sooner had Nick vanished the milk with a second spell than a saltshaker appeared above him and dumped its contents into his hair. This time several other people laughed as Nick leaped to his feet and tossed his head, flinging salt.

Stifling a smile, I glanced at the next table over, fully expecting to see Lance Rathbone behind the saltshaker. Lance was a wizard and Arkwell's resident trickster. Only he wasn't at his usual table either. *What, is this Sophomore Skip Day and nobody told me?* The real culprit, I saw, was a dryad by the name of Oliver Cork.

I glanced past Oliver, continuing my search for Eli. No luck. *He couldn't have done it without magic*, I reminded myself.

I went through the breakfast line and sat down at our table alone. Still no Eli. Where was he?

As if the thought had been an incantation, I spotted Eli coming through the massive wooden double doors of the cafeteria. He looked the same as any other day in his faded jeans and a dark, long-sleeved tee with a band logo on the front. But going by the huge yawn he tried to hide behind a raised fist, I guessed he hadn't slept well. All my speculation ceased as Eli's eyes alighted on me and a wide, cocksure grin slid across his handsome face. My stomach did a little flip at the sight of it, and a funny, achy feeling went through my knees. Good thing I was sitting down. If any ordinary had a diluted strain of siren blood, it had to be Eli Booker. Forget Bob Dylan.

As he walked toward me, I tried to recall all the openings I'd considered for asking him what he'd been doing last night around 11:45. But I abandoned the endeavor by the time he reached me. The whole thing was absurd. Even if Eli *could* do magic, he wouldn't hurt Britney. That sort of thing just wasn't in his nature. He would more likely beat the crap out of whoever had attacked her.

"Hey," Eli said, sliding into the bench opposite me.

"Hey."

He reached across the table and snagged a piece of bacon off my plate and popped it into his mouth. "Where's Selene?" he asked a couple of chews later.

"She's . . . sleeping in."

A single dark eyebrow rose on Eli's face. "Yeah? That doesn't sound like her."

I dropped my gaze from his face. "She, um, didn't sleep well, I don't think."

"That makes two of us." Eli yawned again.

It was the perfect opening, so I started to ask him why, when a loud bang stopped me. I jumped, my heart rate going from resting to overdrive in a split second. My eyes searched for the source of the noise.

Nick Jacobi had knocked over the bench he'd been sitting on. He and Oliver Cook stood across from each other, both shouting and with hands raised in a defensive position. Magic hummed in the air between them like a live wire. The two looked fit to kill. It seemed their little magical roughhousing had gotten out of hand. Neither was playing games now.

Nick's glamour had slid off him, revealing his true form

beneath—black, scaly skin, a single stubby horn on his forehead, and eyes that glowed red. He was an Ira demon, a rage demon, the kind that fed off the anger of others. Consequently, Iras had hot, dangerous tempers themselves.

Oliver, too, was looking more his natural self, his body thinner and taller, oddly treelike, and far less intimidating than Nick.

"This is bad," I said.

Across from me, Eli had already stood and was heading for the demon and dryad.

I moved to stop him. "Don't!" Without magic he would get crushed.

Too late, Eli had grasped Nick's arm and pulled him around before he could attack Oliver. A howl of rage exploded outward from Nick. He shoved Eli in the chest with both hands and Eli flew back, crashing into the upturned bench.

Nick's rage remained focused on Eli. He charged toward him, ready to strike again. I jumped up, my mind racing for the right spell to stop the demon, but panic made it hard to think.

I raised my hand. "Alexo." The shield spell burst out from my fingertips in a streak of purple light. But before it could form over Eli, it *vanished*. But that was impossible. Stuff like that only happened when The Will was in place.

I opened my mouth to cast the spell again, but before I could, Nick froze mid-attack. His body was jerked into the air as if hoisted by an invisible pulley.

I gaped up at him as he struggled against whatever unseen bonds held him.

Eli got to his feet and stepped over to me. "You all right?" He touched my arm, sending tingles over my skin.

I huffed. "Oh, right. Worry about me, because *I'm* the one that just got tossed like a football by a pissed off—"

I broke off when I saw four strange men entering the cafeteria. They looked as if they'd gotten lost on their way to a Renaissance festival. They wore waist-length red robes like some kind of tunic over black pants. Sweat broke out on my skin, and all my muscles contracted from a sudden spurt of terror at their appearance—bloodred on black, just like Marrow had worn.

"Who the hell are they?" Eli moved closer to me as if he intended to shield me with his body.

The men marched farther into the cafeteria, silence spreading out before them. I looked around for a teacher or staff member, someone who could tell me whether or not it was time to make a run for it, but I didn't see anybody.

The nearest man headed right for us. He carried a wizard's staff that he held before him, pointed directly at Nick's floating body.

A few feet from Nick, the man came to a stop. He looked like a retired prizefighter with his massive square jaw and squashed nose. His shoulders seemed wider than his arms were long. The scowl he leveled first at Nick then at Eli, and finally at me, made the hairs on my arms and neck stand up.

"That's enough rule breaking for one morning." The man made a downward slash with his staff, and Nick crashed to the ground with a loud thud. He let out a groan then scrambled to his feet. His black, scaly skin and horn vanished as his glamour slipped back into place.

"Who are you?" Eli demanded, placing his hands on his hips.

A low murmur echoed around us. I wanted to disappear into the cracks in the stone floor. I didn't know who this guy was, but one thing was for sure—he wasn't somebody you should challenge unless you could back it up. In the ordinary world, Eli was badass enough to take on anybody, but this was the magical world.

A wide, toothy grin stretched across the man's face. "Me? Why, I'm the Captain of the Will Guard."

Will Guard, like Will-Workers. Well, at least I could dismiss my original fear that these guys were Marrow supporters come to take over the school. The gold insignia on the left breast of the man's tunic bore the Magi Senate crest of the tree, wand, and flame, symbolizing the three sects of magickind: naturekind, witchkind, and darkkind.

"What's the—" Eli began.

The man tapped his staff against the floor, and Eli made a choking sound, reaching for his throat. Some kind of powerful magic crackled in the air around us. I grabbed Eli's arm, trying to steady him.

"What did you do?" I took a step toward the man, outrage belying my better judgment to stay quiet.

In answer, the man tapped the staff again. An invisible hand seemed to grip the back of my throat and tongue. I tried to shriek, but no sound came out. It was some kind of gagging spell. I remembered my mom using the same spell on me whenever I started to make a scene in public when I was little. I knew from experience it was best not to fight it. I forced my body to relax, and at once the pressure in the back of my throat eased enough that I no longer felt like I was going to hurl.

With a self-satisfied glint in his eyes, the man turned away from me. Resentment made my skin burn. This guy had no right to come in and start casting spells at students. And after all the stuff with Marrow, I wasn't about to just cower down to him because he might be here on Magi business. I reached out with my mind-magic and tried to grab the staff from his hands.

Without access to their magical instrument, a witch or wizard couldn't perform most magic.

Some unseen force blocked my way. The man jerked his head in my direction then smirked before turning back. He motioned toward the overturned bench with his staff and it righted itself. He stepped onto the bench and then on top of the table. He turned in a circle, surveying the room.

The cafeteria was absolutely silent, all eyes turned on this stranger. In a loud, gruff voice, he said, "My name is Captain Gargrave. I am head of the Will Guard. We have been sent to Arkwell by the Magi Senate to perform the duties of The Will. This means that all the combative magic violations you students have been perpetuating these last few chaotic months have officially come to an end."

Another murmur went through the crowd, this one tinged with something like defiance. It wasn't that we couldn't do magic before The Will. It was just that people didn't dare try most spells for fear they would be restricted. I didn't think this Will Guard was likely to have much luck reinstating that kind of fear, not now that everybody had gotten used to the freedom.

Captain Gargrave must've sensed that rebellious spirit as well for he said even louder, "If you dare to challenge my authority or the authority of any of my men, you *will* reap the consequences." He made an upward slash with the staff.

Nick let out a yell as he was hoisted into the air again. This time Captain Gargrave spun him around in several fast, nauseating circles. Eli and I both backed up instinctively, in case Nick tossed his cookies.

Just when I thought Nick was going to lose it, Captain Gargrave let go and Nick dropped to the floor again. He landed hard, but still on his feet. Gargrave stepped down from the table without another word. As he passed me, I felt the gag in my throat lift. The captain joined the others, and they started patrolling the cafeteria.

Eli and I exchanged a look. I could tell he was anxious to talk about what just happened, but we both knew it was better to let things settle down so we weren't overheard.

His stomach grumbled. "I'll be back in a minute," Eli said, before stalking off to the breakfast line.

I sat down again as the silence in the cafeteria slowly began to dissipate. But the conversations remained subdued and nobody was doing any magic, legal or otherwise. I glanced at Gargrave who was eyeing the crowd like a hawk on the hunt. *Way to make a nasty first impression, dude.*

I had a feeling the nasty was only getting started.

~ 4 ~

Tragical History

While I waited for Eli, I contemplated my eggs and bacon for a couple of minutes, and then got up and threw the contents of my breakfast tray into the garbage. Something inside the trash can growled, and I realized too late that I'd forgotten to sort out my silverware. A moment later the fork came hurtling out of the can like a missile and whacked me in the forehead.

"Hey," I said as I rubbed my stinging skin. Good thing I hadn't used a knife this morning.

A head covered in scraggly brown hair emerged over the top of the can. The trash troll fixed a glare at me with its huge black eyes. It looked like a really ugly, twisted version of a Mr. Potato Head with a head and torso twice as long as its stubby legs and arms. It bared its teeth at me, mumbling incoherent words.

It dawned on me that I was being scolded. By a trash troll. Glaring, I shooed at it. "Go on, get back in there. It was just an accident."

The troll muttered something more then stuck its tongue out at me before disappearing. I backed away from the trash can, on the lookout for more projectiles. It seemed even the trash trolls had developed their own spirit of rebellion, same as us students.

Eli arrived back at the table at the same time I did, his tray laden with food. I sat down across from him and watched with mild interest as he began shoveling. "Looks like the senate finally decided to do something about all the fighting," Eli said between mouthfuls.

"It's something all right." I flashed a scathing glance at Gargrave. "But I'm not sure it's the right something."

"What is it?" Eli's gaze locked on my face.

"Someone attacked Britney Shell last night."

He stopped mid-shovel, a bit of egg falling off the tip of his fork. "What? How? What happened?"

I spent the next few minutes telling him about my adventures last night. He was thrilled at my success on getting such good details out of the sheriff, but when I got to the part about the almost-Paul, Eli dropped his fork onto his plate with a loud clang. "*He* was in the dream?"

I flinched at the vehemence in his tone. It was deserved—Paul had betrayed both of us to Marrow—but I was the one he'd pretended to date for several weeks leading up to it. I should be the angry one, but mostly I wanted to forget it.

"Yeah," I said, "but I don't think it was actually him. He looked different. And Lady Elaine said it didn't mean anything since Britney's not a dream-seer and her dreams are just dreams." *Good thing, too,* I thought. *Or you would be a suspect in the attack by now.*

The bell rang before Eli could ask any more questions. I waited while he dumped his tray with considerably less trouble from the trash troll, and then we walked together to homeroom. For reasons unbeknownst to us, Eli and I had the exact same schedule. I didn't mind. Any excuse to be with him. And walking was the best part, the way he leaned into me, our bodies touching more often than not. Every time his hand brushed against my fingers, my heartbeat lost its rhythm as I hoped that this would be the time he would finally take hold of my hand.

The morning announcements lasted three times longer than usual. The principal started off reminding us for at least the hundredth time about volunteer opportunities still available for the Beltane Festival on May first. They'd been hyping the festival for months now. Normally, Arkwell held its own celebration on campus, including a dance, the magickind equivalent to prom. But this year marked a centennial for the foundation of Lyonshold, the capital city of magickind in the United States, and the Magi Senate decided that the students should join the huge celebration. Volunteers would get to do stuff like light the bonfires and dance in some of the rituals.

Yeah, there was a negative two percent chance that I would volunteer for such a thing. Still, I was looking forward to going as a regular spectator. I'd never been to Lyonshold. Since it was hidden on a magical island somewhere in the middle of Lake Erie, students only visited during holidays and celebrations. Or capital trials, I supposed, thinking about Paul.

Next Dr. Hendershaw went into a detailed, and wholly unnecessary, introduction of the Will Guard. Then she delivered even more bad news when she informed us that not only was the Guard authorized to use magic on us, they could also hand out detentions.

Awesome.

Afterward, Eli and I headed to first period.

"So I wonder who attacked Britney," Eli said as we walked along.

"No idea."

Eli glanced down at me. He was so tall my head barely reached his shoulder. "You know that the Dream Team is going to have to investigate this, right?"

I scrunched up my nose, a little embarrassed by the current name of our amateur detective agency. But Eli had picked it and that made me love it a little bit, too. "Aren't we supposed to wait until we get *hired* before investigating?"

He snorted. "Eventually. But until we get established, we're mainly pro bono."

"Hey," I said, my brain making a sudden and completely unrelated connection. "Why wasn't Lance at breakfast?"

Eli looked puzzled but said, "I think he's sick. I had to turn off his alarm because he slept through it. When I woke him up he was really out of it so I just let him go back to sleep."

"Huh." I chewed on my bottom lip, thinking it over. "You don't think he was out after curfew, do you?"

Eli shrugged. "Probably. I didn't see him at all last night. I had dinner with my dad off campus and didn't get back to the dorm until late. He wasn't there."

We arrived at the classroom and took our usual seats toward the back. "Didn't that seem a little weird to you?"

Eli set his bag on the floor, chuckling. "This *is* Lance we're talking about. He sneaks out all the time to set up his pranks."

"Oh, right." I scowled at the memory of one of Lance's pranks that had been directed at me. A few hours before my restroom-cleaning detention with Ms. Hardwick last semester, Lance had stopped up every toilet and sink in the first-floor bathroom of the administration building. I still needed to pay him back for that.

"Why are you so concerned about Lance this morning?" Eli paused, frowning. Then he rolled his eyes. "Please don't tell me you think he attacked Britney, because that's absurd."

I scoffed. "Shouldn't we consider *everyone* a suspect until proven innocent?"

In truth, I hadn't been thinking about Britney at all, but Selene. The idea that the two of them were out together might be far-fetched, but it wasn't outside the realm of possibilities. Selene and Lance had dated for a while freshman year, and over the past few months they'd been developing a strange love-hate relationship, not exactly friends but not quite enemies either. Lance had been pretty upset about Selene getting hurt during our fight with Marrow, although he never admitted it outright. I only knew from Eli. Selene refused to believe it entirely. But there was no denying that every time the two of them were to-gether the air seemed to crackle. Maybe they'd finally given in.

That would explain Selene's reluctance to tell me. I'd be ashamed of a midnight rendezvous with Lance Rathbone, too. Sure, he was good-looking, but he was also a bona fide jackass with a capital *J*.

"Yeah, well," Eli began, but he broke off as a girl with long brown hair entered the room. His ex, Katarina Marcel.

Actually everybody in the classroom went silent at Katari-na's arrival. She was a siren, same as Selene; only she didn't go around trying to downplay her beauty. Just the opposite. Today she wore a tight, sage green top that laced up the front and a pair of skinny jeans. She looked like she'd just stepped off the runway at a fashion show. Her beauty was so mesmerizing, even I had a hard time not staring at her.

It helped when she leveled a nasty, hate-filled look at me. The look lasted only a second before she turned her gaze on Eli, a stunning smile rising to her lips.

I heard Eli's quick indrawn breath, and jealousy stung my insides. Ever since Eli had broken it off with Katarina, she'd been doing her best to get him back. Well, the best she could without truly invoking her siren magic. That was half the reason he'd broken up with her in the first place—he couldn't be sure his attraction to her was genuine.

I sort of hoped the other half was his attraction to me, but so far he hadn't given me any proof beyond that one kiss, which he'd never once mentioned.

Katarina strolled past our line of desks and sat down a few feet away. The smell of her perfume as she went by made me feel faint, in a dreamy, buzzed kind of way. *Stupid sirens.*

"All right, class," our teacher Miss Norton said from the front of the room. "Let's begin. Please open your books to page eighty-four."

I pulled out my well-worn copy of *The Tragical History of the Life and Death of Doctor Faustus.* The best thing I could say about the book was that it was light and easy to carry around.

"Now." Miss Norton motioned to the dry-erase board where two lines from the play were written in her neat handwriting. "This quote is from act five, scene one, which all of you should've read overnight." She began to recite, gesticulating wildly. "'Her lips suck forth my soul: see, where it flies! Come, Helen, come give me my soul again.'"

Norton ceased her dramatic performance, pushed her wire-rim glasses back up her nose, and then surveyed the room. "Who would like to guess what magickind inspired Christopher Marlowe to describe Helen thusly?"

Silence met her question. A dozen possible answers occurred to me, but I wasn't about to voice any of them to this group. The various kinds had been getting more and more sensitive to any comments about their nature that could be considered derisive.

Just last Thursday, passive, quiet Britney had dumped a beaker full of bloom-and-grow potion over Lance's head after he referred to all naturekinds as tree-huggers during our alchemy class. Lucky for Lance, the potion wasn't toxic, but it did make his face break out in tiny, green leaves, which soon covered his whole head until he resembled a walking, talking Chia Pet. Pretty funny, really, although a little overreactive on Britney's part. Lance had said hundreds of worse things before.

Apparently, I wasn't the only one aware of the dangers of voicing such opinions, as the silence stretched onward, nobody willing to raise a hand.

Miss Norton ran her gaze over the group again. I sank down lower in my chair, hoping her attention wouldn't land on me. She appeared exceptionally bright-eyed and awake this morning. Her alleged Coke addiction (the drink, not the drug) seemed to be under control lately. As a fairy, Miss Norton was prone to the intoxicating effects of sugar.

"Anybody?" Norton said into our continued silence. She sighed and then opened the top drawer of her desk and pulled out her infamous talking stick. It looked like an exceptionally crooked wand, although I didn't think it was. As a naturekind, Miss Norton had no need of a wand or any other magical instrument to wield her magic.

"All right. This is your last chance." Norton made a sweeping gesture with the stick toward the room at large. "If I don't get a volunteer, I'm going to have to choose someone."

Come on, somebody speak up. I glanced expectantly at Katarina. She hardly ever let a chance of being the center of attention go by. But no such luck. Katarina had her eyes carefully focused on her book, although I caught her taking a quick peek at Eli.

"Suit yourselves." Miss Norton let go of the stick. It hovered in the air before her for a moment and then began to move about the room, sweeping this way and that as if it had a mind of its own. I cringed each time it made a pass in my direction.

Finally it zoomed to the other side of the room and hung suspended over Nick Jacobi's chair. I let out the breath I was holding, glad to have dodged the bullet.

Next second the stick did a mad race back across the room right at me. It moved so fast, I actually ducked, certain it would strike me in the head.

But instead it swerved right and stopped inches away from Eli's face. He stared at the stick, his eyes going crossed and his mouth twisting into a frown. Then exhaling loudly, he seized hold of it, resigned to the inevitable.

"So," Miss Norton said, smoothing the folds of her fluffy, flowered housedress. "Which magickind do you suppose it was, Mr. Booker?"

Eli shifted in his seat. I swallowed back guilt. I should've raised my hand.

"Any day now," Miss Norton said.

Eli looked up. He fixed his gaze on Miss Norton, as if pretending she was the only other person present. He took a deep breath and then said in a quiet voice, "Siren."

Eager whispers broke out in response to this, and nearly everybody turned their gaze on Katarina, the history between them common knowledge. My skin went red, both in vicarious embarrassment for Eli and a sudden swell of pity for Katarina. I didn't like her, but I imagined the statement must've hurt.

It was even possible Eli wasn't referring to her at all. Katarina hadn't done anything so heinous to him as to be compared to a soul-sucker. No, I had a feeling Eli was thinking about what Paul had done to me. He was only a half siren, but that was plenty enough.

"And what makes you believe it was a siren?" Miss Norton said.

I closed my eyes. This couldn't get any worse.

Wrong.

"It was me." Katarina's voice cracked. "He thinks I used my siren powers on him."

Eli turned a smoldering look on her. "This has nothing to do with you." He turned back to Miss Norton. "I just meant that sirens are capable of bending people's wills, which is a lot like stealing someone's soul. Plus the reference to flying could be literal since sirens really can fly. And Helen is supposed to be extremely beautiful, so the description fits."

"Aw," Miss Norton said, pointing a finger in the air. "But what about some of the demonkinds that really do feed on the soul?"

"I haven't heard of any that are supposed to have the kind of beauty Helen did," Eli said, thrusting out his jaw.

"Wait," Nick Jacobi said. He slapped the top of his desk. "Are you trying to say that demonkind are ugly?"

"Yeah," Royce Davidson said from beside Nick. Royce was a Metus demon, the kind that feeds on fear. "What about succubi? Could've been one of them."

"That's right," Nick said. I could tell he was still on edge from the fight in the cafeteria. The hint of red flashed in his eyes through the glamour. He turned those eyes on me, his face twisting into a glower. "Or it could've been a Nightmare." He paused. A vicious grin parted his lips to reveal large, pointed teeth. "Oh, never mind. I guess Nightmares aren't pretty enough, are they?"

Eli stood up, the legs of his combo desk-chair scraping against the stone floor. He pointed the talking stick at Nick. The vision of him in Britney's dream swam in my head. "You shut your mouth."

Nick stood, too. "Go ahead and try. *Ordinary.*"

"No, boys," Miss Norton said, moving to intervene.

Nick extended his hand. "Hypno-soma!" A jet of red light flew out from his fingertips.

Eli ducked sideways, just barely missing it. "Fligere," he shouted back, aiming the stick.

What was he doing? He couldn't work magic.

But the spell erupted from the tip of the talking stick. Miss Norton, still in motion, stepped in front of it. The spell struck her in the chest. Her eyes went wide, and she tipped backward, landing in a heap on the floor.

A silence louder than the shouting and flying spells descended in the room.

I turned my head toward Eli, my stomach sinking.

So much for the no-magic defense.

～ 5 ～

The Sheriff, the Student, and the Oracle

The Will Guard arrived seconds later. Captain Gargrave came through the door first, pointing his staff at Eli, who went rigid, his arms pinioned at his sides. Across from him, Nick stood in a similar state. The principal had said the Will Guard was armed with magic detectors. Apparently, they were really good ones.

"Are you all right, Miss Norton?" said Katarina, helping the fairy to her feet.

Miss Norton let out a groan as she rubbed her chest where Eli's jab jinx had struck. I did an inner double take at the thought. Eli had done magic. There was no denying it. I'd seen it with my own eyes. Heard it with my own ears. But how was it possible?

I looked Eli up and down, half-convinced he was someone else in disguise. The dark, dangerous expression on his face was familiar, but also inscrutable. He could be thinking anything.

"This is the second time I've had to break you two up," Gargrave said, glancing between his captives. Then he turned toward Eli and yanked the talking stick out of his hand. "And according to my information, you're not supposed to have a wand, Mr. Booker. Where did you get this?"

"It's mine." Miss Norton stepped forward and seized the

stick from Gargrave. "It's . . . it's just a classroom tool." She hugged it close to her chest as if fearing Gargrave would take it back.

But the captain shrugged and returned his attention to Eli. "Come with me. I think the principal is going to want to hear about this."

The spell holding Eli in place let go, and he shook out his arms as if to get the blood flowing again.

"Why just him?" I said, unable to stand idly by. "Nick cast a stunning spell first."

Gargrave scrutinized the Ira demon, considering the matter. He shook his head. "I don't think so. He's a demonkind and therefore entitled to a little more tolerance."

Although Gargrave didn't say it, the word *ordinary* seemed to sound throughout the room. It echoed over and over again inside my head.

"That's not fa—" I began, but Eli cut me off.

"Leave it, Dusty. I'll be fine."

With an effort, I closed my mouth.

Gargrave turned toward the door, and Eli followed after him. Our eyes met for a moment, and I saw he wasn't angry at being the only one punished. Instead he seemed resigned to his fate.

As soon as he and the Will Guard were gone, Miss Norton ordered all of us back to our seats. We spent the rest of the period in silent reading. Although I kept my eyes glued to the page, none of the words registered. My head was too crowded with questions and doubts all vying for my attention like unwelcome houseguests. The image from Britney's dream kept coming back to me. I didn't want to believe Eli was involved, but I couldn't ignore what I'd witnessed—he had done magic. Was I wrong about Eli like I'd been wrong about Paul? Feeling sick, I wrapped my arms around my chest.

I wanted desperately to talk to Eli, but by the time first period ended, he hadn't returned. I walked to my spell-casting class alone, ignoring the gossip filling the hallways. Everyone was talking about the ordinary boy who'd somehow done magic.

When I descended the stairs into the tunnels and caught a familiar whiff of canal water, my thoughts turned to Britney. Guilt and relief battled inside me. If I had told Lady Elaine about Eli being in her dream, he would be in even more trouble. Then again, if he'd been the one to attack her . . .

Stop it, Dusty. Not everybody is a power-crazed villain in disguise.

With an effort, I forced the thoughts from my mind. The task proved easier once I arrived at spell casting. Today we were working on illusion spells, a subject we'd been studying nonstop since the semester began. According to our textbook, there were three levels to illusion spells, starting with the simplest and working up to the hardest. We'd already learned the level-one stuff, which involved transforming the appearance of an existing object into something else. We started small, first turning pennies into quarters, and then textbooks into pillows.

Now we were moving on to level two: duplication. Five minutes into my attempts to make a duplicated illusion of a penny appear beside a real one, sweat broke out over my skin, and I started panting from the effort. No matter how hard I tried, I couldn't remove the telltale blurriness from the false penny. Who knew creating something out of thin air would be so difficult?

Still, I was grateful for the distraction as the period slipped by quickly. I only checked the door twice, hoping Eli had arrived, and I was too busy concentrating to be concerned about what he might or might not have done.

But when class ended, my worry came back full force. Wishing I'd just asked Eli for the truth when I'd had the chance, I hesitated at the stairs leading up from the tunnels to Monmouth Tower and my history class. Then, on impulse, I turned and doubled back, making a right at the next intersection. If I hurried I would have time to swing by the administration office in Jefferson Tower to see if I could find out what was keeping Eli so long.

Halfway there I realized it was a stupid plan and a little on the desperate side, but it was too late to turn back. Besides, the substitute teacher we'd been stuck with for history since our old teacher Mr. Marrow had turned out to be a power-hungry murderer, wasn't much concerned with tardiness. Mrs. Rosencrantz was a hamadryad and well past ancient. With her treelike patience, she spent most of the class dozing while we were supposed to read from the text.

I marched through the door into the administration main office intent on asking the secretary about Eli, but when I arrived, the reception desk sat deserted. The only sign of life came from the large plant in the corner behind the desk. I had no idea what it was—biology was a junior-level class at Arkwell—but it was definitely of the magical variety. Its leaves kept rustling in random spurts, and the multiple yellow flowers perched on the tops of its stems had turned toward me when I entered the room, their dark centers like large eyes watching me. Thank goodness it didn't have vines; otherwise I would be worried it might reach out and grab me. No plant should show so much interest in a person.

I ignored the creepy feeling crawling over my spine and peered down the hallway behind the desk that led to the principal's office as well as to a couple of conference rooms. I thought I heard the sound of voices down there. Deciding that a quick peek wouldn't be too big a risk, I slipped past the desk and tiptoed down the hallway.

A familiar, gruff voice froze me in my tracks as I reached the door to the first conference room on the right. I stopped just outside it and listened as Sheriff Brackenberry said, "So you claim that Britney left your little"—there was the sound of paper ruffling—"Terra Tribe, the Society for the Betterment of Nature, meeting at nine P.M., and that you two were the last ones there."

Brackenberry stopped speaking. I strained my ears to hear the person answer, but it must've been a nod or a head shake for the sheriff continued, "And you don't know where she went and you never saw her after that." Another pause. "And you went straight back to your dorm." A third pause.

Brackenberry let out a doubtful sigh. "Well then, as it stands now you were the last person to see her before she was attacked. I'm not saying that you were involved, but if you remember something, I would encourage you to report it at once. You can find me at this number."

There was another sound of sliding paper.

"You're free to go."

Gulping in panic, I turned, dashed down the hallway and back around to the reception desk. I leaned my arms on top of the desk and lowered my gaze, trying to appear nonchalant. My heart pounded so hard in my chest I was certain everyone in a two-mile radius could hear it. The plant rustled its leaves, letting me know it had seen me. I hoped it couldn't talk as well.

I didn't look up at the sound of approaching footsteps until the person was almost next to me. When I did I saw it was Oliver Cork. I smiled at him, trying to appear friendly but worried I looked mostly guilty. Why were the police interrogating him?

Did that mean they hadn't fingered Eli for the attack? And what the hell was the Terra Tribe?

When I spotted Sheriff Brackenberry scowling at me from behind Oliver, the questions stopped midstream and the smile vanished from my face.

"What are you doing here?" Brackenberry said, hands on his belt.

"I . . . um . . ." I glanced over my shoulder, stalling until Oliver had left. I turned back to the sheriff. "I just wanted to know if Eli was still here."

Brackenberry frowned, not buying it.

I willed the guilt out of my expression. Coming to find out about Eli *was* the reason I came. The eavesdropping about Britney was just an unintentional bonus.

"Eli's not here anymore."

"Oh." I began to twist my fingers through the strands of my hair hanging down over my shoulder. "Did he go back to class?"

The sheriff shook his head. "They've taken him over to Lyonshold for the rest of the day. The Magi Senate is very interested in learning how an ordinary suddenly started casting spells."

I wasn't sure what to make of this news. On the one hand, it meant they hadn't yet found Eli guilty of anything to do with Britney. On the other, a trip to the magickind capital city to be interrogated by the Magi Senate spelled big trouble.

"Oh, okay." I took a step back from the desk, preparing to leave.

"Not so fast," said Brackenberry. "We planned on waiting until this afternoon, but since you're here." He waved at me to follow as he headed back down the hallway and reentered the conference room.

I walked in behind him, each footstep heavier than the last. Brackenberry motioned for me to sit while he pulled a cell phone off the clip on his belt and slid his finger over the touch screen, opening it. The cell must've been brand-new because it didn't give him any trouble as he dialed.

I glanced around the room, taking in the long, glass-topped table and the dozen matching high-backed chairs upholstered in a bright pattern of blue and yellow roses intermixed with sprites—tiny winged creatures with humanoid bodies and chameleon-like skin. A folder sat opened on top of the desk, and I wondered if it was the case file on Britney. I leaned in for a better look, but Brackenberry flipped it closed.

A moment later he said into the receiver, "It's me. Destiny Everhart is in the administration office right now . . . she was asking about Eli . . . yes, I know. Are you on campus yet? I figure it would be better if she heard the news from us. I'm sure some of the senators' kids already know." He nodded his head a couple of times. "Uh-huh. Right. See you in a minute."

Brackenberry ended the call and returned the cell to the holster on his belt. Then he sat down on the opposite side of the table from me and folded his hands across his ample belly. The buttons on his navy blue policeman's uniform bulged outward, the fabric beneath them strained. "Lady Elaine will be here soon."

I bit my lip. What could be so bad they would have to tell me about it in person? A thousand possibilities flitted through my mind like a flock of rabid birds, each one pecking away at my ability to sit here in this seat and pretend not to be having a panic attack.

Then the worst possibility occurred to me. It could be about my mom. She'd been in England for the last two months, but was due to come home soon. I didn't know when exactly, because she kept pushing back the date. But what if something had happened? Cold sweat beaded on my forehead and the back of my neck. I gnawed on the inside of my cheek, bracing for the worst.

But when Lady Elaine arrived some five minutes later, she didn't bring me bad news about my mother. Even so, what she had to say hit me with the force of a wrecking ball.

"Today," she said, her voice grave and her frail body rigid as she stared down at me, "the Magi Senate decided to drop all charges against Paul Kirkwood. He has been set free and will be resuming classes here at Arkwell in a few days."

My heart seemed to freeze up inside my chest and my blood turn to ice water. Paul Kirkwood, free? It had to be a joke. And yet I knew it wasn't. Lady Elaine wouldn't lie to me. Not about this.

I swallowed. Paul Kirkwood. Ex-boyfriend. A murderer's accomplice who tried to bend my will into serving the Red Warlock. The guy I thought I would never see face-to-face again.

He was coming back.

And I knew without a doubt my life was never going to be the same again.

6

Confidential

As if the first bit of news Lady Elaine delivered wasn't bad enough, she delivered another bomb seconds later.

"We want you to spy on him."

"What?" I blinked, repeatedly, my brain slipping like an engine stuck in neutral.

"Hold on, please," Sheriff Brackenberry said to Lady Elaine. He stood up and walked to the door, which Elaine had closed when she arrived. I watched as he ran a hand over the door frame, uttering an incantation.

While he worked, Lady Elaine walked once around the room, trailing her fingers along the wall and speaking the same incantation. Slowly, I felt the atmosphere in the room change. The air seemed to grow denser, the sounds muffled.

"There now," said Brackenberry, resuming his seat. "That should ensure we aren't overheard."

My curiosity piqued, I sat up straighter in my chair. "Who would be listening in?"

Brackenberry drummed his fingers on the table. "That's not your concern."

I huffed, crossing my arms over my chest. "Yeah, sure. Because being asked to spy on my ex-boyfriend doesn't have anything to do with you sound-proofing the room. So, what, am I here to take meeting minutes?" I motioned toward the conference table.

Lady Elaine sat down next to the sheriff, ignoring my sass for once. Before I could register my disappointment, she said, "First, I must emphasize that what the sheriff and I are asking of you is strictly voluntary. You are not required to participate." A dark expression crossed Lady Elaine's thin, ancient face, worry in her eyes. "And no one would think the worst if you refuse. It's liable to be very dangerous."

A chill slid over my skin, and I trembled. I tried to think of some wiseass remark—sarcasm was a great avoidance tactic—but nothing came to me. The fear I felt was too real, too present.

Paul was free. Paul would be on campus in a few days. And I would have to face him. I wanted to believe that seeing him again would be easy, that I could use my hatred of him as a shield. Only, I wasn't sure I did hate him, at least not enough to resist his siren's charm. I'd never considered the possibility that I would have to deal with his siren magic or my feelings toward him ever again. He was supposed to have remained locked up for a very long time.

I let out a slow breath. "Okay, I'm listening."

Lady Elaine glanced at Sheriff Brackenberry, and he nodded.

She turned back to me, pulling up the sleeves of the dark green, wool sweater that had fallen over her hands. "The main reason we sealed the room is because this is *not* an official meeting. Neither the sheriff nor I are acting in our normal governmental roles at present, and none of the Magi know what we are instigating here."

I looked between the two of them, more confused than ever. "Is this some kind of rogue operation?"

Brackenberry snorted. "You watch too many movies."

"That certainly is true," said Lady Elaine, a suspicious curve to her lips.

"What this is"—Brackenberry leaned over the table toward me—"is a secret. And before we tell you anything else, you must agree to maintain the same secrecy. So even if you turn us down, you must not speak about it to anyone else. Understood?"

A couple of months ago, I might've stood up and left the room right then. Forget this clandestine, liable-to-be-dangerous crap. But the stuff with Marrow had changed me. I wouldn't say it had made me any braver—even now, I felt like my heart might burst its way out of my chest and go galloping across the table—but it had made me a little wiser. I knew I couldn't run away from the bad and scary things in my life. Better to face those things head-on then to get caught from behind.

I slowly nodded, although I wasn't exactly ready to swear an oath of silence. I didn't plan on blabbing about it, but I wasn't sure this kind of news was something I could keep from Selene or Eli.

"Good," said Lady Elaine. "Now, I'm sure you have lots of questions."

"You can say that again." Some of the tension left my body now that I'd made up my mind to stay and hear them out. "Why did they let Paul go?"

"Officially," Sheriff Brackenberry said, "the Magi Court has dropped all charges against him due to his age and the lack of indisputable evidence that he contributed to any of the significant crimes."

"What?" My fingers clenched into fists. "But what about my testimony? And Selene's and Eli's? My mom's? We spent hours in those deposition meetings telling everybody what went down with Marrow. How is that not evidence?"

Lady Elaine raised both hands. Deep crevices lined her palms and ran down her twig-like fingers. "Calm down, Dusty. It is evidence, but there's more going on here. For one thing, Paul put on a convincing display. He said he was sorry for the things he'd done and voluntarily shared the password to his administrator account on the reckthaworlde.com website."

The sheriff growled. "Fat lot of good it did. The blasted thing was already completely offline by the time we got into it. And we've had no luck tracking down the host servers. Paul claims he doesn't know where they are. We've checked Marrow's apartment, Paul's dorm room, and even his uncle's house, but no luck."

I leaned back in my chair, my breath coming in angry gulps. Of course they hadn't been found. Paul was too clever. I didn't understand how anybody could let him off. What kind of idiots were running the magickind government, exactly?

"There's no point in being angry," Lady Elaine said, addressing Brackenberry as much as me. "The deed is done. Now all that matters is how we handle what comes next."

I sighed. "I guess you're right. But what exactly do you want me to do?"

Lady Elaine dropped her gaze from my face and began to pick at a fingernail. "We want you to resume your relationship with Paul."

I stood up so hard, I banged my knee against the table, sending a sharp stab of pain down my leg. "No way. Ew . . . and . . . *gross.* There's no way I'm going to pretend to be that creep's girlfriend."

Sheriff Brackenberry tsked. "I told you she wouldn't go for

it. These kids are all the same. Only concerned about themselves."

My skin prickled. It was so unfair, so insane. How could they ask me to do it?

And then the more obvious truth occurred to me.

Gritting my teeth, I said, "Even if I was willing, it wouldn't work. Paul doesn't like me. He never did. He just pretended to date me because Marrow told him to." My voice broke as I finished speaking, and unexpected tears stung my eyes. I opened them wide, trying to hold them back.

Sympathy filled Lady Elaine's gaze as she looked at me. "I know you feel that way, but I've spoken to Paul several times and have kept an eye on his behavior. I do not believe that all of his feelings for you were on account of Marrow."

At once, those stupid tears burned my eyes again, and a bubble of emotions rose up my chest into my throat. I swallowed it down, unable to deal with it. Especially not in present company. "That's impossible. He's just fooling you the way he fooled me. It's what he does."

Lady Elaine nodded. "Maybe, but if so, then he must have an ulterior motive for putting on such an act. In either case, I believe he will be receptive toward any advances you might make."

I sat down, my stomach roiling.

"We're not asking you to resume any kind of sexual relationship with the suspect," Sheriff Brackenberry said.

I flushed. "I never . . . I didn't . . . I mean . . ."

Lady Elaine cleared her throat. "We just want you to spend some time with him. Get him to trust you if possible. Just enough that you can keep a lookout for any suspicious behavior."

Like luring girls to their deaths?

I tried to picture myself spending time with Paul again, pretending to like him. I couldn't do it. I was the wrong person for a job like this. They needed someone like . . . like . . . Katarina, a siren full of confidence and staggering beauty. Not someone like me.

Then the absurdity of the entire situation occurred to me. I shook my head and started smiling. "You guys don't need me to spy on him. I mean, come on. You're the freakin' government. Don't you have professionals for this sort of thing? Won't you be keeping tabs on him all the time already?"

Sheriff Brackenberry sighed. "Well, that took less time than I thought."

Lady Elaine shot him a look. "I *told* you she's far cleverer than you give her credit for."

"Hey." I stomped my foot, annoyed at the implied insult. Not that Brackenberry's doubt about my intelligence came as a surprise. "I'm sitting right here, you know. And I *can* hear you."

That got their attention.

"Why do you need me?"

"Because we don't have anyone else we can trust," said Lady Elaine.

I shook my head. "Not buying it."

"It's true," she insisted. "Under normal circumstances, the government *would* keep close tabs on Paul, but nothing about this situation is normal."

I scooted to the edge of my seat, intrigued again despite my disbelief. "What do you mean?"

Brackenberry brushed a hand through his long, shaggy brown hair, a strange look on his face. I couldn't decide if it was worry or skepticism. Maybe both. "It seems that somebody has been pulling strings concerning Paul. There are some worrisome signs that someone inside the senate has orchestrated his release."

"Yes," Lady Elaine said. "Not only is Paul being released after providing such a small amount of information, but it appears that no plans are being made to have him regularly monitored beyond the absolute minimum. All we've been able to confirm they've done is to confiscate his personal computers and place heavy restrictions on his student account."

A sound close to a growl escaped the sheriff's throat. "That's right. My department hasn't received any orders, and every time I try to figure out which department *is* taking responsibility for it, I'm given the runaround."

I frowned, a little intimidated by the scope of this thing. My dealings with magickind law enforcement had only been with the sheriff's department, but there were others out there, including the magickind equivalent of the CIA and the Secret Service.

"Given that," said Brackenberry, "we've decided to take matters into our own hands until we can uncover who's behind Paul's release and what that person hopes to gain from it. The answers lie with Paul, but he's clever. We believe that *you* are the best way to get the truth from him."

I once again considered the idea of running out of here, but a new possibility occurred to me. "Paul's uncle is a senator. Couldn't he be pulling the strings?"

"Doubtful," said Lady Elaine. "Titus Kirkwood has been the biggest roadblock to Paul's plea deal."

That made sense. Magistrate Kirkwood had always despised his nephew. I gulped, suddenly emotional again. Half the reason why I couldn't truly hate Paul was because of the abuse he'd suffered at his uncle's hands.

"So are you going to help us or not?" said Brackenberry, suddenly impatient. His sharp gaze seemed to pin me in place.

I looked away, drawing a ragged breath.

"This is very important, Dusty," Lady Elaine said.

I swallowed, searching for my voice, which seemed to have gotten lodged in my throat. "Why? Marrow is . . ." I searched for the right word. He wasn't dead. As far as anyone knew he couldn't die—not with an immortal phoenix as a familiar, one capable of resurrecting him time and time again. "He's gone, right? I mean, he hasn't come back yet, has he?"

"No," Lady Elaine said, firmly. "We don't believe he's back. But he has his supporters. Surely you've seen how quickly animosity is spreading among the different kinds. Not all of the unrest can be attributed to the loss of The Will. We believe Marrow's followers are behind most of it. Including what happened to Britney last night."

I resisted the urge to fidget. Now would be a good time to come clean about Eli, but I couldn't bring myself to do it. "Why do you think that?"

Brackenberry scowled. "Because we were finally able to analyze the curse used on her. It's black magic, of the sort that hasn't been seen in centuries. Only someone like Marrow could've known the spell. We believe he passed it on to some of his chief followers who are now acting on their own to continue his work."

I shuddered. This kept getting worse and worse.

"This also means," Lady Elaine continued, "that you and Eli should focus your dream sessions on Britney's attack. In light of this new evidence."

I sighed, the last of my resolve giving way. I might hate every minute of my time with Paul, and I was nearly as frightened by the idea of facing him as Marrow returning. But I knew I had to.

"Okay," I said, meeting both of their gazes and somehow managing not to flinch. "I'll do it."

7

The Client

I left the conference room a few minutes later and nearly bumped into the principal lurking beyond the door.

"What are you—" I broke off at the dangerous flash in Dr. Hendershaw's eyes, the look magnified to an absurd level by her Coke-bottle glasses. Considering how long it had taken me to complete the heinous restroom-cleaning detention she'd given me last semester, the last thing I wanted was to get in trouble again. Besides, the loud, annoyed huff I heard from behind let me know Lady Elaine would be all over the principal's nosiness.

I made my way to my history class, walking faster than I meant to, the frenzy of my thoughts having a direct effect on my feet, it seemed. I walked through the door into the classroom, not bothering to announce myself. Mrs. Rosencrantz probably wouldn't notice.

"Excuse me," a deep, raspy voice said.

I jerked my head to the front of the room. With a jolt of shock, I realized it wasn't Mrs. Rosencrantz sitting behind the teacher's desk, but an old and rather horrible-looking man. His bald head gleamed in the overhead lights. Two narrow strips of steel-gray hair fanned the tops of his lips in a severe mustache. The same gray color formed the bushy eyebrow hanging over his right eye. There wasn't a left eyebrow at all. Where it should've been perched the top of a black eye patch that seemed to be affixed directly to the man's skull.

I froze halfway into my seat, gaping in surprise. "Woah, you're not Mrs. Rosencrantz."

The man fixed his single eye on me. "Very observant, Miss Everhart. Please sit." He waved at the chair with one hand, the knuckles disproportionally large.

I remained in that awkward halfway position even as my leg muscles began to burn. Sitting seemed like a bad idea, akin to running away from a snarling dog. But as the man took a step toward me, I plopped down into the chair with an audible thump.

He stopped right before my desk and stared down at me. How someone could look so imperious with only one eye, I couldn't guess. But it made me understand the unnatural quiet in the room. This guy commanded respect.

"Do you have a note explaining your tardiness?" the man said, brushing a bit of dust off the sleeve of his dark gray, oddly militaristic blazer.

"Um." I began to fidget, running my hands over the pockets of my jeans, even though I knew I didn't have one. I hadn't bothered to ask. "No, but—"

He silenced me with a single jerk of his chin. "I see. Then I'm sure you will understand the detention I must give you in light of this oversight."

"But—"

He turned away before I could say anything more. "After class tomorrow. Room three thirty-seven, Monmouth Tower. I expect you to be on time."

Choked by the injustice of it all, I glanced sideways, only now registering that Selene was present. She gave me a sympathetic look, but shook her head when I started to mouth a question at her.

I swallowed and forced my gaze to the front of the classroom where One-Eyed Pirate Man now stood before the teacher's desk—*his* desk now, apparently. I wanted to shout and rail at him. I'd been doing something important. Something for the *government*. I shouldn't be punished. But I held back, realizing that I couldn't say any of that.

The teacher addressed the class at large. "As I was saying before our interruption, the city of Atlantis, as described by the philosopher Plato, was comprised of three concentric ring-shaped islands separated by motes." The man raised his hands, and a swell of powerful magic filled the room, making my skin tingle. "It resembled something like this."

An involuntary gasp escaped my throat as a holographic image appeared in the air above the man's head. It was as real and detailed as one of Eli's dreams. The image depicted a city, one with a strange assortment of buildings. A few looked like Egyptian monuments while others appeared to be straight out of ancient Greece or Rome. Three ringed islands formed the city with a wide expanse of bright, blue water separating each one. A series of stone bridges served as the only connection linking them.

The largest, most prominent building stood at the center of the inner island. It was a towering cathedral-like structure with tall pillars surrounding its entrance. At the very top of the structure, a single tower stretched upward like an ancient space needle.

"But . . . sir," someone said. I pulled my gaze away from the image toward the speaker. Never in my life had I heard Travis

Kelly refer to one of the teachers as "sir." As the son of a senator, Travis ran with Lance's crowd, which meant he considered himself too important to bother showing such respect to a lowly teacher.

Until today. I wondered exactly how many detentions this guy had given out already.

"Yes, Mr. Kelly," Pirate Man said. It was starting to bug me that I didn't know his name. I scanned the dry-erase board to see if he'd written it up there, but the magical hologram obscured my sight.

"That can't be Atlantis," Travis said.

"Why do you think so?"

"Because it looks just like Lyonshold."

I turned my gaze back to the vision, intrigued by Travis's claims.

"Ah, yes, the resemblance is true. But what about now?" The teacher gestured with his hands, rotating the image until a massive gateway appeared front and center. Two statues of a half-horse, half-fish creature perched on each side of the gates like stone sentinels.

"Guess I was wrong," said Travis, sounding crestfallen. "There aren't any statues like that in Lyonshold."

"Indeed not," said the teacher. "Lyonshold is guarded by stone lions, not hippocampus." He fanned his fingers and the horses transformed into two regal lions with shaggy manes and wide mouths opening into a snarl.

"Yeah, that's it," said Travis, brightening.

Beside me, Selene raised her hand.

"Yes, Miss Rivers," the teacher said. He lowered his hands and the vision of Atlantis disappeared.

"Why the similarities?" asked Selene.

The man smiled at her. I got the impression it wasn't something he did very often. His teeth looked alarmingly yellow and sharp. I wondered what magickind he was. I looked around for an item that might be a wand or staff hidden by a glamour, but couldn't find any. So either he wasn't a wizard or he had the object hidden beneath his blazer.

"That's a good question," the teacher said. "The exact one that we will attempt to answer in the coming weeks as we delve into the dark, tragic history that was the rise and fall of Atlantis."

Despite my resentment toward the man, I couldn't help the excitement that came over me at this news. I already knew what ordinaries believed to be a myth was actually real, and the idea of Atlantis intrigued me. A lost island, swallowed by the sea? Definitely cool. I wondered if there were magickind archaeology teams who went around excavating stuff like that. *Sign me up for that career choice, please.*

The teacher turned to the dry-erase board and wrote down our homework assignment. I quickly pulled out my notebook from my backpack and copied it, managing to finish just in time for the bell sounding the end of class. Then I scooped up my things, and Selene and I hurried out the door together.

"Geez, what a jerk, huh?" I said, peering at Selene.

She pulled her pink-and-gray camouflage baseball cap out of her bag and yanked it down over her braided black hair, frowning. "He's definitely strict. Made me take this off when class started." She pointed to the cap.

I grimaced. Most of the teachers didn't care if we wore hats to class, even though it went against school policy. I wondered if this guy would enforce the no-gum-chewing rule, too.

"Sucks about your detention," said Selene.

"Yeah, no kidding." I grimaced. "So what's his name anyway?

And if you tell me it's Blackbeard or Sparrow I'm totally going to lose it."

Selene adjusted the strap of her olive green messenger bag hanging over her shoulder. "Close. It's Corvus."

"How's that close?"

"He said it means raven."

I snorted. "Well then it *is* just as bad. What kind is he?"

"Didn't say."

"Weird. I wonder why he would keep it a secret."

Selene glanced sidelong at me, a familiar patient expression on her face. "Isn't it obvious?"

"Uh . . ."

"He doesn't want us to know."

"Why not?" I said, stepping closer to her to avoid a collision with a tuba someone walking the other way was carrying.

Selene exhaled, her voice low, conspiratorial. "There are some kinds that always try to keep their identities secret, like vampires and hags, even some of the fairy races. And certain demonkinds, of course."

I grimaced. "The darkest of the dark, you mean."

Selene nodded. "The administration and all the teachers will know, but not students." Then her expression hardened. "Not that I blame him for wanting to keep it secret. Stops people from judging you based on your kind."

I didn't say anything, understanding her bitter tone all too well. Nightmares had been hunted to near extinction all because the rest of magickind feared we would suck their souls out through their dreams. And everybody assumed sirens were manipulative and vain and that their only value lay in their beauty.

We walked along in silence for a couple of minutes as we

navigated the crowd of students making their way to the cafeteria. The pre-lunchtime ruckus seemed at a fever pitch today despite the presence of the Will Guard watching from alcoves or trolling the hallways, their red tunics like warning flags.

But once we reached the underclassmen cafeteria, Selene said, "So why were you late to class?"

I looked around to see who was nearby. It didn't seem like anybody was listening in, but you never could tell with magickind. Used to be I didn't have to worry about people paying attention to me. I was just a nobody, a halfkind and a Nightmare, the lowest of the low. But after all the stuff with Marrow, my classmates had started taking more of an interest. I didn't think it was a good idea to risk it. I shook my head as we stepped into the lunch line.

A hurt look crossed Selene's face. For a second, I didn't understand, but then I remembered our argument from the night before. "It's not like that," I said. "I just can't tell you here. It's secret and a pretty big deal."

Selene pursued her lips. "Does it have to do with Eli?"

I paused, caught off guard by the question. Then I remembered English class. "What'd you hear?"

"That he stole someone's wand and tried to kill Miss Norton with it and almost succeeded."

I rolled my eyes and then relayed the honest, unembellished story about our English class. I resisted the temptation to point out that she would've seen it for herself if she hadn't ditched this morning. She listened, intrigued as we traversed the line.

"I wonder how he was able to do it," Selene said when I finished.

"No idea."

Selene readjusted her ball cap. "Maybe it has to do with The

Will being gone. He could have witchkind blood somewhere far back in his family."

"I guess it's possible," I said.

Starving after my skimpy breakfast, I decided on a hamburger and a heaping mound of fries. To my surprise, Selene chose the same, forgoing her usual soup and salad combo. Maybe she needed to refuel after her busy night with Lance.

Ew.

We sat down at our usual table, side by side to make for easier whispering. Then with our heads practically touching, I told her about my meeting with the sheriff and Lady Elaine.

"I can't believe they're letting him go," Selene said when I finished. She drummed her fingers on the table, each hard tap emphasizing her dismay.

Nodding, I picked up my water goblet and took a drink.

"And how dare they ask you to go all femme fatale on him. Minus the fatale, of course, since he's the bad guy."

I choked as an image of me in an exotic stripper getup flashed in my mind. Water dribbled out of my mouth, and I wiped it away. "Ugh, don't describe it like that."

Selene huffed. "And I can't believe you agreed to it."

"Like I had a choice with so much at stake. You know how dangerous he is. How dangerous all of Marrow's supporters are."

Selene gave a little shiver. "I guess you're right."

Wanting to change the subject, I told her about last night and all the stuff with Britney. When I got to the part about seeing Eli in the dream, she didn't react at all. I nudged her with my elbow. "Don't you think that's a little odd?"

Selene shrugged. "Weird, maybe, but I definitely don't think he had anything to do with it if that's what you're suggesting."

I picked up my napkin and wiped the salt from my lips. "Even after what happened in English?"

"Oh, come on, Dusty." She wrinkled her nose. "This is Eli you're talking about. He would never hurt Britney, and we know he's not a Marrow supporter. His presence was just coincidence. I bet Britney has a crush on him."

"She's got a funny way of showing it." I popped a fry into my mouth and chewed dejectedly. The idea of Britney liking Eli hadn't occurred to me, but it was definitely possible. Eli's attractiveness transcended all the kinds. I'd even seen Irene Stark checking him out once, the same person who believed so strongly in the superiority of her kind that she often refused to talk to someone if they weren't a fellow fairy.

"It's not as if most of us can control what we dream about the way you can," Selene said. The note of reproach in her tone distracted me from my jealous musings about Eli.

I supposed she had a point. But then the image of that plinth and the unreadable letters rose unbidden in my mind. She was wrong about my ability to control my dreams, at least lately. I shuddered, remembering the deep, empty feeling inside me from the need to reach that plinth and discover those hidden words. I felt it even now.

Fortunately, a distraction appeared a moment later as Lance Rathbone walked into the cafeteria. He paused, surveyed the crowd, and then approached our table. Right away, I could tell there was something off about him. His clothes were in disarray, one pant leg stuck halfway inside a black kneesock while the opposite leg sported an untied shoe and a blue sock. One side of his shirt hung lower than the other from the misaligned buttons.

I looked up and saw his face was puffy and that two dark circles rimmed his cheekbones. His light brown hair lay plastered against his skull on one side and stuck straight out on the other. He peered down at Selene, blinking a couple of times as if in a daze. His green eyes, usually bright, seemed dull.

"Rough night?" I said, smirking. I winked at Selene, but she frowned back at me, her expression confused.

She stared up at Lance. "What happened to you?" she said with no trace of irony in her voice.

It was my turn to be confused. I examined Lance more closely, guessing my assumption had been wrong. The puffiness and bruises were too extreme to have been brought on by a sleepless night. He looked like he'd been beaten up. I knew Selene could be a feisty one, but I didn't think she was into the kind of stuff that would leave her love interest looking like he'd had a run-in with a pissed-off gorilla.

Double ew.

Lance didn't answer as he rubbed his eyes with his knuckles, leaving them even redder and puffier than before. "You seen Eli?" he finally asked, directing the question at me.

I shook my head. "Not since English. He got sent to the principal's office."

Lance surveyed the cafeteria. "And he's not back yet?"

Selene and I exchanged a look. He was really out of it. If Arkwell had been a normal ordinary high school, I would've assumed he was stoned or something.

"You haven't heard?" said Selene.

Lance slid a leg over the bench opposite us, whacked his knee on the table, and then plopped down, groaning.

I considered him a moment, shocked to find myself actually

feeling concern. I'd never seen the guy looking so disoriented and clumsy.

"Heard what?" Lance said, rubbing his knee.

Selene relayed the story about Eli doing magic in English class.

"Huh," Lance said when she finished.

Selene reached across the table and whacked him once on the top of the head.

"Hey." He winced, putting a hand over his brow.

"What's wrong with you?" said Selene.

Lance's mouth opened but no words came out. It was as if what little part of his brain he normally used had a short in it. He closed his mouth, knuckled his eyes again, and then glowered back at us, looking more like himself than he had so far today. "Nothing's wrong with me. I found this note and I wanted to show it to Eli."

He reached into his front pocket and pulled out a folded slip of paper. "Seems kind of important."

Selene and I grabbed for it at the same time, but she got there first, ripping it out of his hands. She set it on the table and flipped it open, revealing a typed message on the inside addressed to the "Dream Team." My eyes read the words at once, but my brain took several seconds to absorb the meaning:

Meet me in the library tunnel alcove. 10:00. About a case. Life and death.

"When did you find this?" I said, my voice constricted by fear. It couldn't be a coincidence, not given the time and place.

"Uh . . ." Lance stuttered. "This morning."

Selene narrowed her eyes. "Are you sure?"

Lance scratched his chin as if the question required deep introspection. Gritty black marks rimmed his fingertips. "I think so, only I kind of remember seeing it last night maybe, but I thought I dreamed it. It's weird, but everything after dinner yesterday is fuzzy."

"Um, that's a little more than weird," I said.

Selene waved at Lance. "Let me see your necklace."

"Why?"

"Just let me see it," she snapped. Selene normally wasn't this rude to people, but Lance was the exception, part of their strange love/hate thing.

Scowling, Lance obeyed, pulling the thick silver chain out from underneath his shirt collar. "Happy?" he said.

"Never with you," said Selene. "Take it off and place it on the table."

Lance grunted but again did as she said. He unclasped the chain and dropped it in front of her.

Selene didn't pick it up, but held her hand over it. Then she closed her eyes and began to hum. My skin tingled with the familiar, pleasant feeling of her siren magic. The chain and the round, flat charm attached to it began to glow. At first it shone bright yellow but then little tendrils of black began to seep through like bloodstains through clean gauze.

I examined the charm that I'd first taken as some kind of Catholic saint medal, but then I realized it was an engraving of the Joker, Lance's pop culture hero. I flashed Lance a you're-a-moron look, but it was wasted as he wasn't looking at me. Instead his eyes were fixed on the joker playing card he was shuffling back and forth in his hands. From the beat-up look of the card, it was time for a new one. A piece was missing from one of the corners.

I returned my attention to Selene, who stopped humming and pulled her hand away. The glow on the necklace vanished.

Lance returned the card to his pocket and, with something like his normal swagger, said, "Well, my little Sherlock, what did you deduce?"

Selene didn't answer at once. She picked up the note and ran her thumb over it. I half-expected her to start humming again, but she didn't. Finally she said, "I think you've been cursed." She hesitated, biting her lip. "At least, there's some kind of unpleasant magic lingering on your necklace. It's a talisman, right? And you never take it off?"

Lance nodded, his gaze fixed on the joker charm as if seeing it in a new and sinister light.

I touched Selene's arm. "How can you tell?"

She turned her eyes on me, the irises a startling shade of violet. "It's a detection spell we've been learning in my musemancy class. We're studying siren defense right now. It's supposed to reveal the presence of any magic on an object to let us know if it's safe to touch." She grimaced. "I guess back in the day, a lot of witchkind and even some ordinaries used to enslave sirens with magical necklaces and bracelets and things. Pretty nasty business."

"No kidding." My mind drifted back to the conversation with Brackenberry and Lady Elaine about the unrest between the kinds. I had a feeling that Selene wasn't studying siren defense right now because the curriculum called for it.

Lance picked up the necklace and put it on. "So you're saying somebody cursed me?"

"I think so," said Selene, "although I'm not really skilled at the spell yet. But the magic I detected is residual, not active. And it's clear *something* happened to you. Question is, who would want to harm you?"

"Um, anybody that's met him?" I offered.

"Ha, ha," Lance said, rubbing his temple.

Selene's brow furrowed. "Who was the last person you remember seeing?"

"Eli probably. Who else? He is my roommate."

I rubbed my arms, warding off a sudden chill at the coincidence. Was it possible Eli had seen the note, too? If so, it might've given him reason to be down in the alcove.

Selene started to ask Lance another question, but someone called his name from across the way. Lance stood up, his eyes lingering for a moment on Selene. "See you later." Then he turned and walked off.

Selene made a noise like a grunt, although it was far too feminine and delicate a sound to be labeled one. "Typical." She returned her focus to the note. "Looks like somebody wants to hire us for a case. I wonder who it is."

"I've got a pretty good idea," I said, a little surprised Selene hadn't come to the same conclusion already. Then again, I hadn't gone into details about where Britney had been found.

Selene arched her eyebrows. "Who?"

"Britney Shell. The library tunnel alcove was where she was attacked, and assuming the note did arrive yesterday, then the timing lines up, too."

Worry clouded Selene's expression as I finished speaking. She began to trace a finger along the pink scar that ran down the side of her face from her hairline to jaw. I knew the gesture was a recently developed nervous habit. I could tell she was connecting the dots just as I had. Two people cursed in the same night, one unconscious in the hospital and one with unaccountable memory loss. And the only things connecting them were a note and . . . Eli.

"Are you still so sure Eli had nothing to do with it?" I asked, hating the doubt rising up inside me. I wanted to believe his complete innocence, but always the memory of Paul haunted me. And this was the magical world where anything was possible. He could be under a spell, or maybe it wasn't Eli at all but some kind of shapeshifter. Either way, I had to get to the bottom of it.

Selene's finger stilled on her face. She stared back at me, her eyes thoughtful. But she didn't answer. There wasn't one to give.

～ 8 ～

Conductor

That night, I headed to my dream session with Eli, dreading it more than I had in months. The school day had ended with no sign of him, but he'd sent me an e-mail a few hours after dinner saying he was finally back.

Can you come to our session early? he'd written. *We've got lots to talk about.*

He had a gift for understatement.

I took the direct route to his dorm room, through the commons. The rain had finally stopped, but the air remained damp and chilly. The wet surfaces of slanting roofs, archways, and parapets of the dark stone buildings that comprised Arkwell's medieval-esque campus glistened in the pale sliver of moon overhead.

By the time I reached Flint Hall my shoes were sodden and my hair twice as poufy from frizz. I climbed the stairs to Eli's floor trying not to squeak with each step. When I walked in, the living area of the dorm Eli shared with Lance was empty. I glanced around, surprised by Eli's absence.

I cleared my throat. "Anybody here?"

Eli stepped through the doorway of the thin divider that separated the sleeping quarters from the living area. He was shirtless. I stared, openmouthed, unable to help myself. He wasn't just shirtless, he was wet. Droplets of water glistened on his chest that was hard with muscle and absolutely perfect, even with the three scars that ran diagonally from his shoulder to his rib cage. The scars, like the one on Selene's face, were still pink with newness, the wounds suffered in our fight with Marrow. On the left side of his chest perched a black scorpion tattoo.

I forced my gaze up, a warmth that had nothing to do with my brisk walk across campus heating my body. Eli's black hair stuck up at odd angles, wet and sexy as hell. I wanted to brush it out with my fingers.

Finally, I dropped my gaze to his face. Eli had frozen, too, and was looking at me looking at him. Something vibrated in the air between us. The sweet, tingly memory of that one kiss overwhelmed my senses as if it had happened a moment ago instead of weeks.

A slow, mischievous grin stretched across Eli's lips and the intense feeling broke. I let out the breath I'd been holding and felt my body relax. I could handle the playful Eli a lot better than the smoldering, serious one of a moment before—*that* version of Eli scared me. In all the right ways.

"Sorry," he said. "But I had to squeeze in a quick shower. I was smelling a little funky."

At the word smell, I took a deep inhale and immediately regretted it as my thoughts went fuzzy from the impact of his soapy, masculine scent. Nobody should smell that good.

I closed my eyes and shook my head, forcing my mind to focus. "Why'd you wait so long to take one?" I said, once I felt marginally in control again. I opened my eyes and dared another look at him. It proved to be bad timing as he was in the process of threading his arms through a T-shirt and pulling it over his head. The muscles in his arms and chest moved in alarming ways, all sinewy and popping.

He caught me staring again as his head emerged from the top of the shirt. I dropped my gaze from his bright, knowing eyes, my skin reddening from head to toe.

"I didn't mean to wait so long," said Eli. "But I had a dozen things come up when I got back and just now had a chance." He turned and sat down on the nearby sofa. "Anyway. It's no big deal, right? I mean, you don't seem worried about it."

Even though I knew he was only teasing, my temper flared. It had been a long couple of months of suggestive looks and tentative touches as we danced around what had happened and what this thing was between us. "No, what I'm worried about," I said as I shoved my hand into my front pocket and withdrew Britney's note, "is this."

I stepped toward the sofa and chucked it at him. The action didn't work as well as I planned, the lightweight paper floating toward him rather than dive-bombing. Irritated even more at my failure for good dramatic effect, I gave the note a hard shove with my mind magic. It smacked Eli in the face.

Whoops.

"Ouch." He grabbed the note and shot me a glare. "You really need to work on your aim."

"You need to work on your reflexes."

He stared at me, his expression turning toward the dangerous side, like a panther contemplating a good chase. Then he shrugged and examined the note, pulling it open. "What is this?" His eyes moved across the message, then he flipped it over and read the Dream Team addressee. He raised his gaze to mine, his mouth open in confusion. "Where did you get this?"

I cringed at his choice of words. What I wanted was a clear, absolute denial, not an ambiguous response. "I don't know. You tell me?"

To my dismay, Eli smiled. "Why are you pissed at me? Don't get me wrong, I kind of like it, but . . ."

I flushed again, hating how easily he knocked me off-kilter. "I'm not pissed. I'm concerned. I'm pretty sure Britney wrote that note. Lance gave it to me at lunch, says he found it here in your dorm. Only he can't remember when. His memory is all messed up because somebody cursed him last night. But the last person he remembers seeing is *you*."

The playfulness vanished from Eli's face. "What are you implying?"

I folded my arms over my chest and backed up, leaning against the desk that sat across from the sofa. I had to know for sure, paranoid or no. "Where were you last night between ten and eleven forty-five?"

Eli's eyebrows rose. "You're kidding, right?"

I shook my head.

He stood and took two steps toward me, close enough that I had to lean my head back to keep my eyes fixed on his face. "I was right here. In this dorm. And why the hell are you treating me like I'm Pa—"

He broke off, but I heard the rest of what he was about to say anyway. *Like I'm Paul.*

I swallowed, suddenly swimming in doubt. Eli's anger came off him in waves. Why had I accused him so quickly? So tactlessly? I bit my lip, hating how crazy he made me. Or maybe I was just going crazy in general.

I exhaled, letting the air escape through my teeth slowly. "You were also in Britney's dream."

Eli craned his head sideways, frowning. "What?"

I brushed back strands of my red hair that had fallen in my face. "It's true. I saw you with a wand in your hand attacking her while she tried to run away."

"Let me get this straight." Eli took a few steps back from me. "You think I first cursed Lance and then ran down to the library alcove and cursed Britney and then was stupid enough to leave evidence like this hanging about." He waved the note in the air.

I winced. Spoken like that it did seem absurd and completely out of character for Eli. But it was too late to retreat now. "Something like that."

"Oh, and I suppose you have a motive for why I would attack her, yeah?"

"No, but you've never been able to do magic until now and . . ." I trailed off, my suspicions about him weakening by the second.

Eli opened his mouth to respond then closed it. I held my breath, waiting for him to explode or, even worse, to transform into a stranger, the way that Paul had transformed right before my eyes from a caring boyfriend to a betrayer.

Finally, Eli said through gritted teeth, "I had nothing to do with what happened to Britney or Lance. I've never seen this note before, and I've never done any magic until this morning in English class." He paused and drew an uneven breath. "And I can't believe you'd think for a second that I might've done it. Dreams aren't real, Dusty. You know that. Only my dreams have any meaning. The ones we share together."

Another wave of guilt crashed over me, followed by remorse. He was right. And I was wrong. Even worse, I could tell I'd really hurt him. The tension in him went deeper than anger.

"I'm sorry." I closed my eyes and pinched the bridge of my nose, unable to bear the weight of his stare. "It's just so much has been happening. And it felt like more than coincidence. And I guess I'm just a little paranoid." I let my hand drop and looked back at him, hoping he believed me.

He clenched his teeth. A muscle ticked in his jaw.

"If it helps, I didn't tell Lady Elaine about seeing you."

Eli put his hands on his hips. "Oh, yeah? And why not?"

"To protect you, and maybe because deep down I knew you didn't have anything to do with it. And I really am sorry. I guess I'm having a hard time trusting these days." I spoke the last sentence without really meaning it, at least not at first. But once it was out, I felt the truth behind it. I'd been denying it for months, but I *was* having a hard time trusting. And sleeping. And doing anything normal. I kept seeing Marrow's face in every stranger. Kept remembering how much it had hurt to find out the truth about Paul.

Some of the hardness in Eli's expression softened, and he stepped toward me again, vanishing the distance between us. He gripped my shoulders, his hands warm through my shirt. "It's all right. I understand why you've got trust issues. But I'm nothing like him. Nothing."

I nodded, unable to speak. He was so close I could feel his breath. All I wanted was to lean toward him, vanishing the last of the space between my mouth and his. His head tilted downward by an inch, his fingers squeezing my shoulders.

And then he turned away from me and sat down on the sofa. I drew a deep, ragged breath, my head swimming and my whole body on fire.

Eli shifted his position on the sofa a couple of times before turning his attention to the note once more. He cleared his throat. "Maybe we can use this to help us figure out what really happened. I haven't talked to Lance at all today, but I will first thing in the morning."

"Yeah, good idea," I said, my voice breathless. At least the prospect of a new case would lighten Eli's mood. "Oh, and I'm supposed to focus your dream on Britney's attack. Lady Elaine thinks it might be connected to some of Marrow's supporters."

"Makes sense." Eli slid the note into his pocket.

I considered telling him the rest of it, but decided not to. For one thing, Lady Elaine and the sheriff had sworn me to secrecy. For another, telling him about that would inevitably lead to telling him about Paul. Didn't take a genius to guess that such a revelation wouldn't go down too well at the moment. I figured Eli hadn't heard about his release yet—he would've said something straightaway.

I pulled out the chair beneath the desk and sat down. "So tell me about your trip to Lyonshold."

Eli arched a single eyebrow at me. "How did you know I was there?"

"Oh." *Crap.* I searched for an explanation and decided a partial truth was better than a lie. "I bumped into Sheriff Brackenberry on campus today. He told me."

"What was he doing on campus?"

I leaned forward, only now remembering. "He was interrogating Oliver Cork. I guess he was the last person to see Britney before she was attacked. They were attending some meeting about a group called the Terra Tribe. I think it's like a student organization, but I'm not sure. Ever heard of it?"

Eli shook his head. He stood and walked to the desk, bending down next to me as he opened the drawer to retrieve a pen. I couldn't help myself. I took another deep inhale of his clean scent. His hard shoulder brushed my arm, and I caught myself leaning in toward him. But he moved away, using the desk's surface to write the name Terra Tribe down in the little notebook he'd started carrying around in his back pocket after we formed the Dream Team.

"I'll research it later," he said, returning to the sofa. He yawned. "Anyway, my trip to the capital was pretty interesting. A couple of people interviewed me about what happened, and then I spent several hours playing lab rat to a group of magickind scientists." He screwed up his face. "More like mad scientists."

I had a vision of a bunch of wizards poking and prodding at him with needle-tipped wands and resisted a shudder. "What'd they figure out?"

Eli brushed a hand through his hair, his calm, nonchalant expression belying the sudden excitement I sensed in him. "They think I'm a Conductor."

"Like a train conductor?" An image of Eli dressed in a blue and white striped pair of overalls popped up in my mind, and I started to grin.

"It's not funny." Eli crossed his arms. "It's kind of cool, actually." A smile broke across his face, his excitement refusing to be contained a moment longer. "It's really rare and not something anyone has seen since before The Will, but a Conductor is an ordinary who has the ability to channel magic from inside a contained source."

I tilted my head, thinking it over. "What does that mean? A contained source."

He shrugged. "All magical objects I guess. From what they've told me so far, stuff like wands and staffs have a magical core, kind of like a battery. You know how witchkind require an object to focus their magic?"

I nodded, envisioning my favorite analogy for this phenomenon—a witchkind's magic was the computer and the magical object the mouse and keyboard.

"Well, it's the core that does the focusing," Eli went on. "Their magic flows through the core, but it doesn't really use it. Conductors, on the other hand, channel the magic *inside* the core. It's a more limited source of power, but still magic. Enough for minor spells at least."

The scene from English class replayed in my mind. The fligere spell wasn't very complicated, but given how hard it had struck Miss Norton, I wasn't sure I would call it minor. And that had been only his first attempt.

"In other words," Eli said, "I can do magic now." I looked at him, surprised by his bubbly, kid-on-Christmas-morning tone. He was grinning in earnest, our earlier argument forgotten. "I'm supposed to pick out a wand sometime tomorrow."

The reality of what he was saying finally dawned on me. Eli Booker, the only ordinary at Arkwell, could now do magic. All my worry about him being in Britney's dream faded away in genuine happiness at this news. He would no longer be the outsider. No longer have to watch from the sidelines, only studying the theory of magic but never practicing it himself. He would finally be a part.

I beamed at him. "Congratulations. I'm so happy for you."

"Thanks." He leaned back, putting his hands behind his head. "I think this makes breaking The Will totally worth it."

I frowned. "So The Will was set up to prevent Conductors from doing magic the same as halfkinds?" It was this reason, more than any other, why Paul had become Marrow's follower.

He was a halfkind, cut off from his magic at birth by the spell all because the Magi Senate wanted to keep the kinds from intermixing. But not anymore.

Eli dropped his hands into his lap. "Looks like it."

"Did they say why?"

"I asked, but nobody had an answer."

"Huh." I thought back to the reason Marrow had given for why halfkinds had been blocked—the Magi feared them because they tended to be so powerful. I wondered if the same was true of Conductors.

Eli glanced at his watch, excitement still buzzing around him. "Then again, I don't know how I'm ever going to fall asleep for our session without The Will to help me."

I laughed. "I don't blame you."

"For real." Another huge grin seemed to split his face in half. "Do you know any sleeping spells?"

I shook my head. "Nope. Even if I did, they wouldn't work on you."

"Right. Good thing, too, or we would never have beaten Marrow."

I smiled, remembering with grim satisfaction how the spell I'd cast at Eli had ricocheted off of him and struck Marrow. It was a rare moment of brilliance for me and had only worked because, as my dream-seer partner, Eli was impervious to my magic.

He shifted sideways and laid his head on the arm of the sofa, stretching out his long, lean body, his feet dangling over the edge. "I guess I'll have to do it the old-fashioned way."

I nodded, but didn't say anything, an uneasy feeling tightening in the pit of my stomach. My happiness for him was truly genuine, but now a trickle of worry began to seep in. Magic had a way of changing people. Look at what it had done to Paul. Just the hope of possessing its power had been enough to turn him from a decent person into someone willing to lie, cheat, and kill to get what he wanted.

It would change Eli, too. Inevitable, really.

And as I watched him fall asleep, his breath slowing as his chest rose and fell, I could only hope it wouldn't change him too much. Or for the worse.

9

Dream Share

Nearly twenty minutes later, Eli finally fell asleep. I didn't need the slow rhythm of his breath to tell me. I could smell the fictus coming off him as he started dreaming, my desire for it a bone-deep ache.

I stood and crossed the room to the sofa, climbing on top of him as gently as I could. It wasn't that I feared waking him, but rather that I was hyperaware of my body touching his. My attraction to him made this dream-feeding business more complicated than it already was. I'd long since considered the possibility that our dream-seer connection was half the reason why Eli never mentioned kissing me, and why he'd never taken things a step further. It was definitely one of the reasons why I never brought it up.

Sighing, I slid my leg across his chest and sat down. Then I touched my fingertips to his forehead and felt the familiar, swooping rush as my consciousness left my body and entered the world of Eli's dreams.

Bright colors swirled and danced around me, vivid and hyper real. There were colors in here that didn't have names, colors that defied imagination. His dream tasted so much sweeter than Britney's, his fictus so much more satisfying. It had been such a long time since I'd dream-fed on anyone else that I didn't realize how accustomed I'd grown to him until now. Like an addiction. For a moment as the dream world formed around me, I felt completely at peace and safe, all the worries about Paul and Britney and Marrow nothing but a distant memory.

The good feeling evaporated as I took in my surroundings. I appeared to have arrived in some medieval torture chamber. Strange metal devices sat on a row of wooden shelves nearby while more devices hung from the walls, including several pairs of manacles. In the center of the circular room stood a rectangular stone table inlaid with an assortment of gems and engraved with mystical symbols. Eli was lying on top of the table, seemingly asleep or unconscious. He was shirtless. Again. *Great, even more distraction.*

But at least Eli wasn't the only person present. Three other people stood around the table, two men and a woman, all of them wearing long robes of light blue. One of the men held a clipboard, the other a stethoscope. The woman held a wand that she was waving back and forth over Eli.

The clipboard and stethoscope gave me pause, and I turned in a circle, taking a closer look at my surroundings. This place wasn't a torture chamber. It was a science lab. The marbled walls had thrown me off, but the instruments on the shelves were the kind we used every day in my alchemy class—glass beakers and vials, jars of herbs and magical ingredients, even microscopes.

Feeling a little calmer, I approached the table, sidestepping around the trio of scientists. "Hey, Eli. Wake up."

His eyes fluttered opened, and he stared up at me, confused at first. Then he smiled and sat up, giving me a nice shot of his muscle-covered backside. He swung his legs over the side of the table and peered around.

"Wow," he said. "I can't believe I'm dreaming about this place. Thought I'd had enough of it."

I took a step back, making sure we kept a safe distance between us. "Is this where they did all those experiments on you today?"

"Uh-huh." He jumped off the table and pushed his way through the scientists who remained oblivious to his presence. He examined the room. "Well, more or less."

I didn't bother asking him what the differences were. Now that I knew the place, it didn't hold much interest.

I clapped my hands. "Are you ready?"

"Yep. Take us to the scene of the crime."

Ignoring the cheese factor in his words, I closed my eyes and concentrated on the library tunnel alcove. I drew on my memories of both the actual place and the way I'd seen it in Britney's dreams. For a while, nothing seemed to happen. I could still hear the scientists murmuring behind me. I focused harder, willing my imagination to set the scene.

Finally, I felt the dream world respond, and I opened my eyes to see a gray mist swirling around Eli and me. Then without warning, the mist vanished and the world snapped into place. It happened so hard, I staggered forward, just managing to catch my balance. I straightened and looked around. With a horrible swooping sensation, I realized we hadn't arrived in the tunnels.

We were in *my* dream. My nightmare.

I stood on the top of that tall tower again, the black blanket of sky overhead seeming near enough to touch. A ferocious wind buffeted my body, forcing me back and away from the stone plinth set at the tower's center. The moment my eyes saw the plinth all reason fled my mind as the need to read those letters took hold of me. I lurched forward, throwing my weight and the force of my will against the wind. It screamed in answer, blowing harder, determined to stop me.

I dropped to my knees and began to inch my way forward. Somewhere, as if from far away, I heard Eli shouting. "Dusty! What are you doing? Where are we?"

I glanced up long enough to see that he wasn't far away at all, but standing over me, completely unaffected by the wind or those hidden letters on the plinth's surface.

I tried to respond but couldn't. Speaking would require too much effort, effort I needed to reach the plinth.

With agonizing slowness, I made my way to it. Eli's voice and all his meaningless questions and concerns were nothing but a dull hum in my ears, a noise barely distinguishable from the wailing of the wind.

"Seriously, Dusty, you're scaring me. What's going on? Why aren't you changing the dream?"

I stretched my hands toward the plinth, my eyes fixed on the faint imprint of letters. I ran my forefinger over them, again trying to read it like Braille. I could almost make out the first one.

"Come on, Dusty, talk to me. Talk to me or I'm going to kick you out of this dream, I swear it."

His warning registered in my brain. I couldn't let him evict me. Not until I saw the letters.

"Got to read this," I said, panting.

"Read what?" Eli squatted down beside me. I recoiled from him, afraid we would touch by accident.

"The letters." I clawed at the plinth, my nails quickly wearing down to nubs. I pressed on, frantic now, uncaring of the blood streaks I left on the stone as I scraped away the flesh on my fingertips.

"Stop it, Dusty. Stop it right now." Eli stood up, looming over me.

"Don't touch me," I hissed, and on some distant plane I heard the insanity in my voice. It frightened me somewhere deep down, but not enough to break through the plinth's spell.

"If you don't stop I'm going to touch you." Out of the corner of my eye, I saw Eli clenching his hands into fists. "Dammit, Dusty, what's wrong with you?"

I shook my head, using my palms now. I could almost see it. A straight edge and a curved top, a P and yet that didn't feel right. It could be a B or an R. *P or B or R or P or B or R. Which one?* Eli stooped toward me again, and I sensed his hands reaching for my frantically clawing arms.

"Don't!" I screamed.

Boom.

Something struck the tower, and it gave a violent lurch as if from an earthquake.

Eli stumbled backward while I fell forward into the plinth, my forehead smacking stone. Dazed, I pushed myself back into a kneeling position as the tower gave another shudder.

"What the hell?" Eli turned and ran to the tower's edge, looking out at the night sky surrounding us.

Only as I struggled to my feet, I realized the sky wasn't dark as it had been when we arrived, but was suddenly bright, as if lit by an unseen sun. The unnatural sight of that brightness broke the plinth's hold on me at last. With my limbs trembling as hard as the tower, I hurried to the edge, wanting to see what was happening.

I looked down at a sparse forest, populated by giant, ancient trees, some of them nearly as tall as the tower. At once, I found the source of all the shaking as a giant fireball shot up from the ground and struck one of the trees. It exploded on impact. Fire and debris spewed outward.

Boom-boom-boom.

The explosions were everywhere now, closing in around us.

Another fireball struck the tower, this one from far below, at its core. It rumbled upward, almost slowly. The ground shot up beneath my feet like a sinkhole in reverse. I pitched forward and slammed into the wall. The fissure spread and widened. The wall broke, huge chunks of stone falling over the edge. For a second I struggled to catch my balance, but then I lost it completely, helpless to stop my forward propulsion. Helpless to do anything as I plunged over the side.

The rush of wind ripped the scream from my throat. My body was beyond my control, my limbs locked in place by the momentum of the fall. Even still I twisted and turned through the air like a performance skydiver. I tried to pull back from the dream, but I was too afraid to concentrate. Far above me I saw Eli leap off the edge of the tower. He dove toward me, arms stretched forward. No fear showed in his face, only determination.

Several long, terrifying seconds later, his body struck mine with the force of a meteor. The dream world exploded around us. Pain tore through me, my entire existence seeming to shatter.

The next moment we were back in Eli's dorm. I tumbled sideways off the sofa. My head cracked against the stone floor, Lance's designer rug doing little to soften the impact. Starbursts covered my vision, and a sick feeling expanded in my stomach. I lay there, motionless, but I could still feel myself falling through the air, plummeting to my death from that tall, crumbling tower.

I kept my eyes open, afraid to shut them as I willed away the pain and terror. I'd never been afraid of heights before, but I had a feeling that might change after this.

Eli's face filled my vision as he leaned over me. "Are you all right?" He reached for my arms.

I tried to nod, but the motion made my head pound even harder. Eli took hold of my wrists and pulled me upward. I let him, but only because I thought I would get sick if I opened my mouth to speak. When I was in a sitting position, he let go of my wrists. At once I began to fall backward, my equilibrium still screwed. He grabbed me, cursing beneath his breath as he dropped to his knees and wrapped his arms around my shoulders.

I sagged into him, vaguely aware of the tears wetting my face.

"Shhhh." He stroked my hair. "It's okay. It was just a dream."

But we both knew that wasn't true. His dreams weren't normal dreams. Not the ones we shared together. If I had fallen all the way, if I had struck the ground . . .

I shuddered, my body convulsing with another surge of terror. He held me tighter.

Slowly the fear began to pass, and I forced my sluggish brain to start working again. How had we ended up in my dream? How could it be so powerful to make me lose control like that? I tried to remember all the things I knew about dream-walking. Some Nightmares were powerful enough to infiltrate dreams from afar. Was it possible someone was interfering with both my dreams and Eli's? I couldn't imagine what else besides magic could affect me like that. My compulsion to read those letters went far beyond the level of normal dreaming. Even now my head buzzed with the desire.

I heard Eli draw a breath, and I braced for the inevitable questions, but none came. He seemed to understand that I wasn't ready to talk. He just held me instead, his arms a strong, comforting force around me, his hand gentle as he stroked my hair.

I don't know how it happened, but sometime later, my body shifted toward his, and I felt his warm breath on my face, a slow in and out. Inch by inch, I turned my face toward that warmth. His lips grazed my cheek. And then he was kissing me, his mouth full on mine, hot, wet, and demanding, as if he'd longed for it as much as I had. His hands slid up my neck beneath my hair until he cupped the back of my head between his palms, locking me in place. Tingles coursed through my body, explosions of pleasure erupting over my skin.

It ended much faster than it began. One second he was kneeling on the floor, kissing me, the next he stood and backed away, leaving me suddenly cold and struggling to hold myself up.

"Sorry," he said.

I blinked once, twice, my head swimming with sensation and emotional overload. He was sorry? What for? He was acting like there was something wrong with kissing me. Or maybe the kiss had been bad.

I stopped that train of thought before it could continue any further down the tracks. I was already straddling the crazy line as it was. The last thing I needed was that kind of self-doubt. I'd kissed boys before him, and no one had ever complained.

But none of them were Eli.

Shut up.

I started to push myself up, nearly slipped, but then felt Eli's hand on my arm, steadying me.

"Are you okay?" he said.

I pulled away from him, refusing to look in his eyes, afraid of what I might find there. I turned and sat down on the sofa, dropping my head into my hands. Now that the thrill of the kiss was gone, the pounding had returned full force, made even worse by my embarrassment.

"Why are you sorry?"

Eli shook his head. "It was wrong. I shouldn't have done it. You're hurt . . . and . . ."

"Oh, okay," I said, still embarrassed and wanting the subject over.

He sat down beside me, keeping a careful distance between us. "So what happened?"

"I . . . I don't know." I ran both hands through my hair, relishing the pain in my skull as my fingers caught on snags. "But that place with the tower and the plinth . . . I've seen it before."

"Where?"

I turned my head toward him, risking a glance. But he didn't seem embarrassed or flustered at all. The kiss might never have happened. His expression registered only concern and interest.

"In my dreams," I said. "Last night and a couple of times before, I think."

"Really?"

"Really."

"Huh." He leaned back against the sofa, his hands falling into his lap. "That's pretty crazy."

"Yeah, tell me about it." I crossed my arms and leaned back, too, hating the distance between us and yet wishing it was bigger. I wanted to be worried only about the dream, but that kiss and his reaction to it kept trying to press its way to the forefront of my mind. Was he really sorry simply because I was hurt and he thought it bad timing?

"Have you told Lady Elaine about the dreams?" Eli said.

"No, of course not." An odd possessive feeling came over me

at the idea, one I didn't understand but couldn't deny. They were my dreams and nobody's business but my own. The word on that plinth was meant for me; I could sense it. A tinge of resentment went through me at the knowledge that Eli had seen it. I wished I could take it back. Never mind that he was forced to share his dreams with me time and time again. That dream was different. I knew it, and I could tell by Eli's tense silence that he knew it, too.

"Well," he said, stretching out his hand to pat my knee, "we'll have better luck next time."

"Sure." I tried not to tense at his touch. It was hard. My lips still felt wet and swollen from our kiss. *Sorry,* he had said. Sorry.

So was I.

~ 10 ~

Mind Games

Paul Kirkwood returned to Arkwell the very next day. I spotted him walking down the cafeteria hallway before breakfast. At first I didn't recognize the tall boy with the short-cropped blond hair and lean, serious face. Then it struck me, and I pictured a ponytail and flyaway hairs on the boy's head. Of course they would've shaved his head in jail. In some matters, magickind liked to emulate the ways of the ordinary world.

I stumbled to a halt, limbs numb. Paul's eyes locked on mine, and my heart seemed to plunge into my stomach. For a second, I hoped he didn't recognize me. We were still so far away; I must look different, too. But recognition lit his expression. He didn't smile or wave. He froze in place as if seeing me was as much a shock to him as it was to me.

I ripped my gaze away from him, spun on my heel, and darted into the girl's restroom. My heart had clambered up my throat now, my pulse a flurry of beating wings beneath my breastbone. I wasn't ready for this. I didn't think I would ever be ready.

I turned to the nearest sink, twisted on the cold water, and splashed my face. At least I didn't have to worry about smearing my makeup. I wasn't wearing any. It had been well past mid-night by the time I returned to my dorm, and I'd barely slept afterward. When I woke this morning, I was too tired for mascara.

I looked down at my outfit, a hastily donned long-sleeved T-shirt of a colorless gray and a pair of loose-fitting jeans over sneakers. I couldn't face Paul looking like this. Why hadn't anyone warned me he would be here? A girl needed the right clothes, let alone makeup, to face her murderous apprentice ex-boyfriend with any kind of confidence.

For a second, I thought I might be sick, but then the door opened behind me, and Selene's voice said, "Dusty?"

I faced her, feeling considerably calmer in her presence.

She frowned at the sight of me, her lower lip sticking out in something close to a pout. "You're not seriously going to let him affect you like that, are you?"

I swallowed guiltily and then felt a flicker of anger. Both at her for pointing out my weakness and at me for letting it happen. She was right. The more I allowed him to bother me, the more he won. I refused to let him.

Tugging down the end of my shirt, I stood up straight, raising my head high. "No, I'm not."

Selene bared her perfect teeth in a smile. "Well, good. Because Eli and Paul are about to get in a fight. Which might not be too helpful in your get-him-to-trust-you quest."

"What?"

I stormed past her, the sound of raised voices beyond the door registering in my ears. I had to push my way through a wall of bodies as I exited the restroom. It seemed every student in my year and probably several others had gathered in the hallway to witness the fight.

Only Eli and Paul weren't fighting. Not yet. As I broke through the crowd, I saw them circling each other like a pair of teenaged lions. Eli had stripped down to a T-shirt, and the muscles in his forearms bulged in and out as he clenched and unclenched his fists.

Across from him, Paul held his ground, his hands fisted, too, but his expression less intense than Eli's. He looked resigned to the fight, rather than hungry for it.

Eli was hungry though, his face livid, eyes narrowed to pinpricks. But I knew he wouldn't strike first. It went against his code.

But from the look of it, he would be waiting a long time. That was unless magic became a factor. Worried, I searched Paul up and down for a wand or staff. He wore a thick silver band on his left hand, and I guessed that was it, hidden by a glamour. I couldn't believe the Magi Senate would deny him his computers but allow him access to magic.

I looked around, wondering where the Will Guard was, but I couldn't see beyond the crowd.

"I don't want any trouble with you." The sound of Paul's voice went through me like a lightning strike, setting my nerve endings afire. I knew it so well. The memory of the way he'd sounded that last time, when he used his siren powers to try and force me to serve Marrow, haunted me.

I shut my eyes and counted to three, forcing those memories away. Then I opened them again, trying to figure out what to do next.

"I don't care what you want." Eli stepped forward and Paul retreated. He kept his head down, almost in submission, but I caught the hard glint in his eyes. He was doing everything he could to keep his temper in check.

"You're a liar and a backstabber and a killer," Eli went on. "You killed Rosemary Vanholt. You tried to kill Dusty and Selene and me."

Paul's head shot up, the wary weakness of a moment before gone. "I didn't kill Rosemary."

Eli spat. "You helped."

The crowd murmured around us, people hungry for such juicy tidbits.

"And I would never hurt Dusty." Paul's gaze flickered to my face for a second, and I flinched. When his expression darkened, I knew that he'd seen it.

Great, way to rock the femme fatale, Dusty.

"Don't you dare look at her." Eli spoke each word slowly, deliberately. I could tell he was on the verge of exploding, and I knew it was all because of how much Paul had hurt me.

But I couldn't let him take this any further. What Paul had done didn't matter anymore. Only what he would do next.

I stepped forward, forcing my way in between them. I placed a hand flat against Eli's chest and pushed. "Leave him be."

Eli didn't budge. For a moment, I didn't think he'd heard me at all. I pushed again, this time, digging my fingers in a little. Eli's gaze shifted from Paul to me. A sound like a hiss escaped his throat.

"Stay out of it, Dusty." He grabbed my hand and pushed it away, his touch gentle even in his anger.

I steeled my resolve. "No." This time I shoved him with both hands, forcing him to take a step backward to maintain his balance. "Leave him alone."

Eli's mouth fell open. "Why are you defending him?"

"I . . ." My voice trailed off as I wracked my brains for an explanation. The dozens of people watching us were listening so loudly I could almost hear their ears straining. I tried to plead with him with my eyes, to convey to him that it was a secret I would share with him later, but he wasn't looking at me. He kept his gaze trained on Paul, his body braced for an attack.

"You don't want to do this," I said, grasping for any words that would do. "You've been in enough trouble lately. And he hasn't done anything." *Yet*, I thought but didn't say.

Eli's hands dropped to his side, his expression incredulous. "I can't believe you can say that after all he did."

I took a deep breath, hating the betrayal in Eli's voice that I was standing against him on this, of all things. But I'd given Lady Elaine my word. "Everybody deserves a second chance. Even him." I managed to sound sincere, even to my ears. It helped that I wasn't looking at Paul directly.

Eli didn't respond for several long, strained seconds. From somewhere behind me, I heard the arrival of the Will Guard, loud voices shouting for people to break it up.

"I guess we'll see about that," Eli said at last. Then he turned and strode away, his back so rigid, his muscles might've been made of iron.

I watched him go, my throat tight with a dozen nameless emotions. I should've warned him last night when I had the chance.

Sorry, he had said.

I guess we both were now.

I turned toward Paul, trying to think of something to say, but nothing came to me. There was still too much between us. I walked past him without a word. I'd done enough for one day.

I knew I needed to explain things to Eli, but by the time I'd gone through the breakfast line, he'd already decided to sit at Lance's table. It wasn't the first time he'd chosen to sit there instead of with Selene and me—he did it fairly often, maintaining his friendships as it were—but this morning I knew his motivation wasn't so diplomatic. I couldn't bring myself to go over there, not with Katarina sitting across from him. I decided it best to give him some time to cool off first.

I sat down with Selene, determined to ignore Eli completely for now. This proved especially hard as Selene failed to provide much distraction. She was too sleepy for a deep conversation as she kept yawning around bites of her fruit and yogurt parfait. When I'd come in last night she was still awake and only just changing into her pajamas. I didn't bother asking what she'd been doing. I had a pretty good feeling she wouldn't tell me. Selene could be private to a fault. Nothing could make her spill her secrets until she was ready.

With little else to do, I pulled out my eTab and switched it on. The animation-resistant personal tablet responded quickly, the home screen appearing a second later. It was the one piece of electronic equipment I owned that wasn't temperamental, and therefore I loved it. I stroked my fingers across the rune mark engravings around the edge of the screen with undisguised affection.

I checked my e-mail first. The only new one was from Lady Elaine. I opened it with a surge of trepidation that proved anticlimactic. The e-mail informed me that Paul would be starting classes tomorrow (read: today) and that I should be prepared. *Yeah, way to get the message through on time there, Ms. I Can Predict the Future.* It also included his new class schedule so that I could stalk him more conveniently.

Even better.

Closing down my e-mail, I opened an e-net window and typed in a search for the Terra Tribe. Might as well do something useful. I didn't expect to find much—the Magi Senate censored all questionable material on the enchantment-net—but in seconds I spotted a link to a page on Spellbook, the magickind equivalent of Facebook. I clicked on it. The info page for the Terra Tribe popped up on the screen with this basic information:

Group: Student Organization
Interest: Changing the world
Membership: Private

Frowning, I clicked on the JOIN button. A pop-up message asked me if I wanted to send a request to join the Terra Tribe, and I clicked yes. Then another message displayed saying the request had been sent. That was it.

Disappointed by my lack of progress, I looked up Oliver Cork's Spellbook page. The Terra Tribe was listed as one of his interests, and when I perused his friends page, I came across Britney's profile in the *S* section. I clicked on it and read through the information. She and I were already friends, so everything was visible to me, including all the messages on her wall telling her to get better soon. I scrolled through, alarmed by the hostile tone in some of them. Several people threatened bodily harm to whoever had attacked her while others blamed various darkkinds and even some witchkinds.

I stopped reading when the screen had to refresh and closed the window, a leaden weight settling across my shoulders. If Marrow's supporters were behind the building unrest among the kinds, they were doing a great job. Arkwell was becoming a decidedly scary place to be. I supposed a lot of ordinary students felt the same when it came to school shootings and having to walk through metal detectors to get to class. The difference at Arkwell was that our weapons couldn't be screened anymore, not with The Will gone. And so far the Will Guard hadn't proved much more effective than your average rent-a-cop.

I put the eTab away and focused on breakfast, trying not to worry about the things beyond my control. It wasn't like I could go back in time and undo what had happened with Marrow.

When the bell rang for homeroom, I peered over at Lance's table, wondering if Eli was still too pissed to walk with me. Not only did I want to explain about Paul, but I wanted to know if he'd learned anything more about what happened to Lance. I believed that Eli hadn't cursed him, but somebody had. Who? And why?

Under different circumstances, I would've considered Lance a suspect. Eli had said that Lance wasn't in the dorm room when he'd gone to bed the night Britney was attacked. And it was possible Lance had seen the note and gone down there. Hell, he even had a possible motive of revenge for the bloom-and-grow spell fiasco in alchemy. But none of that explained how he'd been cursed, and I was certain he wasn't faking it. Lance had too much ego to go around looking like that much of a train wreck on purpose. Not to mention the evidence in Selene's detection spell, and the fact that he hadn't been in Britney's dream. I shook my head. None of it made sense.

Eli's answer came through loud and clear as he darted for the door without so much as a sideways look at me.

Crap. I should've plucked up my courage and apologized, Katarina or no. Now I would have to wait until lunchtime, trusting in the cafeteria noise to make sure we weren't overheard. Sighing, I said goodbye to Selene then headed for homeroom.

As I suspected, Eli avoided me through first and second. I contemplated writing him a note explaining things in third period, but the lecture that day proved too distracting—we'd finally gotten around to the sinking of Atlantis and how it had triggered the first War of the Kinds.

When the bell sounded for the end of third period, Mr. Corvus called Eli's name, asking him to stay behind. I glanced at the teacher, suspicious for no good reason beyond curiosity. I lowered my gaze and started slowly packing up my things. I contemplated dropping the contents of my folder on the floor for an excuse to linger even longer.

Before I could, I heard Corvus clear his throat in my direction. "Your detention isn't until this afternoon, Miss Everhart."

I jumped at the sound of my name, and I whipped my head toward him. He gave me a knowing look. I was tempted to say something smart, but my courage wavered at the idea of even more detention, and I hurried up and left the room.

Eli missed lunch, not showing up again until halfway through our psionics class afterward. Psionics is the study of mind magic, and this quarter we were studying telepathy. Our new teacher Mr. Deverell, who'd taken the position a few months ago when my mom left for England, asked us to break off into partners to work through some of the basic exercises. With an uneven number in class today, I ended up practicing with the teacher.

Not that I minded. Mr. Deverell was young, and even though I swore I would never say such a thing about a teacher, super-hot. In his early twenties at most, he had shoulder-length dirty-blond hair and pale hazel eyes that looked like two pieces of polished river rock. He hailed from somewhere down south, but his accent was slight, just enough of a drawl to be attractive. The first moment he spoke, every girl in the class went gaga. Except for me, of course. I managed to internalize all my gaga. Well, mostly. If you didn't count the drooling.

"What's on this one?" Mr. Deverell asked, holding up a flashcard across from me with the picture hidden from sight.

I focused my gaze on it, while I took deep, even breaths, trying to achieve the proper concentration necessary to see the image reflected in Mr. Deverell's mind. Yeah, I'd have better luck trying to see through mud. The harder I pushed the murkier it became. Then finally, something did appear in my mind, but I knew without a doubt it wasn't the image on the card. It was the plinth with its hidden word. I clenched my teeth, forcing the image away.

"You can do this, Dusty," Deverell said in response to my struggle. In his accent, my name sounded surprisingly sexy. He made it easy to understand why so many romance novels were about cowboys.

Concentrate. Concentrate. Oh, screw it. "Apple," I said, settling on the first random image to occur to me. I'd heard someone a few desks down say the same thing a moment ago and figured it was worth a shot.

An amused smile broke across Deverell's face as he shook his head. "Sorry. You were close though." He flipped the card over, revealing a purple ball.

"Yeah, sure. Similar shape anyway."

"Yes indeed." He motioned to the cards lying on the table between us. "Whenever you're ready."

I pulled off the topmost card and examined the image of an orange triangle. I slowed my breathing once more and tried to project the picture outward so Mr. Deverell could see it, but the image of the plinth forced its way to the front of my mind again. For a second, it was so powerful that I almost forgot where I was, the desire to discover the hidden word as strong as ever.

"Dusty?" Mr. Deverell said, his voice breaking through my distraction. "Are you all right?"

With an effort I looked up at him. I tried to smile. "Yeah, I'm fine."

Deverell stared at me, unblinking. "That image, the stone pedestal, what is it?"

I felt the color leave my cheeks. I hadn't meant for him to see. *What's wrong with me?* "It's nothing," I said, trying to make my voice as light as possible. I shrugged. "Just something I dreamed about last night."

Mr. Deverell leaned back in his chair and scratched his chin. "It didn't seem like nothing. It seemed like a—" He broke off and turned his gaze to the doorway. "I think Mr. Booker is about to arrive, and if I'm not mistaken, he will be able to take my place."

Confused, and wishing he'd finished his comment, I turned my gaze to the front of the room just as Eli appeared. He was carrying a wand. *His* wand. He held it in one hand, the tip pointed to the ground as if it were a knife he feared stabbing someone with accidentally. The class fell silent, all eyes following Eli as he crossed the room toward Mr. Deverell and handed him a note. Deverell read it quickly, looking delighted.

"Congratulations," he said, folding the note. "Let's see it then."

Eli held up the wand, a dazed expression on his face as if he couldn't believe it was his. It wasn't much to look at, hardly more than a short stick of dirt-brown wood polished smooth, but I understood his awe completely.

"Very nice," said Deverell.

I smiled my agreement, but I couldn't help but notice that not everyone in the class looked happy. Travis Kelly in particular wore an expression that was borderline hostile. I started to glare at him, but Mr. Deverell's voice distracted me.

"Back to work, everyone," he said, addressing the class. He returned his attention to Eli and gave him a quick summary of the task at hand.

Eli nodded and sat down across from me. Deverell clapped him on the back and then walked away to observe the rest of the class.

"It's awesome," I said, indicating the wand, which Eli had set on the table in front of him. He picked it up, set it down, and picked it up again.

"Thanks. You first." He motioned to the cards with his wand. It seemed clumsy in his large hands.

Wincing at his curt tone, I picked up the next card and went through the focusing process again. This time when the image of the plinth rose up I was able to squash it down. Eli stared at the back of the card for several minutes, his fingers clutched tight around the wand.

He surprised me when he answered. "It's a rectangle."

"What color?"

"Um . . . yellow, I think."

I turned the card over, showing him he was right. A half smile lifted one side of his lips. I returned it with a full one, hoping he was getting over our argument this morning. The situation with Paul would be hard enough without Eli so against it. We might've stepped into troubled water with the kissing last night, but we were friends first. I wanted his support.

I pushed the cards nearer him and waited as he selected the one on top. Then I focused again, trying to pull the image from his mind. To my surprise a picture formed behind my eyes of something with several pointed edges. I concentrated harder, willing the blurriness away.

"It's a pentagram. Blue."

"Yep." Eli flipped the card over.

It got easier as we went along. He answered the next two correctly and in half the time. He missed the third, but it was mostly my fault. He'd interrupted my concentration when he leaned across the table and whispered, "Lady Elaine told me about you and Paul and the trouble in the senate."

I frowned. "Why did she tell you?"

"She found out what happened this morning and was worried I would mess things up."

Yes, that sounded like Lady Elaine. So he knew the truth, but he was still upset about it.

"I'm sorry I didn't tell you earlier."

"It's okay."

Not knowing what to say next, I returned my attention to the picture of the wooden rowboat. The image was more complicated than the ones before, harder to project, especially with the plinth still lingering in the back of my mind.

Eli rolled the wand through his fingers, his focus on me and not the card. "You don't have to do it, you know. You could say no."

My grip on the card slipped, and it fell to the table, picture side up. "But I can't. They need my help."

Eli reached forward and laid his hand on mine as I went to pick up the card. "They can do it without you. We should focus on the dreams. That'll uncover the truth far faster." He paused. "And safer."

The idea was tempting. It really was. Except, we both knew

that reading dreams was no easy task. The answers didn't just reveal themselves. Not unless it was too late to make a difference.

Reluctantly, I pulled away from his touch. "The dreams won't be enough. If they were, Lady Elaine would never have asked me in the first place."

Eli pinned me with his blue eyes. "But Paul's put you in danger before. You should stay away from him."

I sighed. "I can't." Eli started to argue further, but I cut him off. "I won't."

His mouth fell open then closed again with an audible clack. The bell rang a moment later, and Eli got up and walked away without another word.

Need Not Apply

Fortunately, there was little opportunity to continue my argument with Eli in our next class. Math was one of the few classes at Arkwell that was more or less the same as in ordinary high school. It seemed math was a universal idea. And there weren't any algebraic functions that could calculate the magical intensity of spells or anything. It was completely boring and easily my second-worst subject.

Alchemy and science afterward was my absolute worst subject, and with Britney absent, I stood no chance of changing that. She was half the reason I'd managed to scrape a C last semester. I wondered if she was doing any better, and I resolved to go visit her at Vejovis this weekend if I could get a pass.

Finally, the beaker and Bunsen burner hell that was alchemy ended, and I made my way to gym class. At least Selene seemed more awake as we changed into our gym clothes.

"You think I'm doing the right thing, don't you?" I asked after I finished telling her about Eli's reaction.

Selene considered the question long enough that I knew I wouldn't like her answer. "I don't know, Dusty."

I stood up from the bench and shut my locker. Then I turned

to face her, trying not to sound as upset as I felt. "How can you say that? Don't you think Paul should be stopped before he hurts more people?"

Selene ran a finger over the scar on her face. "Yes, but . . ."

"But what? Come on, for all we know Marrow has already risen from the ashes and is just waiting for his faithful servant to return."

Selene snorted. "I'm sure if Marrow is alive again that he's not waiting around for Paul Kirkwood. We know he's got more important servants out there than a seventeen-year-old boy."

I tapped my toe. "How do you figure?"

"Well, somebody let him out of his tomb over in England, right?"

I exhaled, some of my annoyance evaporating. "Good point." I shrugged. "But still, it's not like letting Paul run around unwatched is a good idea."

"You're right," Selene said, her tone placating.

Even still, I heard the "but" in it again. "But . . . ?"

Selene fixed her gaze on me. "I don't think blindly trusting Lady Elaine and the sheriff is a good idea. They're government officials same as the people responsible for letting Paul go."

Her bitter tone took me by surprise. It was one she reserved for subjects she cared about deeply, like the sexual objectification of sirens and her disdain for all things Lance Rathbone. "What do you mean by that?"

Selene bit her lip and waited as a girl walked past, heading for the exit. "Just that the government isn't always right, you know? Those people don't always make the best choices. Some of their decisions are stupid and unfair. But come on, we're going to be late."

She turned toward the door. I fell in step beside her, trying to make sense of her sudden antigovernment sentiments. It wasn't that she was a big fan of the government before, but she seemed downright hostile now. I glanced sideways at her. "Something you want to talk about?"

Selene pushed her long black braid over her shoulder. "I just think they shouldn't be able to force you to do something you don't want to do. And they shouldn't be able to keep you from doing what you do want to do. Especially if it's in your nature."

"Huh?" I said, not understanding her vague generalities. But she didn't get a chance to explain further as we emerged on the gym floor and were immediately beckoned forward by Coach Fritz.

"Come on, girls." He waved his clipboard at us. "Hurry up and get out here already."

I quickened my pace, leery of pissing off Fritz. He still hadn't gotten over me hitting him with a stumbler curse last semester, never mind the hours of toilet-cleaning detention I'd endured as punishment for it. If I gave him so much as half a reason, I'd end up doing push-ups for the entire class period. Fritz was a fairy with typical fairy vindictiveness. He'd tried making me run laps the first couple of times, but running was one of my hobbies so it wasn't very effective. Push-ups, however, left me feeling like I'd been dragged around by the arms for an hour by a herd of elephants.

Selene and I sat down with the rest of our classmates, congregated around the coach. Behind him, a giant tentlike structure was stretched across the length of the gym floor. It looked a bit like one of those tunnels people trained dogs to run through in agility competitions. No prizes for guessing who the dogs would be in *this* scenario. I took one look at the pitch-black, yawning entrance into the thing and shuddered.

"Your goal," Fritz was explaining, "is to make it through the Gauntlet."

That's all? I wondered what would happen if we *didn't* make it through.

Fritz slid the clipboard under his arms and put his fisted hands on his waist. "Now before you start complaining, I promise you won't face anything in there that you're not equipped to deal with, and there's nothing that will do you *serious* harm. Just keep a sharp lookout and react with what comes natural." Fritz's eyes shifted to my face. "Most of you shouldn't have any trouble at all."

I swallowed and dropped my gaze, pretending to be completely absorbed by the fine cracks in the polished wood floor.

"And you might as well get used to it," Fritz went on. "The Gauntlet will be a new regular feature in this class. Nothing will be timed or scored for now, but that will change as the semester goes on."

I groaned inwardly, resisting the urge to roll my eyes, a surefire method of provoking Fritz's anger.

He blew the whistle. "All right. Get into your safety suits and line up."

Everybody responded to this command with varying degrees of enthusiasm. I took my time, crossing to the wall where the safety suits hung from pegs. I selected one in my size and pulled it on. It resembled a wet suit, but the material was surprisingly supple and easy to get on, even with the hard, plasticlike shielding on the arms, chest, back, and thigh areas. All too soon I was ready to go.

Lance and Eli were close to the front of the line, the latter wearing a suit for the first time ever with his new wand clutched in his hand. He looked even better than I'd imagined in the snug-fitting getup.

As Eli approached the entrance, Coach Fritz shook his head. "Not this time, Booker." He eyed the wand with a blatant smirk. "I doubt you've got enough juice in that thing to handle the Gauntlet. You can wait out class over there." He pointed to the benches.

Eli's body went rigid. Outrage coursed through me. It wasn't fair. Fritz had no right to deny him the chance to participate. I braced for Eli's response, expecting him to argue, but he only turned around and replaced his suit on the wall. Then he stalked off toward the benches. But instead of sitting, he raised the wand and started practicing some of the defensive moves we regularly studied in class. Well, at least he would get to do something. Maybe with enough time Fritz would change his mind.

Yeah right, I thought as I took a second look at the coach and saw the smirk still on his face. I turned toward Selene, wanting to complain about Fritz, but I froze when I caught sight of Oliver Cork pulling on his helmet a few feet in front of me.

"Catch you later," I whispered to Selene, then I darted toward Oliver, falling in place right behind him. I accidently kicked him in the back of the shoe, and he turned around, startled.

"Whoops." I flashed my cutest smile and pointed at myself with both thumbs. "Clumsy. Did I break your foot or anything?"

Oliver surprised me when he smiled back. Maybe I was getting better at this whole flirty thing. "S'okay. I'm pretty tough."

I laughed. "Tough like a tree, right?"

The smile vanished from Oliver's face.

Crap. Open mouth. Insert foot. Swallow.

"Are you making fun of me for being a dryad?" His dark eyes hardened.

My eyebrows shot up my forehead. "What? No way. I think it's cool. I love trees and nature."

Oliver scowled. "Whatever." He started to turn back, but I grabbed his arm. It did feel surprisingly like a tree limb, strong but sort of bendy.

I let go at once. "Wait a sec. I wanted to ask you something."

He faced me, looking cautious but not hostile. Thank goodness dryads were known to be extremely patient and slow tempered, an effect of the bond they shared with their respective trees. "Yeah?"

"Um." I bit my lip, wishing I'd planned this out a little better. "I want to know about the Terra Tribe."

His eyes narrowed beneath the crest of his helmet. He crossed his arms, the gesture made awkward by the strips of shielding on the safety suit's sleeve. He looked like an overgrown beetle. So did I, for that matter.

"What for?"

I frowned. This wasn't the answer I'd been expecting. It was a student organization, after all, and I was a student. "I just want to know more about it."

The suspicion in his gaze increased, and I had a feeling he was connecting the dots back to his interrogation by Sheriff Brackenberry and my conspicuous presence right outside.

Thinking fast, I added, "Britney told me a little already."

Oliver chuckled. "I doubt it."

Again, this wasn't the reply I expected. "Sure she did. And I want to join."

Now Oliver laughed outright, sounding genuinely amused.

I blushed, the unpleasant awareness of being the butt of

some inside joke making my eyes burn with tears coming to the ready. I fought them back. "What's so funny?"

"It's impossible for *you* to join the Terra Tribe."

"Why?"

"No darkkinds allowed."

His words hit me like a bucket of ice water to the face. "What . . . what . . . *why*?"

"It's for naturekinds *only*. Which you would've known if you really had talked to Britney about it." He swung around in a clear dismissal.

I stood there, reeling from shock and indignation.

Tears threatened again and I resisted a strong desire to punch him in the back of the head. I contemplated returning to Selene, but I didn't want to give Oliver the satisfaction of seeing me retreat.

Not that it mattered. Oliver kept his back to me the whole time, talking and laughing with one of his friends. I told myself it wasn't about me, although I suspected it was—the darkkind who dared to mingle with naturekinds. A blush of shame blossomed over my skin, and I was glad for the helmet covering my face.

When it was my turn to enter the Gauntlet, I went in without hesitating, grateful for the chance to escape the crowd. I had a feeling my conversation with Oliver had been overheard and that everyone in the class knew about it by now. All I wanted was to be by myself.

Two steps into the Gauntlet though, and I knew I wasn't alone. Not by a long shot. A murky, uneven light illuminated the tunnel in places, casting long, dark shadows. Some of the shadows were moving, writhing like something alive. I couldn't see the walls or ceiling of the Gauntlet. It might've been five miles long or only a couple of feet. I took a deep breath and walked on, braced for whatever.

A few steps in, a portion of the floor sunk beneath my right foot like a lever depressing. There was a loud pop and a hiss. I froze as the stench of sulfur burned my nostrils.

Something flashed, and I jumped back as a wall of flames burst up in front of me.

"Crap." I stared at it, trying to calm my racing heart, which proved difficult as I caught a whiff of something burning. I ran my hands over my helmet and down the front of my suit, checking for fire as I tried to decide what to do next.

Then I remembered my simple goal—get to the other side. I pointed my hand at the flames. "Hydro-rhe." A jet of blue light shot out from my fingertips. The flames sizzled and hissed then disappeared. That was one spell I didn't struggle with anymore.

I moved on. Several more obstacles rose up to block my way, but I took care of them easily, relying on spells and techniques we'd learned in class.

After a while the obstacles began incorporating a more physical element. This was gym class after all. A magically propelled tire rolled out of the darkness, barreling right toward me. I jumped left, dodging it, but then I had to twist to the right to avoid the next one that came quick on the heels of the first. The third, I hit with a deflector spell. It careened sideways, out of my path and was swallowed by the shadows once more.

Next, I had to vanish a creek of boiling green liquid, probably some kind of acid. The fumes made my eyes water, and the stench of it lingered in my nose long afterward.

But really, the Gauntlet was proving to be pretty tame for gym class, full of obstacles a blind person could see coming. My mind soon began to wander. I found myself thinking about what Oliver had said, the shame and embarrassment coming over me as strongly as before. It was so unfair. Like there was anything wrong with darkkinds. We were all more or less the same, right?

Whack.

I reeled backward, clutching my pounding face. *What the . . . ?* I turned in a circle, searching for whatever had hit me.

Whack.

This time the something struck me in the back of the head. I dropped to my knees on instinct. A wooden bat swung through the air above me. It was moving comically slow. A baby could've dodged it—if they'd been paying attention. I cast a restraining spell at it, and the bat stopped midair, giving a slight tremble as it fought to get free of the magic.

I stood and walked past it, my head back in the game as I strained to see more obstacles. I shouldn't have let myself get distracted. Always a bad idea in gym class. With my right eye watering, seeing grew harder and harder. The skin where the bat had struck felt tight and puffy. But somehow I managed to get through the rest of it with only a couple of minor scratches and a bruised shin to add to my injuries.

By the time I emerged from the end of the Gauntlet, my eye had almost swollen shut.

Coach Fritz grinned when he spotted me. "Run into trouble, did you?"

"Nope. I'm just trying to start a new fashion trend—black-eye foundation," I said, cupping a hand over my eye. The pain made me forget the dangers of mouthing off, but to my shock, Fritz chuckled.

"Well, then, I'd say you're off to a great start."

Asshole.

But Fritz's sudden receptiveness to my sarcasm put me on edge, and I dropped all the snark from my voice as I said, "Um, can I go to the infirmary?"

Fritz's grin widened. "I don't think that's necessary. A little bruising never hurt anyone. You can wait until after class."

"But I have detention after class."

Fritz's shoulders rose and fell in an exaggerated shrug. "Not my problem. But I'm sure the teacher will understand if you're late." Something about Fritz's triumphant tone told me that he knew very well who my detention was with and that Corvus would be about as understanding as a swarm of pissed-off killer bees.

Resigning myself to the overall injustice in the world, I walked to the back of the line. I kept my head down, hoping nobody would give me crap about my face.

Once again, I was stuck behind Oliver. This time I seriously contemplated punching him in the back of the head. It was his fault I'd gotten hit by that bat. If I hadn't been so distracted by his idiotic naturekinds-only club, I would've been paying better attention.

But once again, I managed to restrain myself. I even got lucky as class ended before I had to go through the Gauntlet again. I quickly changed out of my gym clothes, doing my best to dodge Selene's probing questions into my bad mood.

"Come on, Dusty," she said, hands on hips. "What's bothering you? You must be really upset to have gotten hit by that bat. You haven't done anything that clumsy in a long time. You've gotten really good."

I tried to roll my eyes, then wished I hadn't as a fresh spurt of pain shot down the right side of my face. "You're wrong there. I'm as bad as ever at this magic business."

"Yeah, right. So what's up?"

I could tell by the firmness in Selene's tone that she wasn't going to drop it.

"Okay," I said, gingerly pulling my shirt down over my head. And then I told her what had happened with Oliver. I braced for an explosion. She was darkkind, too, and bound to be just as upset about the discrimination.

But Selene didn't explode. Instead a sad, almost haunted look rose to her face, and she sat down on the bench across from me with an audible sigh. "That really sucks. I'm sorry."

"You don't seem surprised."

She sighed again. "Well, stuff like that's been happening for ages among magickind."

I swallowed, knowing she was right but hating it just the same. It was so stupid—excluding people just because they were different.

"But don't let it bother you," Selene said. "For what it's worth I doubt it's personal to you, and really, who cares what they think? We both know you're awesome." She beamed at me, and I felt a flush of gratitude, lifting my spirits.

Selene and I finished getting dressed in silence then I headed off to detention.

Despite Selene's pep talk, my thoughts remained unpleasant company as I climbed the winding staircase to the third floor. The door into Room 337 stood open, and I went in, forgetting to knock. I froze at the sight of the familiar room. I hadn't recognized the number, but of course it made sense. There was the large desk, cluttered with books and papers. There were the shelves full of strange items, the spyglass and the wooden compass with the endlessly spinning needle. Even the smell was the same, something spicy, like an old man's cologne.

This had been Marrow's office. But all of his things should've been removed. What was the senate playing at, leaving this stuff here? It could be dangerous. It could be connected to *him*.

My pulse quickened, and I contemplated making a mad dash out of here, but the room was empty and curiosity got the best of me. With my imagination working on overdrive, I stepped into the office and started pulling the books back on the shelf one by one, checking for a latch to a secret chamber. It might've seemed stupid, a cliché right out of a B horror movie, but it was definitely possible. Especially here. At Arkwell. During my detention with Ms. Hardwick, I'd learned the location of several secret passageways and hidden rooms on campus.

As I moved along, checking book after book, I realized that this was Monmouth *Tower*. A tower like the one in my dreams. What if there was a connection?

You're being paranoid, Dusty.

Better paranoid than taken by surprise like last time.

A familiar, gravel-filled voice spoke from behind me. "Just what are you doing, Miss Everhart?"

I spun around so hard that I knocked a row of books from the shelf. The loud crash as they fell made me jump. Then I let out a scream.

Marrow stood in the doorway.

~ 12 ~

J Marks the Spot

"What are you looking for in my office?" the man said again. I blinked as his features blurred into Mr. Corvus. *Not Marrow. Never him.* It was just my imagination. How could I have not noticed the eye patch even for a second?

A dozen answers to this question flitted through my mind, including lack of sleep and the possibility of impending insanity, but I ignored them as I noticed the person standing behind Mr. Corvus. That awful sense of déjà vu came over me again.

Paul was looking at me with an alarmed expression. "What happened? Are you okay?"

Catching onto the focus of his gaze, I raised a hand to my cheek and gingerly ran my fingers along the bruise. His concern, especially the genuine sound of it, took me by surprise. It didn't help that he was looking as handsome as ever. Maybe even more so with his short hair and that haunted look in his eyes like something had broken on the inside, something that needed to be fixed. That *I* could fix.

Don't fall for that, I reminded myself. *This is Paul, a manipulative siren, capable of forcing sympathy.* A part of me winced at my easy use of stereotyping, but sometimes it was hard not to judge a person by their kind. Especially when combined with their past actions.

"I'm fine," I said at last.

Mr. Corvus made a disgruntled sound. "You still haven't answered *my* question, Miss Everhart."

I blinked, coming back to my senses. "Oh, I was just . . ." I stooped and started picking up books, my face aflame. "Just . . ."

"Snooping?" Mr. Corvus said. Startled by what sounded like humor, I glanced up to see he'd raised his one eyebrow in a somewhat amused expression. "I've heard you've a habit of doing that."

"It's more like a compulsion," I said, encouraged by the slight change in his attitude—subzero to only icy was still an improvement. "I just can't help myself sometimes."

"You've got lots of reasons to be suspicious," Paul said in a quiet voice, his eyes fixed on the floor now.

Mr. Corvus cleared his throat. "Reason or not, that's no excuse for you to invade my privacy."

I swallowed. "I'm sorry, sir. The door was open and I didn't think about what I was doing."

"That much is clear." Mr. Corvus ran his thumb and forefinger over the two halves of his mustache. "Apology accepted. Now clean this up. We need to get started with your detention."

I nodded, picking up the pace.

"Give me a moment, Paul," Mr. Corvus said, "and I'll find the book I promised you."

I looked up, suspicious again. What business did Paul have with Mr. Corvus? An unpleasant memory of how Paul would sometimes meet Marrow after class rose up in my mind.

Marrow could be anybody, I realized. The couple of times I'd asked about it, nobody seemed to know just *how* his return to life would be. Would he even look like himself or would he resemble someone else entirely?

A violent shiver went through my body. *Stop with the paranoia already.* I needed to focus on the real-life dangers present in this very room. Namely, Paul Kirkwood.

He knelt down and started helping me with the rest of the books. "So what did happen to your face?"

I sighed, risking a glance at him. The eye contact thing was getting easier. "Gym class. What else?"

He smiled. "I hope you feel better soon."

I stood, not saying anything. The awkwardness of the situation was making me antsy, and I wished Mr. Corvus would hurry up so Paul could leave already. There was something wrong about exchanging pleasantries with this guy like we were old friends. Never mind that it was what I was supposed to be doing.

"Ah, here we go." Mr. Corvus pulled a book from one of the drawers on his desk. He held it out to Paul. I stared at it, trying to read the title but not having any luck. The inscription on the black cover had faded long ago. "Be sure you return it as soon as you've finished."

"I will, sir," Paul said, accepting the book. He tucked it under his arm, gave me a final smile, then left.

"So," I said, turning to Mr. Corvus and trying to act casual. "What was that book, anyway?"

He raised his eyebrow again. "Do you know what some would say about your curiosity?"

Sensing a trap here, I tried the cute and innocent defense. "Um, that it's an admirable side effect of my smart and inquisitive nature?"

Mr. Corvus did not smile. Instead the eyebrow lowered,

making his expression even more intimidating. "Nosy is what they would say. Or better yet, mind your own business."

I gulped, feeling thoroughly chastised.

"Now, take a seat and we'll begin."

I did as he said, pulling out the chair in front of the desk and plopping into it, my nervousness bringing out my clumsiness.

Mr. Corvus withdrew yet another book from the desk drawer and set it down in front of me with an audible thud. I'd never seen a book so large and heavy before. Like the one he'd given Paul, this too had a black cover that was clearly made of some kind of leather, but I had a feeling it wasn't cowhide. The texture seemed too hard and scaly. Lizard maybe. And utterly creepy. Strange silver symbols were engraved on the front. They didn't look like any of the rune alphabets I'd seen translated in various textbooks, but more like pictographs, Egyptian hieroglyphs maybe, although without any of the typical cranes or ankhs.

Mr. Corvus opened the book to a page bookmarked with a white feather. The top half of the page consisted of a single large symbol, which I took to be an illustration rather than a pictogram. It showed three linked circles, one on top and two on the bottom, but all joined in the middle. Beneath the illustration were more of the strange pictographs like on the cover. They ran in lines down the center of the page, arranged like a poem.

"Your task for this detention is simple," Mr. Corvus said. "You will translate the first line of this text."

My jaw fell open in disbelief. "Um, how the heck am I supposed to do that?"

"You mean you can't read this already?"

I did a double take, my eyes darting to the pictograms and

then back to Mr. Corvus. His expression remained deadly serious, and his tone suggested that he had doubts about my intelligence in general. "Uh . . ."

"I'm only teasing, Dusty." A ghost of a smile flickered across his face.

Yeah, I wasn't seeing the funny in this one.

"If you *could* read it without any effort, then it wouldn't be a very effective punishment, now would it?"

I shook my head. I was beginning to think my new history teacher was two rungs shy of the top of the crazy ladder.

Mr. Corvus fetched a third book from his desk and plopped it down next to the other. This one was equally as large, although it had a normal-looking cover. "This is the translator. You'll find everything you need in there."

I reached out and pulled it open, dreading what I would find. As I expected, the book was organized by symbols that appeared as random as the cracks on the gym floor. "How am I supposed to look anything up without knowing how stuff is ordered?"

"The old-fashioned way, I suppose. One by one."

"Right," I said through gritted teeth.

This was going to take forever.

Forever turned out to be three hours. By the end of it, my eyeballs felt as if some tiny creature had been running a vacuum over their surface all afternoon, and I was so hungry my stomach had started to gnaw on itself. As detentions went, this one wasn't much better than the toilet-cleaning duty. *Way to go, Mr. Corvus. The crappy teacher award has got your name on it.*

As if he'd heard my sarcastic thoughts, Mr. Corvus set down

the book he'd been reading, pulled off his single eyeglass, and then fixed his gaze at me. His one eye was so dark a blue it was almost black, the color like a raven's wing in sunshine.

"Let me see your progress so far," Mr. Corvus said.

Dread now pounding in my temples, I picked up the paper with my scrawled notes and handed it to him. I'd written the definition beside every picture after verifying each one three times, and still it made no sense:

Circle
Break
Twelve
Blood
One

Mr. Corvus examined it for a moment and then handed it back. "Nicely done."

"Really?" I read the words again, wondering if I'd missed something.

"Yes, it's very close."

"So what does it mean?"

Mr. Corvus leaned back in his chair and tented his fingers in front of him. "Well, the *meaning* is so obscure it would take hours for me to explain properly, but I assume you don't wish to spend those hours."

I shook my head, although the idea of spending all that time on the stupid thing and still not understanding it irked me. Then I remembered I was dealing with a teacher, and I rephrased the question. "What does it *say* then?"

Mr. Corvus smiled, clearly pleased as he leaned forward and

took the paper back. He grabbed a pen lying nearby then scribbled down a sentence. He turned the paper around so I could see it.

"Only the blood of the twelve can undo the circle," I read aloud.

Mr. Corvus nodded. "Well, that's as close to a literal translation as possible."

"It sounds a little morbid."

"It *is* a little morbid."

I started to ask him what the book was about, but my stomach let out a huge grumble.

Mr. Corvus cleared his throat. "You may go." He folded the slip of paper with my translation and dropped it into the trash.

Feeling light-headed and more than a little annoyed to see my hard work chucked in the garbage, I turned and headed for the door. It was too late to catch dinner, and I struggled to remember what edible items we had stashed in the dorm. Probably nothing. I could always hit one of the vending machines but the idea of forcing down some of that sugar-free, taste-free crap made me gag.

What I really wanted was a big fat, calorie-packed candy bar. Yep, bring on the sugar rush and the instant—if temporary—relief from my headache and sleepiness. But contraband like that wasn't easy to get ahold of at Arkwell.

Fortunately, I knew a guy. If I could track him down at this time of night that was. I thought I might be in luck, though. I even felt pretty sure that he would answer the door for me. I hadn't spoken one on one with Mr. Culpepper—Arkwell's resident maintenance man and the chief purveyor of black market items—since my short stint in the infirmary after we defeated

Marrow, but every time I passed him in the hallways and corridors, the dark, surly look on his face would vanish for a second and a friendly smile would flash across his features.

I decided to try him in the maintenance office first. If he wasn't there, I would try his secret hideaway out in Coleville Cemetery. We'd end up out there regardless; unless I got lucky and he was carrying around a Snickers bar in his pocket.

As I reached the bottom floor of Monmouth Tower, I turned immediately toward the corridor leading to the tunnels, even though the weather outside was nice enough for walking. The library tunnel alcove was on the way to Barbary Hall, where the maintenance office was located. I'd planned on investigating the crime scene with Eli, but considering how badly today had gone, I wasn't sure that would happen. It wasn't likely I would find anything useful, but I wanted to give it a try at least.

When I reached the alcove's large entryway some ten minutes later, I stopped and stared in at it, trying to reconcile the images from Britney's dream with the real thing. It wasn't hard. Aside from some distortion differences, the two visions were a pretty close match. I stepped into the alcove and walked slowly around the pool searching for anything out of the ordinary. Eli was far better at this than me, but I did my best to emulate the methodical way he let his eyes scan back and forth.

Yeah, this was a waste of time. Nothing looked out of place. How could it? Aside from the water in the pool and the thin layer of slime on the floor, there was nothing here.

I stepped out of the alcove and walked to the place where Eli had stood in the dream. Here, her attacker had stood here. Most likely, anyway. I cast a fire spell and knelt down to examine the ground. The flames perched in the palm of my hand danced about, the shifting light more of a hindrance than a help. I focused on the spell, willing the fire brighter and steadier.

It didn't make a difference. Once again, there wasn't anything to see. The ground here was covered in the same, thin layer of slime and that was all. It wasn't even dense enough to leave footprints. Sighing, I stood up and took a couple of steps farther into the tunnel itself, guessing that the attacker had come this way.

Then I saw it, a little piece of . . . something . . . lying very close to the wall. Trash, most likely. It was so small, at first I couldn't believe I'd seen it at all. I stooped down and picked it up, praying I wouldn't regret touching it. It looked like paper, but you never could tell with magickind. It could easily have been a piece of manticore eggshell, which wasn't as poisonous as the creatures housed inside them, but which could still make you sick if you held it too long.

But it wasn't trash or anything magical at all. I picked it up, pinching it between my fingers. It was a thin piece of plastic-covered cardboard. A pattern of red and white swirls marked one side of it, and on the other was a black letter *J*.

J

As in Joker.

It seemed Lance Rathbone had been down here after all.

13

The Guilty

I swear I don't remember anything," Lance said as he paced the length of Room 013. It was the unofficial headquarters of the Dream Team, in the basement of the library. "I've tried, but I just can't *remember*."

"It's okay, man. We believe you," said Eli.

I glanced sideways at him, eyebrows raised. Fortunately, most of the swelling from my run-in with the baseball bat had gone down overnight, and the gesture didn't hurt overly much. *I* didn't believe Lance. Not yet anyway. The fact that I was even *willing* to believe him had mostly to do with Selene.

After I found the joker card, I still managed to track down Culpepper who gladly gave me a full box of Milky Way Midnight bars, as well as his cell number in case I ever needed it. Then I came back to the dorm and immediately showed the card to Selene. I was all prepared to e-mail Lady Elaine with the info, when Selene asked me to wait and hear Lance out first. *Of all the times for the love part of their love/hate thing to kick in.* But I'd agreed and spent a long, frustrating day in classes fretting about it. That was, when I wasn't fretting about Paul. I'd only seen him from a distance once or twice, and I still had no idea how to go about getting close to him.

"I wouldn't speak for all of us," Selene said, distracting me from my musings about Paul.

"Yeah, same here," I said.

Selene smiled at me, but it vanished a second later as the chair she was sitting on gave a little buck beneath her. "Cut it out, Buster," she said, kicking the chair with one boot heel.

I stifled a grin. For some reason, the animation phenomenon was ten times stronger in Room 013 than anywhere else on campus. Enough so that one of the chairs had taken an unnatural liking to Selene. She'd fought off its attentions at first, but now she seemed to regard it as more of an unruly pet. She'd even given it a name.

Lance stopped his pacing and glared at me, ignoring Selene completely. "Why the hell would I attack Britney?"

"That's easy. Because she dumped that bloom-and-grow potion on your head."

Lance rolled his eyes. "Give me a break. My version of retaliation is a little more eye for an eye, as *you* should know firsthand."

I grimaced, realizing he had a point. I had several unpleasant memories from our feud last semester. Thank goodness we'd called an unspoken truce after the stuff with Marrow.

"Besides," Lance continued, "I already evened the score on that one. Put a little pennyroyal in her tea."

I gaped at him. "Pennyroyal is poisonous."

"Not to mermaids it's not." Lance bared his teeth in a huge grin. "Just makes 'em sweat. A lot."

I grimaced, remembering clearly the day Britney had been sweating so much in our alchemy class that the air around us felt as humid as a tropical rain forest.

"Typical," Selene said, folding her arms.

Lance pointed at her. "And you said I'd been cursed, so who-ever attacked Britney must've attacked me, too."

"Maybe," said Selene. "But why were you down there in the first place?"

"The note, obviously," said Eli, not looking up. He was stand-ing over a table with his wand pointed at the joker card and its remnant, their torn edges aligned. "Diorthon," he said, and a wisp of yellowish light puffed out from the tip of his wand.

I jumped up from my seat. "What are you doing? Don't mend it. That's our only proof he's guilty."

"Excuse me?" Lance said.

"Doesn't matter anyway," Eli said through gritted teeth. "It's not working." He gave the wand a flick, engaging the glamour. The piece of wood vanished and a thick gold ring appeared on his palm. He slipped it onto his index finger then faced me, his expression hard. "And he isn't guilty of anything other than be-ing in the wrong place at the wrong time."

I put my hand on one hip. "How do you figure?"

Eli waved at Lance. "He must've found the note and decided to investigate it himself. It did say it was a matter of life or death. And he couldn't have known when I was going to get back from dinner with my dad."

"Yeah." Lance bobbed his head in agreement.

Selene snorted. "Why would you even care what the note said?"

Lance shuffled his feet, looking uncomfortable.

"Because he wants to join the Dream Team," said Eli, grin-ning. "It's an excuse to be near Selene."

Lance jerked his head toward Eli, a scowl twisting his fea-tures. "Thanks, man. A lot."

Eli shrugged. "Sorry. But hiding your feelings is just stupid. Being upfront is always better."

Look who's talking, I thought. He and I had spent another day sitting in the same classes and *not* talking about that kiss. Actually, if it hadn't been for me finding the piece of that joker card, I didn't think Eli would've talked to me at all today. He was still unhappy about the Paul situation.

Frustrated all over again, I pointed my hand at the joker card and the piece I'd found. "Diorthon." A bright flash of yellow light erupted from my fingertips. The magic struck the two pieces, and a loud crack echoed around the room. The bigger one shot up five feet into the air while the smaller one burst into flames.

Eli reached out with his right hand and snatched the bigger piece as it fell, and with his left he stamped out the flames before the desk caught fire. "Nice."

Lance clapped his hands, grinning. "Bravo! So much for evidence."

I plopped down into my chair, annoyed with my shortcomings. I scooted over next to Selene and Buster. Selene's face looked slightly pink, but I knew the blush wasn't on account of my embarrassment. She was used to my magical mishaps and probably relieved that she hadn't been in the line of fire this time. No, she must be thinking about what Eli had said about Lance. I suppressed the urge to gag.

"Are you *sure* you don't remember anything from that night?" Eli said as he brushed the ashen remains of the card off the table onto the floor.

All the computers in the room beeped at once, the noise like a high-pitched foghorn going off. I jumped in my seat and nearly fell out of it. Selene wasn't so lucky. She tumbled to the floor as Buster gave another hard buck and rolled to the right.

"I'm sorry!" Eli shouted to the room at large. It wasn't the first time one of us had upset the place. "I'll bring a vacuum next time. I promise!"

The computers beeped again in final scolding then fell silent.

"Great headquarters you got here," Lance said, rubbing his ears.

"Just one more reason for you not to join us," Selene said, getting to her feet. Buster wheeled toward her, but she put a hand up. "No. You stay. I warned you last time what would happen if I fell off again."

If it were possible for a chair to look crestfallen, Buster did.

Lance shook his head, his expression both amused and disgruntled at the same time. He turned to Eli. "To answer your question. No, I can't remember a thing. But I think the curse is still having an effect. I'm having a tough time sleeping, and I can't focus at all."

Despite my aversion to doing such a thing, I took a good long look at Lance. Deep, dark bruises rimmed his cheekbones beneath bloodshot eyes. And it was clear from the baggy jeans and ripped up sweatshirt that he hadn't put his usual level of effort into getting dressed this morning. I wondered if his socks matched today.

"You should go to the infirmary," Selene said, the tiniest hint of concern in her voice.

"I can't," Lance said, not looking at her. "Not now."

"Why not?" I asked.

"Because they'll want to know what happened to him and *where*," said Eli.

I frowned, coming to grips with the truth that we weren't

going to turn Lance in. Only, who was I kidding? I'd known from the start we weren't going to. He was our best clue yet, but if the sheriff found out he'd been there, who knew when we'd have access to him next.

Holy crap, I'm turning into Eli.

I exhaled, not entirely displeased with the revelation. "What we really need is a way to jog Lance's memory."

Eli turned to me, his expression brightening for the first time since he failed to mend the joker card. "That's a great idea."

I blinked. "Um, you know that jogging a memory is just an expression of speech, right?"

"Not among magickind it's not. With mind magic it's possible to *extract memories*."

Duh, I realized. We learned about that particular police procedure after the fight with Marrow.

"We need to ask Deverell how it's done," Eli went on. "If anybody would know, he would. Tomorrow, I'll—"

"No," I said, cutting him off. "I'll do it. He likes me better."

Selene giggled. "You mean *you* like *him* better."

Eli glanced between the two of us, frowning. "What do you mean?"

"Dusty thinks he's hot."

I felt a blush threaten to warm my face, but I managed to fight it back. I shrugged my shoulders instead and grinned. "Well, it's true." I glanced at Eli, wanting to see his reaction. He was watching me with his mouth opened and eyes narrowed.

"You can't be serious?"

I smirked. "No harm in looking. And besides, of all of us, I'm the most capable at psionics. It's my strongest subject."

"Nuh-uh." Lance pointed a finger at me. "No way am I letting you mess around in my brain. You might incinerate it."

I rolled my eyes. "Like you'd even miss it."

"Ha, ha."

Eli cut off any further remarks with a whistle. "Don't start." He glanced at me, his expression still dark. "You talk to Deverell then, but do it soon. If Lance is still under the curse we need to figure out a way to break it as quick as we can."

I tilted my head and gave Lance an appraising look. "I don't know. I think it might be an improvement."

Selene snorted.

Lance opened his mouth to say something, but I waved him off. "I'll leave lunch early tomorrow and try to catch Deverell before class."

After that, the meeting adjourned. Selene darted for the door, in a hurry to make it to her Musemancy Club meeting on time. Lance followed her not long after.

I lingered behind on purpose, same as Eli.

"So," he said, running his fingers through his hair.

"So." I waited, breath held for him to go on. There were a thousand things I wanted to say to him, questions I wanted to ask, but I couldn't find the nerve.

After a few seconds, I couldn't stand the silence any longer. "Can you bring the moonwort key to dinner tonight?"

Eli cocked his head. "Sure, I guess. Why do you want it?"

I searched for a safe response, knowing I didn't dare tell him the truth—that I wanted it to break into Paul's locker. I decided on a half-truth. "I want to check Britney's locker, see if there's anything useful in there." I hadn't planned on doing that, but once the idea occurred to me it seemed a worthwhile task.

"Okay," he said, "I'll bring it."

"Thanks." I opened my mouth to ask him about that kiss,

but my courage failed me as I saw his expression. He seemed so cold, so distant, as unapproachable as a snarling hellhound. I picked up my backpack and turned to leave.

"Hey," Eli called as I reached the doorway.

I glanced over my shoulder. "Yeah?"

He ran his fingers through his hair again, not looking at me. As I watched him struggle with what to say, my gaze fixed on his parted lips, and my body tingled, the memory of our shared kisses always so close to the surface. I wanted to run over and kiss him again. If only I could be certain he would welcome it, not back away and tell me he was sorry. But his swings from hot to cold left me too confused for such courage.

Eli drew a breath and then said on an exhale, "Never mind . . ."

Swallowing my disappointment, I turned and walked off, wishing that I hadn't stayed behind in the first place.

Eli brought the moonwort key to dinner that night, but once again he decided to sit at Lance's table. I didn't want to read anything into his decision to sit there, but I couldn't help wondering if he was still avoiding me. I kept glancing over at him, fuming each time I caught Katarina flirting at him. At least he brushed her off same as always.

Nevertheless, as I fell asleep that night, it was with horrible images of Eli and Katarina dating again, swirling in my head. I half-expected those images to follow me into my dreams.

They didn't.

I dreamed of the plinth again. Everything was the same as before, the tower, the wind, the all-consuming need to read the word.

Only this time, after hours of digging and clawing and

scratching, I finally uncovered not just one but two of the letters.

B E

That was all. A consonant and a vowel and only two out of eight. And yet here, in this place, this dream, those were the two most important things in the world.

～ 14 ～

Locker Room Recon

Eli didn't come down for breakfast the next morning, but I decided that was a good thing. It gave Selene and me freedom to discuss my plan to raid Paul's locker. I didn't expect to find much—the guy was way too smart to carry around a notebook detailing his evil schemes—but I figured there was a good chance I could find out what the book was he'd borrowed from Mr. Corvus. I doubted that it mattered, but you never knew. The book might've been another one of Marrow's trinkets left behind, full of secret messages and black magic spells. Or, that could just be my imagination running away with me again.

Selene and I arrived at English class a few seconds before the bell rang, our timing perfectly orchestrated. Miss Norton was already sitting behind her desk, which conveniently stood right next to the door. Trailing behind Selene, I walked in, clutching my stomach and moaning.

Miss Norton eyed me suspiciously. I wasn't the first student to attempt to fake an illness, after all. I ignored the look, my eyes half-closed from the imagined pain as I stumbled into the room and took my usual seat. Eli arrived moments later, his hair disheveled and cramming down the last few bites of a granola bar. To my general horror, Katarina followed right behind him. He sat down next to me, but Katarina took the desk on his other side, flashing a cold smile my direction.

I started to glare, then remembered my sick routine and coughed instead.

As soon as the bell rang, Selene said in a loud voice from the chair beside me, "Are you sure you're okay, Dusty?"

"I'll make it." I coughed into my hand then followed up with a groan.

Katarina scoffed. "The rest of us won't." She raised her hand. "Miss Norton? Can Dusty be excused? She's flooding the room with her germs."

Selene and I exchanged a look, both of us holding back a grin. Who knew Katarina would prove so useful?

Miss Norton sighed. "Yes, of course. Go on down to the infirmary, Dusty."

I stood up slowly. "Thank you." I coughed in Katarina's direction once more before I walked to the front of the room and accepted Miss Norton's proffered note excusing me from class. As I exited, I caught a glimpse of Eli's confused stare, and I smiled reassuringly, hoping he would guess I was off to break into Britney's locker. I didn't want to think how he would react if he knew Paul was my primary target.

Even with the note, I kept up the sick act as I made my way to the cafeteria building where all the student lockers were located. I checked Britney's first, keeping an ear out for hall monitors and members of the Will Guard. It was empty, and I guessed the police must've cleaned it out in their search for her attacker.

I moved onto Paul's next. He was using the same locker he had been before. The e-mail Lady Elaine had sent me with his schedule also contained the location of his lockers and his new dorm room. As I slid the moonwort key into the master lock, it vibrated in my hand, the magic in the thing kicking on. A second later the lock clicked, and I swung the metal door open.

Aside from a math textbook and a handful of loose papers lining its bottom, the locker was empty. I sighed. I'd expected as much, but I couldn't help being disappointed. Especially because this meant I would have to activate plan B.

Ignoring the sick feeling in my stomach, I shut the locker as quietly as I could and then made my way to the Phys Ed building, where Paul had gym first period. I quickened my pace as I spotted the door into the boy's locker room and the empty hallway before it. If I hesitated, I knew I would chicken out.

A second before I reached it, I heard a door open behind me and a gruff male voice say, "Stop right there."

I spun around, fear-fueled adrenaline rushing in my ears. Captain Gargrave stood a couple of feet from me, a suspicious scowl on his face. He held his wizard's staff in one hand pointed at me. It was as long and straight as a broom handle, the top curved downward in a slight hook set around a red stone.

I flapped my arms at him in alarm as a vision of me dangling in the air flashed through my mind. "Whoa! I'm just on my way to"—I held up the balled paper in my hand, the panic-ruined remains of Miss Norton's note—"the infirmary."

Gargrave's thick, bushy eyebrows sank lower on his forehead as he thought it over, the task appearing to be quite an effort. This was the closest we'd been, and I saw he had a slow look about him, as if whatever had squashed his face like that had squashed his brains, too.

"This isn't the infirmary."

Less nervous now that he'd lowered his staff, I touched a finger to my chin, and said, "Really?" I took a look around, doing my ditzy routine. Beyond the door marked GYMNASIUM I heard the squeak of sneakers. Sounded like Coach Fritz had his senior class doing laps. I turned back to Gargrave. "I wondered what that smell was."

Yeah, he wasn't buying it. "You need to get back to—" Gargrave's words cut off so abruptly for a second I thought someone had hit him with a silencer jinx.

But then another voice spoke from behind me, this one familiar and as smooth as melted chocolate. "Is there a problem, Captain?"

I glanced over my shoulder, unable to keep from smiling as my eyes alighted on Mr. Deverell. He was dressed in his usual classroom attire of khaki pants and a short-sleeved polo shirt that displayed his tan forearms, but his hair looked wet. He must've spent his free period making use of the fancy whirlpool Coach Fritz had obtained for his gladiator team last summer.

I turned back to Gargrave. He seemed to be sizing up Mr. Deverell, as if he wasn't sure who held more authority in this situation. I took a step nearer to Deverell. My bet was with him.

"She claims to have gotten lost on her way to the infirmary," said Gargrave.

I coughed into one hand while I held out the other one carrying Miss Norton's note to Deverell. He took the note, uncrumpled it long enough to read it then returned it to me.

"Well, the sick part is true, regardless," Deverell said. He motioned toward me. "If you want, Dusty, I can escort you to the infirmary."

I nodded, feeling flustered on multiple levels now.

"Is that all right with you, Captain?" Deverell arched his eyebrows.

Gargrave grunted and then turned on his heel and strode away, disappearing around a corner.

A smile teased Deverell's lips as he looked down at me. "He's not exactly friendly, is he?"

"About as cuddly as a hungry grizzly bear."

Deverell chuckled. "An apt description." The smile slid from his face, and his brow furrowed. "So you're feeling sick?"

"Yeah, a little." I considered coughing to play it up but decided not to. Deverell looked genuinely concerned for me, and the idea of deceiving him made me want to squirm.

"Not sleeping well, are you?"

I frowned, uncertain if that had been a question or a statement. "No, I'm not, but . . . how did you know?"

Deverell took a few steps away from me and leaned his back against the wall. He slid both hands into his front pockets. "I sensed it, connected to that image from your dream I saw when I was helping you with the projection cards."

"Oh, that." A vision of the plinth flashed as clear as a photograph in my brain, the *B* and *E* on its surface like pieces of art, lovely to behold even to my waking mind. I pushed the vision away. "It's nothing."

Deverell shook his head. "I'm afraid that's not true. I think you might have the beginnings of a block, as we call it in psionics."

"A block?"

He nodded. "It's when an abstract object such as an idea or an image or even a thought gets lodged inside your mind."

"Ouch. Sounds painful."

He shook his head. "Not really, but the longer the block is allowed to continue the deeper it can get lodged."

"Is it dangerous?"

"Only to your grades." He smiled, heading off my horrified look. "It hampers your mind-magic."

"Oh," I said, catching his drift.

"Most of the time the block goes away on its own. But I do know a few techniques we can try to help it move along more quickly if you want."

I bit my lip, uncertain. On the one hand, I would love to stop obsessing about the stupid thing, but on the other, I didn't like the idea of anyone else besides me seeing the plinth and reading that word.

Still, I didn't want to reject him outright. "Thanks for the offer. I'll think about it."

"Sure. I understand."

"But there is something else you could help me with," I said, suddenly remembering my afternoon mission.

"Yes?"

I bit my lip, trying to think of the best way to phrase it. "Do you know anything about how to extract memories?"

"A little," Deverell said, his voice cautious now.

"Any chance you could show me how to do it?"

"Why?"

Knowing I couldn't mention Lance, I spun the first yarn that came to mind. "I have this friend, you see. She's a fairy, and well, she has a little bit of a sugar problem, you know?"

Deverell compressed his lips as if he were resisting a smile. "I do."

Feeling encouraged, I flipped my hair back behind my shoulders. "Well, she went on this bad binge last weekend and thinks she did something really stupid, but she can't remember what. Or with *who*, if you catch my drift."

He nodded, still looking on the verge of smiling.

"And now she's asked me to try to help her remember." I stopped speaking and drew a nervous breath.

Deverell scratched his chin, and I could tell by the look on his face the answer would be no. "I'm very sorry, Dusty, but I can't simply show you how to do something as complicated as that. It's far too advanced and delicate a technique. Not to mention the moral complications involved in possessing such a skill."

"Right." I sighed, seeing his point.

Deverell nodded, checking his watch. "Now I suppose you don't *really* need me to show you how to get to the infirmary?"

"I think I can manage."

"Good. But make sure you're feeling better in time for my class."

He bestowed one last smile on me and then turned and walked off.

Once more alone in the hallway, I exhaled, fighting back a wave of nerves. Then with a huge effort of will, I turned and faced the door into the locker room. I took a deep breath, bracing for the stink, and stepped inside.

The smell was even worse than I feared, the BO stench having seeped into the walls themselves. Covering my nose and mouth, I moved quietly down the rows of lockers, searching for the right number. Unlike ordinary high schools, all the lockers at Arkwell were assigned to make sure that each locker suited the needs of whatever kind it belonged to.

Paul's locker was in the farthest corner and adjacent to the shower area entrance. It looked more or less like my gym locker, and when I opened it with the moonwort key, I was glad to find it wasn't stinky. Just the opposite, I discovered, as I impulsively leaned toward the shirt hanging from a hook and breathed in. The familiar, pleasant smell filled my nose, the combination of laundry detergent, shampoo, and deodorant that formed Paul's particular scent. The smell brought back so many memories that I stood there for a second, overwhelmed by them all.

Then I remembered where I was, and I reached into the locker and started rummaging through his backpack. I found the book at once. It was the largest thing in there, resting in between a three-ringed folder and a government textbook. I pulled it out, surprised by how dense it was.

A photograph that must've been stuck to the book fluttered to the ground and landed at my feet. I bent and picked it up, turning it over in my hands.

My own face stared back at me. I swallowed as a nameless emotion tightened in my chest. It wasn't fear, exactly, but something akin to it. I recognized the photo, of course. It was from my freshman-year soccer season. Paul had asked me for a picture when we first started dating, and this was the only one I'd had at the time.

Why had he kept it? And what was he doing carrying it around in his backpack?

The simplest answer was that Lady Elaine had been right—he did have true feelings for me. But things were never simple with Paul. I didn't know much about black magic, but I knew that a person's likeness could be used against them in certain spells and curses. The thought sent a shiver slipping over my skin.

Swallowing back the ball of nerves in my throat, I slid the photo into my pocket and returned my attention to the book in my hands. The title on the cover and spine was faded beyond discernment. The leather cover was flexible like a Bible, instead of firm, making it hard to hold.

I turned and set the unwieldy thing down on the nearest

bench. Then I flipped over the front cover to the title page. In a fancy, swirling script it read:

The Atlantean Chronicle

BY NIMLOT OF SAIS

TRANSLATED BY ALTHEA BROWNE

Puzzled, I started to leaf through the thin, flimsy pages, being careful not to tear them. Why would Paul want a book on Atlantis? He was a senior, not a sophomore. I couldn't say for certain, but for the most part it seemed the curriculum at Arkwell varied by grade the same as it did in ordinary schools. And I knew for sure the magickind government regulated what the students were taught. Which meant Paul should've studied Atlantis two years before.

Not that I could blame him for his interest in this book. Although there was plenty of text on the pages, there were also dozens of extremely detailed and fascinating illustrations. Some depicted the buildings while others showed genuine Atlanteans who really didn't look very different from the students and teachers at Arkwell aside from their archaic clothing. But the clothing itself was strange enough for studying. One picture showed a woman wearing a pointy hat nearly as tall as she was. Another was of a man wearing a robe with hanging sleeves so long I had to wonder how exactly he accomplished certain bathroom functions without taking it off.

As I continued to flip through, the illustrations grew broader in topic until I reached a section full of intricate maps. The first few showed the entire city itself while further in they grew more specific, some revealing the layout of important buildings and some looking more like architecture drawings than anything else.

And to think it was all real, and all buried somewhere out in the ocean. The thought made my imagination come alive with possibilities, wonderment like the sudden feel of weightlessness as a roller coaster breasts the first hill.

The loud crash of a nearby door slamming open brought me right back to reality with a sickening plunge. *Crap oh crap oh crap.* I leaped up, slammed Paul's locker shut, and then dove for cover behind a nearby towel cart. I would've dove into it and hidden beneath the towels—disgusting or not—but this early in the morning it was empty.

A few seconds later, more than a dozen boys crowded into the locker room, all of them sweaty, loud, and alarmingly male. But the swearing and shouts didn't bother me nearly as much as some of the topics of conversation. My ears burned so hot I feared they would shrivel up and fall off. If I listened too long, I would be scarred for life. Even though the bin hid all of me except for my feet and ankles, I felt completely exposed and vulnerable.

I squatted down with my back leaning against the wall and positioned my face so I could stare out through one of the grommets in the rough woven fabric that formed the towel bin. From this vantage point I had a clear shot of Paul as he entered the locker bay. I held my breath, mentally kicking myself for being so stupid. *The Atlantean Chronicle* felt like a giant rock in my hands. Why hadn't I put it back? Paul was bound to notice it missing the second he picked up his backpack.

As he started to undress—giving me a flash of glistening, sweat-drenched skin over hard muscle—I turned away, a blush heating my body from head to toe. *Stupid move, Dusty. Really stupid.*

Fortunately when I peeked out a few moments later, it was to watch him walk off with his shower caddy in hand and a fresh white towel wrapped around his waist. I raised my head high enough to glance over the top of the bin. With any luck most of the boys would be in the shower, and I could make a break for it.

Crap. Frank Rizzo, one of the few senior boys I knew by sight, was standing in front of his locker only half-undressed. He was a Mors demon, the kind that feed on death magic, with a reputation for being nasty. Still, he was the only person around at the moment.

Acting quick before my nerves talked me out of it, I raised my hand toward the ceiling and cast a darkness spell. The spell was one of the first ones I'd ever learned, a necessary survival skill for Nightmares. For once my magic worked perfectly. All the lights in the room went out, the darkness like thick, black drapes being drawn over my eyes.

Shouts echoed down the way toward me. I blinked a couple of times, willing my eyes to adjust faster. Fortunately, my half-Nightmare side let me see well in the dark. Not perfectly, the way a full-blooded Nightmare could, but enough that I was able to dart out from behind the towel bin and start running for the door without fear of running into anything.

Only, I hadn't accounted for the book, so big and awkward. I rounded a corner too tight, striking the locker with the top of the book. It tumbled out of my hands, struck the ground, and scooted several feet, disappearing beneath a bench. I dove for it, heart ramming against my rib cage.

I couldn't find it at first and started to panic. Any moment now someone would figure out what was going on and utter the counter spell to turn the lights back on. Finally, my hands closed around it, and I lurched to my feet. I clutched the book to my chest like something that would break if I dropped it again then darted for the exit.

Just as I reached it, a hand closed around my arm, fingers pinching. I shrieked at the same time as a familiar voice spoke my name.

"Hypno-soma," I said automatically. A bright burst of magic exploded from my fingertips, highlighting Paul's stunned face as the spell struck him in the chest. He stumbled backward, his grip on my arm slackening.

I turned and bolted through the door, and I didn't stop running for a long, long time.

～ 15 ～

A Crow's Feast

I hid *The Atlantean Chronicle* on the top of a storage shelf inside one of the secret passageways of Vatticut Hall. Only Ms. Hardwick ever used the passage, and she was several inches shorter than me, guaranteeing she wouldn't see it unless she went climbing—not very likely given her plumpness.

Keeping the book with me was a bad idea. It was evidence that I had been in the locker room, and I knew there wasn't a chance in hell that Paul wouldn't come looking for it, looking for me.

Damn. Why does everything always have to go so wrong?

There was no answer to my silent question as I made my way to spell-casting class. I'd briefly considered going to the infirmary for real, but Miss Norton had written down the time on the note excusing me, and I was well beyond it. I figured it better to try my luck with Mr. Carbuncle than attempting to account for my whereabouts for the duration of the last class period to the infirmary nurses.

Mr. Carbuncle was in a generous mood, and I got off with only a verbal reprimand for my tardiness. But despite my good fortune, I was a nervous wreck when I left the classroom to head to third period. I expected Paul to ambush me around every corner. And whenever I spotted the red and black uniform of a Will Guard, I braced for them to stop me. The darkness spell wasn't exactly illegal, not for Nightmares, but casting it during school hours—and in the boy's locker room, no less—surely was.

But for whatever reason, everything went smoothly. That was, until lunchtime. Eli had stopped off at his locker before heading to the cafeteria, and one look at his face as he arrived told me he had heard the rumor about the locker room prank and had figured out what I'd really been up to during English class.

"You said you were going to look around Britney's locker," he said, holding out his hand for the moonwort key.

I couldn't bring myself to look in his eyes as I gave it to him. "I did. Like I said, it was empty."

"Right. But you failed to mention you were checking Paul's locker, too."

I began to fidget with my napkin. "I'm sorry. I didn't want you to be worried."

He slid the key into his pocket. "So you were just trying to protect me, huh?"

"Yes." I dared to meet his gaze.

"I'm not the one in need of protection." I started to argue but he cut me off. "I understand why you did it, and I also realize that you're too stubborn to drop this crap with Paul, so I'll make you a deal. I won't fight you on it anymore if you promise to be honest about what you're doing and to let me help."

I stared at him, unsure how to respond.

"I just want to keep you safe," Eli said. Then without waiting for my answer, he turned and walked off.

The subject didn't come up again throughout the rest of the

day or at dinner that night, but only because Eli had gone out to dinner once more, this time with his grandma.

"I wonder what Paul wants with that book," Selene said for at least the tenth time as we ate. I'd told her about the photograph, too, but she'd dismissed it as unimportant by comparison. I didn't quite believe her, but then again, it wasn't like she could know his motivations for having it anyway.

I shrugged. "Beats me. But I'm going to go over every inch of it before I put it back in his locker."

Selene nodded. "And I would like to try the detection spell on it. But we need to do it fast. If Mr. Corvus finds out you stole the book, there's no telling what kind of trouble you might be in."

I swallowed, remembering the torturous hours I'd spent deciphering that ancient text. "Good point. I'll sneak it out on my way home from my dream session with Eli tonight."

The next few hours after dinner passed maddeningly slow. I spent the time in the dorm with Selene, doing my best to resist the urge to head down to Vatticut Hall and fetch *The Atlantean Chronicle*. But it was too risky. Until curfew, Paul could be anywhere. He could be out *after* curfew, too, I knew, but I figured it was a lot less likely.

Absolutely refusing to do homework on a Friday night, I wasted time on the computer, checking and rechecking all my favorite websites and reading through my Spellbook feed. As usual of late, Selene wasn't proving to be much of a distraction. She was working on some sewing project for the home economics class she was taking this semester. The very idea of such a course made my skin crawl, but she seemed to be enjoying it.

"What are you working on?" I asked, eyeing the black coat draped over her lap and the needle and thread in her hands.

The thread was strange. It was silvery in color and oddly textured, flimsy and light like gossamer. If I didn't know any better I would've thought it was spider's silk.

Selene glanced up. "Just a costume project."

I frowned, taking a longer look at the garment. She seemed to be making some kind of alteration to the back of it. "For what?"

This time she didn't look up. "Um, the drama club is putting on a play."

"Fun," I said, returning my attention to the computer screen.

Finally, the time came for me to leave. I slipped on my black leather moccasins, said good-bye to Selene, who was in the bedroom changing for bed, and then left the dorm. Eli was sitting at his desk in front of the computer when I arrived, the screen opened to a Spellbook page.

"Hey," he said, not looking up as I walked in.

"Hey." I sat down on the sofa, keenly aware of the lingering tension between us. I cleared my throat. "What are you looking at?"

Eli glanced over his shoulder, his smile clearing the air a little. "I'm trying to figure out what this Terra Tribe is all about."

"Oh, yeah, that. I forgot to tell you in all the excitement of finding the joker card, but I know a little more about it."

"Yeah?" Eli swung his chair around to face me.

I nodded, less than enthused by the idea of reliving the scene with Oliver Cork. But it was too late to stop now. I gave Eli the short version, leaving out the aftermath and how I'd gotten hit by the baseball bat inside the Gauntlet. I would go to my grave without telling him about that one. Fortunately, the story stung less than I thought it would, but it still left an unpleasant taste in my mouth.

By the end of it, Eli was scowling. "You've got to be kidding? Arkwell really allows that kind of stuff to go on?"

I wrinkled my nose. "Apparently. Selene says stuff like that has been happening for ages."

Eli grunted and ran a hand through his hair. "No wonder I haven't gotten a response to my request to join."

I sat forward on the sofa. "Yeah, I'm sure that's why I haven't gotten one either. Talk about adding insult to injury."

"For real." Eli turned back to the computer and started clicking the mouse. "And it definitely paints the group in a different light."

"You mean sinister?" I stood and walked over, coming to a stop behind his chair. He'd navigated to the Terra Tribe's Spellbook page, but when he clicked on the friends' list all he got was a message stating membership to the group was private and that his request to join was still pending.

Eli drummed his fingers on the desk. "What we need is someone who belongs to the group who's willing to talk to us."

"Yeah, but who?" I bit my lip. "Are you friends with Oliver on here? We might be able to find the members that way."

Eli shook his head. "Nope. I'm not even friends with Britney. I don't really friend people unless they ask me to. Too much hassle."

I made a noncommittal "mmmm," although the childish, prone-to-be-jealous part of me was secretly glad Britney hadn't friended him.

"Actually, I think the only naturekind I'm friends with is Irene Stark," Eli said, his fingers striking the keys as he entered a search.

I rolled my eyes at the back of his head. Britney would've been far preferable to Irene.

In seconds, Eli had pulled up Irene's wall. He clicked on her info, and we both saw the Terra Tribe listed as one of her groups.

"Bingo," Eli said.

I caught myself grinding my teeth and stopped. "What makes you think she'll talk to you about it?"

"I don't know if she will or not, but I'm going to give it a go."

Perfect.

"Are Oliver's friends hidden or can you see them?" I asked, bending toward the desk.

"No idea." Eli searched for Oliver and clicked on the link.

We could see the list all right. And it was long. Half of the people I didn't recognize, many of them adults. I suspected quite a few might be Arkwell graduates. There were a number of photos of people wearing jerseys from the various international magickind universities.

Eli scrolled slowly through the first hundred or so then started moving through the rest more quickly. I recognized a couple of people but none that I knew well enough to try and get them to spill the beans on the Terra Tribe's inner secrets.

That was until a familiar face caught my eye.

"Wait a minute." I touched Eli's shoulder, hyperaware of how warm he was and how close. "Go back up."

Eli did as I asked, and he stopped in the right place without any prompting from me. He knew exactly which person I'd recognized. He beamed up at me. "Perfect. You can get her to talk for sure. She owes you big time."

I nodded. Melanie Remillard did owe me, a little anyway. She had asked me to discover her best friend's murderer, a task that eventually led to the showdown with Marrow. Still, I wasn't wild about the idea of asking her about the Terra Tribe.

She seemed nice enough, but after the way Oliver had behaved, I wasn't sure I could count on her to help. Nevertheless I said, "I'll ask her about it as soon I can. I'll get Selene to come with me. She knows Melanie better."

"Sounds like a plan." Eli tapped his wand ring against the desk. "She might not be willing to tell us much about the group, but she should at least be able to shed some light on Britney's activities that night. And it's not like we have any reason to believe there's a connection between the Terra Tribe and what happened to her."

"Good point." I smiled, feeling better about the whole thing.

Eli stood up without warning, going from beneath my eye level to towering over me. I took a step back, my senses on overload. An odd expression crossed his face, and for a second, I allowed myself to believe it was disappointment that I had moved away.

"You ready?" I said.

In answer he turned and lay down on the sofa, his body covering the expanse of it with at least a foot of leg hanging off the end. "I will be soon."

I leaned against the desk and waited for him to drift off. Then I climbed on top of him and into his dreams like I'd done so many times before.

But unlike all those dreams before, the world I emerged into was blurred and foggy like a picture out of focus. The ground beneath me seemed to be nothing but smoke and mist, and I experienced a moment of vertigo, feeling like I would fall right through it.

"Whoa," I heard Eli say from somewhere to my left. "What's going on?"

I turned my head, wishing there was something I could hold

on to, to steady myself. A second later a tall-backed chair appeared in front of me. I reached for it, and the vertigo stopped.

"You okay?" Eli said as he emerged from the fog.

I nodded, not trusting myself to speak yet.

Eli halted a few feet from me and motioned to the formless world. "Are you doing this?"

I shook my head. My reply came out a croak. "I'm not doing anything."

Eli didn't appear to hear me. His attention had shifted to the world beginning to take form around us. It was like watching a painter filling in the blank spaces of a sketch.

We were in some kind of large chamber with a high-vaulted ceiling. Tall stained-glass windows decorated the stone walls at regular intervals with marbled statues of various magickind in their native forms set on the floor in between them. In the center of the room stood a long rectangular table, a massive wooden slab polished to a bright shine. The tall-backed chair I was leaning against was one of several set around the table.

"Wow," I said, recognizing the place from various pictures in the magickind news outlets. "Have you been to Senate Hall before?"

Eli didn't look at me as he answered. "Yeah, the day I found out I'm a Conductor. One of the scientists was pretty friendly. She thought I might enjoy seeing it. I guess they don't let civilians in here very often."

"Yeah, I've heard that, too." Across from me, several suits of armor were just coming into focus, lined up along one section of wall. They were far grander than the ones at Arkwell, with vivid indigo plumes on their ornate helmets and glistening shields engraved with the Magi Senate crest. I wondered if the real-life ones were as lively as those at Arkwell. It would make for interesting meetings.

"I've never even been to Lyonshold," I added, a little envious.

"You'll get to see it soon," Eli said as he moved down the table that, like the knights, was still taking on form around us.

"How do you figure?"

He picked up an object from the table that looked like a stick or maybe an overly thick wand. "The Beltane Festival."

"Oh, yeah. That."

"I've been thinking about volunteering for it." Eli held the object up higher. "I really hope this isn't a regular feature at senate meetings."

I took a longer look at it and noticed a little piece of string sticking out from the end of the stick. "Is that dynamite?"

"Yep." Eli leaned toward the table and set it down much more carefully than he'd picked it up. I understood his caution. Dreams were a lot more real than most people realized. Especially Eli's dreams.

"Yeah, I think that would be out of place even among magickind."

Eli grinned. "Not unless Culpepper suddenly gets elected to the senate."

"Let's hope not," I said, picturing Culpepper's secret storeroom of illegal items. It included not only candy bars and black magic objects but also entire crates full of dynamite and other dangerous explosives. Yeah, not exactly the type of guy I wanted in charge of things.

Eli started to say something more but stopped. I turned to see what had stolen his attention. More of the table had come into focus by now, and with a sickening drop in the pit of my stomach I realized that we were no longer alone in the vast chamber. People now sat in the chairs—twelve of them in all.

And they were all dead.

I gasped and took an involuntary step backward, repulsed by the sight of their slackened faces and dulled, unseeing eyes. Even worse was when I realized they were people I knew, school-mates and friends. There was Britney, her head craned back over her chair, her long strawberry blond hair spilling downward be-hind it. Beside her sat Oliver Cork with Melanie Remillard next to him.

The girl in the chair nearest me was Katarina; her torso was slouched forward, braced against the table. Selene was next to her, her position upright and the most normal of those I'd seen so far, but still undeniably dead.

Terror twisted in my gut at the sight of my best friend. I ran forward and touched her arm, trying to remind myself this was only a dream and failing. Her skin felt frozen beneath my fin-gers. I let go of her at once, tears stinging my eyes. I looked away, only to be faced with more horror. There was Lady Elaine and Sheriff Brackenberry. There was Eli. And there was . . .

Me.

I closed my eyes as vertigo came over me again. Vomit burned the back of my throat, and I swallowed it down.

Crack.

I opened my eyes again to see the scene had altered. The bodies were still there, congregated around the table like revel-ers at a macabre feast, but now dozens of crows had joined them. They were everywhere, perched on the backs of chairs, on the table, even on top of the people themselves.

They were pecking at the dead bodies. I watched one rip

away a piece of ashen skin from Bethany's face. I covered my mouth, too frightened and revolted to scream.

"What is this?" Eli said, moving down the table.

I was amazed he could speak at all given how pale he was and green around the edges. I shook my head, unable to respond. I wanted to look away but couldn't. My eyes continued to roam, transfixed by the gruesome horror as I watched the crows feasting.

When my gaze reached the head of the table, I realized the man sitting there was Eli's father.

Eli had realized it, too.

"Dad," he said, choking on the word. He rushed over to him, trying to shoo away the crows. But the birds only cawed and clacked their beaks at him. I moved to help, engaging my Nightmare magic. If the birds wouldn't respond to Eli, I would imagine them away.

Only, I froze mid-step as my eyes registered the face of the woman in the chair to the right of Eli's dad.

My mom.

The crows had eaten the eyes from her skull, leaving behind red, raw pits. As I watched one of them dipping in for another taste, rage exploded out from me. Screaming, I lunged for the birds, all reason forgotten.

As I reached my mother's body, a cloud of dense fog swooped down, and the world vanished. I once more found myself shrouded by smoke and mist.

"What the hell?" Eli said from some far distance.

Then just as quickly as it had vanished, the world snapped back into place.

We had returned to the tower once more.

"What are you doing, Dusty?" Eli screamed at me from a

few feet away. "We have to go back. That dream was important."

I could only stare at him, my thoughts already giving in to
that powerful, obsessive need to reach the plinth and read the
word. The first two letters of it seemed to sing to me, beckoning
me with a power stronger than any siren. I staggered toward
them, struggling against the wind.

"Take us back, Dusty," Eli said, charging over to me.

I dropped to my knees in front of the plinth and started
scratching at the space beyond the *E*.

Eli stooped and shouted into my ear, "Take us back!"

I flinched away from him, but I didn't stop. I couldn't. Nothing else mattered but that hidden word. Already I could see the
shape of the next letter. A vertical straight line with another
running horizontally out from its base. It could be an *L* or a *Z*
or another *E*.

"If I help you do this will you take us back?" Eli said, his
voice loud in my ear, but oddly distant, like the buzz of some
far-off machinery. He knelt right next to me, but he might as
well have been a thousand miles away. He didn't matter.

But then he touched the plinth. I screamed, outraged by the
violation. My need to defend it rose up so strong I reached out and
smacked his hands away with no thought of the consequences.

The dream world disintegrated around us as agony shot
through me. A second later my consciousness slammed back
into my body. With a garbled cry, I slid off Eli onto the floor. I
lay there, unable to move until the pain receded.

Eli rolled over on the sofa, and his face appeared above me.
"I can't believe you touched me on purpose."

"You and me both," I said through gritted teeth. I hadn't

done anything that stupid in a dream since my very first time. At least the madness I was under hadn't followed me into the waking world. But what was wrong with me?

"Are you okay?" From the sound of Eli's voice, I knew he was wondering the same thing.

I sat up, and he rolled back, making sure our heads didn't collide. "I'm fine."

Eli swung his legs over the edge of the sofa, moving into an upright position. He didn't offer to help me get up, just sat there, staring at me with an expression that made me want to check my face in a mirror to make sure nothing red or hairy had sprouted there.

Vivid memories of our last dream-session came back to me, and I understood why he avoided touching me. He didn't want the same thing to happen again. Something hot and unpleasant burned behind my eyes for a second.

I pushed myself to my feet, wiping the hair out of my face. "I'm sorry I fumbled it. We'll try again next time."

I turned to leave, but Eli jumped up and grabbed my hand, stopping me. It never ceased to amaze me how fast he could move, his reflexes catlike. I faced him, trying to ignore the way my pulse in my wrist danced beneath his touch. His fingers felt like heat-wrapped steel. I didn't pull away, wondering how long he would keep holding me.

He let go the second my eyes found his.

He didn't look away but said in a soft voice, "We need to talk about what happened."

I shook my head.

"What's going on with you and that stone table thing and those letters? What does *B E* stand for?"

I folded my arms across my chest and glared at him. "I don't know. It's just something I've been dreaming about lately."

"But why did you manipulate the dream? We needed to stay and observe that scene in Senate Hall a helluva lot longer than we did."

"I didn't manipulate it. Not on purpose. It just happened." I took a deep breath, forcing my irrational temper back inside its cage. It was just that stupid plinth affecting me again.

Eli scratched his cheek, thinking it over. "Do you suppose someone's interfering with us?"

"I guess it's possible. . . ." I exhaled, wishing I were better equipped at lying. But I couldn't. Not about this. Not to him. "But Mr. Deverell thinks I've got some kind of block in my brain connected to that dream."

Eli frowned, his eyebrows drawing closer together. "A block?"

I nodded and then explained it to him.

When I finished, Eli said, "Why didn't you take him up on the offer to help?"

I bit my lip, searching for any answer other than the truthful one—that I was afraid of anybody else seeing that word, being in that place. "I haven't had a chance yet. But I will. I promise."

He stared at me for several long minutes as if unsure whether or not to believe me. I wasn't sure I believed me—only not getting help was stupid, and I knew it. I just had to get past this inexplicable impulse to protect the plinth and its hidden word.

"Okay," Eli said. "So what do you make of what we did see in the dream?"

"That something bad is coming." The image of all those

dead people and the crows swam before my mind's eye. I tried to draw comfort in the knowledge that dreams were nearly always symbolic. The only time Eli's dreams depicted reality was right before the event in question was about to take place.

Eli nodded. "I wonder what the crows represent. They could be a person, like how the black phoenix represented Marrow."

"Maybe."

We spent a couple of minutes speculating, but there was so little to go on at this juncture. At least talking about it made it less scary, that is, until I left, taking the tunnels so I could get to Vatticut Hall unobserved and retrieve *The Atlantean Chronicle*.

As I walked along, I tried to push the thoughts and fears from my mind, focusing instead on my surroundings. The danger of being down here alone late at night and with Britney's unknown attacker still on the loose was more pressing than dreams and blocks and dead friends.

Dead mothers.

No, don't think about that. Don't you dare.

For a moment, my homesickness for my mom was so strong, I nearly burst into tears. We'd never been close, our relationship strained for years by the impact of my parents' divorce, but things had changed between us after we took down Marrow. I needed to see her, to hear her voice and assure myself that she was all right. Tomorrow I would give her a call. A simple e-mail wouldn't do.

By the time I arrived at Vatticut Hall ten minutes later, I'd gotten my emotions under control. To my relief, *The Atlantean Chronicle* was just where I left it. I tucked the book beneath my arm and then hurried back to Riker Hall.

As my dorm room door came into sight, I grinned in relief at my success.

But when I reached the door, a hand closed around my arm, and for the second time that day, Paul Kirkwood spoke my name from out of the darkness.

～ 16 ～

Trust Issues

I didn't panic. I didn't scream or respond with an attack. Instead my whole body went numb. My heart gave one horrendous thump against my chest and then seemed to cease beating altogether.

"Dusty," Paul said again.

I turned slowly toward him, and he released my arm. My eyes met his, and we stared at each other for several long seconds. I could see his pulse beating in his throat. A muscle twitched in his jaw as he held his teeth clenched tight together.

"I need that back," Paul said, finally breaking the silence. His voice did strange things to me, oddly welcoming and repulsive at the same time.

I clutched the book tighter to my chest. "No."

"Please."

I frowned, stunned by his sincere tone. It wasn't what I'd expected. This wasn't the Paul I'd faced that day with Marrow, the boy desperate for power and as ruthless and cunning as Marrow himself. Still, I didn't trust him. If it came to magic, I would have the edge, but he was easily big enough and strong enough to take the book by physical force. He could've done it already when I had my back turned.

"Why?" I said. "What's so important about it? I know you don't need it for class."

He took a step toward me, and I fought off the urge to retreat. I'd forgotten how tall he was. Not quite as tall as Eli, but enough that I had to lean my head back. I could almost taste the memories as his familiar scent filled my nose.

Paul fixed his unwavering gaze on my face. "I want to tell you, but I don't know yet if it's the right thing to do."

I glowered back at him. "What do you know about right?"

"I know you've been asked to spy on me."

My mouth fell open. "How did you—" I cleared my throat. "That's absurd."

Paul grinned. "I don't think so. If I were in their position, I would do the exact same thing. You're more than capable." The smile vanished as quickly as it had come, leaving his eyes cold, distant. The difference it made in his face was so startling for a second I wondered if he'd developed some kind of split personality.

"But I know it's true, Dusty," he went on, that sincerity back in his voice. "You don't have to lie to me. I understand why you're doing it."

I glanced away, shaken up by his unexpected directness. I stared at the floor for a moment, regaining my composure, and then faced him once more. "Okay, if we're going for the honest approach, why don't you tell me what you're really up to? How did you get them to let you off, who are you working for now, and what's your endgame?"

Paul didn't react to the accusation behind each question as I spouted them off, except for the tiniest flinch of his eyes. I couldn't tell if he was hurt by my questions or offended. Maybe both. For a second I pictured Lady Elaine's and Sheriff Brackenberry's reactions when they found out how badly I'd blown project Paul Recon. Not good.

He took a long time to respond, as if weighing his answer carefully. He sucked in a breath and let it out slowly. "I *want* to tell you, Dusty. I really do. But I can't."

I tightened my grip on the book. "Same old Paul. Full of secrets and schemes."

This time his flinch wasn't little at all. He looked like I'd slapped him. I expected him to come back with an angry retort, but when he spoke his voice was softer than ever. "That's why."

I tapped my toe. "Why what?"

"Why I can't tell you." He pinned me with his gaze, the green in his eyes visible despite the dim light. "Because you wouldn't believe me."

"Try me."

Paul tilted his head to the side, a humorless smile curving his lips. "Here I thought we were going for the honest approach."

I scowled at him, infuriated by his words. I wanted to slap him for real. I wanted to . . .

My anger eased off as I realized he was right. I wouldn't believe him. No matter what he said. That trust had been broken.

I exhaled, annoyed to be seeing things from his perspective. "I guess you've got a point."

Paul nodded, a forlorn look in his eyes. He folded his arms over his chest. "So here we are."

"Yep. Here we are."

He took another step toward me, and I tensed. It was almost painful to be this close to him again. His voice came out a husky whisper. "Is there anything I can do that will allow you to believe me?"

I closed my eyes, my head fuzzy with emotions and memories rising to the surface. I found myself remembering all the kisses we'd shared and the way his body had felt pressed to mine.

I swallowed and forced my eyes open. It occurred to me that he might be using his siren powers on me, but I dismissed the idea at once. I knew he wasn't. Not yet, anyway. Or if he was it was so slight that he might not be doing it on purpose. I remembered all too clearly what it felt like when he *was* doing it on purpose.

"Take it all back," I said, my voice tight with emotion. "Take back all the things you did."

Paul looked down. "You know I can't do that, Dusty. Nobody can change the past. Not even magickind."

Would you even want to? I wanted to ask him. *Would you change all of it or just the part where you got caught?*

I kept the question to myself. I could guess the answer he would give, but he was right—I wouldn't believe him.

Paul took one last step toward me, this one putting him close enough we were almost touching. Then he did touch me, laying his hands on top of mine where they still clutched the book.

"Read it," he said, pushing *The Atlantean Chronicle* toward me. "Search it for clues and secrets and all the worst things you think of me. And when you don't find anything, give it back. Deal?"

"Deal," I said, my voice catching.

He stepped away from me, his hands sliding off mine. He turned and started to leave, but paused after a few steps. He looked over his shoulder at me and said, "I'm sorry." Then he turned back and disappeared into the shadows at the end of the hallway.

I felt better once I stepped inside my dorm, safer. Physically at least. I locked the door, including the dead bolt. Too bad I couldn't turn a lock in my brain and block out all the thoughts. There were so many things to think about—the Senate Hall dream, Paul, the stone plinth and what the new letter might be, Paul, *The Atlantean Chronicle,* and Paul.

Yet more pressing was the sudden realization that I was alone in the dorm room. Selene was gone. Again. I walked into the bedroom and switched on the light to be sure. Her bed wasn't just empty, it was still made.

But when I came back into the living room I spotted a hand-written note propped against my eTab.

Hey Dusty, went out for a walk. Don't wait up for me.—Selene

Glad we had progressed to the note-leaving stage of whatever secret she was keeping, I sat down and pulled my eTab out of its cradle. I didn't want to write a dream journal, but I didn't dare skip it. Submitting them late—or not at all—was one of Lady Elaine's biggest pet peeves. Even if what I wrote was garbage, just getting it in would save me a lot of trouble. Mostly I didn't want to write it because I wasn't ready to face the implications of that dream and what all those dead people meant—myself included. I shivered.

At least I could leave out the part about the stone plinth. I would do as I promised Eli and get Mr. Deverell's help, but there was no reason to divulge my secrets to Lady Elaine and whoever else in the magickind government read my journals. I had a right to some privacy, same as anyone else.

I switched the eTab on and as I moved to open the dream jour-nal app, I saw an instant message waiting for me. It had arrived more than an hour before from OracleGirl, Lady Elaine's on-line handle. I clicked on it, read the brief message, and then started to grin. I might be overwhelmed with questions right now, but at least one of them would be answered very soon.

Britney Shell was awake.

～ 17 ～

Sympathies

I slept in later than I'd wanted the next morning. When I rolled over to check the alarm clock I saw it was almost eleven. Crap. I wanted to try and get to Vejovis today to see Britney, but securing a pass and finding a ride would take time. School policy stated only a parent or legal guardian could sign out an underclassman from Arkwell. I'd asked Lady Elaine if she could bend the rules for me, but she shot me down. Focus on Paul, she insisted—Britney wasn't my main concern anymore and she needed time to rest.

Oh, well, at least I'd had a good night sleep for once—no dreams or nightmares about flesh-eating crows or the stone plinth. I yawned and stretched and slowly sat up. Across the room from me, Selene was still in her bed. I was glad to see it. When I finally passed out last night, she still hadn't come back yet.

As if she'd heard me thinking about her, Selene stirred and rolled toward me.

I gasped when I saw her face. "What happened to you?"

Selene's eyes fluttered open, and she blinked stupidly at me for a second, too drowsy to understand the question.

"I mean your face." Scratches and welts ran down one side. She looked like she'd picked a fight with a thorn bush and lost.

Selene blinked again and then grimaced. The gesture appeared painful. She winced and then raised her right arm and examined it. More scratches and welts ran down from her wrist to her elbow. "I had a little accident."

I threw my bedcovers off and sat up. "No kidding. What happened?"

Selene sat up, too, brushing her black hair behind her shoulder. I noticed a leaf stuck in the long, silky strands. Selene saw it as well and plucked it out. "I tripped and fell."

I folded my arms across my chest, unable to keep the disbelief from my face. Selene was far too graceful for things like tripping and falling. "During your walk last night?"

She nodded, a blush rising on her skin. "Yes. I was in Coleville and it was dark. You know how much stuff there is to trip over in there."

She was right, I did. The place was packed with stuff—grave markers, stone statues, bushes, trees, flowerbeds. I'd tripped in there more than once myself. "So you were by yourself?" I asked, watching her reaction carefully.

She narrowed her eyes. "What does it matter?"

That was a definite no. But I wasn't happy that she still insisted on hiding her activities. "It matters because you're . . . you're keeping secrets from me. You're my best friend." I cringed as I blurted it out. It was so childish, but I couldn't help it. What could she possibly be doing that she couldn't tell me about?

Selene dropped her gaze. "I'm not trying to keep secrets from you on purpose. It's just . . . you wouldn't understand."

Angry, unexpected tears filled my eyes. I hadn't realized how much it had been bothering me. "Fine. Don't tell me." Holding them back, I stood and turned to leave.

"Wait!" Selene cried. The sound of her raised voice stopped me cold. Selene almost never shouted or lost her cool.

I stopped and looked back at her.

"Just hear me out," she said, meeting my gaze.

I huffed and then sat down on my bed again, arms crossing automatically.

Selene ran both of her hands through her hair, looking more anxious than I'd ever seen her. "I've been dealing with some things lately. Really personal things that I haven't wanted to talk about to anybody. Stuff about who I am and what it means to be a siren. You can understand that, right?"

I swallowed, nodding. Of course I could. When I first found out the history behind Nightmares, I'd spent several weeks trying to cope with the knowledge that my kind had done so many heinous deeds to other magickinds that the Magi Senate had sanctioned the killing of Nightmares until there were hardly any of us left. It happened years and years ago, long before The Will, but that didn't lessen the impact of knowing that evil might be a fundamental part of my Nightmare nature. I didn't really believe that, but sometimes when I was feeling down on myself I had to stop and wonder.

"But you've been struggling with that since I've known you," I said, softening my voice. Now that I had her talking, I didn't want to blow it. Sometimes getting Selene to open up was like trying to convince a feral cat to let you pet it. One hasty move and it would retreat. "I mean, what with all the sirens-are-more-than-sex-objects stuff. So what's different now?"

"It's just"—Selene hesitated, her gaze dropping to the floor—"everything that happened with Marrow really opened my eyes to a lot of things. I'm still trying to sort it all out."

At Marrow's name, I felt my pulse quicken. "What does Marrow have to do with it?"

Selene looked up and held my gaze as she spoke. I could tell it was an effort. "Only that some of what he said is true." She bit her lip. "The world we live in is kinda messed up."

I took a deep breath, struggling to stay calm. Was my best friend really sympathizing with Marrow? The Red Warlock? The impossible-to-kill, evil wizard who wanted to be supreme dictator of the world? It was all I could do not to shudder.

"How so?" I said, trying not to freak out on her.

Selene looked relieved. "It's not fair how the Magi force us to live a lie all the time, disguising ourselves as ordinaries, blending in. Why do we have to fit into their world? Why can't we just have our own and be who we're meant to be?"

"Well, for one thing," I said, my mind bursting with counter arguments, "you can't dismiss the dark ages. You've heard what it was like. The ordinaries killed thousands of us back then and that was long before the invention of guns and viral weapons. Just imagine what they could do now."

Selene frowned. "But who's to say that ordinaries would react that way? All that persecution was a long time ago when human beings were superstitious and ignorant."

"Time doesn't necessarily change things. Look at all the fights going on among magickind now that The Will's gone." I pursed my lips, trying to imagine what the world would be like if magickind came out in the open. What would people do when they learned that Metus demons derive their power from the fear of others or that Mors demons fed on death? I couldn't say for sure, but I doubted most ordinaries would be open-minded about it.

Selene grimaced. "Well, you might be right. But still, why can't we live apart then?"

"We do. Sorta."

"We're still expected to blend in. We have to hide so much and pretend we're not what we really are."

"You're right. It sucks," I said without much conviction. I could see her point, but I thought the restrictions justified in some cases. The true natures of some magickind were downright scary. I was pretty sure if given the freedom to do so, hags like Ms. Hardwick would toss the candy bars in favor of little children.

Selene smiled and stood up, relieved at my agreement, no matter how feeble. "I'm sorry for being a little nutzo lately. It'll get better. I promise." She turned toward the closet. "Are you hungry? I'm starved."

I started to point out that she really hadn't told me anything about what was actually going on with her, but I held back, sensing she needed more time. "Sure," I said.

Ten minutes later, Selene and I headed down to the cafeteria to grab a late breakfast/early lunch.

Eli was waiting for us when we arrived. I'd sent him a text message about Britney. Unfortunately, Lance was with him, too, but that couldn't be helped.

"So are we all going?" Eli said as Selene and I sat down with our trays.

"I'm going," Lance said, bringing his fist down on the table.

"Easy, killer," I muttered.

Selene took a drink from her water goblet, wiped her lips, and set it down with the kind of elegant finesse that belied the likelihood of tripping and falling. For once, she'd actually put on makeup to hide the scratches on her face. "We can't all go to the hospital. I'm sure there's a limit to the number of visitors she'll be allowed at once."

"Yeah, and she might not want to see us at all," said Eli. "Who knows what kind of condition she's in right now?"

I looked at Lance, barely suppressing a smile. "I'm pretty sure she won't want to see *you*, period."

Eli kicked my shoe under the table.

"What?" I said assuming my most innocent expression. "It's true."

"Not helpful."

"I think only Dusty and I should go," said Selene. "We're better friends with her than either of you two."

"Yeah, but you might miss something important," said Eli.

I scoffed. "It's not my first time questioning somebody. Plus, you know how Britney is. She's so shy she might not say anything with you there."

Eli nodded. "Yeah, I guess you're right. Any luck on getting a pass?"

"I got one," Selene said. "My mom already called it in."

I sighed. "I'm still working on mine. My mom's cell is going straight to voice mail. She probably forgot to charge her battery or dropped her phone in a toilet. I e-mailed her but considering she does most of her e-mailing on her cell I'm not hopeful. I tried my dad but he's not answering either. He gets up early on Saturdays and goes for long hikes, minus his cell. Says it's his only chance for a little peace." I scrunched up my nose. "I think he's just lucky he hasn't gotten lost and eaten by bears yet."

Selene snorted. She'd met my dad a couple of times last summer, and found his absentminded-professor routine amusing. I usually found it dangerous, especially when he did things like leave the oven on for seven hours *after* finishing dinner. My dad was a classics professor at Chickery College, a private—and ordinary—liberal arts school.

"Yeah, no luck here either," Eli said, an odd strain in his voice. "My dad's working a case, I guess."

I understood his worry at once, remembering the dream. "You haven't talked to him at all?"

"No, but I called the department this morning and they told me."

I smiled. "I'm sure he's fine."

Lance looked between Eli and me, his brow furrowed. "Well yeah, he's fine. Why wouldn't he be?"

I inclined my head toward Eli, allowing him to decide whether or not to respond. I'd told Selene about the dream before we came down to breakfast, of course, but she was part of the Dream Team and could definitely be trusted. The verdict remained out on Lance.

Eli cleared his throat and looked around for eavesdroppers, but the cafeteria was pretty empty, typical for a Saturday. And to my delight, Katarina wasn't present. Still getting her beauty sleep, no doubt.

Satisfied it was safe, Eli recapped the dream from last night. *His* portion of it, anyway, keeping mine a secret. I couldn't help the upsurge of affection I felt for him at his thoughtfulness. It was just his tendency to do stuff like that which made it so hard not to have feelings for him. Well, that and his overall hotness.

Lance appeared to listen to the story with some difficulty, the effects of the curse still plaguing him. The bruises beneath his eyes were deeper than ever, and he kept yawning as if he hadn't slept for days. He seemed to be doing his best to cope with the curse, but I had a feeling it was going to catch up to him sooner or later.

"So what do you think it means?" Lance said when Eli finished.

Eli set down his goblet. "I'm not sure. It could mean lots of things. I did some research on crows and their symbolism. There's a lot of it. War, death, famine, plague."

"All kinds of bad, in other words," I said.

Eli frowned at me. "Did you really think it could be anything else?"

I grimaced, doing my best not to picture the gruesome scene from last night. "No."

"Crows can also be messengers from the dead," said Selene.

We all turned to gape at her.

She shrugged. "It's pretty rare, but there are historical accounts in magickind history."

Eli's eyebrows shot up on his forehead. "Wow. That's incredible." He paused, then shook his head. "But I don't think it applies to the dream."

"Yes, you're probably right. But I thought it worth mentioning," said Selene. "Only . . . aren't crows more or less ravens, but smaller?"

"Hmmm, I think *so*." Eli turned his gaze to me. "Can you check for us?"

"Sure." I picked up my eTab, which I'd brought with me in case either of my parents decided to e-mail me back. I did a quick search on the ordinary Internet. The e-net was too likely to come back with mixed, confusing results. "Yep, according to this, the most obvious difference is their size. They're different species, technically, but they share the same genus. It's—" I froze, the eerie prick of coincidence striking my spine as I read the word on the screen.

"Corvus, right?" Selene said.

Once again we all turned to face her.

Her expression turned magnanimous. "The first day of class Mr. Corvus said his name means raven. I told you that, Dusty."

"Right." That conversation seemed to have occurred ages ago, but was really only a few days. His name had been just an afterthought and a joke. But now . . .

"You think those crows represent Mr. Corvus?" Lance said, a skeptical note to his voice.

Selene shot him a scathing look. "If you're going to be negative, you can butt out."

A devilish grin spread across Lance's face, and he winked at her. "Aw, come on, you know you'd miss me."

"Sure she would," I said before Selene could respond. "But only because you make such an easy target."

Lance flipped me the finger.

I grinned. If he was already stooping to physical gestures instead of verbal ones, then victory accomplished. Only, I had a sinking feeling he'd stooped because his curse-addled brain was incapable of generating a smart-ass remark at the moment. The knowledge deflated my sense of accomplishment and compounded my worry.

"And for your information," Selene said, "it's *very* possible the crows represent Mr. Corvus in the same way that the black phoenix represented Marrow."

I started to nod my agreement, but Eli's reply gave me pause.

"I thought that too at first, but when you think about it, the black phoenix represented itself. It was always real. As far as I can tell, Mr. Corvus doesn't have a pet crow hanging around."

I bit my lip, mulling it over. Eli was right about the black phoenix and Marrow, but there were things about Mr. Corvus that unsettled me, and not just his eye patch. He was so strict and hard, for one thing. For another, he'd taken Marrow's place as history teacher *and* had moved into Marrow's office with some of his things still on the shelf.

Selene traced a finger down the scar on the side of her face. "That doesn't mean he's not one of Marrow's followers. Anybody could be one."

Eli's nostrils flared as he inhaled a deep breath. "That's true. Okay, so we'll check him out. See what he was up to before he came here to teach."

"Right, good idea," I said, although a part of me wondered why, if he was one of Marrow's supporters, he would've put himself in a position so likely to make us associate him with Marrow. Or maybe that was the point. Maybe it was a ruse to try and throw us off.

Selene motioned to the boys. "Why don't you two work on digging up the dirt on Corvus while Dusty and I talk to Britney?"

"All right," said Eli.

"Assuming we actually get to visit Britney," I said, returning my attention to the eTab. I clicked on my e-mail, but when it refreshed a second later, there were no new messages.

Across the table, I watched as Eli took a bite of egg casserole, made a face, and then set his fork down. "I think I'm done. Anybody want some of this?" He motioned to the surprising amount of food still on his tray.

I stared at him. Eli normally ate enough for two people. "Are you not feeling okay?"

"I'm just really worn out." He shrugged, running a finger over his wand ring. "This magic business is a lot harder than I thought it would be."

Lance clapped him on the back. "Don't worry, man. It'll get

easier the more you practice. I mean, look at Dusty. She hasn't blown up anything in at least twenty-four hours. Might be some kind of record."

I smirked at him. "That's only because I was waiting for you to be around. Wouldn't want to waste a good explosion."

Eli grinned. "I'm glad to see you guys are getting along so much better these days."

An offended look crossed Lance's face. "We could always resume our competition. We left off with a tie, I'm pretty sure."

"Oh, give me a break," Selene said with a dramatic eye roll. "Dusty totally beat you."

"I have *never* been beaten." Lance thumped his chest.

Selene started to reply, but I elbowed her. "Don't encourage him. We know who won for real, and that's good enough."

Eli shook his head at the lot of us. Then he stood, picking up his tray. I looked up at him. The dark spots beneath his eyes were more noticeable from this angle. I wondered if his exhaustion today had less to do with magical exertion and more to do with worry over his dad.

An image of Mr. Booker's dead body being eaten by crows popped up in my mind with shocking clarity. I sucked in a breath, and forced the image away before I saw my mother again. All my humor vanished with it, leaving fear behind.

I hoped my mom responded soon.

∽ 18 ∽

Vejovis

Typical of my life experience, the more I wanted something to happen—like an important e-mail popping up in my inbox—the less likely it was to happen. Even worse, the likelihood decreased with every press of the refresh button.

When I wasn't obsessing over my inbox, I spent the day reviewing *The Atlantean Chronicle*, but I didn't find a single thing of note. Selene's detection spell was a bust, too.

Finally, an hour past curfew, a message came in from my dad:

> *So sorry sweetheart. Just got your voice mail but I figured it's too late to call. I was at a symposium all day. I'll call you in a pass first thing tomorrow. Love, Dad.*

I sent him a quick reply and closed the eTab. I texted the news to Eli and then asked if he'd heard from his dad, but he texted me back saying no. He also told me to get a new phone because it was changing every other letter of my texts into symbols, making it nearly impossible to read. The symbol-changing was new, but the crappy phone wasn't.

Tell me something I don't know, I texted back, but Eli didn't reply. Maybe my phone had been offended and eaten his response.

Eager to be off tomorrow, I turned in early. Selene came in not long after and lay down. I was a little surprised at her arrival. She'd gotten a phone call from Lance an hour before and had gone out to meet him.

Selene cleared her throat and then announced into the darkness, "So Lance just told me there's a little more going on with Eli than him being tired."

I rolled over, focusing my gaze on her vague outline. "What do you mean?"

She exhaled. "Some witchkinds have been giving him crap about being a Conductor."

I leaned up onto my elbows. "Like what?"

"A couple of threatening notes left in his locker and some anonymous e-mails calling him a cheat and a fake."

"Why on earth for?" My voice echoed loudly in the still room.

Selene exhaled again. "It's stupid. But I guess a lot of the witchkinds aren't happy about an ordinary using *their* magic. They're acting like he stole it or something."

I gasped, outraged. "That the dumbest thing I've ever heard."

"I know," Selene said, a dark tone to her voice. "And it gets worse. Lance told me that his dad and the other witchkind politicians are unhappy that he's being allowed to use magic at all. They tried to stop it. They say it's dangerous to let an ordinary do magic."

"What? But that's so unfair." I wanted to hit something, but the only thing available was a pillow, and that would be less than satisfying. No wonder Eli was so distraught. He'd been so happy to discover his magic, but now he was getting heat for it. My heart hurt for him. I wondered why he hadn't told me.

"What does Lance say about it?" I asked, bracing for the worst.

I heard Selene shift on her bed. "He's angry. More angry than I've seen him. He had a big fight with his dad about it on the phone. Senator Rathbone wants him to put in a new room-mate request, but Lance refused. He's no plans on ditching Eli." Something like awe, or maybe pride colored Selene's voice.

My mouth fell open. I couldn't believe it. I never would've expected Lance to stand up to his father. I guess this meant he wasn't quite the total jackass I'd always taken him for. "I'm glad to hear it," I said.

Selene didn't respond for several long seconds. Then she said in a soft voice, "Me, too."

We fell silent after that, each of us no doubt thinking about the boys in our lives as we drifted off to sleep.

Despite our good intentions, Selene and I both slept in late the next day. We hurried to get dressed. The cafeteria would be closing soon, and as much as I wanted to eat a Milky Way Midnight bar for breakfast, I figured it was a bad idea. Maybe afterward.

I opened the door to leave but froze when I saw my mother standing in the hallway, one hand raised as if she were just about to knock. I stared at her a full thirty seconds before registering that it was really her.

Moira put a hand on her hip, her vivid red fingernails flashing. A scathing look crossed her face. "I haven't possibly been gone long enough that you've forgotten me."

A huge smile spread across my face. "Mom!" I jumped forward, grabbing her so hard around the waist that she grunted.

But she hugged me back and kissed my cheek. "I missed you, too."

I pulled away from her, a dozen questions on the tip of my tongue, but Mom held up a piece of paper, distracting me.

"I just got in this morning, but I hear you're looking for a day pass," she said, grinning smugly.

I grabbed the paper and examined it more closely, confirming it was legit. "You're the best, Mom."

Moira tilted her head, her blond hair—longer than it had been the last time I saw her—brushing against her shoulder. "I know." She waved. "You two ladies go grab your coats. Let's head out now."

Fifteen minutes later, I climbed into the passenger seat of my mom's neon orange-and-black pin-striped Dodge Challenger. Magickind were supposed to blend in with ordinaries whenever they traveled out in the ordinary world, but my mother tried to blend in more with teenage boys and old men with too much money and too little hair.

I looked over my shoulder at Selene sitting in the back. "Put on your seat belt."

She arched an eyebrow. "Why?"

"Oh, you'll see."

Mom shot me a look as she turned the key. "My daughter is implying that I'm a bad driver."

"I'm not implying. I'm saying it outright."

Moira opened her mouth to argue as she started to pull out of the parking spot, but she dropped the clutch too soon, and the car gave a huge buck as the engine revved and then stalled. Magickind should never be allowed to buy stick shifts, especially not my mother. I couldn't figure out how she'd convinced the dealer to sell it to her. With magic, no doubt.

"Whoops." Moira put the car back into first and started the engine.

Behind me I heard the click of Selene's seat belt as she fastened it.

Mom had better luck the second time, and once she reached cruising speed we were out of danger of stalling. For the time being, at least. But we weren't safe by any means. Right away Mom pressed me for information on Britney, Paul, and Eli's latest dreams. I told her everything, but it wasn't easy as she insisted on looking at me while I talked. Consequently, she kept drifting left of center or driving up on the curb.

"Watch the road, Mom!" I said as I finished. A horn blast and the screech of tires drowned out the sound of my voice.

My mom jerked the car back seconds before a collision. Then she smiled over at me, perfectly at ease even though I was trying to convince my heart to go back into my chest.

"Honestly, Dusty," Moira said, patting my hand, wrapped around the emergency brake so hard my knuckles were white. "You're far too uptight."

"Right, because *dying* is nothing to get uptight about."

She waved me off.

"So how was your trip to England?" Selene squeaked from the backseat. "Did you discover who let Marrow out of his tomb?"

I glanced back to see she'd gone completely white. Poor girl. But I had warned her.

"No," Mom said, for once keeping her eye on the road. "But whoever it was is no longer in England."

I looked at her profile, trying to gage her level of worry. "Then where is he?"

Mom glanced at me. Her longer hair made her look younger than she really was, but her eyes looked old. "I'm pretty sure he or she is in Chickery."

I exhaled, not entirely surprised. It only made sense that whoever had set Marrow free would've followed him here. But why hadn't the person been there when Marrow tried to reclaim his ancient, powerful sword, the Excalibur of legend? Not that I was complaining. If he had been there, things might've turned out differently.

"But don't you worry," Moira said. "I'll find him sooner or later."

I nodded and then pulled out my cell, remembering I needed to text Eli. I sent him a message that we were on our way to visit Britney, and I asked about his dad. Fortunately, the text must've gone through without being garbled this time, because he replied right away, telling me that he'd spoken to his dad and that everything was fine. Funny how easy it was to sense his relief even through a text message. He finished up by giving me a couple of reminders for the interrogation.

Against all reasonable likelihood, we made it to the hospital in one piece. Vejovis was located on the waterfront. To ordinaries it looked like some kind of warehouse, a big brick-sided building with only a couple of windows. Hospitals were one of the few institutions magickind kept completely separate from ordinaries. There were just too many kinds with strange anatomies to treat them anywhere else. A glamour charm could hide those differences, sure, but doing so would make it impossible for a physician—ordinary *or* magickind—to treat them successfully.

We checked in with the receptionist first, a thin, frail woman with gray scraggly hair and ashen skin. At first I thought she was a newly made vampire, not yet fully decayed, except vampires always disguised their corpselike appearance with a glamour. But then the unpleasant keenness in her voice gave her away as she told us Britney's room number. I'd heard banshees were a regular fixture at magickind hospitals—their ability to sense encroaching death a useful tool in helping the doctors prevent it—but this was the first time I'd ever seen one in person.

"Only two of you can go in at a time," the banshee said. "And only if the patient gives permission."

My mother winked. "Oh, I'm sure she will."

The three of us climbed into the elevator, and Mom hit the button for the fourth floor. I was a little concerned about using the elevator. None of the buildings at Arkwell had them and for good reason—it was too risky with the animation effect.

As the elevator lurched into motion, I grabbed hold of the rail and clenched my teeth, hoping we wouldn't plummet to our deaths.

Mom must've sensed my concern for she gave me a knowing smile. "Don't worry. They're not run on electricity. Everything in Vejovis is run on magic."

Selene's eyes widened. "Really?"

"Yes. It's one of the few magical institutions that does."

"What are the others?" I asked, relaxing a little. Magic could be unpredictable and dangerous, but most of that depended on the skill of the person working the magic. Whoever built this place was probably the skilled of the skilled.

"The only other place nearby is Lyonshold," Moira said.

My eyebrows climbed up my forehead. "The entire *island*?"

"Hypocrites," Selene muttered under her breath.

It was a fair point, but I didn't comment, even as an uneasy feeling came over me. Marrow wanted all of magickind to turn away from ordinary technologies. When he'd said it, I'd assumed such a thing would be impossible. But apparently I was wrong.

As the elevator doors opened, we stepped out and made our way to Britney's room. A werewolf sheriff's deputy stood guard outside her door. In seconds, my mom convinced him to allow Selene and me inside to see Britney. I had a feeling the normal protocol would've been to ask the patient if she wanted any visitors, but my mom had a way of making people forget normal stuff.

When the deputy stepped aside giving us clearance, my mom waved us on without her. I didn't question her actions. Talking to Britney would be easier without her.

The room looked nothing at all like an ordinary hospital room. Thick green tapestries embroidered with gold and silver runes and other magical symbols covered the walls, and the bed was made of wood with more of the same symbols carved into its frame. I guessed they were there to promote healing. In one corner of the room sat a massive porcelain tub with clawed feet. It looked big enough to swim in, or at least big enough for a mermaid to fully submerge.

My eyes turned to Britney, lying on the bed. With a pang of guilt, I saw she was asleep. The black stitches still marred her face, but her color had lost its zombie-ish hue.

I glanced at Selene. "Should we wake her?"

Selene sighed. "I'm afraid we have to. We came all this way and might not get another chance anytime soon."

"Right." I took a step nearer the bed. "I'll do it." I leaned over and gently touched Britney's shoulder. She reacted at once, her eyes snapping open. For a second she looked like she might jump up and run away. She was staring at me like some kind of monster that had come to eat her.

I took a step back, my hands raised in an attempt to calm her. "It's okay. It's just me, Dusty."

Britney frowned, her eyes narrowing. "I know who you are."

"Oh, I thought . . . never mind." I smiled. "How are you?"

She pushed herself into a sitting position. "What are you doing here? Nobody's supposed to be here."

Selene clucked her tongue. "Good to see you, too, Brit."

Britney's gaze wavered between Selene and me, as if she couldn't decide which of us posed more of a threat. She'd always been on the flighty side, but this was downright paranoid. I wondered what kind of damage the spell had done to her.

"I mean it," Britney said. "You're not supposed to be here."

"We just, uh . . ." I broke off as my cell started ringing. "Sorry." I reached into my pocket and pulled it out. Glancing at the number, I felt my stomach flip over. I'd deleted Paul's contact information off my phone ages ago, but it didn't matter. I had the number forever memorized.

I debated answering for a second, but then I pressed the END button and the phone fell silent.

"We just need to talk to you about what happened the night you were attacked." Selene came forward and sat on the foot of the bed.

Britney recoiled away from her, drawing her legs up to her chest. She was wearing a green robe, thicker than an ordinary hospital gown, but not by much. More runes and magical symbols had been stitched around the collar and the hem of the sleeves. "I don't want to talk about it. I don't remember what happened."

Right away I knew she was lying. Eli had drilled the signs into me during our last "case" when we'd gone together to interview one of the suspects. Britney was displaying all of them—rapid blinking, short responses, defensive behavior, and so on.

"It's okay, Britney. You can tell—" My cell sounded again, this time alerting me to a text message. Of all the times for the stupid thing to start working properly. "One second." I pulled the cell from my pocket. It was Paul again:

Are you with Britney Shell?

Now my stomach contracted into a tight ball. How did he know I was here? The idea that *he* was spying on *me* made all the hairs on my neck and arms stand at attention.

I closed the text without responding and slid the phone back into my pocket.

I returned my focus to Britney. "You can tell us anything," I continued. "Selene and I are here to help. We want to find out who did this to you and make them stop."

Britney's mouth fell open, and for a second, she looked at us like we were insane. She shook her head. "You can't help. You *can't.*" She sounded half-angry and all-the-way scared.

"Yes, we can. Eli's helping, too." I said, stumbling over the words in my embarrassment. "You heard what we did, right?"

"You defeated the Red Warlock," Britney said in a low, desperate voice.

I nodded vigorously and then brushed back the hair that had fallen into my face. "That's right. So whoever you're afraid of has got to be easy by comparison."

Ice crept into her expression. "You have no idea what you're saying."

I winced, because it was mostly true. I was trying to make it sound like we'd gone into the fight with Marrow with a clear plan of victory. In actuality, we'd just gotten lucky. Me in particular when I delivered the blow that killed him—well, his current incarnation.

"Then why don't you tell us what's really going on?" Selene pressed.

My cell went off again. "Crap." I yanked it out, getting annoyed now.

So was Selene. She turned a stony gaze on me. "Who is it?"

I didn't answer her. I couldn't.

Leave now, Dusty, Paul's message read. *It's dangerous. Don't talk to her. Don't do anything except get out.*

An automatic jolt of fear went through me at his words. But doubt followed quick on its heels. What kind of danger could we be in inside a hospital? I glanced back at the door, which we'd left open. My mom was right there, peeking in on us every couple of seconds as she kept the police officer busy.

"Nobody," I finally answered, closing the text once more. Selene returned her attention to Britney. "We know that Lance was in the alcove. Do you remember that?"

Britney paled. She opened her mouth to speak, but no words came out.

"You do remember, don't you?" I said in a soft voice.

Tears filled Britney's eyes. "Is he . . . is he all right?"

I tilted my head, surprised by her answer. It wasn't what I was expecting. "Mostly . . . but he's been cursed and we're not sure what it was or how to take it off."

Without warning, Britney let out a huge sob then burst into tears. "I'm sorry. It's my fault. I did it. I didn't mean to. It wasn't supposed to be him. I messed up. I didn't want to do it, but I had to. I *had* to."

Selene and I exchanged a look.

"Wait, slow down." I raised my hands. Britney sobbed again, her words disintegrating into garbled cries.

Selene reached out and touched Britney's leg. "Shhhh. Try to calm down."

A few seconds later, her cries died away.

"Okay," Selene said, exhaling in relief. "Are you saying that *you* cursed Lance?"

Britney didn't respond, just sat there, red-eyed and frozen.

"You can just nod if you want," said Selene.

I sucked in a breath as Britney did. It didn't make sense. If Britney attacked Lance then who had attacked her?

"Why did you attack him?" Selene said. The sound of her voice made my skin tingle, and I realized she was invoking her siren magic. Not much, just enough to lure Britney out of her paralyzing fear.

"I didn't mean to." Britney's voice quavered. She pulled the bedcovers up over her arms.

Selene patted her again. "It's okay. So you didn't mean to attack Lance. Your target was someone else, right?"

"Who?" I said, and Britney flinched.

Selene didn't glare at me, but I got the feeling she wanted to. It seemed of the three of us on the Dream Team, Selene had the best knack for interrogating. With her siren skills, she should always play good cop.

"Who did you mean to curse?" Selene said, her voice almost singsong now.

For a second I didn't think Britney would answer, but then she said, "Eli."

A weakness struck my knees and I grabbed the bed rail to steady myself.

Without any prompting, Britney went on, the words spilling out of her. "I left the message in his dorm room, knowing he would meet me in the alcove. But when Lance showed up instead, I panicked."

"Why did you want to curse Eli?" I said.

Britney looked at me, clamming up once more.

"Who wanted you to do it?" Selene said. The question took me by surprise. It seemed Selene had made far more sense out of Britney's crying fit than I had.

Britney bit her lip.

"Come on," Selene said. My skin tingled again, and I could almost hear the hum of magic on the air. I half-expected Selene to start singing. "Tell us who wanted you to do it."

"I can't," Britney cried. "You don't understand. He has something on my mother. He knows—"

My cell chimed again. I closed my eyes, fury heating my skin. I yanked it out of my pocket, determined to shut it off this time.

Please, the message read. *Please, Dusty. Don't do this.*

My hand lingered over the END button. If I held it down long enough, the phone would shut off.

"Who knows?" Selene said, not bothering to ask me about the cell this time. "And knows what?"

Britney shook her head, tears in her eyes again.

"Who is it?" Selene pressed.

"I can't tell you." The tears spilled over.

"Yes, you can." The definite hum of music sounded in Selene's voice, and the room filled with her siren magic.

I could see Britney struggling against it, caught between her terror and the desire to give into the siren's call.

"Stop it, Selene," I said.

She didn't hear me, but asked her question again, the music-magic intensifying.

"Stop it, Selene," I said again, louder this time. I knew what it felt like to have that power used against you. It wasn't right to do it to Britney.

"It's—" Britney's voice cut off. For a second nothing happened. She just stared at us, frozen in place.

But then the mermaid began to shriek.

~ 19 ~

The Target

It wasn't a normal scream, but the fierce, terrible sound of a mermaid in pain, the kind of thing that was dangerous to hear without the high density of water to attenuate the frequency. The handheld mirror sitting on the end table beside the bed cracked. I covered my ears and hunched over, that noise like a hatchet to my skull. On the foot of the bed, Selene was doing the same, both of us paralyzed by the screams.

I forced my eyes on Britney, trying to make sense of her terror. She'd fallen back against the headboard and was thrashing around like a horror movie demon. Struggling against some unseen force, she raised both hands to her neck and started pulling at the collar of the robe against her throat.

A second later I realized what was wrong—the robe was getting smaller. Already I could see where the fabric pressed into her skin, making it bulge around the seam. Britney's shrieks lessened as the pressure increased around her chest, cutting off her air supply.

The pain in my head eased, and I jumped forward, able to move again. Selene ripped the bedclothes off. The robe was shrinking everywhere, cutting into Britney's wrists and ankles. It no longer looked like a gown but like a bodysuit, the fabric pressed against every inch of her body, crushing the life out of her.

I tried to grab the edge of the fabric and pull it off, but it was like trying to slide my fingers beneath two pieces of metal welded together. I searched my mind for some spell to use, but I'd never learned anything to combat this.

"Mom!" I screamed over my shoulder. Where was she? Neither she nor the deputy was visible in the doorway. I searched the room for some way to call for help, but there wasn't a phone or any other recognizable device in the room. Abandoning the attempt to pull off the robe, I spun around and dashed to the door. There had to be someone nearby.

The hallway was empty. I raced down to the nurses' station in the distance, but it was deserted. I searched behind the desk for a way to page a nurse, but again there wasn't any recognizable device. My mom hadn't been kidding when she said this place was run completely on magic. *Mom,* I thought, trying to focus my mind the way we did in psionics, *where are you? I need you.*

My chest bursting with panic and frustration, I raced back to Britney's room.

Selene was singing at the top of her lungs, trying some kind of siren magic to free Britney from the robe, but it only seemed to be slowing down the pace of the robe's shrinking. Britney's face had gone a sickening shade of blue-gray, her lips like slate.

I pointed at her. "Alexo." The magic left my fingertips, but when the shield spell hit Britney it dissipated uselessly.

"Aphairein," I said, but the correction spell bounced off.

Britney's thrashing started to slow, and for a moment I thought Selene's magic might finally be reversing the curse. But the dread pounding through my body told me otherwise. I'd witnessed death once before, that slow giving in to the inevitable.

Mom, I cried again, putting all the force of my mind behind it.

A dead silence descended into the room as Selene stopped singing. Britney lay motionless on the bed, her body bound as tight as an Egyptian mummy.

I closed my eyes, too horrified to scream or cry.

Click-click-click.

The familiar sound of high-heeled shoes striking stone broke the hold of my despair, filling me with hope.

I turned to see my mom striding into the room. Her expression was dead calm, her eyes focused on Britney. She raised her hand toward the mermaid and spoke an incantation. I didn't recognize it, but at once magic filled the air around us like a powerful wind. My skin tingled from the force of it.

There was a loud crack followed by a ripping sound. I looked down to see the robe falling off Britney. Her naked body beneath was a ruin of bruises and swollen flesh. I turned away, shielding my eyes from the gruesome sight.

I felt my mom's arms slide around me. She began to pull me toward the door. "Come on now," she said. "She's going to be fine. I promise."

I didn't believe her. Couldn't. Damage like that must surely be fatal.

We spent the rest next few hours inside a private lounge in the hospital waiting for news.

Across from me, Selene sat in the corner, her head in her hands, crying silently. My mom and I both tried to console her, but she wouldn't listen.

"It's my fault," she said, her voice raw. "I shouldn't have pushed her the way I did."

I exhaled, desperate to hug her, but I knew she wouldn't want me to. Not yet. Selene prided herself on always being tough and strong. But right now she was broken.

"You couldn't have known what would happen," I said.

But *I* had known. Paul had warned me.

I'd managed not to cry so far, but guilt pressed in on me every second, making it hard to breathe. I should've listened to Paul. We should've left. Britney might still be okay then.

How did he know?

I closed my eyes, aware I could drive myself crazy wondering about it. But I swore I would find out soon.

As we waited, my mom explained her disappearance. "There was a fight in the opposite wing, as far from Britney's room as it was possible to be, it seems," Moira said. "It was between a Mors demon and a Werra fairy who somehow managed to escape the psych ward. You can imagine the havoc it might've caused." She made a face.

So did I. A magickind psych ward? A Werra fairy gone insane? What a horrible thought.

"I went to help as well, not knowing the danger I'd left you girls in." My mom looked first at Selene and then at me. "I'm sorry. I didn't realize how serious this situation was. I've been away and out of touch for too long, it seems."

"What made you come back to the room?" Selene said, gratitude in her voice.

Mom smiled. "I heard Dusty calling."

I returned my mom's smile, glad it had worked. Mr. Deverell had told us in class that it was possible to communicate telepathically over long distances so long as the two people shared a strong bond. It was nice to know that included me and my mom. I would never forget the way she had charged in and saved Britney. We didn't always get along, but right now, in this moment, there was nothing I wanted more than to be like her.

Finally, one of the doctors came in and confirmed what my mom had said from the beginning—Britney had survived. She was hurt badly, but they were sure she would recover in time.

Selene finally stopped crying, and the hopeless knot in my stomach began to unwind.

Sheriff Brackenberry and Lady Elaine arrived not long after that. I told them everything, including the stuff about Lance being cursed. He was officially off the suspect list, and it was about time someone stepped in to help him.

The moment I finished, Selene said, "That was *Paul* texting you?"

I squirmed beneath her accusing stare. "Yeah."

Her nostrils flared. "Why didn't you tell me?"

"I didn't believe him."

"But—"

"Let me see the phone," Lady Elaine said, cutting off whatever accusation Selene had planned to say. I handed the phone to Lady Elaine. She examined the texts—navigating the cell's functions far better than I would've expected—and then gave it over to Sheriff Brackenberry, who did the same.

"I'm going to need to keep this as evidence." Brackenberry set the phone down on the end table beside his chair. "I'll have one of my men pick Paul up as soon as we're done here."

I frowned, unhappy at losing both my phone and the chance to be the first to talk to Paul.

"Are you sure you want to do that?" my mom said, crossing one leg over the other.

Brackenberry cocked his head to the side, eyeing her suspiciously. The animosity between the two of them was well known. "Of course, I'm sure. Clearly, Paul is connected to the attack somehow. This is just the break we've been hoping for to put that young man where he belongs. In jail."

I flinched at the animosity in Brackenberry's tone. I didn't think it was so much that he hated Paul, but more that he hated the idea of a guilty person going free.

Moira tossed her blond hair behind her shoulder. "Well, do what you judge best, but if you want my opinion, I think you should hold off bringing him in." She sat up straighter. "In fact, I think you should pretend that Dusty never showed you the texts at all."

Brackenberry stared at my mom as if she'd gone insane. But Lady Elaine looked intrigued by the idea. "Why do you think that?"

A smug smile crossed my mom's face. "Because that text message is a dead end. It proves nothing at all. And I'm quite sure that you'll have no better luck getting the truth out of Paul Kirkwood this time than you did last time."

A huge, wolfish grin spread across Brackenberry's face. For a second, his eyes seemed to glow yellow. "Oh, I wasn't the one interrogating him last time."

A chill danced across my neck. I'd never particularly liked the sheriff, and now I had a better idea of why. There was something bloodthirsty about him.

Moira scoffed, completely unimpressed. "Whoever orchestrated his release in the first place won't let you alone with him for more than a minute, and we both know it."

Brackenberry's grin disintegrated into a scowl.

"What do you suggest?" Lady Elaine asked.

The constant attitude my mom gave the sheriff lessened some

when she addressed the older woman. "Let Dusty do it. Paul has already reached out to her through those texts. If you give it some time, she'll be able to uncover all the buried secrets. I'm certain of it."

I was completely taken aback, and not just by her faith in me. Her stance on this was a complete one-eighty from what she would've done a few months ago. I'd noticed the change earlier when she didn't comment on the sheriff and Lady Elaine recruiting me to spy on Paul, but I'd dismissed it as a fluke. I couldn't dismiss this, though.

Brackenberry leaned back and rubbed his beard, his eyes thoughtful. "I suppose you might have a point." It sounded like the admission pained him.

To my mother's credit, she resisted rubbing it in.

Lady Elaine turned her gaze to me. "Are you okay with this strategy?"

I scratched my head, unsure of how to answer. At the moment I was too numb with shock to be certain of anything. "I guess so."

Lady Elaine frowned, her lips a thin tight line. "You need to be certain. Clearly, the situation is even more dangerous than we first suspected."

"How so?"

Lady Elaine gave me one of her patient looks. "It's obvious that you are as much of a target for whoever this madman is as Britney was."

"What?"

"Honestly, Dusty," Moira said, snapping her fingers. "You need to get with the picture."

I might've held back my temper when it came to Selene, but my mom was a different story. "Don't talk to me like I'm stupid."

"Then prove to me you aren't." Mom shifted in her seat, uncrossing and recrossing her legs. "You told us that Britney admitted she was waiting down there to attack Eli. Well, there's only one reason why he would be a target of the same people who helped Paul escape punishment."

Slowly, the answer came to me. Actually, it had been there the whole time—I'd just refused to admit it. The only reason why they would target Eli, an ordinary with only the smallest recourse to magic now that he was a Conductor, was because . . .

"He's a dream-seer," I said, my voice catching.

My mother nodded, her expression both proud and worried.

"Yes," Lady Elaine said. "Whoever targets him, targets you both. Always."

～ 20 ～

A New Client

I texted Paul six times that night when Selene and I finally got
back to Arkwell. I said the same thing in each one:
We need to talk.

He ignored them all.

I turned in around midnight, plugging in my cell and setting it beside my pillow. Even with the juice pumping to it, the
stupid thing would probably shut itself off before morning. But
in case it didn't, I wanted to hear any incoming text messages.
I had a feeling Paul wouldn't ignore me forever.

I was right as sometime later, my phone chimed. I blinked
the sleep out of my eyes and stared at the screen.

We will. Soon. I promise.

Irritated by the short, useless message, I tossed the cell onto
the floor. It beeped at me in protest then fell silent—turned off
at last, no doubt. I rolled over and fell back into a fitful sleep.

I dreamed of the plinth again. The urgency to learn that word
was stronger than ever. Even inside the madness of the dream,
I seemed to understand that I must finish uncovering it soon.
Everything depended on it.

I scraped and clawed and dug until all the skin on my hands was torn away, leaving the bones exposed.

By the end of it, I'd uncovered the next two letters—*L L.*

B E L L

I woke the next morning with the image of those four letters burned inside my brain. *BELL.* What did it mean? Was it something obvious, like a literal bell?

Only, there were still four more hidden letters. BELL was just the first part of a larger word. Of course, it was possible the word didn't mean anything at all. I had no idea if the subject of a block held any significance. It could be something random and stupid, the mental equivalent of an earworm.

I sighed and got out of bed. It was time to take Mr. Deverell up on his offer. I still harbored reservations about someone else learning the word, but if the person behind Britney's attack wanted the dream-seers out of the picture, then there must be something big coming. And given that small glimpse we'd seen in the Senate Hall dream, it would be all kinds of bad. I needed to get my dream-mojo working correctly again.

In the meantime, there was Paul to focus on. Remembering my discarded phone, I picked it up from where it had fallen beside my bed. Surprise, surprise—it was turned off. I hit the POWER button and then stuffed it into my pocket, knowing it would take a good five minutes to turn back on.

"I'm heading down now," I said to Selene, who was still getting dressed. She nodded, her face expressionless and her eyes red and rimmed with dark spots. I tried to think of something to say to make her feel better, but I knew only time and finding the bad guy would be able to do that.

More determined than ever, I marched out the door and down to the cafeteria. My phone chimed from inside my pocket halfway there. It was from Paul and had arrived around three this morning. I tried to read the text but couldn't. Half of the letters had been replaced with symbols.

Ugh, of all the times for the animation phenomenon on it to worsen.

Afraid I would crash into something if I attempted to decipher it while walking the hallway, I returned the cell to my pocket and hurried to the cafeteria. Eli beamed at me from across the room the moment I arrived, his eyes lighting up. He waved me over, quite unnecessarily—as if I would go anywhere else.

"How are you?" Eli said as I reached the table. He lifted the strap of my backpack and slid it from my shoulder, setting it down on the table for me.

I blinked up at him. "Um, I'm fine. What about you?"

"Just glad you're all right." He squeezed my shoulder.

As I sat down, I realized he must've heard about what had happened at Vejovis. I wondered who told him. Selene and I had gotten back far too late to tell him in person and it wasn't something I'd wanted to send in an e-mail.

"What all do you know?" I asked as he took the spot right next to me, near enough that I could feel the heat of his body. I thrilled at his closeness even as unsettling memories of our last kiss and its disastrous non-results afterward came over me. I did my best to ignore them and retrieved a pencil and notebook from my bag.

"Most of it," Eli said. "Lady Elaine filled me in last night right after they came and took Lance to Vejovis to try and figure out what's wrong with him."

I froze midway through pulling my cell out of my pocket. "They took him to the hospital?"

"Sure, where else?"

"I dunno. Maybe somewhere safe."

Eli grinned, a dimple appearing on one cheek. "Could it be you're starting to care whether Lance Rathbone lives or dies? Miracles and wonders abound."

"Shut up." I returned my attention to the message on the screen. Deciphering it was going to be a lot harder than I thought.

After a moment Eli asked, "What are you doing?"

I scrunched up my nose. "Trying to decode a text message."

He snorted. "I told you that thing needs to be replaced."

"Yeah, well, my birthday's not until September."

"I know," Eli said. "September first."

I glanced at him, surprised. I couldn't remember us ever talking about when my birthday was, but the fact that he knew made my insides tingle. "Right." I forced my gaze back to the cell.

"Who's it from?" Eli leaned over me to look down at the screen, his chin brushing my shoulder. His breath tickled the side of my face, sending shivers down my neck. I resisted the urge to close my eyes and savor the feel. It was too risky—not knowing how Eli would react, not being certain if he felt the same. I stiffened at the reminder.

"Something wrong?" Eli said, his hand coming up to rest against my lower back.

I gaped at him, incredulous that he could be so clueless.

"What?" he said, frowning.

"Just . . . just don't, okay?"

"Don't what?" He cocked his head.

I clenched my teeth. *Stupid handsome, confusing boy.* "It's just . . . hard to take you being all . . . touchy and stuff. Not

215

after . . ." I closed my eyes and took a deep breath. "After that kiss," I blurted out.

Eli's hand fell away from my back, and I opened my eyes to see him run his fingers through his hair hard enough to draw back the skin on his forehead. "Dusty, if you only . . ."

"What?" I said, shivering again. Even hearing him say my name made my body react in ways I couldn't control.

"It's just—"

He broke off as Selene arrived.

"What's up?" she said, sitting down across from us.

I tried to smile, hoping she wouldn't sense the tension—fat chance, of course, considering this was Selene. She looked between Eli and me, puzzling it out.

"I'm trying to figure out this text," I said, before she had a chance to ask any probing questions. As much as I wanted to know what Eli was going to say, it needed to be a private conversation. I held up the phone. "It's from Paul."

"Awesome," Eli said, putting a little distance between us.

Pretending not to notice, I examined the message and started making notes, decoding each word through simple trial and error.

Finally, I determined that it read: *Meet me by my locker after first period. Alone.*

"So what does it say?" Eli asked as I set the pencil down.

"Nothing. He just wants me to meet up with him after English."

Eli cleared his throat, the sound suspiciously close to a growl.

I braced for him to tell me not to go, but he didn't. Before I could wonder why, he changed the subject to what had happened to Britney. He wanted a blow-by-blow account, full of the details most people would've thought meaningless, but from which Eli was sometimes able to glean clues.

Selene and I told him what we could. When we finished, Eli spent a good five minutes in brooding silence while Selene and I focused on breakfast. The look on Eli's face as he contemplated the details we'd given him could only be described as inward. He was present physically but checked out mentally, lost down whatever path his thoughts had taken him.

Finally, that inward look broke, and he picked up his goblet and took a drink.

"Well," I said, "what did you figure out?"

Eli set down the goblet hard enough that milk sloshed over the side. "Not much, but at least we know where to start looking."

"How so?" I knew better than to be skeptical. Eli had a knack for this detective stuff. He was the only person my age I knew who had a good idea of what he wanted to be when he grew up. I kind of envied him that. For me, I just wanted to survive the next two years of high school.

Eli tapped the table. "Britney. We've got to figure out what she was doing that got her caught up in all of this."

"Yes, that makes sense," Selene said.

Eli pointed a finger. It was crooked, bending inward at the last knuckle. "But that means the two of you need to ask Melanie about the Terra Tribe. I'll give it a shot with Irene Stark. Between the two of them, we might figure out what the group is up to."

Selene nodded. "I'll see if Mellie can stop by the dorm tonight or tomorrow."

The bell rang a few minutes later, and the three of us made our way to English class. I barely paid attention to Miss Norton's impassioned lecture on Alexander Pope's inappropriate characterization of sylphs in *The Rape of the Lock*. My thoughts kept returning to Paul as I wondered what he would have to say.

When class ended, though, I finally understood why Eli hadn't protested.

"What are you doing?" I said as he made a right at the bottom floor of Finnegan Hall instead of the left that would take him to our second-period spell-casting class.

Eli's brow furrowed. "Going with you."

I sighed. "You can't. We both know he won't talk with you there." As Eli started to protest I placed my palm against his chest, fingertips barely touching him. He sucked in a breath. The raw sound of it sent a quiver through my belly and down my legs, and I pulled my hand away. "I need you to run interference with Mr. Carbuncle. Make up some excuse if I'm late."

As I started to leave Eli caught my wrist and turned me back toward him. "Paul's dangerous, and you shouldn't be alone with him."

I pulled my hand free of his grasp, trying to strengthen my resolve. "It's a hallway. Full of lockers and students. I won't be alone."

A muscle ticked in Eli's jaw. "I promise I'll behave."

"Not trying to kill him isn't exactly going to get him to talk." I flashed him a bright smile. "I'll be fine, Eli. And we both know how important this is."

That muscle ticked twice as fast, but then his expression relaxed and he exhaled. "Okay. But if you're more than five minutes past the bell, I'm coming after you."

For one awful second, I was tempted to tell him that even if he did come to rescue me he wasn't likely to succeed. Paul's magic was strong and came to him naturally—something I'd learned in just the few short minutes after Marrow had broken The Will. But Eli was struggling with even the most basic spells. He didn't have the same problem I did, with his magic being explosive and unruly. His was just weak, like a shower with low water pressure. It would be a no-contest.

But I didn't say it, ashamed for even thinking it. I wanted the opposite for him—wanted him to be strong and capable. Why did magic have to be so complicated?

"All right," I said. "But I wouldn't even be in danger of being late if we weren't wasting time arguing."

He shooed at me. "Go on, my little red-haired Nancy Drew. Hurry up. Be careful."

I grinned at him, and then turned and raced away, almost sprinting. I didn't know how long Paul would wait for me.

Long enough, it seemed. He spotted me the moment I turned the corner into the hallway housing his locker. His eyes fixed on mine, his expression odd. He looked pleased to see me, but he was clearly trying to hide it. I slowed down, wanting to evaluate the situation.

Paul pulled his gaze off me, returning his attention to his locker. He started rummaging inside it. I approached him cautiously, my "Eli-instinct," as I'd come to think of it, making me hyperaware of my surroundings. The hallway was crowded with other students, talking and switching out books. Nobody seemed to be paying any attention to me or the handsome boy with the shaved blond head.

Down at the end of the hallway, I spotted the red and black uniform of a Will Guard. I'd seen the big, gruff-looking dude before, but I had no idea of his name. I was just glad he wasn't Captain Gargrave.

I stopped beside Paul's locker and leaned against the one adjacent to it. "You wanted to see me?" I said, speaking low.

Paul nodded, not looking up. "Yes, but we can't talk here."

I frowned. "Why not?"

Paul turned his gaze to me for a second, and I saw how tense he was, like a bowstring pulled taut. "It's not safe."

I huffed and folded my arms, more afraid than I cared to admit but also annoyed by his clandestine behavior. I just wanted to know what was going on. Screw this runaround crap. "Don't be so paranoid. It's the middle of the day. We're surrounded by people our age."

"I'm serious." Paul's voice sounded close to a plea. "We have to be careful. Can you meet me after school in Coleville?"

My body temperature seemed to plummet ten degrees and gooseflesh erupted down my arms. I was starting to rethink convincing Eli to stay behind.

"You don't have to come alone," Paul said, the urgency in his voice giving way to something melancholy. "Bring Selene . . . or Eli, if you want. Whoever will make you feel safe being near me."

I swallowed, guilt swelling in my chest for no good reason I could think of. Just the opposite. I had *reason* not to trust him. But why did I suddenly feel bad about it?

A smile twisted Paul's lips. "Actually, bring them both. I've got a case for the Dream Team."

"What?"

"Shhhhh." Paul brushed a finger over his lip. "No details here. But everything later. I promise."

I exhaled, both exhilarated and terrified at the same time. "Okay. We'll come. But where?"

"My family crypt. Do you know it?"

I nodded. Of course I did. It was one of the largest structures in Coleville, and Rosemary Vanholt had been murdered less than twenty feet from its entrance. The connection there had never occurred to me before, but now that it did all the guilt I felt for not trusting Paul vanished in a second.

He must've sensed the change in my attitude, for he stiffened. "All right. Meet me there at seven tonight." He swung his locker closed, gave me a final tentative smile, and then stalked away.

I watched him go, my feelings a big, jumbled mess inside me. I didn't know it was possible for one person to feel so many contrary emotions at once. I decided it was a good thing he wanted the whole Dream Team to come tonight. Eli was right—being alone with Paul was dangerous.

For my sanity.

~ 21 ~

The Ghost and Rumpelstiltskin

My sanity remained a point of concern all through my next two classes and halfway through lunch. My forthcoming talk with Mr. Deverell filled me with the kind of dread usually reserved for public speaking and other forms of torture. The only distraction I had was telling Selene and Eli about our seven o'clock appointment with our latest client.

"You've got to be joking," Eli said, grimacing.

"Nope." I made a face. "I figured you'd be happy. Because the alternative is me going to meet him alone. After dark. In a cemetery."

Eli grunted. "And you're just crazy enough to do something that stupid."

"You wouldn't love me any other way." I said it jokingly but the sudden shift in his expression, from mildly annoyed to dark and brooding, gave me pause.

Fortunately Selene stepped in. "Stupid or not, we're definitely going." The look on her face made it clear arguing wasn't an option.

Not that any of us did. For me, seven couldn't get here soon enough, not compared to how little I wanted to talk to Deverell.

Nevertheless, fifteen minutes before the end of lunch, I forced myself to get up and walk to the psionics classroom. I froze in the doorway, my gaze taking in the odd assortment of things scattered across the floor at the front of the room. Normally empty, the space now looked like a mini summer-camp obstacle course, minus the mud pit. Orange traffic cones, fluorescent batons, red playground balls, and big blue plastic cubes were scattered here and there with bright pink pieces of string connecting them.

Deciding today was going to be an interesting class, I turned my gaze toward the desk where Mr. Deverell sat reading a newspaper.

"I didn't know people still did that anymore," I said.

He looked up, not a bit startled by my sudden appearance. "Did what, Dusty?" As usual, his slow drawl made my name sound like something special.

I coughed once. "Read the newspaper."

"Ah, yes. Well, I'm old-fashioned that way, I suppose. But at least the paper rarely gives me an attitude the way the computers around here do."

I chuckled. "Good point."

He lowered the paper and folded it neatly back into position. Then he stood up and waved me forward. "Come on in. No need to stand in the doorway. Just be careful of the minefield. It's our next telepathy exercise. You'll each take turns navigating it blindfolded."

"Fun," I said as I dropped my backpack on one of the desks in the front row. Then I faced him, trying to figure out how to begin.

Deverell smiled. "Do you have a question about the homework?"

I shook my head. *BELL,* the plinth said. *BELL.* What did it mean?

At my silence, Mr. Deverell came around the desk and perched on the side of it. "Is this about the block then?"

"How'd you know? Did you, um, see it?" I tapped my forehead.

He cleared his throat. "I'm not in the habit of forcing my way into my student's minds."

"Right." I blushed. "Sorry."

He smiled. "I only guessed because I couldn't think of any other reason why you would sacrifice part of your lunch hour to talk to me." He dropped his gaze and examined his hands, probably checking for newsprint smears. I'd never noticed before how oddly long and thin his fingers were. He looked up. "I take it you're ready to accept my help?"

"Yeah, I guess I am."

"Good. I'm completely swamped today but we could start tomorrow, if you'd like." He glanced at the minefield. "We can do it in here, say around four-thirty?"

"Oh." I bit my lip. "Okay, that works."

"You sound disappointed."

"No, it's just . . . is there anything I can do to start working on it in the meantime? I need to get past this thing quick. It's interfering with my dream-seeing."

"Yes, I see." Deverell picked up a pen from his desk and began to roll it in between his fingers. "Well, the best thing is to go through some of the meditation techniques we've been studying. That will help prepare you for the *nousdesmos.*"

"The what?"

"*Nousdesmos,*" he said, more slowly this time. "It's a mind link. I will join my mind with yours and then help guide you to a resolution of the problem. A bit like our minefield exercise, actually, only completely within your head."

"Huh. So it's like a Vulcan mind meld."

Deverell chortled. "That's a fairly apt description, I suppose. But it won't be invasive like it's portrayed in that show. Before we begin, I will teach you how to prevent me from seeing anything you don't want me to see."

This was good news—there were plenty of memories I didn't want him to see, particularly the most recent ones with Eli—but it did little to alleviate my main worry. "What if the thing I don't want you to see is the subject of the block itself?"

He tapped the pen against his chin, considering the question. "The block is concerned with the stone pedestal I already saw, yes?"

"Yeah," I said through gritted teeth, an irrational anger threatening to rise up inside me. "But it's something *on* the pedestal I don't want you to see. There's something written on it."

"Hmmm. So the reason you don't want me to see has nothing to do with it being embarrassing or personal."

"Not at all."

"Then what *is* the reason?"

"That's just it." I waved both hands through the air. "I don't have one, other than a gut feeling that nobody else but me is supposed to."

Mr. Deverell's eyebrows rose so high on his forehead, they disappeared beneath his blond bangs. "How strong a gut feeling?"

I grimaced. "Strong enough that when Eli saw part of it during a dream-session I broke the first rule of dream-walking and slapped him." I paused then added, "We're not supposed to touch the subject."

Deverell didn't respond, looking lost in thought.

I swallowed. "Is the block more serious than you thought?"

His gaze focused on me again. "No, this just makes it more complicated." He stood up. "Now, I know you don't want to, but I need you to tell me about the dream. Don't go into details. Just give me the gist of it."

"Okay," I said, mustering my willpower. Then I plunged on, describing the tower and the ever-present wind and finally the plinth itself. "There are eight letters on it, all hidden. At least at the start, but I've uncovered the first four. *B E*—"

Deverell waved at me to stop, the pen in danger of flying free of his grip. "Don't tell me."

I frowned, even as relief flooded me. "Why not?"

"Because it's a *name*. It must be."

"Whose name?"

"Who or what," Deverell said. He fell silent for a couple of seconds then nodded, as if in agreement to some private debate in his head. "Yes, you must not let me, or anyone else, know the letters."

I folded my arms across my chest, trying to still the jitters tap-dancing through my body. "But it feels like once I learn the letters the block will go away. The word seems to be the whole point."

Deverell nodded, his lips compressed into a thin line. "I'm certain you're right. Learning the word is the key to undoing the block. And I will still be able to help you, but I'll have to be careful not to see the letters myself. I've read about similar cases. We shouldn't ignore your instinct on this or we might make things worse."

Trying not to freak out by the foreboding in his tone, I said, "Why is the name so important?"

"Because names have power, Dusty. Especially *hidden* names. It's an ancient truth that naming something gives you power over it. On the most basic level it's a symbolic sign of ownership, such as when parents name their children or even when you name your pet. The act of naming is what makes the thing yours."

I scratched my forehead. "But once you name your kid you tell people about it."

"True, hence the symbolism." Deverell punctuated his words with the pen. "Not so when we're talking about magical things."

I wrinkled my nose. "There's a surprise."

"Did you know witchkind *name* their magical instruments?"

"They do?"

"Oh, yes. Within days of taking ownership of a wand or a staff, they give it a name but share it with no one. To learn the name of a wizard's wand is to gain mastery over it. Any magickind can use the power in a magical instrument without knowing the name, but *using* the power is not the same as mastering it."

Names have power, I thought. I wondered if Eli had named his wand—surely Lance had told him about the practice, even if the witchkind senators were being jerks about him doing magic.

"So you can see why they are kept hidden, yes?" said Deverell.

I shrugged. "Sure, it's like putting a password on your e-mail account."

He scoffed. "That's putting it extremely mildly, but the idea is correct, to prevent someone from taking what's yours. But the power in names is so much greater than magical instruments. Take the story of Rumpelstiltskin, for example. Do you know it?"

"More or less. That's the one where the girl has to learn

Rumpelstiltskin's name or lose her baby. And he's like a goblin or elf or something."

"Actually, he was an imp." Deverell gestured with the pen again and the cap popped off, hitting the floor with a small clink.

I reached out my hand and summoned the cap into my palm. "Let me guess," I said, handing it back to him. "You're getting ready to tell me that the story is true, right?"

Deverell's smile was more of a grimace as he recapped the pen and set it on the desk. "Oh yes, I'm afraid it is." He glanced up at the clock above the door. I followed his gaze and saw we had only a few minutes left before the bell rang.

"But let me summarize," he continued, walking back around the desk. "Basically, the story you know is mostly true, only the girl was a witch and not an ordinary miller's daughter. She really could spin straw into gold, although it was just an illusion spell. She made an unwise bargain with Rumpelstiltskin, and when he came to collect she refused to pay. But there's no breaking a deal with an imp. At least not while it lives."

I cringed. That was the problem with the true version of fairy tales—they managed to be even more gruesome than the original Brothers Grimm, and that was saying something. "Let me guess. They're not so easy to kill either."

"Not at all." Deverell slid open a drawer and pulled out a pile of ornate blindfolds made of black velvet studded around the edges with silver beads and set them on the desk. "The witch managed by learning the imp's true name. Every living being, ordinary and magickind alike, has a true name, you see. It's one we're born with and not given. Most of us never learn our true name. The knowledge remains buried deep inside our unconscious until we die. To know your true name in life is incredibly dangerous."

"I would think it would be helpful."

Deverell shook his head. "The spirit of a living thing is similar to magic. And as magic can be harnessed through words and incantations, so can your spirit be harnessed by your true name."

I chewed on my bottom lip, dreading the direction this story was headed.

Deverell continued, "Now, imps like Rumpelstitlskin are an exception when it comes to true names. They're born knowing theirs—the knowledge the only way for them to tap their magic. So once the witch learned it, she gained the same mastery over Rumpelstiltskin's magic, which she then turned against him. Since she didn't have enough of her own power to do it, she forced him to perform the asunder curse on himself."

I gaped. The asunder curse did exactly what it implied—ripped things in half. It wasn't a banned black magic spell, but it was so dangerous only law enforcement officials and the like were permitted to learn it. "But how is that possible? Curses can't be self-administered."

Mr. Deverell wagged a finger at me. "Oh, but it wasn't. Once the witch knew the true name, the imp's spirit and his magic became hers to command and control however she wanted. Rumpelstiltskin died a slave."

"And in pieces," I muttered, shuddering.

With an effort, I forced my mind away from the story and back to the problem at hand. "I still don't see what all of this has to do with the name on the plinth, though."

Deverell flashed a confident smile. "I'm certain that once

you learn the name, whatever entity it belongs to will present itself."

"Entity?" The word had an ominous ring to it. "You mean it's something *alive*?"

"Not necessarily. But it's something that has magic, to be sure, and therefore some kind of spirit. It could be a magical creature or more likely a ghost or some other transcended spirit."

My breath grew shallow. "I thought ghosts are just an imprint of a dead person, like an echo."

"That's the ordinary version of it." He sighed. "Real ghosts are not so benign. They're not an imprint of the living thing, but the thing itself, only broken, incomplete."

"I think I like the ordinary version better."

"So do I," said Deverell. "But a ghost trying to show you its true name is a call for help. A spirit without a body is like a raw, exposed nerve. It's pain beyond comprehension. Constant and maddening. The only rest for a ghost is to find a new vessel to house its spirit. The ghost wants you to know its name so that you can have the power to force it into a host."

I felt the blood drain from my face. "You mean like possession?"

"Yes, of a sort, but not in the Hollywood movie sense you're thinking of. Inanimate objects serve far better." He gestured toward the minefield. "Even these cones and boxes would suffice, although they lack a certain elegance for the task."

He was right about that. I couldn't think of anything less suited to housing a spirit. A tremble went down my spine at the ghoulish turn of this conversation. "But why did this happen to *me*?"

Deverell glanced at the clock again. We had less than a minute left. "Wrong place, wrong time," he said, looking back at me. "A ghost has no control over whose psyche they latch on to. It's a matter of proximity and perhaps the bad luck of whoever is near enough at the time the death occurred."

"But I haven't been around anyone dying. Not recently, anyway." It was such an odd thing to say, but true, and I felt a moment of vertigo at how strange my life had become.

"No one in the last year?" Deverell asked, gently.

My mouth fell open. "This could've been going on for a year? Are you kidding me?"

"Well, a year might be extreme, but it does take time for the spirit to draw enough energy to manifest its need. If it is a ghost, I would guess the death happened weeks ago at a minimum, but more likely months."

My stomach clenched as I realized I'd been near the death of four people in that time frame—Rosemary Vanholt, Arturo Ankil, my ancestor Nimue, and the person who had murdered all three of them—Ambrose Marrow. The Red Warlock.

I ran my hands up and down my arms, shivering. The idea that Marrow could be connected to me through my unconscious mind, a literal block in my brain, made me want to scream and run away.

I fought the impulse back with all the reason I could muster. It couldn't be Marrow. For one thing, he wasn't really dead, thanks to his bond with his immortal familiar. And for another, his spirit and remains had been swallowed by the black phoenix. The only thing the giant bird had left behind had been The Will sword, Excalibur of legend.

I swallowed then said, "Are you sure that once I learn the name I can get this thing to stop haunting me?"

"Quite sure," Deverell said as the bell rang. "You will become its master in every way."

I nodded, praying with every fiber of my being that he was right.

~ 22 ~

Latin Lessons

I didn't give Eli the details about my meeting with Mr. Deverell, and he didn't ask for any.

"So long as you're working to fix it, then I'm good," he said.
Thank goodness for that. I had enough to worry about without
adding Eli's concern over me being haunted by some unknown
ghost into the mix.

As if in contrast to my bleak mood, the weather outside had
taken a pleasant turn toward nice. All during sixth-period alchemy, everybody else in the class and I kept taking long, longing looks out the window at the bright sunshine. We suffered
through gym afterward and then Selene, Eli, and I made a mad
dash for the commons.

So did the rest of Arkwell. The place was packed with students. One group was attempting to pass a Frisbee back and
forth with only moderate success—magickind tended to struggle
with hand-eye coordination—while another group was kicking
a soccer ball with even worse results.

But most of the students were lounging in the sunshine,
sleeves rolled back and faces turned toward the sun. The grass
was too wet to sit on, so people were squatted on the cobblestone
paths or on the low stone walls separating the pathways from

the grassy areas. Eli, Selene, and I found a place to sit on the latter.

Nobody felt much like talking. Selene pulled out a book to read while Eli leafed through the pages of his case notebook. I closed my eyes and leaned my head back, letting my thoughts wander as the sunshine lit up the thin skin of my eyelids.

But a few minutes later, the sound of an approaching noise pulled me out of my happy place. I slowly opened my eyes and peered around, blinking to clear the spots from my vision.

"What the hell is that?" Eli said from my right.

A moment later I saw a group of people in brown cloaks walking down the main pathway toward the center of the commons. The hoods on the cloaks covered their faces, but as they drew nearer I realized they were chanting.

Selene tensed beside me, and she covered her mouth with her hand.

"What is it?" I said, glancing at her a second before returning my attention to the newcomers. They were filling up the center of the commons now, more than twenty of them at least. The lounging students were giving way to them as if repelled by those strange words. But I didn't think it was an incantation. The words lacked the characteristic under-hum of magic. Yet there *was* magic nearby. I could feel the faint prickle of it on my skin.

"*Fiat justitia ruat caelum*," Selene murmured in time with the brown cloaked figures.

I turned my head, gaping at her. "How do you know that?"

"It's Latin."

Latin, I thought. Selene would know. She'd been studying the language for the last two years.

"What does it mean?" Eli said, standing up. Nearly every-one else was doing the same, all eyes fixed on the unfolding scene.

The cloaked figures had formed a circle in the middle of the commons, facing outward. In the center of the circle several of them carried a long glass case, like pallbearers. Inside the glass, lying on a blanket of flowers, was a person I had no trouble recognizing.

Britney Shell.

Except, it wasn't. It was someone else pretending to be Brit-ney. An odd blurring around the girl's face gave it away, an in-dicator of an illusion spell. Putting an illusion spell on a living thing was upper-level magic. And these cloaked figures had done a subpar job of it.

As more and more people recognized the person in the glass case, I heard Britney's name whispered over and over again. It seemed most people didn't realize it was someone else in disguise.

"Is she dead?" they whispered.

"When? How did it happen?"

And all the while the brown cloaked figures chanted, "*Fiat justitia ruat caelum. Fiat justitia ruat caelum.*"

It slowly dawned on me that this was a protest, the magic-kind version of a sit-in. But the phrase they were chanting didn't seem like a peaceful one. And displaying Britney—who most certainly was not dead—inside a glass coffin was nothing short of antagonistic.

Eli grabbed my wrist. "Come on. This is going to get ugly."

I nodded, and as he started pulling me away, I grabbed hold of Selene and tugged her along, too. By the time we reached the nearest walkway leading away from the commons, the crowd had started to shout at the assembled group, the tension close to an explosion.

Then it happened. Someone in the crowd let fly a spell. I turned to watch as a jet of red light soared toward the brown cloaked figures and smashed into the case. It shattered, spraying glass everywhere, and the girl inside it screamed as she fell. For a second the scene seemed to freeze in place.

In the next, chaos erupted. The cloaked figures retaliated with a barrage of spells and other magic. Shouts of outrage and screams of pain filled the air. Eli was dragging me now.

"Let's go," he shouted over his shoulder. "This isn't our fight."

He was right, and I knew it. Already I could see the flash of red as the Will Guard began to converge on the scene. They would subdue the crowd in moments, and I didn't want to be in their line of fire.

Still, as we turned down a path, I took one final look back at the fight, my gaze drawn to two of the cloaked figures. Both of their hoods had fallen back in the struggle, revealing their faces. A shock of recognition went through me. With an effort, I ripped my gaze away and returned my attention to the path ahead.

We managed to escape the fight and the Will Guard, running all the way back to Riker Hall before coming to a stop.

I hunched down, recovering my wind. The adrenaline pumping through my system had my heart and lungs doing double-time. "I saw their faces," I said between pants.

"Who?" Eli asked, wiping a trickle of sweat off his forehead.

"Oliver Cork and Melanie Remillard. They were wearing the brown cloaks."

Eli froze in place, his hand still against his forehead as if in a salute. "But they're both members of the—"

"Terra Tribe," I finished for him. "Just like Britney." I looked at Selene, grimacing. "What was that phrase they were chanting?"

"It was Latin, right?" said Eli.

"Yes." Selene paused and drew a long breath. "*Fiat justitia ruat caelum,*" she recited. "Let justice be done, though the heavens should fall."

~ 23 ~

Paul's Secret

The fight on the commons was all anybody talked about during dinner that night. Every table I passed by people were telling some version or another of what went down. I didn't bother to listen. School gossip rarely reflected reality. Not once did any of them mention the Terra Tribe. Given the secretive nature of the group, I had a feeling that most of the students didn't know it existed, let alone that it had been behind the demonstration.

Not that it really mattered. All that did was what the Terra Tribe would do next. The Dream Team was determined to find out.

But first we had to deal with Paul.

We stayed in the cafeteria until ten minutes to seven, and then we headed out to Coleville. In the aftermath of the fight, and with twilight descending around us, campus was nearly deserted, the few people we did pass, subdued and unfriendly.

As we rounded the corner into Coleville's main entrance, I shivered with a sudden sense of déjà vu at meeting Paul in this place where so much had happened before. Even without the history, Coleville was spooky with all the crypts and statues covered in ivy and the headstones with their crumbling edges and wind-worn names and dates.

When we arrived at the Kirkwood mausoleum, a giant stone structure with a facade as elaborately engraved as an ancient Roman temple, there was no sign of Paul.

"I knew it," Eli said, leaning against a gravestone.

"He'll be here." I glanced at the shadows moving around us as a breeze rustled the trees and bushes.

"I am here," a voice called from somewhere near the mausoleum.

I squinted at the doorway. In the dim light and deep overhang, it was a big black hole. But a distinctive shape moved out from the shadows, slowly transforming into Paul.

"We talk in here." He waved us forward.

I wrinkled my nose, my stomach churning at the idea of entering the mausoleum. Unlike the crypt we'd broken into last year during our investigation of Mr. Culpepper, I was certain this one actually contained dead bodies. I'd done enough dwelling on dead people for one day, thank you very much.

But I didn't have much choice as Selene strode forward and disappeared into the open doorway with no hesitation at all. I moved to follow her, but Eli stepped in front of me, ensuring I entered last. I rolled my eyes at his backside. Like that would help if Paul had some deadly trap waiting for us. I noticed that Eli didn't even bother to draw his wand.

Damp, musty air moved over me as I stepped in. It held an odd, slightly sweet stench that made the back of my throat burn as I took my first full breath. The taste of dead people.

Great.

A single lit torch hung from a holder beside the door, casting weak, flickering light into the burial vault. More than a dozen stone tombs sat in ordered fashion across the floor. They were as elaborately engraved as the outside of the mausoleum. It seemed the Kirkwoods didn't care much for stark simplicity. Other tombs were stacked inside deep shelves running from the floor to ceiling along the perimeter of the vault.

As soon as we were all inside, Paul pulled the door closed, the ancient wood groaning in protest. Then he faced us. The light from the torch cast long shadows across his face, giving him a sinister look.

"What's this all about, Kirkwood," Eli said at once.

Paul didn't look at him, but kept his gaze fixed on me as if I were the only person present. "I know who attacked Britney Shell."

Eli folded his arms across his chest, the gesture emphasizing the breadth of his shoulders. "So we guessed."

Again, Paul ignored him.

Selene let out an annoyed sigh. She waved at Eli and then Paul. "Would you two like to just have it out right now and get it over with? Because I'm not going to sit here and watch you stomp around each other like a couple of gorillas. So either put up or shut up. Which will it be?"

I held back a smile, enjoying the way both boys squirmed at Selene's scolding. When neither of them said anything, she sighed again. "Thank you." Then she turned her gaze back to Paul. "So who was it?"

For the first time since I'd stepped inside the burial vault, Paul looked away from me. Then with absolute certainty in his voice, he said, "My uncle, Titus Kirkwood."

Nobody spoke for several seconds. My first reaction was to believe him. I'd seen enough evidence in the past to know that at a minimum Magistrate Kirkwood was physically abusive. He'd once put his nephew in the hospital with a broken cheekbone and ankle after a punch to the face and a push down the stairs.

Except . . . Paul was the source of that evidence. Paul who had lied to me, who had been working with Marrow all along.

"Is that so," Eli said. "Now, why would he?"

Paul took a deep breath, turning to Eli. "I'm not sure *why*. At least not yet."

"Of course." A smirk spread across Eli's face.

Selene leveled her fiercest glare at him. "Drop the attitude. It's not going to help us get anywhere."

"Selene's right." I said.

I faced Paul, trying to make my expression as neutral as possible while inside me a private battle ensued. On the one hand, I knew not to trust him, that everything he said could be a lie, but on the other, my gut instinct—the same one that Mr. Deverell had been so insistent we follow—was telling me that Paul wasn't lying this time. That he would never lie when it came to his uncle. He hated the man far too much for that. Even more, his uncle hated him. "Why do you think he's behind it?"

Paul visibly relaxed. He turned, walked to the nearest tomb, and then hopped on top of it. "It's probably best if I start at the beginning."

"Novel idea," Eli said. Then he too turned and climbed up onto one of the tombs. Selene and I exchanged a look. Neither of us would be jumping on *that* bandwagon. *Ew.*

"It actually starts back on the night that you defeated Marrow," Paul began. "Do you remember when we found Mr. Culpepper's client files where he kept records of all purchases?"

"Yes," Selene, Eli, and I said almost in unison. There'd been a file on my mother and more than half of the faculty at Ark-well in there.

Then I remembered. "There was a file on your uncle."

Paul nodded. "Believe me, it was a shock to find out that someone as hard-nosed about rules and traditions as my uncle would purchase black market items from someone like Culpep-per."

"What was in it?" Selene asked.

Paul started to swing his legs back and forth as they dangled over the side of the tomb. "Not much. Made it easy for me to get through it all before Culpepper chased us out. The only significant item was a chain made from the scales of a Levia-than."

"What's that?" asked Eli.

"Leviathans were ancient sea monsters," Selene answered be-fore Paul could. "They're nearly extinct now. Magickind used to hunt them down to make armor out of their scales. Levia-than scales are impervious to magical attack."

"They made a lot of ancient weapons out of them, too," Paul said.

A memory popped up in my mind. "You're talking about the garrote that Marrow used to kill Rosemary, aren't you?"

"Yes." Paul dropped his gaze to the floor. I couldn't tell for certain in the weak light, but I thought his face looked flushed. If this was an act, then he'd been taking classes.

Eli scoffed. "That's ridiculous. You were there when Rose-mary died." He pointed at Paul. "So either you already knew your uncle purchased that chain or you're making this up."

A vein pulsed in Paul's temple as he gritted his teeth. "I'm not lying. I had no idea where Marrow got that chain. That's how he works. He always deals with his followers individually, never more than two or three at a time. It was the only way to safeguard his identify until he was ready to reveal himself as the Red Warlock. I knew about Bethany Grey, and she knew about me, but that was it. Everyone else was kept secret."

It made sense, in an odd mafia boss, Godfather kind of way. "How do you know that your uncle purchased the chain for Marrow?"

"I didn't for sure. Not until later. But that's a specific kind of item and not something most people could afford. Culpepper's records said my uncle paid thousands of dollars for it. It's possible he wanted to make a talisman out of it for protection. I've heard of people doing that. But I don't think he did. It was too much of a coincidence to be anything else."

I let out a humph, in complete agreement with him on this point at least.

Selene wrapped her arms around her chest. "But how did you find out for sure then?"

Paul's lips peeled back in a smile so cold it made me want to shiver. "My uncle came to see me when I was in jail, wanting to know all about the reckthaworlde website and how much I knew about the members. His nervousness was all the proof I needed. I didn't even have to tell him about Culpepper's records. The second I threatened to expose him to the senate as one of Marrow's supporters, he was willing to deal."

"Holy shit." Eli slapped the top of his leg. "Your uncle's the one who got you off."

"Yes, that's right."

I shook my head. It was incredible. In every news report I'd come across, Titus Kirkwood had been the most adamant about his nephew's guilt. His performance was so believable he'd even convinced Lady Elaine and Sheriff Brackenberry he couldn't possibly be involved.

I swallowed, forcing my eyes to Paul. "Why should we believe you when you've lied so much before?"

Paul flinched, but he held my gaze. "Because liars deal in truths. It's the only way we can get away with it."

Nobody spoke for a moment, all of us digesting this awful reality. Not for the first time in recent months, I wished the world were more black-and-white, right and wrong easy to distinguish.

Selene broke the silence first. "Assuming you are telling the truth about everything, why would your uncle bargain with you? If he's the kind of man who would attack an innocent girl like Britney, why wouldn't he just kill you?"

"Just so we're clear," Paul said, motioning to the three of us. "The only time my uncle gets his hands dirty is in the privacy of his own house. Someone else attacked Britney, but they were following his orders. Several someones, most likely. It's the only way he could've pulled it off both at Arkwell and Vejovis."

I was about to ask him why, if he knew so much, he hadn't done anything to stop it. Then I remembered that he had tried. I just hadn't listened. I cleared my throat. "That still doesn't answer her question. Why didn't he send someone to take care of you?"

Paul sat up straighter. "Because I have something he wants."

"And what's that?" said Eli.

"I'm the only person around who can identify all of Marrow's followers."

My temper flared. "You just said that Marrow kept everybody secret from each other."

Paul didn't squirm as I thought he would when caught in a

lie. Instead he remained steady. "Just hear me out. I don't know who all the followers are, but I have a list of all the member information of everyone who ever joined reckthaworlde.com. I've never read it, but I have access to it. I made a backup copy of the reckthaworlde.com database from just hours before the website went offline."

"How's that possible?" I said, thinking back. "Sheriff Brackenberry said they searched Marrow's apartment, your dorm room, and your uncle's house for the servers and didn't find them. And I know that database servers aren't small enough to stuff under the floorboards in your bedroom."

Paul snorted. "True enough. But the servers were kept somewhere else. I don't know where. Marrow had me set up all the hardware at his apartment, but then he moved it. The sheriff was wasting his time looking for them at my house. Someone else besides me took the website offline. Obviously, since I was in jail at the time."

"Oh. Right." I puffed out my cheeks.

"But once Marrow moved the servers," Paul continued, "I administered everything remotely. All it takes is an Internet connection and an administrator account."

Eli slid off the tomb, his boots making a dull thud on the stone floor. Then he stood up to his full height, fixing a hard stare at Paul. "This is crap. There's no way you were able to make a copy of an entire website database remotely without big-time equipment."

Paul returned his stare, unimpressed. "I didn't copy the entire database. Just the user information tables. It was a virtual backup, and the data, once compressed, is very small. All I needed was a laptop. And that *is* small enough to hide under the floorboards. So to speak."

"But," Selene said, unconsciously running a finger down her scar, "if you had access to that information all this time, how can you claim you never knew who the other followers were? Surely you took a peek."

"I'm not stupid." Paul snorted. "If I slipped somehow and Marrow found out, he would've killed me. But he didn't know enough about technology to realize what I could do with my administrative access. I set up the virtual backup without his knowledge."

"But why do it in the first place?" I asked, although I had a feeling I knew the answer already.

"Insurance," Paul said, not looking at me. "I knew the information was important, and I wanted to have it in case I needed it later." He looked up, unapologetic. "I'm glad I did. It's what has kept me alive ever since."

I stared at Paul as awed by his cleverness as I was repelled by it. I always knew he was ultra-intelligent, a computer genius, but I was just beginning to understand that he was a survivor, too.

"So Magistrate Kirkwood hasn't had you killed yet because he wants the list?" Selene said, brushing something off her arm. It looked suspiciously like a spider and I squirmed.

Paul took a deep breath. "That and he's afraid that if he tries and fails, I'll give it over to his enemies in the senate."

I tapped my foot. "You make it sound like the senate is a bunch of cutthroat politicians out to kill each other off to gain power."

Paul arched a blond eyebrow at me. "Well, it is. All the conflict between the kinds, like the fight on the commons today, that's been going on within the senate, too."

It was a sobering thought.

"Where's the data now?" Eli said, the hint of doubt still in his voice.

"Dusty has it." Paul waved at me.

I put my hands on my hips, indignant at the accusation. "No, I do not."

Paul held his hand out to me. "Can I see your phone?" When I didn't respond he said, "Please."

Huffing a little, I pulled my cell out of my back pocket.

Paul slid off the tomb and stepped toward me, only to have Eli block his way. Paul stared down at Eli's hand on his arm. Then he met Eli's glower. "I meant what I said. I would never hurt her."

"I meant what I said. I'll never let you get close enough to try." The veins in Eli's forearm bulged out around taut muscles.

I touched Eli's shoulder in a silent request.

He glanced back at me then slowly nodded and stepped away.

I held the cell out to Paul, and his fingers brushed my hand as he took it. His touch made me jump as if from a tiny electric shock. I expected him to retreat back to his seat, but he didn't. Instead he remained where he was, less than a foot from me, close enough to touch without even trying.

Paul did something to the phone that I couldn't see, but a second later he turned the screen toward me. It was opened to an app I'd never seen before, some kind of menu screen with a bunch of nonsensical file names listed.

"What is that?" I said, breathless with shock.

"Those files contain information on all of Marrow's followers," said Paul.

Eli held out his hand. "Let me see it." Paul gave him the cell with no hesitation. I watched as Eli selected one of the files. A passcode prompt appeared on the screen, one only Paul knew, no doubt.

Sighing, Eli handed the cell back to me. "Those file names look like legit computer files. I hate to admit it, but he might be telling the truth."

I stared down at the screen, my face draining of color. "How did you get it onto my phone?"

"Simple," Paul said. "That's not yours."

"What?" Selene and I said in unison. Beside me, Eli looked on the verge of something violent. I glanced at Paul and then down at the phone. It *looked* like my phone. It was definitely my case, anyway. It was too beat-up for me not to recognize it as mine.

Paul took a precautionary step back from Eli, slowly nodding. "I switched them out. That phone is the same make and model as yours, of course, and it has your original SIM card, but it contains some of my own modifications, including the app I just showed you. It's hidden and encrypted with a password. Please don't bother trying to figure it out. Three incorrect attempts and the program will self-destruct. Actually, the whole phone will self-destruct."

Eli's hands clenched into fists. "What the hell?"

Paul put up a hand, trying to calm him. "Don't worry. Worst it'll do is burn her fingers if she tries. It's not magic but mechanical."

"Oh, sure, because that's such a comfort," said Eli.

Pushing Eli aside with my shoulder, I poked Paul in the chest. "Where's my real phone? How'd you do it?"

Paul didn't move to defend himself. "The day you stole *The Atlantean Chronicle*. I made the switch that night. There was nobody in the dorm so I broke in and replaced your old phone with this one."

"Oh, this is just great." Venom dripped in Eli's voice.

I gritted my teeth, outrage making my head swim. "Is that why my phone started changing letters to symbols?"

"Probably. Sorry about that." A sheepish grin crossed Paul's face.

Eli took a threatening step toward Paul. "But why give it to Dusty in the first place?"

This time Paul stood his ground. "Because I knew it would be safe with her. And because my uncle would never expect it. It's not like he's been content just to trust me not to expose him. He's been looking for the data nonstop. And I'm pretty sure he's a lot smarter about technology than Sheriff Brackenberry and the rest of magickind."

My fingers tightened on the phone automatically, some of my anger giving way to astonishment. He hadn't exactly said that I was holding his life in my hands, but if he was telling the truth about Magistrate Kirkwood, then I most definitely was.

I started to put my phone back in my pocket, but Paul stopped me.

"Do you mind if I make sure it's hidden again?"

I frowned, realizing the gravity of what my phone now held. I handed it back to him. I wanted to stay angry with Paul, but I couldn't manage it. What he'd done was horrible—not to mention a little scary—but the fact that he would trust me with something so huge meant a lot. Even if I didn't want it to.

He gave the phone back a moment later, and I stowed it in my pocket.

I faced Paul once more. "Explain how your uncle was behind the attack on Britney."

Sighing, he took a step back. "I spent a little time at his house right after my release, and I didn't waste it. I couldn't believe he would support Marrow. He craves his own power too much. So I wanted to figure out what he was up to now that Marrow is out of the picture. I hacked his e-mail using the same laptop that I used for the website backups. It was hidden in my room the whole time. Brackenberry didn't find it because they were looking for magical concealment, but I had it hidden in an ordinary secret compartment. They didn't think to check for those."

I shook my head, once again astounded by his cleverness.

Paul continued on, unaware. "Several of the e-mails I found were written in code. They had names and references to things that don't exist. One of them, I was pretty sure was a reference to the attack on Britney. And when I found out she was awake, and that you and Selene were going to talk to her, I guessed she would be in danger." He paused. "I was right."

"How did you know we were going to visit Britney?" Selene asked.

Paul shifted his weight, squirming a little. "Dusty texted Eli about it. I've been monitoring the phone just in case . . ." He leveled a defensive look at me. "In case you told Brackenberry something important about me."

I crossed my arms over my chest. "You've been spying on me?"

Paul nodded. "But no more than you've been spying on me."

I pressed my lips together, unable to decide on a response.

Paul pulled his gaze from me and glanced at the other two. "The attack on Britney is only the start of it. From what I saw in those e-mails, my uncle is planning something big. A way to make himself consul. It's what he wants more than anything."

Selene raised her hand to her mouth. "You think he's going to assassinate Consul Vanholt?"

"What else?" said Paul.

I gaped—the consul was the same as the president.

"I don't know how yet," Paul said, "but based on the code words, I think it's going to happen during Beltane. And the place is Lyonshold. My guess is it's going down during the festival. But the e-mail also talked about Atlantis. I haven't figured out what it means yet."

He stopped speaking, giving us a chance to digest this. I turned the notion over and over inside my head. Was it possible? Could Titus Kirkwood be planning a coup? I stared at Paul, trying to decide if I could trust him. Something about the way his face looked in the torchlight reminded me of Bethany's dream. *He* had been in the dream. No, that wasn't right. Someone that looked like him but wasn't him. Someone like . . .

Titus Kirkwood.

The realization dawned on me as bright as a searchlight. Titus and Paul shared a strong, almost uncanny resemblance given that they were only uncle and nephew and not father and son. But it was one close enough that I was certain Britney had been dreaming about Titus and not Paul.

I glanced at the other three and told them about Britney's dream. "It all fits," I said when I finished. "And Britney was supposed to curse Eli to keep us from seeing what's coming in his dreams. This must be why."

Eli nodded. "I suppose it makes sense."

"That's why you borrowed Mr. Corvus's book, isn't it?" I asked Paul.

"Yeah, I wanted to see if there was a record of any assassinations that took place on the island. I figured my uncle might try to copy it. Of course, I, uh, didn't get very far." A playful grin flashed across his face for a second.

It was my turn to squirm.

"Who were the e-mails to?" Eli asked, scowling.

Paul's grin vanished. "There wasn't a salutation, but the address was thecrowking@gmail.com."

Eli and I exchanged a look.

Paul's brow furrowed. "What do you know?"

I gave him a quick summary of the Senate Hall dream and the connection between Mr. Corvus and crows.

"I suppose he might be involved," Paul said when I finished. "But I don't know much about him. We should check him out."

Frowning at the "we" in his statement, I said, "Now wait a second. All this might be true, but if so, why haven't you gone to Sheriff Brackenberry with it? Why come to us at all?" I waited, expecting Paul to finally be stumped, but he answered as quickly as before.

"Because I don't have any concrete proof. Sure, his name is probably in the data, but so are hundreds of others. That's not enough. And the stuff about Britney and the assassination is all guesswork. It's not like they're going to take my word for it, not considering my history. No, I can't go to the authorities without indisputable evidence. My uncle is too powerful. There's no telling how many people he has working for him. He'll try to kill me if he thinks I'm going to turn him in, data or no. If I'm going to take that kind of risk, I want to make sure it's worth it. I want to make sure that he pays."

I flinched at the hatred in his voice, like the hard crack of a whip. It was shocking to learn the reality of his life now, the perilous tightrope he had to walk every second. Not that it wasn't his fault.

But I decided his reasons were valid. With an accusation this big, they weren't liable to take my word for it either. Titus

Kirkwood was a magistrate, and you didn't get that high up without lots of support. Besides, we hadn't seen any definite signs of this in Eli's dreams that I could tell.

"Okay," Selene said. "I'm convinced."

I glanced at her and then at Eli. He slowly nodded. "Me, too."

I turned back to Paul. "I guess this means we're on the case. But you've got to promise me something first." I pulled the cell out of my back pocket again and held it up. "Once we've taken down your uncle and you're no longer in danger, we give the phone and the password over to the sheriff."

Paul hesitated, but only for a second. "I promise."

His hesitation worried me, but there was nothing I could do about it at present. "All right," I said to the room at large. "So I guess we start with Mr. Corvus and the Terra Tribe."

"Yes," Eli seconded. "And we've got one week to figure this out."

One week until Beltane.

I hoped it would be enough.

～ 24 ～

Dream Remix

y session with Mr. Deverell the following afternoon wasn't at all what I expected. It was less like *Star Trek* and more like Luke Skywalker being tortured by Obi-Wan with the blast shield and the training remote. Not that I pointed out this comparison to Mr. Deverell. I didn't want him to think I was a *total* sci-fi geek.

We started off doing some mental "exercises" designed to strengthen my mind and to make sure I could keep the important stuff hidden, then he performed the *nousdesmos*. It seemed a lot like being hypnotized. In seconds I found myself slipping away, not falling asleep, but more like entering a dream. Except there wasn't a dream or even a dreamer. There was nothing but empty blackness all around me as if I'd been submerged in an ultra-advanced sensory deprivation chamber.

Mr. Deverell's voice spoke to me from somewhere in the darkness, encouraging me to visualize the plinth. "Let your instincts guide you."

Yeah, he might as well have said "stretch out with your feelings, Luke" for all the help it was. I didn't feel any instinct about anything. All I felt was nothing at all, just one big black everywhere. It was frightening and yet oddly peaceful at the same time. *Unbeing.*

But slowly I managed to reach the plinth and focus on the words, willing them into sight. It was hard, but infinitely better than scratching away at them the way I did in my dreams. I didn't have any fingers to scratch with in this state.

But by the end of the two-hour-long session, I'd managed to uncover only two letters: *A N.*

B E L L A N

It wasn't as much as I wanted, but at least it was a step in the right direction.

"Let's try again on Friday," Deverell said afterward.

"Why not sooner?" I asked, trying to hide my disappointment.

He shook his head. "Your mind needs time to recover from what we did here today. The brain's a muscle, same as any other, and we just put it through a rigorous workout."

I wanted to argue but could tell it was no use. As I left the classroom, I decided I would have to try again in Eli's dream during our session tonight. Deverell had said it was dangerous to let anyone else see the name, but with so much at stake, I knew it was a risk I would have to take.

I told Eli this plan the moment I arrived in his dorm that night for our dream-session.

He thought about it for several long seconds before answering. "Are you sure that's a good idea?"

"What do you mean? Of course it is." I leaned forward in the chair I was sitting in. Eli sat across from me on the sofa, slouched back and looking as hot as ever. The light blue T-shirt he wore was threadbare, as if from hundreds of washings, and it had a rip on the collar, one long enough that I could see the edge of the tattoo on his chest. Try as I did, I couldn't keep my eyes from slipping down to it again and again.

Damn him.

Eli leaned forward, too, the opening in his shirt spreading even wider. "I don't want you to get hurt, Dusty. If Deverell says your mind needs time to recover then we better do it."

"We don't have time. Beltane is less than a week away. I need to be able to manipulate your dreams now. But at this rate, it's never going to happen in time." I stood up and started pacing the room. "And we don't know anything at all. *The Atlantean Chronicle* is super long with no index. There's no telling if we'll find details on an assassination. And we don't know who's involved or where exactly it's going to happen. I know I haven't been there, but I'm pretty sure Lyonshold is a *big* place. So it's not like we can keep on top of everything. And—"

Without warning, Eli stood up from the sofa and pulled me into a hug. I was so caught off guard, I gasped. His arms slid around my shoulders as he drew me to his chest. "Calm down," he said. "I've never seen you so worked up. You're not yourself."

For a second I had no idea what he was talking about, but then I realized he was right. I felt like I was on the verge of a meltdown. But that wasn't like me. I'd been under plenty of stress before and not lost it. So why now?

Eli's hands moved up and down my back. "It must be from the session. You're stressed out."

I nodded into his chest, relaxing against him automatically. I suddenly felt like sleeping. Right here. In his arms.

I felt Eli's hands slide all the way to the small of my back, the movement making every muscle in my body react. I started to lean into his touch, then realized what I was doing, and pulled back, my face flushed.

As he let me go, I saw his was, too. And he was breathing hard. I watched the rise and fall of his chest, more confused than ever. I wasn't completely inexperienced. I could tell when a guy was reacting to me in a not-just-friends kind of way. I remembered that kiss, so hot and steamy it might've scalded my insides. Friends didn't kiss like that. A boy *not* interested in you didn't kiss like that.

I mustered my courage to once again ask him for an explanation, but I didn't get a chance before he deliberately changed the subject.

"I did some digging into Mr. Corvus today," he said, returning to his position on the sofa.

Taking a deep breath, I retreated to the desk, leaning against it. "Oh, yeah? Find out anything?"

Eli made a face. "Not a thing, although that's telling all by itself."

"How so?"

"He doesn't have a past," Eli said around a yawn. "At least not one I could find so far. All the Internet and e-net searches I've done were a dead end. The guy doesn't have so much as an entry on ratemyteachers.com."

I frowned. "He wouldn't, would he? I didn't think magic-kind used that site."

"Some of them do." Eli turned and lay down on the sofa. "There're even a couple of ratings on there for Marrow."

I gaped. "Nuh-uh."

He grinned over at me, his eyes half-closed. "Yep. And they were pretty positive, too."

It was sort of funny to think about, but I didn't laugh. Folding my arms across my chest, I walked to the sofa and looked down at him. "Not being on the Internet doesn't really mean anything. Corvus is old."

Eli shook his head, his eyes slipping all the way closed. "His official school records were a dead end, too."

I shoved Eli's leg with my knee. "How did you see his official records?"

Eli opened his eyes, a smirk splayed across his lips. "Easy. I broke into the admin office today after classes."

I dropped my forehead into my hand. "You've got to be kidding."

"It wasn't a big deal. Dr. Hendershaw meets with the office staff on Tuesdays so I knew I could get in and out without getting caught. Thanks to the moonwort key, that is."

"I'm half-tempted to take it away from you."

Eli pinned me with a gaze. "You wouldn't dare." He wasn't smiling, but I could see the humor in his eyes, and I definitely heard the challenge in his voice. It put me in mind to do something daring, and for a tense moment I imagined climbing on top of him *before* he fell asleep. Better yet, I imagined him grabbing my hand and pulling me there.

Stop it, Dusty. Stop it right now. "Was his file empty or something?"

"Nope," Eli said. "But it only had one entry for prior work experience. He spent twenty years at Castlebank Academy in Scotland."

"Well, that seems normal. Castlebank is just like Arkwell."

"Sure." Eli slid his hands behind his head, his arm muscles flexing from the gesture. "Except he stopped working there ten years ago. And there's no record of what he's been up to since."

I hooked my thumbs into the belt loops of my pants. "Well, that's weird. But it doesn't exactly link him to Magistrate Kirkwood."

"No, not yet. But the next step is to check out his office." Eli sounded eager at the prospect, but I couldn't say the same. Mr. Corvus was fierce. Mr. Corvus would not take lightly to catching someone breaking into his office.

"We'll have to plan that one carefully."

He nodded, his eyes slipping closed. "Did you get anywhere with Melanie yet?"

"No. Selene sent her an e-mail, but she hasn't responded. Then she tried to track her down while I was with Deverell but didn't have any luck. I have a feeling it's not going to be easy."

"Yes, well, it wouldn't be any fun if it was." His voice trailed off, and a few moments later he was asleep. Must be nice to be able to shut off so quickly.

I climbed on top of him, a dull ache beginning to pound in my temples from stress and worry. Still, I had every intention of having another go at the stone plinth tonight, no matter what Eli said. And as long as I didn't hit him again it should work.

I reached for his forehead, ready to enter the dream, but froze as Eli shifted beneath me. It was slight, but enough to make my heart throb against my rib cage. My face went red, and my body temperature spiked. Then Eli's hands, which had been pinned beneath his head, slipped down and landed against my waist, catching on the jut of my hips.

He smiled in his sleep. I considered removing his hands to somewhere less intimate but decided not to. Some things just felt too right to change.

What didn't feel right was Eli's dream. Once again, I found myself surrounded in thick fog, even worse than last time.

"Eli," I shouted, fighting off vertigo. I tried to will the dream to take shape, but nothing happened. This might as well have not been a dream world at all. The sharp teeth of panic nipped at me, but then Eli emerged from the fog.

"I'm here."

I wanted to throw my arms around him, but that would be a very bad idea. "What's going on with your dream?"

"I don't know." Eli looked tense, and I wondered if he'd been close to panic, too. "Do you think this is because of the block?" He motioned to the fog.

I bit my lip, dismayed by the idea. "I . . . I don't think so. I mean, I don't see how. This is coming from inside you, not me." I paused, thinking about the dreams before it. Everything seemed so muddled. I exhaled. "Then again, it might be me. I'll ask Mr. Deverell."

Eli ran his hand through his hair, his lips pinched. "Yeah, that's a good idea. Come on. Let's see if we can figure out where we are. It looks like it's clearing a little."

I followed after him as he moved deeper into the fog. Having something solid to focus on helped with the vertigo, but I still would've felt better holding on to him. If only there was a way around the no-touching rule.

After we walked a few paces, I saw he was right. The fog was lessening. Something like daylight seemed to be brightening it. Ahead of me Eli came to a sudden stop. I saw at once what had caused it—a stone wall. The stone wall of a tall tower.

No, it couldn't be. I stepped up beside him, my heart sinking. We were once again standing atop that tower, *my* tower. If

I turned around and walked a few strides in I would see the stone plinth.

"So maybe the fog is from you after all," Eli said as he gazed out onto the gray nothingness surrounding the tower.

I didn't respond, knowing he was right. I squinted, trying to see through the fog. I could just make out the top branches of the nearest trees but that was all.

Eli faced me. "This isn't where we're supposed to be, Dusty."

"I know." The words came out listlessly. I was suddenly so tired, as if I'd run twenty miles without stopping and hadn't eaten for days. All I wanted was to sit down and rest. But I couldn't. Eli was right. "I'll try to fix it."

I closed my eyes and focused on manipulating the dream. I felt the magic respond, but it was weak and insubstantial, like trying to build a sand castle with dry sand or a snowman with powdery snow. No matter how I pressed and pulled and forced, the shape of it wouldn't stay.

Finally, I gave up, making a sound somewhere between a shriek and a groan. "I can't do it. It just. Won't. Go."

Eli didn't say anything, but I could feel his gaze on me. Frustrated and growing desperate, I strode away from the edge toward the center of the tower where I knew the plinth would be. If I couldn't manipulate the dream, then I would work on the block. No time to waste.

The fog grew denser the farther in I walked, soon becoming so thick I couldn't see more than a foot in front of me. I pressed on, and in moments began to suspect something was wrong. In every other dream, I would've reached the plinth by now, but there was no sign of it. I walked on. Sooner or later I would reach the other side of the tower at least.

I was right. Except as I stepped through the fog, it wasn't the other side, but the same side. Eli was standing right where I'd left him. I'd managed to walk a circle, missing the plinth completely.

I didn't know how that was possible, except this was a dream. A place where *anything* was possible.

I stepped up beside Eli. "You try changing it."

He rubbed his chin, mulling it over. "Okay." Then he closed his eyes, and he held his hands rigid at his side, no doubt mimicking the way I did it.

Nothing happened at first. But then the wind began to pick up. The fog swirled around us. I expected visibility to drop even more, but to my surprise the wind seemed to be dissipating the fog.

Out of the corner of my eye, something bright caught my attention. I turned toward it automatically, walking closer to the edge of the tower. But I didn't lean against it, the memory of plummeting over the side all too vivid.

I didn't need to get to the edge to see what the bright thing was. The top of one of the trees was on fire, the branches like a thousand torches bound together. Soon more of the trees caught fire, not from the wind blowing or any other natural phenomenon. They just ignited as if from the inside.

"What's going on?" Eli said, opening his eyes. He turned and surveyed the scene.

I glanced at him. "You're not doing this?"

He shook his head. "If I am, it's not on purpose."

I started to reply, but a loud rumble went through the tower and the floor began to shake. Beyond the wall, one of the trees fell over with an ear-splitting crack.

Eli and I both backed away from the edge. But it didn't matter. The rumble grew louder, the stone beneath us breaking apart. It split right down the middle, right where we were standing.

We turned to look at each other, the same thought going through our minds. Then we reached for each other just as the tower began to fall.

We woke with our arms wrapped around each other, our quick breaths mingling, our panic mutual from a brush with death inside the dream.

I started to roll off him, but Eli's grip tightened. I froze and then gave in, letting my body relax into his. For once I didn't question it. We didn't speak, didn't move. Just held each other, finding comfort in the embrace and acceptance in our shared silence.

∼ 25 ∼

Loyalties

For the first time since it had started, I reported the tower dream in my dream journal. I did it as soon as I got back to the dorm. The fire and the tower falling seemed too meaningful not to tell Lady Elaine, especially not now that we suspected something would happen at Beltane. I even mentioned how the tower was originally my dream, and how the plinth that was supposed to be there was missing. Then I sat and waited for an IM from OracleGirl. Surely she would have something to say about it.

Only she didn't. Not that night and not the next morning when I checked it again. I didn't know if I should be relieved or worried by her lack of response, so I ignored it instead. Either there was a hidden meaning in the dream or there wasn't. It wasn't as if Lady Elaine had to tell me one way or the other. For all I knew, in the last few months all of Eli's dreams could've been pointing to this impending doom at the Beltane Festival.

Or maybe Paul is lying.

I knew it was possible that he had made up the stuff about his uncle for some unknowable reason, but I wasn't about to drive myself crazy worrying about the what-ifs. He *hadn't* made up the stuff about Britney. I knew the key to solving this was finding out the reason she was involved.

Clinging to this certainty, Selene and I decided to make Melanie and the Terra Tribe our priority today.

"I figure we leave lunch early and try to catch her in the upperclassmen's cafeteria," Selene said as she ran an ivory-handled comb through her dark hair. "If that doesn't work, we ditch gym early and wait outside of her last class."

I froze in the process of applying my mascara, afraid I would give myself raccoon face if I didn't. "Why not try and catch her during breakfast?"

Selene sniffed. "Would you be inclined to cooperate so early in the morning?"

"Good point," I said, and then resumed applying my mascara.

To my surprise, Paul was waiting for us in the foyer when we came down the stairs. I couldn't tell for sure, but it seemed like Frank and Igor were giving him the evil eye, their spears pointed a little lower than was usual. Paul on the other hand seemed completely unconcerned about them. He flashed a dazzling smile at me the moment he saw me.

I smiled back, automatically. For a brief second all the bad history between us vanished, and he was the Paul I first met—smart, handsome, and obviously into me.

"What's up?" I said, coming to a stop in front of him.

"I just found out this morning that the Terra Tribe is holding their next meeting tonight at eight in the theater house."

Selene frowned. "How do you know?"

Paul shrugged. "Spellbook isn't the most secure site around. I hacked into their page and saw the announcement."

I beamed at him, thrilled that something had finally gone right. "That's perfect."

"Hmmm," Selene said, sounding less enthused by the idea.

I turned toward her, surprised. "What's wrong?"

She folded her arms over her chest. "Nothing. I just think we should give Melanie a chance to help us first before we resort to spying on them."

I frowned. "We've spied and snooped on other people, and it's not like the Terra Tribe has exactly been innocent."

"I'm not saying we shouldn't go through with it, but we should spy only as a last resort. We wouldn't want anybody spying on us when we're doing stuff in Room 013, after all."

I started to point out that we weren't involved in anything potentially dangerous to other people, but then decided not to as I realized that to an outsider we probably did look like we were up to nothing good half the time. What with breaking into crypts and stealing books from the boy's locker room.

"You're right. We'll talk to Melanie first."

Selene nodded. "I hope she cooperates."

"Me too," I said.

But I should've known better.

"Why do you want to know?" Melanie slammed her locker door closed so hard, the ones next to it shuddered from the impact.

"We already told you," Selene said, in her most patient, persuasive voice. After a failed lunchtime attempt, Selene and I had finally managed to track Melanie down after classes. Good thing Coach Fritz let us out a few minutes early. Given the look on Melanie's face the moment she spotted Selene and me, I knew for sure she'd been avoiding us. The knowledge stung. A couple of months ago, I'd been her hero.

"We're just trying to help Britney," I finished for Selene.

Melanie glared. "Britney's already got all the help she needs."

"What do you mean?" asked Selene. When Melanie refused to answer, Selene dropped the softness in her tone. "Come on, Mellie. Why are you treating us like pond scum? I thought we were friends."

Melanie's glare faltered then faded. But her manner remained cool. "We are, but . . . things aren't so easy as they used to be."

Melanie looked at me, her huge eyes suddenly watery, but I didn't think it was from sadness. "We're just getting tired of always being the victim."

I arched an eyebrow. "Who's we? And victim of what?"

"Naturekinds is who." Melanie thrust out her chin. "First Rosemary was murdered and now Britney's been attacked twice. She was in a *hospital*. Who does that?"

Selene and I exchanged a look. We had a pretty good idea who, but neither of us was about to mention that to her. Finding out another witchkind was behind the most recent attack on her kind wasn't going to do us any favors in getting her to talk.

"But Britney survived," I said. "My mom saved her."

Melanie shrugged. "If Britney hadn't been there in the first place, she wouldn't have needed saving."

"What's that supposed to mean?" Selene said. It was a good thing she'd spoken first, because my response would've been more along the lines of *Thanks a lot, you ingrate.*

Melanie ran her hands over the bottom of her blouse, smoothing nonexistent wrinkles. "There's just a lot of talk among the naturekinds about"—she seemed to search for the right word—"independency from the other kinds."

Selene's brow furrowed. "Like setting up separate institutions just for naturekinds? Like schools?"

"And hospitals." Melanie tapped her foot. "Britney's mom

hadn't wanted her to go to Vejovis in the first place, but the government officials insisted on it. The idiots. But Britney's safe now. She's in a secure location surrounded by her own kind only and nothing bad has happened to her since."

Nausea burned in my gut. The attitude behind these events was so wrong, so *regressive*. It was just as stupid as the witch-kinds harassing Eli for being a Conductor. "But you're acting as if the attack on Britney was *because* she's a naturekind."

"That's because it was."

"No, it wasn't." I bit my lip, hesitating. "We don't know why she was attacked yet, but I doubt her kind had anything to do with it."

Melanie stood up straighter, emphasizing how much taller she was than Selene and me. "She wasn't attacked by a nature-kind, that's for sure. And that's what matters."

I was unable to keep my temper in check any longer. "All the bad stuff lately has nothing to do with kinds. Rosemary wasn't the only one Marrow killed, remember? He murdered Mr. Ankil, too, a *witchkind*. And my great grandmother, a *darkkind*."

A crimson stain spread over Melanie's cheeks. "You're just a halfkind. You wouldn't understand. You don't know the first thing about *loyalty*."

I raised my hand, ready to curse her. Sweat broke out on my skin from the waves of anger rippling through me. I'd never been so insulted, so outraged in my whole life. I knew about loyalty. And it had nothing to do with someone's kind.

"You're nothing more than a mule," Melanie said, taking an ominous step toward me.

I moved to defend myself. "Flig—"

An invisible pressure seemed to wrap around me, forcing my hand down to my side before I could cast the jinx. Across from me Melanie too was struggling against some unseen force holding her in place before she could fire her own spell at me. Selene was caught as well, but she wasn't fighting. She seemed frozen in shock.

"That's quite enough of that," a rough, male voice said.

I craned my eyeballs as far to the right as I could and saw Captain Gargrave walking toward us, his staff held out before him, the ruby winking in the lights overhead. He came to a stop a few feet from us, setting the end of the staff down on the floor with a hard clack.

"Fighting is against the rules," Gargrave said.

"No kidding, Captain Obvious," I said.

All the color blanched from Gargrave's face only to surge back into it, tomato red. I exhaled, wishing like hell that he'd used the gag spell on me. I had a feeling my sassy response didn't bother him half as much as the unintentional captain pun. I mean, how often is the person you say something like that to an *actual* captain?

"Detention, Miss Everhart," Gargrave said. It might've been my imagination, but it seemed as if the magic holding me tightened its grip. My breathing grew shallow, and I began to feel lightheaded. "Seven o'clock. In the kitchens."

Great, I thought, remembering the Terra Tribe's meeting tonight. The timing couldn't have been worse.

I started to complain, but then stopped, keeping my big fat mouth shut for once.

As usual, too little too late.

~ 26 ~

The Terra Tribe

The only good thing about scoring a detention in the kitchens was . . . wait . . . nothing. There was nothing good about it. Predictably, the kitchen staff assigned me dish duty. I spent more than an hour loading dirty plates, goblets, and silverware into a giant metal machine that had developed a prankster personality from the animation effect. This meant that every time I turned my back on it, the dishwasher sprayed me with warm soapy water. When I shouted at it to stop, it sprayed me in the face. With the dirty water.

I tried to console myself by remembering that at least Selene, Eli, and Paul were still available to check out the Terra Tribe's meeting tonight, but it didn't help very much. I desperately wanted to be with them.

At half past eight, the kitchen manager—a witch who would've made a perfect Mrs. Claus with her white hair, prodigious belly, and red cheeks—told me I could leave. I bolted for the door, pausing only long enough to flip the bird over my shoulder at the stupid dishwashing machine. As I escaped through the door, I thought I heard it make a gurgling noise that sounded suspiciously like laughter.

I checked my cell phone as soon as I was out of the kitchen

and read a text message from Selene informing me that she, Eli, and Paul were staked out in the theater hall and that they were going radio silent until it was over.

"I'll fill you in when I get back to the dorm," her message concluded.

Selene and the boys had another thing coming if they thought I was going to sit this one out. Not after the stuff with Melanie. If the Terra Tribe was up to anything even remotely dangerous, I wanted to play my part in taking them down.

I sprinted all the way across campus to the theater hall, stopping just outside the door only long enough to catch my breath. Lights were still on inside, and I figured I'd gotten here in time. I opened the door and walked in, trying to look completely at ease, as if I had business in this building. A late-night appointment with a teacher perhaps. Maybe even another detention.

I needn't have bothered. There was no one in the foyer or down the long hallways leading off in both directions as they wrapped around the theater. The only guard the group had stationed was a sign hanging on the main doors into the theater:

PRIVATE MEETING IN SESSION
DO NOT DISTURB

I peeked through the narrow window beside the sign, saw a group of people standing on the stage, and then moved past the door, down the hallway on the left. When I came to a door marked BALCONY, I opened it as quietly as I could and slipped inside.

It was completely dark in here, the only light the faint gleam around the door seams. It was enough that I could make out the first couple of steps leading upward, but that was all. I walked toward them, placed my hand on the banister, then started climbing.

As the darkness increased, I considered doing a fire spell, but I held back, hoping to come across another door soon. And at least I had the banister to guide me. At last I saw the faint glow of the door ahead. Without a window on the door, I had no idea what I would be stepping into, so I crouched down, pulled it open, and slipped through as quickly and quietly as I could.

It was brighter up here, but not by much. I heard voices down below, and I crawled into the nearest row of seats. I waited for someone to sound the alarm that they'd spotted me, but when the timbre of the voices didn't change, I risked a peek around the edge. I was too far up to see much, except for the blurred shapes of maybe twenty people congregated on the stage. Some of them appeared to be wearing the brown cloaks from yesterday.

Even worse than not being able to see them, I couldn't make out what they were saying. The Terra Tribe might be meeting in the theater hall, but they weren't exactly practicing for a play. I pulled my head back behind the cover of the seats and then glanced around, trying to figure out if I was small enough to squeeze *underneath* the seats. Yeah right. A toddler would have a hard time managing it.

Sighing, I slowly crawled out from the row and made my way down the aisle, sticking as close to the nearest edge as I could and trying not to speculate when the last time the carpets had been cleaned. I wondered where Selene and the boys were hiding out. If they'd only told me.

I pressed forward, focusing on the sounds ahead. Soon I was close enough to catch snippets of the conversation. One voice rang loudest of them all—Oliver Cork. He seemed to be giving a speech:

"I know some of you are feeling nervous after what happened yesterday at the demonstration, but believe me, things will be different at the festival. Our message will be heard and seen and no one can stop it."

There was a murmur of agreement. I crawled on, finally close enough to start making out a couple of faces. Melanie was there, wearing one of the brown cloaks, same as Oliver. So was Irene Stark as well as a boy from my English class.

"It's time we let the magickind world know that we won't tolerate it anymore, the abuse of the earth, the constant rape of her natural resources. They take, take, take with no thought or concern about the consequences. It's bad enough that we let millions of ordinaries tear down forests and pollute the waters, but even our own leaders stand by and let the witchkinds and darkkinds do the same. But change starts here."

I froze in place at once shocked and completely taken in by the fervor of Oliver's speech. Who knew the guy was such a powerful speaker? For a moment my mind filled up with the images from Britney's dream—of poisoned rivers and dead forests, animals starved and deformed.

I shook my head, refocusing. I could hear Oliver just fine, but not the others. I needed to get closer. I moved on more quickly for fear that someone down below would look up and see me.

A hand closed around my wrist, and I nearly screamed. I held back at the last second as I saw Paul's face peering out at me from where he was crouched between the rows of seats.

"What was that?" someone said from down below.

Paul yanked my arm, pulling me into the row and right on top of him. My heart thudded against my rib cage like a hammer against a slab of meat. I was certain they had seen me, although that worry seemed inconsequential when compared to the shock of finding myself lying on top of Paul Kirkwood. But I didn't dare move off him, as I braced for the shouting to start below.

I felt Paul's slow, deep breathing as his chest moved in and out. His hand rested on my waist as if he was worried I would tumble off him. Not a chance given the tight confines between the seats. The familiarity of his touch felt nice and completely wrong at the same time. I risked a glance at his face and saw an amused glint in his eyes. He, at least, was enjoying himself. I resisted the urge to smack him, but only because I didn't think I could manage it silently.

And so I waited, the seconds passing like minutes as I focused on the voices below. Finally, I decided that they hadn't seen or heard me. Oliver was now saying something about their need to practice one more time. Just what they were practicing, I had no idea.

I slowly crawled forward, off Paul and onto the welcome flatness of the floor. I wasn't particularly careful with my knees and feet as I went, and I felt a surge of satisfaction as Paul let out a groan. Served him right.

Once I was off him, I sat up, still safely hidden behind the seats. Paul sat up, too, although he had to stay crouched down to keep his head from peeking over the top.

I motioned to the aisle behind Paul and then pointed to my eyes, mouthing, "I want to see."

Paul nodded. He twisted around so he was facing the aisle. Then he lay down on his side, his head close to the edge. He motioned for me to lie in front of him. I took a deep breath, unhappy at the idea of being in such a position, even if there was a good reason for it. Trying to switch positions would've been too noisy, especially after the close call we just had.

I crawled in front of him, resting on my side. I inched toward the edge, then raised my head to see what was going on below. Oliver and the other brown cloaked figures were standing center stage in a circle, each holding an unlit torch. The rest of the Terra Tribe had moved to the outside of the circle.

"Now," Oliver was saying, "it's important that the timing be correct. So let's give it a try." He held up his torch and spoke the fire incantation. The torch burst into flames. "One . . ." Oliver said. "Two . . . three . . ." I waited for him to stop, but he didn't, not until he'd counted all the way to sixty. Once he did, Irene Stark raised her hand and lit her torch. Then she too counted to sixty. Another brown cloaked figure did the same right after her.

On and on it went, until finally the last of them, Melanie, lit her torch. There were twelve torches in all, twelve people. But the demonstration seemed completely pointless. What kind of message could there be in a couple of lit torches?

But Oliver Cork answered this question soon after. "Good job, everybody," he said, extinguishing his torch. "But it'll be a lot more impressive when we do it for real on Saturday. The enchantments on the torches we'll be using have all been applied. Now it's just up to us to move forward with it. And to change the world." He raised both hands over his head in a victory salute as he spoke this last sentence, and the rest of the Terra Tribe cheered and clapped.

I chewed on the inside of my cheek. So the Terra Tribe would be using enchanted torches when they did this live. But enchanted to do what? And I couldn't see how their environmental protest could be connected to Magistrate Kirkwood's assassination plot.

As the crowd below started chattering incoherently, I became aware of Paul's broad hand resting on my hip and his body pressed against mine. I started to fidget, wishing the meeting would adjourn so I could get out of this position. I looked around, wondering where Selene and Eli could be.

No sooner had I thought it than I spied Eli crouched in between the rows directly across from us. It was amazing how much he could express in a single look. I could tell from his dark expression that he'd seen everything that had happened with Paul since I'd crawled down the aisle—and he wasn't happy about it. I wanted to say that he looked jealous, but I was afraid to put that label on it. Things with Eli were far too complicated to chalk it up to something as simple as jealousy.

I looked away from him as I heard the distinctive sound of the main doors into the theater opening, followed by the soft clack of someone wearing low-heeled sandals.

"Oh, hey, Miss Norton," Oliver shouted. The talking died down, and as I fixed my gaze on the stage, I saw Miss Norton step into view. For the first time ever she wasn't wearing a housedress but a pair of jeans. The change in her attire made her almost unrecognizable, at least from this distance.

"Thank you, Oliver," Miss Norton said as she surveyed the crowd. "And thanks to all of you for volunteering for the Beltane Festival. Oliver assures me that everything is in place." Miss Norton clapped her hands once, the sound ringing out almost as loud as gunfire. "I have a feeling it will be a day that will be remembered forever. The day that naturekinds begin their quest to change the world."

I took a deep breath, chilled by Miss Norton's words. It seemed the Dream Team had just identified the next subject in our investigation.

The meeting finally ended, and after waiting a few minutes in case anyone came back to retrieve a forgotten purse or cell phone, I finally crawled out into the aisle, away from Paul. Across from me, Eli stood up, and one row down from him, Selene did the same.

She rolled her eyes when she spotted me. "I knew you wouldn't be able to stay away."

I grinned back at her, grateful for any reason not to talk to Eli right now. He wasn't outwardly angry, but there was a smoldering, dangerous sparkle in his eyes. I decided it would be a good idea to keep myself in between him and Paul for the foreseeable future.

"Well, that was interesting," Paul said.

Eli shot a glare at him. "Not here. Come on." He turned on one heel and then led the way back up the aisle to the balcony door. I followed after him with Paul coming behind me and Selene bringing up the rear. When we reached the bottom floor, Eli double-checked the hallway before stepping out.

Then the four of us made our way to Room 013 of the library. We only had twenty minutes before curfew, but that was enough time to hash out our next steps.

To no one's surprise, Eli's first words were "We check out Miss Norton first thing tomorrow."

"How do you want to do it?" Selene said from her usual seat on Buster. The chair had practically peeled its wheels the moment she had stepped inside. Now it was contentedly rocking side to side. How Selene could stand it without getting sick was anybody's guess.

"We'll hit her classroom during lunch," said Eli. "Tra . . ." He paused and cleared his throat. "Travis Kelly has her fourth period and he says she's always late. That should give us plenty of time."

I flinched at the anger in Eli's voice when he'd said Travis's name. It was enough to tell me that Travis was one of the witch-kinds that didn't approve of Eli being a Conductor.

"Who's going to do it?" asked Paul.

"Dusty and I will," Eli said with no hesitation. "She and I work best together."

I blinked. "We do? Since when?"

Eli scowled. "Now's not the time for jokes."

I smiled back at him, although I wasn't entirely sure I'd been joking. We did work great together a lot of the time, but not always.

"We also need to check out her office," said Selene.

Eli nodded. "That one will be trickier. We *should* wait until tomorrow night, but we can't afford the time. But Dusty and I can ditch alchemy tomorrow to do it. Mrs. Ashbury is the least likely to raise a fuss about our absence. She only cares about misbehavior inside her classroom. And there's a broom cupboard right across from Miss Norton's office. We can hide in there until the bell rings and then break in. With the moonwort key, it'll be a piece of cake."

I tapped my foot. "Now hang on just a minute. Who says I'm willing to ditch alchemy? It's my worst subject." In truth I didn't mind missing it—actually, the idea thrilled me—but I did mind Eli assuming I would do whatever he wanted. He normally wasn't so tyrannical. I had a feeling most of it was because he wanted to make sure I didn't volunteer for me and Paul to do it.

Eli arched an eyebrow. "Would you rather sit it out?"

Darn him. He knew me so well. "No, of course not."

Eli clapped his hands. "Good, then, it's settled." He glanced at his watch. "We better hurry up if we don't want to break curfew."

We all headed for the door. Buster made a pathetic little noise with his chair wheels as Selene patted him good-bye.

Once in the hallway, Paul turned toward me and touched my shoulder. "Be careful tomorrow. And I'll see you later."

He let his fingers trail down my arm as he stepped back. Then he turned and walked away.

Selene, no doubt as aware of Eli's brooding look as I was, quickly said, "We better hurry." She took hold of my hand and started pulling me down the hallway after her. "We'll see you tomorrow, Eli."

"Wait, Dusty," Eli said before we'd gone two steps. "Can you stay for a second?"

"There's really not time, Eli," Selene said over her shoulder.

"Please."

I stopped and pulled out of Selene's grasp. "I'll catch up." She considered arguing for a second, but then nodded once and hurried on, leaving me alone with Eli.

I turned and faced him, my heartbeat already picking up. "What is it?"

Eli ran his hands through his hair, not meeting my gaze. "I . . . I just need you to promise me something."

I didn't respond, but waited for him to go on.

"Just promise me that no matter what happens you won't get back together with Paul," he said in a single breath.

Really? Of all the things he could say that was it? I closed my eyes, disappointment and frustration clouding my good judgment. I opened them again and said, "I can't promise you that. Everybody deserves a second chance. Even Paul." I wasn't being spiteful, although I had no plans of getting back together with him. I really did mean it. If more people believed in second chances and forgiveness, then the massacre of my kind all those years ago might never have happened.

Eli stared at me, his expression masked. I expected him to be angry—I half wanted him to be angry—but he looked only cold, a human ice sculpture. I waited a couple of seconds for him to say something, but he didn't.

I sighed and wrapped my arms around my sides. "And at least he shows some interest in me, even if there is an ulterior motive behind it. It's better than nothing."

Eli flinched, my words hitting the mark. He shook his head, exhaling. "I'm sorry, Dusty."

And there it was again—a nonsensical apology. I'd finally had enough. "You know, I don't get you at all. One minute you're kissing me and touching me like you want something more, and the next you're all whoops, just kidding." I raised my hands in emphasis. "And now this stuff with Paul. I mean, why do you even care if I get back with him? It's not like we're together."

Eli closed the distance between us in one step and put his hands on my shoulders. If he had been ice before, he was fire now. "I can't stand the idea of you with him. And I do want more from you . . . so much more. You have no idea." The look in his eyes as he spoke took my breath away. I didn't move, waiting for him to kiss me, to make good on that look.

Instead he stepped back, letting go of me. "But I can't . . . *we* can't."

"Why not?" I said, breathless, a terrible wrenching in my chest.

Eli lowered his gaze. "I can't tell you." I started to protest, but he cut me off. "I promised I wouldn't and I have to keep my word. But there is a reason, Dusty."

"What reason?" I dared a step nearer him.

Eli stepped back. "Trust me, you don't want to know." And then he turned and hurried out the door. I went after him, but he disappeared down another hallway so quickly it might've been magic. And when I called out for him to stop, only silence greeted me.

I left then too, more confused and hurt than ever and with a sadness tugging on my heart like a sinking anchor. If I wasn't careful, I would drown.

~27~

Shakedown

I decided I believed Eli's reasons for not telling me why we couldn't be together were genuine, but that didn't make the not knowing any easier. I was up half the night thinking about it. I wondered if there was something wrong with him. The whole thing might've been a scene out of a soap opera where one of the characters finds out he's got some terminal condition and he breaks it off with the love interest to try and save her from the heartbreak of losing him. That might be a cliché, but I imagined the premise was true enough.

Only . . . if Eli was sick, why would he have promised somebody else not to tell me about it? It didn't make sense. Plus, the idea of him being sick was too horrible to consider even for a second. Then I wondered if maybe it was the other way around, that there was something wrong with me that I didn't know about. But I couldn't see how that was possible.

No, I didn't think there would be any guessing the truth. I would just have to learn it for myself, some way or another. But not right now. There were too many other important things to worry about.

Nevertheless, stuff between us was weird the next day. We didn't ignore each other, but we were both tense and far too quiet. Selene didn't comment about it, but that was only because I'd told her what Eli had said. To my relief and disappointment she hadn't speculated what his reasons might be. There just wasn't enough to speculate on, I supposed.

When lunchtime rolled around, Eli and I ate quickly and then slipped out. We didn't talk as we walked along, making our way to Finnegan Hall. The air around us seemed charged with electricity.

As we reached the door to Miss Norton's classroom, Eli touched my arm. "You wait out here in case anyone comes by."

I nodded, and he slipped inside. Time seemed to slow as I waited, silently walking up and down the corridor on the look-out for unwelcome guests. Every time I checked my watch, I expected to find that ten minutes had passed, but it always turned out to be one or two.

Then when ten minutes had finally come and gone, I turned to the door into the classroom, ready to pull him out of there. We were cutting it close. But just as I reached for the handle, the door swung open.

Eli jumped, startled to find me standing so close.

"What took you so long?" I peered into the classroom.

He ran his hands down the front of his shirt. "Nothing. I just wanted to be thorough."

The sound of approaching footsteps echoed toward us, and we both darted down the hallway and around the corner, out of sight.

As we climbed down the stairs, I said, "Did you find anything useful?"

Eli sighed. "Not a thing."

"Really?" I craned my head to look at him, and my foot caught on the step. Eli grabbed my arm, keeping me upright. But he let go almost at once, as if touching me was as dangerous as trying to handle a live wire. Yeah, this tension between us was really starting to suck.

But it only got worse later when we squeezed into the broom cupboard across the hall from Miss Norton's office after fifth period. With the two of us in there, I had to practically stand on top of him. As it was, Eli wrapped his arms around my waist, the tight confines demanding it. The only good thing about the situation was that it was too dark for me to see his face. But I could hear his breathing, and each time he moved so much as an inch, my whole body reacted, tingles traveling over my skin in pleasant, yet unwelcome waves.

I tried to ignore the sensation by forcing my mind on the task ahead of us, but thoughts of what it would feel like to lean forward and kiss him in the dark kept pushing their way to the front of my mind. I decided it was a very good thing that I wasn't exceptionally skilled at telepathy. I definitely didn't want to know what thoughts *Eli* was entertaining every time his fingers moved against my back.

Finally, we heard the bell sound for the start of sixth period. Thank goodness. We waited a couple of seconds, and then Eli leaned even closer to me, reaching his hand toward the door. For a second his distinctive smell—something dark and musky and completely masculine—overwhelmed me, making me light-headed.

As soon as the door opened I stepped out, taking a huge breath and blinking in the sudden brightness. Eli looked a little flushed, and the sight of it made my body burn even hotter than it already was. I turned away from him, embarrassed and annoyed at myself. I'd been attracted to him for months, but now that I knew for sure he wanted me too but that we couldn't be together for some mysterious reason, my attraction to him had tripled. Quadrupled even. Go figure.

Stupid, rebellious nature.

Eli brushed past me on the way to the door to Miss Norton's office. He pulled the moonwort key from his pocket, unlocked the door, and stepped inside. I hurried after him, my breath quickening from sudden adrenaline at what we were doing.

I looked around at the untidy sprawl of bookshelves and the paper-strewn desk.

Eli strode to the desk. "Let's get a move on."

He took one side of the desk while I took the other. There was a lot, but at least we were looking for something specific—anything to do with the Beltane Festival.

"Found it," Eli said a few minutes later. He pulled out a folder from beneath the rubble of essays and homework assignments and opened it.

I came around the desk to see the contents more clearly. Eli stepped aside to allow me room, his body rigid as if he feared touching me again. He flipped through the folder's contents. "Here we go." He handed me a slip of paper. "Looks like the list of participants."

I scanned the names, committing the ones I didn't already know to memory.

"And this looks like stage blocking," Eli said, unfolding a map.

I set down the list of names and leaned toward the map to examine it more closely, unsure of what Eli meant. According to the label, this was the inner island of Lyonshold. I searched the map for Senate Hall, knowing it was here somewhere, and saw it was dead center of the island. In the open area surrounding the hall, someone had drawn little circles in a regular pattern.

Inside the circles were written the names of the same Terra Tribe members on the list I'd just read.

"So now we know where they'll be," I said, drawing a line between two of the circles with my finger. "But we still don't know what's going to happen when they light those torches."

"No but—" Eli broke off as the doorknob rattled, making us both jump.

I sucked in a breath. "Did you lock it?"

Eli nodded, his eyes darting around the room, no doubt looking for cover. But there wasn't any, not unless Miss Norton was so drunk her vision was impaired.

"Dusty," a voice called from the other side of the door. "You in there?"

Realizing it was Selene, I dashed for the door, unlocked it, and yanked it open.

Selene fell into the room. "Come on! Miss Norton's on her way."

I didn't waste time with questions—like how on earth she could know that—but bolted through the door, shouting over my shoulder for Eli to follow.

He did, slamming the door closed behind him. The three of us started to move down the hallway, but an outraged scream froze us in place.

"What were you doing in my office?"

We all turned to see Miss Norton charging us, her little fairy ears making her look like a lioness getting ready to take down a herd of wildebeests. I gulped, trying to come up with an excuse. None came.

Sometimes when you're caught, you're caught.

———

For the first time since starting my career at Arkwell, I was sent to the principal's office with two accomplices. I'd sorta hoped that would make it more fun, or at least more bearable, but it didn't. Not really.

There wasn't room for all three of us inside of Dr. Hendershaw's office, so the Will Guard who'd escorted us to the admin building—including Captain Gargrave, much to my dismay—put us in the same conference room where Sheriff Brackenberry and Lady Elaine had first recruited me to spy on Paul.

I wasn't happy to be back here.

Neither were Selene or Eli, but we didn't have time to bemoan our unfortunate luck as we decided on our collective story.

"Let's just tell them the truth," Eli said after several failed attempts at a believable excuse. "We know the Terra Tribe is planning something and this will make sure they get stopped."

"Fine," I said. "But we can't tell them the stuff about Paul."

Eli drummed his fingers on the arms of his chair. "Oh? Why not?"

"Because we promised him we wouldn't until we had proof, and we don't have it yet."

The door behind us opened before Eli could reply. We all turned to look as Sheriff Brackenberry and Lady Elaine stepped in. The former looked bemused and the latter concerned. But neither said anything until after they'd shut the door and sat down. Sheriff Brackenberry leaned forward, resting his thick forearms on the table. "You've got two minutes to convince me you had a good reason to break into a teacher's office."

Eli started to answer, but I spoke over him. I had a lot more experience dealing with Brackenberry, and I didn't trust him not to mention Paul. "We think Miss Norton is helping a student organization plan some kind of protest during the Beltane Festival," I began. Then I told him everything we knew and suspected about the Terra Tribe, including their involvement in the protest on campus the other day as well as Britney's connection to the group.

When I finished, Brackenberry sat back in his chair and stroked his beard. I waited with my teeth clenched. As far as I could tell, this could go either way—big, big trouble or us getting off easy.

The sheriff glanced at Lady Elaine. She shrugged, the gesture weirdly articulate with her bony shoulders visible in the snug turtleneck she wore. "Miss Norton *is* the faculty advisor for the group."

Brackenberry grunted then faced me again. "Do you have any proof that Miss Norton was involved in orchestrating whatever this demonstration is?"

I shook my head, reluctantly. A couple of marks on a map and a last-minute appearance at the meeting didn't constitute proof. Besides, all indicators were that the lighting of the torches was an official part of the Beltane Festival.

"I see." Brackenberry cracked his knuckles, the sound as loud as tree branches snapping. "We'll look into the claims about the festival, but I need to know if in your little investigation one of you took some kind of magical stick out of Miss Norton's classroom. She says it went missing this very day, and that strikes me as quite a coincidence."

It took every ounce of my self-control not to look at Eli. Miss Norton kept the talking stick—surely the object in question—in her classroom, at least during the school day, and he would've had a perfect opportunity to take it if he wanted to. Not that he had any reason for taking it that I knew of.

"No, we did not," Eli replied, coolly.

Brackenberry turned that accusing gaze on me. "Well, then, you won't mind turning out your pockets for me, will you?"

"Nope." I stood up and did as he asked, although how he thought I would be able to hide that thing inside these jeans was beyond me.

"Okay, now the rest of you," Brackenberry said, once he'd seen both of my pockets were empty.

Selene and Eli did the same, and Eli's pockets—which probably *were* deep enough to conceal the stick—were as empty as mine. I wondered where he'd stashed the moonwort key, then decided I didn't want to know.

The sheriff stood up. "All right. You three will stay here until we've sorted this out. And we'll be checking your lockers for the stick, too, just to be sure."

I shrugged. "Knock yourself out." I hoped I wouldn't regret saying that. I hadn't cleaned out my locker in ages, but I didn't *think* I had anything in there liable to get me in trouble.

Well, *more* trouble.

The moment Sheriff Brackenberry and Lady Elaine left, I turned toward Eli. "Was the talking stick in her classroom when you went through it?"

Eli shook his head. "I don't remember seeing it, but it wasn't exactly my focus."

He waved at Selene. "So how did you know Miss Norton was coming?"

Selene grimaced. "Lucky chance. She passed by my classroom. I didn't know for sure she was heading for her office, but I figured better safe than sorry. I asked to be excused and then I sprinted up the stairs, hoping to cut her off. She waddles pretty slow, but there just wasn't enough time."

"Why didn't you send us a text?" asked Eli.

"I was stupid and forgot my phone this morning."

I patted her arm. "At least you tried. But of all the bad luck. I bet the missing stick is the reason she came to her office in the first place."

"Probably." Eli leaned back and stretched his legs out in front of him, crossing them at the ankles.

We did only a little talking after that, which didn't help pass the time any. And there was a lot of it. Sheriff Brackenberry and Lady Elaine didn't return until more than an hour later.

Once again they sat down across from us, but this time Lady Elaine started off the conversation. "It turns out you were correct about the Terra Tribe."

I sat forward, eager for news.

"They were planning a demonstration for the festival," Lady Elaine continued. "The torches were enchanted with messages that would appear in the sky once they were lit. A speech along the lines of the one you heard Oliver Cork give during the meeting."

I frowned. "That's it? Just a speech?"

Brackenberry cleared his throat. "Perfectly harmless, if a little inflammatory. Still, I'm sure the Magi Senate will appreciate *not* having their celebration disrupted by a student protest. But unfortunately, it's too close to the celebration to replace the Terra Tribe volunteers, so they will be permitted to light the bonfires, but they won't have any access to the torches beforehand."

I huffed and leaned back in my chair. I knew I should be relieved they hadn't been planning anything nefarious, but it was hard not to feel a little disappointed, too.

"Speaking of perfectly harmless," Lady Elaine said as she tapped her fingernails against the table. She wore bright pink nail polish. "I wanted to tell you that we've identified the curse used on Lance. It's not deadly, at least not at first, and we should be able to break it any day now."

Selene exhaled, the sound just barely audible. "What kind of curse was it?"

"One designed to inhibit a person's production of fictus." Lady Elaine glanced at Eli. "It prevents him from being able to dream."

It was my turn to exhale. This proved it then. That curse had been intended for Eli. It was the only reason why it would be designed to affect fictus. Titus Kirkwood was definitely trying to stop Eli and me from seeing the future in his dreams.

"Now, if there're no more questions," Sheriff Brackenberry said, "we need to discuss your punishment for today's fiasco."

Eli, Selene, and I all glanced at one another, sharing mutual dread.

"We've decided to let Miss Norton determine your punishment," Lady Elaine said. "She wants two weeks of Saturday school starting next week and suspension from the Beltane Festival."

I gripped the arms of my chair. "How's that fair? Don't let her decide. She was the one behind the protest."

Brackenberry shook his head. "You don't know that for sure, and Miss Norton denies any knowledge of it. The punishment is hers to make as she's the offended party." He paused, a toothy grin stretching across his face. "Just consider yourself lucky that we didn't let Dr. Hendershaw decide. She's not exactly your biggest fan."

That was certainly true. I slumped down in my chair, accepting defeat. This was the worst possible punishment ever—and I wasn't talking about the Saturday school, although that was certainly bad enough. We *needed* to be at the festival. Just because the Terra Tribe wasn't involved in something bad didn't change the likelihood that something bad was coming.

For one brief second I regretted not telling Brackenberry and Lady Elaine the truth about Paul. But then I remembered there was still one more day to go. One more day to find the answers we needed.

But with a terrible sinking feeling in my stomach, I knew if we didn't succeed we would have to tell them anyway. Even though it meant putting Paul's life at risk.

~ 28 ~

Roadblock

The only lead we had left to follow was Mr. Corvus, but after getting caught by Miss Norton, we needed to proceed with caution. Breaking into another teacher's office the very next day seemed the worst of ideas, but we had no choice.

After a long debate, we decided the best thing was for Eli to do it alone during our third-period history class. That way both Selene and I would be present to deter Mr. Corvus from leaving the classroom. There was still a risk of Eli getting caught by one of the Will Guard, but they didn't bother patrolling the floors that were mostly faculty hallways very often.

The moment the bell rang for the start of third period, Mr. Corvus walked up to my desk and fixed his imperious gaze on me. "Where is Mr. Booker this morning?"

"I think he went to the infirmary," I answered with no hesitation. "Said he had a headache. We had psionics last period."

Mr. Corvus flexed his jaw as he decided whether or not to believe me. I kept my eyes on him, not fidgeting. The story had enough believability in it that there was no reason for Corvus not to swallow it. Coming down with a headache after studying mind-magic for an hour was common. And it wasn't like Eli had a reputation for ditching.

"All right," Mr. Corvus said, and then he returned to the front of the classroom and started teaching.

I barely heard a word he said, my ears straining for the sound of Eli's arrival. It was only by sheer force of will that I kept myself from glancing at the door every few seconds.

But less than five minutes after class began, Eli arrived. I frowned at him as he walked in and handed a note to Mr. Corvus. I held my breath. The note was a forgery. A few months ago, during his brief stay in the infirmary after our takedown of Marrow, Eli managed to snag an empty pass with the head nurse's signature on it. He'd since made a couple of copies of it, but this was the first time he'd used one. It wasn't the sort of thing you could get away with often.

Corvus studied the pass a moment then nodded. "Very well. Have a seat."

Eli turned up the aisle and took the desk next to mine. I sent him a questioning look, but he just shook his head. My impatience to learn what he'd found out made the rest of class pass even slower. But when the bell rang, Eli refused to tell us anything until we were in the cafeteria, our conversation safely disguised by the surrounding noise.

"I couldn't get in."

"What?" Selene and I said in unison.

Eli grimaced. "The moonwort key wouldn't work. I put it in the keyhole but nothing happened. It might as well have been just a piece of wood."

I bit my lip and glanced at Selene—she knew more about these things than Eli and I did. "How's that possible?"

Selene sighed. "The door must be enchanted against it. Most people don't bother because moonwort is so rare, but I suppose there are some paranoid enough to protect against it anyway."

Eli thumped his fist on the table. "That's just perfect. Leave it to Mr. Corvus to be paranoid."

I thought about his eye patch. "Well, it does sort of suit him. But yeah, this sucks. Do you know how to pick a lock the manual way?"

Eli leaned back in his chair and crossed his arms behind his head. "Yeah, but I don't have the tools to do it. My dad has some, but it would take time for me to get them, and my dad would kill me if he found out."

Judging by his dark tone, I had a feeling this expression carried more weight with his police officer father than it did for most parents.

I slouched against the table, resting my head on my arms. "So what do we do now?"

Eli scratched his cheek. "We still have *The Atlantean Chronicle.* I'm about halfway through it. I'll try to finish up before our dream-session tonight."

"Okay," I said unenthusiastically. I'd already scanned through each page and hadn't found anything and so had Selene. But Eli insisted that one of us might catch something the others had missed.

"And we might finally have a breakthrough with the dream," Eli added, casting me a significant look.

I didn't reply. I had my hopes set on learning the last two letters of the name this afternoon with Mr. Deverell, but I didn't want to jinx it.

"But what do we do if neither pans out?" asked Selene, glancing between Eli and me.

Eli leaned back and ran his hands over his head. "If we don't, then we have to go to Brackenberry and Lady Elaine with what we do have." He fixed his gaze on me as if he sensed the protest already rising to my lips. "We have to, Dusty. I know it puts Paul at risk, but not telling them could put even more people at risk."

I looked down at the table and took a deep breath. He was right, of course, and I'd already known it. Still, as I nodded, I couldn't help the hopelessness that came over me, and the certainty of coming doom.

The bad feelings followed me into my session with Deverell. I struggled to concentrate, my desire to succeed in direct opposition to my ability to do so. Several times Mr. Deverell admonished me to relax and focus, insisting that I was proving to be my biggest obstacle. I tried to do what he said, I really did. But when the session ended, two hours later, I'd only managed to uncover one letter. *Just one.* So close and yet still impossibly far away.

BELLANA

The name meant nothing to me. Nothing at all.

Except failure.

As I walked away from Mr. Deverell's classroom, my cell phone felt like an iron weight in my pocket. I pulled it out, and for the first time in months, I dialed Paul's number.

He answered on the first ring.

"Can you meet me?"

"Sure. Anywhere."

I thought about it for a couple of seconds, trying to decide on the place. Somewhere outside and public would be best, I knew, and yet I wanted to talk to him alone. To my surprise, the idea didn't frighten me. Somehow these last few days, I'd gotten accustomed to being around him.

"How about . . . our alcove?" I knew he would understand

which one I was talking about, the one hidden deep in the tunnels and where we'd shared our last kiss.

I heard Paul draw a breath, as shocked by the location as I'd been to name it, but he recovered quickly. "All right. I'll be there in ten minutes."

As I walked along the dark tunnel leading to the alcove, I tried not to think about my motives. Everything with Paul was too confused to try and figure it out. With the soft, soothing sound of the canal water echoing off the wet walls, it was surprisingly easy not to think. I kept my gaze partly fixed on the water, drawing some small comfort from its motion. Several times I saw the telltale swirl as a naiad swam by, and once I even caught the colorful flash of a merkind fin. It occurred to me how strange my life was, and yet how wonderful, too, in the quiet, peaceful moments like this.

But when I rounded the corner into the alcove and found Paul waiting for me, the quiet vanished in an instant. Paul didn't smile when he spotted me, but his eyes lit up in that special way of his I remembered so well—the kind of way that made me feel welcome and wanted. *Needed.*

I pushed down the surge of bittersweet memory and approached him.

"Hey," he said. "Do you want to sit?" He motioned to the edge of the small pool where we'd once dangled our feet together.

I shook my head. "What I have to say won't take that long."

"Oh." Paul lowered his gaze, looking diminished. "What is it?"

I shifted my weight from one foot to the other. Maybe I should've sat down. Did bad news go over better that way? People in movies always seemed to think so, but I doubted it would matter much. "I'm sorry, Paul, but it looks like we're not going to find proof about your uncle in time to stop whatever he's got planned tomorrow."

"Nothing panned out with Corvus?"

"Not yet." I exhaled, mustering my courage. "But you see, the thing is . . ."

Paul raised his hand, stopping me. "It's okay, Dusty. I understand."

I blinked, surprised by his certainty. "You do?"

"Sure." A crooked smile crossed his face. "You and Eli and Selene have no choice but to go to the sheriff with what you *do* know."

"Yes . . . that's . . . that's right."

Paul smirked. "Don't sound so surprised. I know you find this hard to believe but I can *sometimes* recognize the right thing to do. Hell, I can even do it occasionally." He flashed that crooked smile again. "Shocking, I know."

I could tell he was joking, but it fell flat. "It's not that I think you don't *know* the difference between right and wrong. I just think you have a tendency to choose badly. A lot."

"I suppose that's a fair statement." He bent over and picked up a couple of pebbles. Then he straightened and started tossing them one by one into the pool. "It didn't used to be that way, you know. All my life I chose good even when my uncle was beat"—he paused, catching himself—"even when things were hard. But then Marrow came along and changed everything."

His voice sounded strange, full of contradictory emotions, both sadness and relief, love and hate.

"Do you regret it?" I asked, surprising myself by the question.

Paul looked up, his eyes bright. He held me with his gaze.

"Yes. There's not a day that goes by that I don't wish I could take it back. Especially Rosemary. I dream about her all the time . . . nightmares that you can't even imagine." He shuddered, at last dropping his gaze. He tossed another stone.

I didn't say anything, still torn between belief and doubt. But then Paul dropped the last pebble into the pool and crossed the small distance between us. He placed his hands on my arms, his touch so light he might've been made of air instead of flesh.

"And I regret what I did to you. More than anything," he spoke in a whisper, and his voice *moved* through me as if my skin were permeable. "I'm sorry, Dusty. And I'll do whatever you want to make things right. So go to Brackenberry. Tell him everything you think you should."

I held my breath, feeling something inside me shift, my internal gauge for him moving from doubt to belief. Then I exhaled as the change brought a sweet relief like setting down a heavy burden I hadn't even realized I'd been carrying.

Acting on impulse, I pulled my cell phone from my pocket and held it out to him.

Paul looked at it as if he'd never seen one before. "What are you doing?"

"Take it. Do whatever you need to do."

Paul's fingers slid around mine, as if he intended to take my hand along with the phone.

"You keep it." Paul pushed my hand into my chest. "Give it to the sheriff. To get to the app press the home button three times and then swipe to the left twice. The pass code is three-eight-seven-eight-nine-seven. It'll open the app and all the files, too."

My mouth fell open, even as my mind repeated the numbers, committing them to memory. "You're giving it to me? But why?"

In answer, Paul leaned forward and kissed my forehead. "You

already know." He let go of me then and started walking toward the mouth of the tunnel. But he paused and turned around. "Say, you, um, wouldn't ever consider maybe giving it a go with me again, would you? That is, assuming I'm still alive come Sunday."

It was such the wrong question at the wrong time, and I found myself wanting to cry and laugh at once. "Just promise that you'll stay alive no matter what and we'll talk about it."

"Deal," he said. And then he disappeared into the darkness.

～ 29 ～

The Circle of Twelve

W here have you been?"

I paused in the doorway of Eli's dorm, wary of his tone and the fierce look in his eye. "I told you, I was tired after my meeting with Deverell and wanted to take a nap." At least, this was the story I sent him when he'd texted me during dinner, wanting to know why I wasn't in the cafeteria. In truth, I'd just needed to be alone for a while, sorting through my thoughts and feelings. Not that I'd managed to resolve anything.

Eli put his hands on his hips, his expression doubtful. "So you *weren't* down in the tunnels with Paul? All alone?"

I frowned. "Were you spying on me?" He of all people would know how to do it without me noticing.

"No, of course not." He scowled. "Selene told me you'd been to see him."

My face flushed. I brushed past him, heading for the sofa. I plopped down onto it and folded my arms. "It was nothing. I just needed to talk to him. I thought he deserved a heads-up about us going to the sheriff. And you've got nothing to worry about. I can take care of myself."

Eli held his breath, his eyes hard. Then he exhaled, the anger seeping out of him. "I suppose you're right."

I frowned, unsure if he was agreeing with me telling Paul or that I could take care of myself.

"I mean," Eli went on before I could ask him, "I don't know why I worry about you so much. You can kick *my* ass, let alone Paul's."

I gaped. Had he really just said that? "You're kidding, right?"

"Why would I be kidding?" Eli came over and sat down on the sofa beside me.

I glanced sideways at him. "Um, because you're a guy and really big and stuff."

He rolled his eyes in my direction. "That hardly matters when magic's a factor." Eli slid the ring from his finger and twisted it to the right, expelling the glamour to reveal his wand. "When it is, I might as well be a ninety-pound weakling."

I cleared my throat. "Still having trouble with it?"

"Oh, you could say that." Eli tossed the wand onto a nearby table. It skidded, clacking loudly, and stopped just shy of falling over the side.

I swallowed, sympathy making my throat tight. How awful for him. Not only was he getting harassed by witchkinds, but he could hardly use the magic they had tried to keep from him in the first place. I patted his leg. "Just give it some time. I struggled for a long while, too . . . heh . . . what am I saying? I still struggle."

Eli snorted. "Sure, more time." He popped his neck. "So what happened with Deverell?"

I closed my eyes and pinched the bridge of my nose. "Yeah, that. Still not unblocked."

"Really?"

"Yes. But I'm close, only one letter to go." I opened my eyes in time to see Eli's disappointed expression. Never mind that he banished it with a smile a second later.

"I guess we both need some more time."

"Sure, which we don't have. At least, which I don't have. I don't suppose you found something helpful in *The Atlantean Chronicle*." I turned my gaze to the desk and saw the book lying opened on top of it.

"No," Eli said. "If there're any details on an assassination in there, it must be a single sentence only. More likely, the Atlantis in that e-mail was code for something else."

I exhaled. "You're probably right." I stood up and faced him. "We might as well get a move on then. Who knows? Maybe we'll find something in the dream this time."

Eli smiled as he shifted sideways, lying down on the sofa. "I'm sure we will."

I waited for him to fall asleep, refusing to get my hopes up. A few minutes later, I climbed on top of him and entered his dream. To my relief, the world I found myself in a moment later was free of the fog that had plagued his last few dreams.

We were in Senate Hall once more, all the details of the place, defined and visible—the stained glass windows and the magickind statues, the row of knights and the long wooden table. Eli stood at the head of the table, examining the chair where in that earlier dream his father had been sitting. All the chairs were empty at present.

I glanced around looking for some sign of what was coming, but nothing stood out to me. The place had an empty, abandoned look, stark and forlorn like a wintry landscape. Directly opposite the foot of the table, but a good fifty feet in the distance, stood the massive doors of the main entrance.

"I want to go outside," I said, turning to Eli. "You up for it? I don't think we're going to find much more in here."

Eli looked up. "Yeah, I think you're right." He walked over to me and together we headed for the door. Two lions were carved into the highly polished wood in the same pose as the ones guarding the main gates into Lyonshold that Mr. Corvus had showed us in class that day.

"I really hope your memory of this place is good," I said as Eli pushed the door open. "Because it might be my only chance to see it since we've been banned from the festival."

Eli laughed. "So much pressure. But I'm sure you'll have reason to visit sooner or later."

"Maybe. But I'd rather see it now." I winked.

We stepped out into a vast entry hall full of more statues and suits of armor. So far so good on the details, it seemed. Then we headed for the main doors across the way, leading outside. Eli pushed them open, and a bright stream of warm sunshine spilled through. I blinked, letting my eyes adjust, then followed Eli outside onto a grand, stone pavilion, like the kind I'd only seen in movies based on books by Jane Austen. I half-expected a horse and buggy to pull up.

"Wow," I said, surveying the endless stretch of green lawn beyond the pavilion, marked here and there by giant, ancient trees and rows of flower beds formed into neat little gardens. Far in the distance, I could just make out the sea separating this innermost island from the other two. "It's so beautiful."

"Yeah it is." Eli raised a hand to his brow, shielding his eyes from the sun. "And just how I remembered it."

I sighed, truly disappointed about not getting to see this in real life. But maybe I could convince my mom to take me to visit the capital city sometime this summer. That is, assuming nothing bad happened tomorrow. I had a feeling if Consul Vanholt was assassinated, Lyonshold wouldn't be open for visitors again anytime soon. And if Magistrate Kirkwood became the new consul, I doubted it would be very much fun to visit anymore in the first place.

"What's that?" Eli pointed, and I followed the direction of his finger until I spotted an odd structure in the distance.

"No idea," I said, even as Eli marched across the pavilion and down the steps straight toward it. I followed after him, trying to look in every direction at once. There were so many things to look at. But as we drew closer to the structure in the distance, it captured my attention completely.

It was a pile of wood, easily as tall as I was, and carefully arranged like an elaborate funeral pyre. The pieces of wood were so varied in color, I had a feeling that several different types of trees had contributed to it. There was even a definite pattern to the colors.

"This must be for one of the Beltane bonfires," Eli said.

I glanced at him. "How can you be sure?"

"Don't you remember what Mr. Corvus said? He told us the bonfires have to be built this precisely because they're supposed to purify all magic when lit during Beltane."

"Oh, right." I vaguely remembered Corvus explaining something along those lines to us. "Well, at least you're dreaming about the festival. That's a good sign. We should keep looking."

"Okay. Let's do a sweep of the area around the hall."

I stifled a smile at his choice of words—always playing the cop.

Making a wide pass, we circled around Senate Hall, which was far larger than I realized. It stood at least seven stories high, judging by the windows, and I guessed it was about as wide as a football field and maybe twice as long. On top of it stood a single watchtower, not terribly tall, but still high enough I couldn't make out the top of it.

Eventually we came to another pyre, shaped exactly the same as the first. We moved on and found a third and then a fourth. By the time we came round to the front of Senate Hall again, we had counted twelve of them.

I sat down on the stone steps of the pavilion when we reached it, feeling the weight of defeat pulling me downward. We'd found nothing amiss. This must be a regular dream after all. The reason it was set at Senate Hall with all the pyres must be because Eli's unconscious mind was still fixated on the Terra Tribe, not realizing that mystery was already solved.

"Are you all right?" Eli frowned down at me.

"Yeah. Just disappointed." I made a sweeping gesture. "There's nothing here. I don't get it."

Eli clacked his teeth, the sound drawing my attention. "Maybe Paul was wrong." He hesitated. "I'm not saying he's been lying, but he could've made a mistake about the e-mail he saw. He's far from perfect."

I exhaled. "You're right." I certainly hoped that was the case, as opposed to it being a lie. I thought about my cell phone lying in my back pocket in the waking world. I hadn't tried to find the hidden data or enter the pass code he'd given me yet. Somehow, trying it seemed like admitting defeat, and I wasn't ready to do that. But now I wondered what would happen if I did try to find it.

Eli kicked a pebble with his shoe, his hands shoved into his pockets. The sun, so bright when we first arrived, was starting to slip behind the horizon. I leaned back on the steps. At least the dream had been calm and peaceful for once. That was a change.

Something in the distance caught my eye, a momentary flash. I sat up. "What was that?"

Eli turned and scanned the lawn behind us. "What?"

"I thought I saw a light. There it is again." I stood, keeping my eyes fixed on the place where it had seemed to emanate— somewhere near the first pyre we'd examined. I started walking slowly toward it, Eli falling into step beside me. But by the time we came within reach of the pyre, I hadn't seen it again.

I stopped. "Never mind, I guess I imagined it."

Eli didn't respond as he stared at the pyre, his eyes glazed over as he did that inward thinking thing of his. He came out of it a second later, and he walked up the pyre, seizing hold of one of the pieces of wood. "I have an idea." He yanked the wood from the top and tossed it over his shoulder, grabbing another one at once.

"What are you doing?" I asked, stepping sideways to avoid one of the flying pieces.

"I have a hunch. Help me tear this thing apart."

I raised an eyebrow at him, not that he could see it with his back to me. Then I shrugged and started helping. Several moments later, we'd dismantled the whole thing. At the very center, sticking out of the earth like a broken cemetery cross, stood a wooden rod. It was roughly the length of a baseball bat although not as thick in circumference. At first, I thought it must've been used to support the pyre, only it was too small to do that effectively.

"I can't believe it," Eli whispered, his eyes fixed on the rod.

"Believe what?"

He didn't reply as he stepped forward, seized the rod with one hand, and yanked it out. He ran his gaze over its surface. I moved closer, examining it myself. Intricate symbols and markings covered its entire surface. So it wasn't an ordinary stick at all, but a magical instrument.

"What is it?" I said, wishing this wasn't a dream so that I could give Eli a poke to get his attention. He was completely absorbed in studying it. "Eli," I said when he still didn't respond.

He finally looked up. "It's a Telluric Rod."

"Say again?"

"A Telluric Rod, also known as an Atlantean Rod."

A chill went through me at the connection. "Why?"

Eli turned it over in his hands, drawing a breath. "It was a handful of rods like this that sunk the island of Atlantis."

Back in Eli's dorm room, I slowly shook off the lingering effects of emerging from the dream and slid off a still slumbering Eli. I stood, then shook him awake. He blinked dazedly at me a couple of times before sitting up.

"So do you really think that Magistrate Kirkwood is going to try to sink Lyonshold?" I said, continuing our conversation from within the dream.

Eli shook his head as he clambered to his feet. "No, I don't think he's going to sink all of it, but a *part* of it, yeah. Assuming that the pyres we saw are the only ones with rods in them, and that makes sense."

"It doesn't make any sense to me."

Eli strode past me to his desk and *The Atlantean Chronicle.* "That's because you didn't do as much reading in this as I did."

I decided not to comment on the fact that it wasn't like I'd had *time* to study the darn thing with so much going on. Instead

I waited until he'd flipped to one of the pages in the back and waved me over.

"See, here it is."

I examined the page, my eyes drawn immediately to a sketch labeled "Telluric Rod." It looked almost exactly like the one we'd seen.

"That's how they sunk Atlantis," Eli was saying. "A bunch of merkind and naiads swam underneath all three rings of the island and planted these rods. Then they set them off with some kind of triggering spell and sunk each one. It's all described in this section. Except, of course, how to make a Telluric Rod. According to this book, the knowledge was outlawed and lost forever."

I folded my arms. "Gee, think I've heard that before."

Eli grimaced. "No kidding."

"But why would Magistrate Kirkwood want to sink part of Lyonshold?"

"Lots of reasons. I wouldn't be surprised if more than a couple of senators and even Consul Vanholt are supposed to be present when those things are set off. They could easily die in the destruction or be assassinated during the chaos while no one is watching. All Kirkwood has to do is stay out of the way and somewhere safe."

I shuddered. "But what about all the people present? They'll be caught, too."

Eli scoffed. "It wouldn't be the first time someone in a position of power was willing to let innocents die to achieve their goal."

I swallowed, knowing firsthand it was true. No wonder Titus Kirkwood was one of Marrow's followers—they were a match made in hell.

"And there's something even worse we haven't considered yet," said Eli.

"What could be worse than hundreds of innocent people dying?"

He ran a hand over his face, alarm in his eyes. "The Terra Tribe. Don't you see? We know, or at least we think we know, that Britney tried to attack me because Kirkwood made her do it. So let's assume that he knows what the Terra Tribe has been planning all along. That means he also knows that they're all *naturekinds*."

I thought about it a moment, my head spinning with details from our history class. "Naturekinds are the ones who sank Atlantis and started the first War of the Kinds."

"Uh-huh. And I bet the trigger for the Telluric Rods is *fire*. It's the only thing that makes sense. Which means tomorrow it's going to look like a group of naturekinds sunk Lyonshold. And with the current state of things you know what will happen next when the witchkinds and darkkinds start pointing fingers."

"Another war." I swallowed as the sound of rushing blood filled my ears. "But why would he want to start a war?"

Eli rolled his shoulders. "Beats me, but I'm sure he sees some advantage in it."

I didn't reply as my eyes fell to the page once more. For a second, all I saw was the Telluric Rod, but then my eyes slid lower and I spotted another symbol that struck a chord of recognition inside me. I gasped.

"What is it?" Eli put a hand on my back as if he feared I might faint.

I bent closer to the book, examining the inscription beneath a three-ringed symbol I knew I'd seen somewhere before. I pointed my finger to it and read the inscription aloud: "'Always from twelve is the circle undone.'"

Eli repeated the words after me, reading it for himself. "What do you think it means?"

I turned toward him. "No idea, but I've seen this symbol before *and* these words. Not exactly as they're written here but close enough there's no doubt of the connection."

Excitement lit Eli's face. "Where?"

"Mr. Corvus." I took a deep breath, forcing myself to calm down so I could explain it correctly—I hadn't thought about the book with the strange pictograms I'd decoded during my detention since the moment it had ended, but everything came rushing back to me now. By the time I finished telling him the details, Eli's excitement had given way to that dangerous, thrilling focus I'd come to expect from him whenever we found a hot lead.

"We need to see that book," he said.

"Do you think Corvus is working with Kirkwood?"

"Maybe." Eli traced the three-ringed symbol with his finger. "Either way this is the first physical clue we've had connecting Corvus to this. Looks like the crows might've symbolized him after all."

"Right."

Eli rubbed his chin. "I wouldn't be surprised if that book contains instructions on how to make the Telluric Rods."

I started to nod my agreement then stopped cold. "But that doesn't make sense. If the book contains dark, secret magic why would he be having students decode it for detention? Seems pretty stupid and risky."

Eli smirked. "We're talking about a guy who might be helping plan the murder of a bunch of people. I don't think rational figures into the picture much."

I frowned, unconvinced.

Eli saw the look and sighed. "Regardless of Corvus's reasons, there's no denying the connection between the two symbols, right?"

"Yes."

"Well, that alone means it's worth checking out. Make that double when you throw the crows into it." Eli put his hands on his hips. "Why are you so reluctant? I thought you wanted to find proof that could save Paul from his uncle."

"I do."

"Well, we might find that proof through Corvus."

"That's just it." I bit my lip, surprised that the problem hadn't occurred to him already. "How are we going to get *into* his office to find the proof?"

I could tell at once that Eli *had* forgotten this little detail. "Shit." He kicked the desk's leg, raking his hands through his hair. "I forgot. If we only had more time. I could get a pass and sneak in my dad's tension wrench from home."

I sighed, my excitement deflated. Once again we were going to be defeated by lack of time. It was so frustrating I wanted to hit something or blow something up just to vent.

Blow something up . . .

An outrageous idea sprouted in my mind. I poked it a couple of times, testing it for viability. It was insane, it really was—but it just might work.

"Eli," I said, drawing his attention. "Mr. Culpepper."

"What about him?"

"He's the maintenance man. He'll have a master key to Corvus's office."

Eli frowned. "But we don't know where he keeps the keys at night. If it's the maintenance office we can break in there, sure, but he might take them home with him, and that would be a much more dangerous mission."

I shook my head. "That's not what I meant. Why don't we just ask him?"

Eli raised his eyebrows, looking at me as if I'd gone insane. "Just ask him if he'll help us break into a teacher's office? In the middle of the night?"

I nodded. "He and I have sorta become friends these last few months. And I know that if we tell him why we need to go in there he'll do it. Especially if he finds out that Titus Kirkwood purchased the garrote that killed Rosemary from him. He cared a lot about her." I paused then added, "Not that I want to tell him that unless we absolutely have to. It would crush him."

"But how would we even get ahold of him this late at night?"

"Easy. I have his cell number."

Eli didn't say anything for several long seconds, just stared at me, his expression oddly blank. Then a huge smile seemed to split his face in half. "Dusty," he said, stepping toward me, "you are a genius."

Without warning, he took hold of my shoulders, leaned down, and kissed me.

The ground seemed to shift beneath my feet the moment his lips touched mine. Desire as hot and sudden as a lightning strike rose up and consumed us both.

~ 30 ~

The Curse

It was so unexpected that for a full second I just stood there, frozen by shock. Then all thought and reason gave way to physical impulse. I raised my hands to his head, sliding my fingers through his hair as I pulled him farther down, deepening the kiss. Eli responded at once. He leaned into me, opening his mouth against mine. He tasted like he smelled—something dark and musky and male.

His hands slipped down my arms to my hips. He took hold of my waist and pulled me into him, his large body seeming to swallow mine. No space existed between us, and still it wasn't close enough. I pushed him with my whole body, forcing him backward across the room until he hit the sofa with the back of his legs.

He fell onto it, taking me with him. He pulled and I climbed until I was on top of him—not in the Nightmare way, but stretched out over him. Our kiss broke but only for a second before Eli captured my mouth with his again. His hands on my waist rose up beneath my shirt. As his rough fingers grazed my bare skin, a violent shiver shot up my back and down my legs. His hands climbed higher, exploring.

Mine did the same, sliding away from his face, down his

neck, then across his chest. Eli turned his head, our lips parting, as he began to kiss his way down my cheek to my neck. My entire body convulsed from the sensation of his lips moving against that sensitive skin. But even as he did it to me, I wanted to do it to him. I pushed his head back, making room as I kissed my way down his neck to his collarbone.

A soft groan escaped Eli's throat. He sat up, lifting me off him. For a second, I thought he was calling an end to things, but then he stood, effortlessly switching our positions as he flipped me onto my back against the sofa. He stretched out on top of me, bracing his weight with one arm as he kissed me again, harder and deeper than before. I struggled to catch my breath, but I didn't care. I wanted this. I had never wanted anything more in my entire life.

I grabbed the sides of his shirt, and pulled up until I was able to slide my hands around his bare waist, the muscles there flexing against my fingers as he breathed in and out, in something close to a pant. This time Eli hissed when I touched him as if in pain. Only I knew by the way he kissed me that it wasn't pain. Not at all.

You should stop, a voice whispered in my head.

I ignored it. I didn't want to stop. Not ever. And neither did Eli. In this moment, I knew it with absolute certainty.

But then Eli jumped backward off of me. I sucked in a breath, completely taken by surprise. I sat up as across the room, Eli paced back and forth, his chest heaving.

"Oh, God, Dusty." He clenched and unclenched his fists. "We can't. Don't you get it? We can't do this. Not *ever*." I flinched at the desperate, agonized tone of his voice. He really believed it, whatever this reason was why we couldn't be together.

I wrapped my arms around my chest, feeling naked despite my clothes. "Why?"

He stopped pacing and stared over at me, his expression torn. I watched his inner turmoil blaze in his eyes.

"Come on, Eli."

At last he drew a deep breath then slowly exhaled. I braced for the truth.

"We're cursed," Eli said.

I just stared at him, his words nonsensical.

"Dream-seers," Eli said, his voice strained. "Our ability to predict the future comes with a curse attached to it."

I sat up straighter, his words now making far too much sense. I'd been living among magickind long enough to recognize the ring of truth in the idea of something so powerful, so useful, also being so costly. "What kind of curse?"

Eli licked his lips. "The star-crossed kind."

"You mean like Romeo and Juliet?"

"No, more like Angel and Buffy."

I tilted my head. "Who?"

Eli exhaled. "Never mind. The thing is, Lady Elaine says that if a pair of dream-seers become involved"—he hesitated, and I could tell he was searching for the right word—"romantically, then they are bound to destroy each other."

I crossed one leg over the other, a shiver traveling over my skin. "Define destroy."

"Like Marrow and Nimue. Just like them." Eli looked at me then looked away just as quickly. "You heard Marrow. He said he was in love with Nimue and then he killed her right in front of us. I don't understand how it works, but the curse turns love into hate."

I slumped back against the sofa, as the memory of Marrow first confessing his love for Nimue and then killing her played through my mind. Even after she was dead he claimed that he had set her free, shown her mercy. It was all so twisted and perverse.

"There's a long history of it," Eli said. "The dream-seers fall in love and then something happens to drive them apart. Most of them end up killing each other."

"Who told you this?"

Eli walked over to the desk and sat down. "Lady Elaine, a couple of days after we fought Marrow when I was still in the infirmary."

I desperately searched for some hole in his story. "But if this curse is true why didn't she tell us about it right from the beginning?"

"I asked her the same thing. She said she'd hoped that given our age and our rocky relationship at the start that she could put it off for a while, but then she saw the way I was after the fight and decided it was time."

I narrowed my eyes. "What do you mean?"

"I was beside myself crazy," Eli said, not quite meeting my eyes. "You were hurt so badly, unconscious. I thought you might be dying. And when they came to take you to the infirmary I freaked out. Didn't want you out of my sight."

My breath caught in my throat. "Really?"

He grimaced. "Yeah. Made a bit of an ass of myself."

I pressed my lips together, wanting to smile but afraid to at the same time.

Eli exhaled. "So Lady Elaine told me the truth, that our attraction toward each other is connected to our dream-seer powers. We're literally drawn together in every way. That's why you and I share all the same classes. We *have* to get close to strengthen our powers. But if we get *too* close that power backfires. She told me all the stories of the dream-seers before us. Most of them died really young, except for Marrow and Nimue, of course, but they spent years battling each other before she finally managed to imprison him in that tomb. Then she condemned herself to the same imprisonment. It's pretty awful when you think about it."

I nodded. It wasn't just awful, it was cruel, like dangling the cure over a sick man, holding it just out of reach while watching him die. I sucked in a breath. "Isn't there a way to break the curse?"

Eli shook his head. "Not according to Lady Elaine. She said it can't be broken, only avoided."

"But how do we know that's true? We don't know that will happen to us. There has to be some kind of choice about it."

"No, Dusty. There's not."

I felt like screaming. "How do you *know*?"

"Because I've seen it."

I glared. "What, did you dream about it or something?"

"No, Lady Elaine had a vision of what might happen. She showed it to me with some kind of mind meld like what you've been doing with Deverell." He drew a long, shaky breath. "It was awful, Dusty. And I don't ever want that to happen to you and me. I care about you too much."

I inhaled, the gesture painful. It was just what I'd always wanted to hear from him. Just what I'd hoped for, but it was never going to happen. The idea made me feel like I was being wrenched apart from the inside out.

Refusing to cry, I put as much steel in my voice as I could. "Why didn't Lady Elaine tell me? Why did she only tell you?"

Eli frowned. "You're not going to like it."

"Oh, there's no doubt about that, I'm sure. But I think I have a right to know."

"She thought, given your tendency to rebel, that if she told you that we couldn't be together it would just make you seek it out even more."

A burst of anger went through me, hot and quick like a firecracker only to sizzle out a second later. It hurt to hear it, but I also knew deep down that it was true. Marrow had exposed that truth to me. The more someone told me I couldn't do something, the more I wanted to do it. Even now I felt that rebellious nature screaming at me to stand up and kiss him again. Forever.

I gave in to it. At first, Eli didn't seem to know what happened as I rushed over to him, cradled his jaw in my hands, and pulled his mouth down to mine in a kiss hot enough to incinerate us both.

For a few seconds we were nothing more than mouth and tongue, taste and heat. But then Eli wrapped his hands around my wrists. I knew what was coming and I fought against it, kissing him harder, trying to express all my feelings in that one act. For a moment, it almost worked, but then he pulled my hands away from his face, breaking the kiss.

Breaking us.

"We can't," he said. "I won't do this."

I pulled away from him, a flush washing over my body, my heart wrenching. I turned my back to him as I fought back tears. Eli didn't try to comfort me, as I knew he wouldn't. But he gave me time, several long painful minutes as I struggled to regain my composure. I had to regain it. I couldn't let him see how much I hurt, and I couldn't be selfish and let this derail us from the task at hand—stopping Titus Kirkwood.

Finally, I wiped the moisture from my lips then turned to face him, making my tone and expression as hard as possible, a difficult task considering how soft and broken I felt on the inside. "So let's call Culpepper, and see if we can't get into Corvus's office."

"Right . . ." Eli said, a thousand unspoken things in his voice. But then he accepted the farce I had presented him. He walked over to the table where his wand still lay. He picked it up, reapplied the glamour, and placed the ring on his thumb. Then he went to the desk and slipped on a thick leather bracelet I'd never seen him wear before. Under different circumstances I might've asked him where he'd gotten it—a gift from his dad perhaps. But not now.

Finally he turned and faced me. "I'm really sorry, Dusty," he said, and the longing in his voice, the sadness, made the broken pieces inside me shatter a little more, some of the breakage as fine and thin as dust.

"So am I," I said. I tried to block out the hurt, to bury the loss deep inside me. I knew if I didn't, the rest of me would break in ways impossible to repair.

Only, who was I kidding. I already was.

~ 31 ~

The Crow King

The sound of jangling keys greeted us as Eli and I came down the third-floor hallway of Monmouth Tower toward Room 337. Faustus Culpepper stood in front of the door, his hellhound sitting beside him.

"Hey, George," I said when the hound turned its head at the sound of our approach. Its eyes glowed like flashlights in the dark light of the hallway. George made a whining sound that I decided to take as his friendliest form of greeting.

"Hey, Mr. Culpepper," Eli said as I bent and gingerly patted George's head, his black coat more like scales than fur. I was relieved George stood still for the petting, but he made it clear that he was simply allowing the affection rather than enjoying it.

"Hello." Culpepper didn't look up from where he was still sorting through keys. A moment later he identified the correct one and slid it into the lock. "You two be quick about this. Don't disturb anything, and make sure you lock up when you're through."

I straightened from my hunched position. "You're not going to stick around until we're done?"

"Nope." Culpepper brushed his knuckles against his head. He wore his hair military short, no doubt a leftover habit from his time in the Marines. Culpepper was a Metus demon, the kind that feeds on fears, but tonight he had his glamour firmly in place, hiding his horns and keeping the green glow out of his eyes.

"Why not?" I asked.

"Well, one, because I trust you not to do anything too stupid."

"That's comforting," Eli muttered.

Culpepper flashed him a dark look. "And two, I don't want to risk being involved if you get caught."

I raised an eyebrow, tempted to point out that his one and two seemed in direct opposition to each other, but really, what would be the point? "All right," I said. "Thanks for doing this." Not only had he answered his cell the second I called him, but he'd headed out to meet us right away. We needed to find this proof quick so I could get back to my dorm and write a dream journal about the Telluric Rods.

Culpepper nodded as he twisted the key in the lock and pushed the door open. Then he turned away, giving the hellhound's leash a soft tug. "Come on, George."

Eli and I waited as Culpepper and the hellhound disappeared around a corner.

"I've got to admit, the guy's growing on me," Eli said. "He still weirds me out, but he's a handy contact."

"I know what you mean," I said, following after him.

Eli searched for the light switch and turned it on. I blinked away the spots in my vision and scanned the room. It looked more or less the same as it had the last time with a cluttering of books and papers across the desk. Eli made a beeline for them while I examined the bookshelf and the objects I knew had belonged to Marrow.

I eyed the spyglass and the spinning compass long enough to observe the layer of dust covering them. The dust was a good sign. It seemed they were just there for decoration, inconsequential leftovers.

Finally, I turned toward the desk. I slid open the drawer where Corvus had kept the book before. It was still there, and I pulled it out and set it on the table.

"Is that it?" Eli came around beside me for a closer look at it.

I nodded, trying to ignore the way my pulse reacted whenever he drew near. *Cursed, we're cursed.* I shut the thought down as tears threatened. "I'll try to find the page. You keep looking."

"All right," Eli said, his voice far too quiet, and I wondered if he'd heard something in *my* voice—the same painful longing made worse by the certainty of knowing it could never be.

I shrugged it off as best I could, focusing on the book. It took next to no time at all to find the page with the three-ringed symbol, because a small notebook had been wedged into the book on the very page.

"Here it is." I pulled out the notebook then pushed the book toward Eli. While he examined the page, I flipped through the notebook. I recognized Mr. Corvus's messy scrawl. Most of it seemed like random notes and gibberish, but then one of the clearer sentences caught my eye.

Only the blood of the twelve can undo the circle.

It was the same sentence I'd decoded during detention. I quickly scanned the rest of the page, and in seconds my skin began to crawl. I couldn't make much sense of it, but there were a lot of references to blood and sacrifice.

"Eli, look at this." I handed him the notebook. His expression grew more concerned with each sweep his eyes made over the page.

When he finished, he raised his gaze to mine. "This doesn't tie him to Kirkwood, but it's worrisome."

"No kidding."

Eli set the notebook down. "Let's keep looking. There has to be proof here somewhere."

"Right." Feeling a welcome burst of energy, one strong enough to temporarily ease the ache in my heart, I resumed my search of the desk.

Eli and I both became so focused on the task at hand that neither of us noticed the door opening a few minutes later. One moment we were alone in the room, and the next two men strode in. I barely had time to register shock when a spell struck me in the chest. It hit hard enough to knock the wind out of me, but I was unconscious before I finished falling.

The first thing that registered when I woke was the instinctual knowledge that moving was going to be painful. My limbs had the aching, numb feel of muscles deprived of proper blood flow from lying far too long in an awkward position. I opened my eyes, holding as still as I could, even as panic began to build inside me. All I could see from my current location was a stone floor, dirty and cracked from age. I was lying on my side, my arms tied behind my back.

All at once the memory of being in Mr. Corvus's office with Eli came back to me. Two men had walked in and attacked us with sleeping spells. But not just any men—Captain Gargrave and one of his Will Guard.

As if thinking his name had conjured him into life, I heard Gargrave say from somewhere above me, "This one's waking up."

"Good," another voice replied. "Just in time."

Closing my eyes, I shifted sideways onto my back and to the direction of the voices. Pain shot through me from the roots of my hair to my toenails. The worst of it was in my shoulders and neck. How long had I been lying like this? Hours for sure.

I opened my eyes to see a low-hanging stone ceiling above me, easily as dirty and cracked as the floor. Right away it put me in mind of a medieval dungeon, although that might've had more to do with the torture currently being inflicted on my body. Bracing one leg against the floor, I tried to roll over onto my other side but couldn't manage it.

"No need to struggle so hard," Gargrave said, his voice suddenly much nearer than it had been before. "Ana-acro."

I screamed as the spell hoisted me into the air by the ropes around my wrists. The magic jerked me to the right then dropped me into a wooden chair. For a moment I couldn't see or think or do anything until the pain receded.

Then finally I looked around, getting my bearings at last. It seemed my first judgment had been correct. This was a dungeon, or at least it was underground. The air possessed that damp smell like the tunnels at Arkwell. There were no windows, and the only light came from torches hung on the walls. So no electricity either, it seemed.

Captain Gargrave stood a few feet in front of me. He was wearing his usual red and black Will Guard uniform, but he had the sleeves rolled up, exposing his thick forearms. I spotted an intricate black tattoo running up his right arm from wrist to elbow. It took a second for my brain to puzzle out the shape. Those black marks were a flock of crows in flight. Gargrave, not Corvus, must've been the crows in Eli's dream.

The moment I made the realization, my eyes fixed on the

man standing a few feet behind Gargrave, his face partly hidden in shadows. Even still, I recognized him. I'd never met Titus Kirkwood in person, but I'd seen his image often enough. Once again I was struck by the strong resemblance he bore to his nephew.

"What are you doing?" I said, struggling in vain to free myself. I couldn't see the rope binding me, but I knew it was silver and made of magic, simply by the painful tingling in my skin where it touched. "Where's Eli?"

"Oh, don't worry," Titus said in a voice that belonged in one of those annoying mud-slinging political commercials. "He's here, too."

I jerked my head around, trying to locate Eli in the semi-darkness. Then I saw him lying a few feet away near the wall. Like me, his wrists were bound behind him.

"Ana-acro," Gargrave said again, and Eli's body rose into the air. He cried out, coming awake at once. Gargrave deposited him into the chair next to me.

"There now." Titus rubbed his hands together. He was a tall, broad-chested man with blond hair slowly giving way to gray and a pointed, severe chin. "The dream-seers together as they should be. It really is a shame that it's come to this. Your talents would've proved useful, I'm sure. I tried to keep you out of the way long enough for me to finish my business, but it seems it wasn't meant to be. You've learned too much."

I glared at him. "How do you know what we've learned?"

A cold smile slid across Titus's face like a snake. "Why, from your own mouth. I knew tonight was your last chance to predict the attack on Lyonshold so I had Captain Gargrave slip a listening device beneath Eli's door earlier this evening. Bugs, I think ordinaries call them. Such a strange euphemism. But highly effective when brand-new and animation free."

My mouth fell open at this news, and I cringed at all the things he must've heard. Not just about the Telluric Rods and our plans to search Mr. Corvus's office, but also about the dream-seer's curse.

"If you didn't want us to find out, you've shouldn't have relied on someone else to do your dirty work," Eli said, surprising me by how quickly he'd recovered and caught up.

Titus examined his hands, the skin around his knuckles oddly discolored. "I only use these for the delicate situations."

I scoffed. "You mean like beating up your nephew?" I expected Titus to react with anger, but his lips parted into a smile revealing a row of perfect white teeth.

"Yes. He's always been a delicate situation, I'm afraid. Just like his mother." Titus clapped his hands. "But enough wasting time." He glanced at the watch on his wrist. "The ceremony will be starting soon, and I need to be away from here when it does."

"Where are we?" Eli demanded.

"Lyonshold. In the dungeon of Senate Hall, to be precise," Titus said. "And I'm well aware that you know what's coming next. Even without the dreams, your detective work has been quite impressive, although it helped that my nephew was so eager to betray my secrets."

"You can't do this." Eli jerked against the rope binding him, but Gargrave pointed his staff, freezing him in place.

"Go head and keep struggling," said Gargrave. "I would hate for this to get boring."

My head buzzed with the realization of where we were and

when. No wonder moving had hurt so much. We must've been under that sleeping spell for nearly eighteen hours. "Abducting us was stupid," I said, trying to draw attention off Eli. "We're the dream-seers. Someone has to have noticed we're missing by now."

Titus smirked. "Oh, I think not. You've been suspended from the festival. Everyone thinks you're back at Arkwell, pouting in your dorm rooms, no doubt."

I started to ask him how he knew about the detention, but I realized Gargrave had been there. Now that I thought about it, Gargrave had been everywhere, he and his men always lurking in the shadows, watching, waiting. Paul was right. His uncle had a long, powerful reach. I'd seen enough of the Will Guard to know how loyal they were to their captain—a man loyal to Titus Kirkwood. Really, using the Will Guard was brilliant. They could be anywhere on campus at any time and no one would question what they were doing.

"Lady Elaine will notice," I said, refusing to admit defeat. "I never entered my dream-journal last night."

Gargrave chuckled. "We entered one for you. What with dreams being so erratic, it was easy to take snippets from your prior entries and mesh them together."

I felt myself pale. This had been well planned, and I wondered how long Titus and his men had been spying on Eli and me. Probably from the moment they decided to sink Senate Hall into the sea. That also meant they'd known the moment Paul had contacted us.

I stuck out my chin. "Our friends will miss us."

Titus cocked his head. "Which one? Her perhaps?" He motioned to the far corner, and my stomach dropped at the sight of a long black braid with hair as glossy and fine as silk. "Wake her," Titus said to Gargrave. "But do it more gently this time. I've had enough screaming."

Gargrave strode over to Selene and muttered a spell. Selene began to stir at once, moaning loudly from the pain of ill-used muscles. Gargrave stooped and picked her up, depositing her in the chair to my left.

I glanced at Selene long enough to determine she was okay. At least for now. I assumed they must've taken her last night when they abducted Eli and me. She wasn't wearing pajamas, though, but the black coat she'd been tailoring for her home ec class. Seeing her here was a blow, but at least there was no sign of Paul.

Titus stepped up to Selene, grabbed hold of her chin, and tilted her head back as he examined her face. He sighed. "It's such a shame we had to bring you into this. I'm quite fond of your mother, and I know she'll miss you terribly. But you shouldn't have gotten so involved with these two." He motioned toward Eli and me. "You know too much as well, I'm afraid."

Selene didn't respond, just sat there, her expression a mask of calm but her eyes livid. I knew in that moment that everything Paul had ever said about his uncle was true. He was a monster, a man who took pleasure in the pain and suffering of others. In a way, that made him even worse than Marrow, who simply didn't care about the suffering he inflicted.

Titus released Selene's face and stepped back. "Now on to business." He reached into his front pocket and withdrew a cell phone. *My* cell phone. "We need to discuss the data my nephew hid inside this. I have a feeling that you know how to access it." Titus approached me and held the phone a few inches from my face.

Right away the instructions and the pass code ran through my mind.

"Oh, she knows," Gargrave said. "She's thinking about it now."

I jerked against the ropes holding me. I felt an odd pressure in my mind, the presence of someone else trying to break in. If it weren't for the sessions I'd spent with Mr. Deverell, I wasn't sure I would've recognized that pressure for what it was. Instinct took over, and I pushed back against it, forcing him out of my mind. Gargrave winced, and I flashed a smile at him, momentarily gleeful in my victory.

But it had come too late.

Titus rubbed his hands together. "Excellent." He took a step toward me. "Now, I'm going to give you one chance to make this easy for everyone. Tell me how to access the data hidden on this phone, and I promise that you and your friends will not suffer."

I gasped as the full meaning in his words reached me. He didn't say that my friends and I would live. Oh, no. He had brought us here to die. It was just a matter of how quick and how much pain we endured beforehand.

"Don't tell him anything," said Selene.

In an almost casual gesture Gargrave backhanded her. Selene's neck rocked back so hard I was terrified it might've broken, my fear intensified by Selene's silence—she hadn't uttered a sound as the blow fell. But then I watched her lower her head back down, and I realized she had held it in with a force of will far greater than any I'd ever known. There weren't even tears in her eyes, despite the blood trickling from the side of her mouth.

"What's your decision?" Titus said.

Doing my best to mirror Selene, I said, "I'm not going to tell you anything."

Titus sighed. "Ah, yes. I figured as much. But no matter. We just need to find the right pressure point. Everyone has one, you know."

My gaze flicked automatically to Eli, bile climbing up my throat of the thought of them hurting him.

But Titus glanced at Gargrave. "Let's try Paul first. Carry him if you must."

Every muscle in my body tensed as I watched Gargrave turn and leave the room only to return a few moments later with an unconscious Paul dangling in the air in front of him, held there by silver ropes. One look at Paul's face told me that he'd needed to be carried in. Shiny black bruises covered his cheeks, and his right eye was swollen shut. His lip was split in three places. Gashes ran down his arms and legs, the wounds visible through his shredded clothes.

The last of my hope that someone would notice we were missing dissolved. There was no one else. Not even Lance, who was still in Vejovis.

Gargrave broke the spell, and Paul fell to the ground with a sickening slap of flesh against stone.

Titus made a clucking noise. "Looks like you need to revive him. Again."

I fought back the urge to be sick, and I realized the reason why he'd chosen to torture Paul over Eli was simply from the pleasure it gave him. Titus pointed his staff at Paul and spoke an incantation I didn't recognize. A moment later Paul's uninjured eye slid open. It swiveled around in his head as he surveyed what he could from that position. He looked terrified.

"Paul," I said, wanting him to know he wasn't alone anymore. "I'm over here."

He turned his head in my direction, and when he saw me his whole body convulsed. "No," he screamed. "Don't you tell him, Dusty. Don't you dare. No matter what."

I flinched at the sound of his fury. There was no lie in him now. He meant what he said. He didn't want me to give his uncle the knowledge no matter what they did to him.

But I didn't know if I could do it.

Mustering all my willpower, I forced my gaze away from Paul and onto Titus. If I could block Paul out, pretend he wasn't there, wasn't suffering, then maybe I could manage it.

But my resolve faltered a moment later when Gargrave kicked Paul in the stomach. "Save the screaming for when it counts."

"Stop it!" I shouted. "Don't hurt him."

Titus flashed a triumphant grin at me. "Oh, yes. I do believe this will work after all." Then he pulled the watch off his wrist and disengaged the glamour to reveal his wand. It was short but as thick as a billy club. He raised it above his head, and for a second I thought he intended to use it as a club.

But he pointed the tip at Paul and spoke a word I didn't know but which made all the hairs on my body stand up on end from the sudden surge of magic. Green flames burst out from the tip of the wand and covered Paul from head to foot, enveloping him like a swarm of insects. Paul writhed on the floor, the veins popping out in his neck as he struggled against the pain, holding in a scream.

"Don't watch, Dusty," Eli whispered from beside me.

I knew he was right, but I couldn't look away. The green flames danced over his body, leaving the skin beneath shiny and red as if burned or bitten. It didn't matter which. What mattered was that it hurt.

Titus broke the spell a moment later, and Paul slumped against the ground, a moan of relief escaping his lips. His skin was red but not blistered and burned as I'd expected it to be. For a second I thought it was over, but Titus conjured the spell again, the green flames brighter than before.

Paul couldn't keep in the scream this time. The spell seemed to rip it out of him. The sound of his pain cut into me like jagged glass. I couldn't bear it. I couldn't watch him suffer when I had the means of putting an end to it.

"Stop!" I screamed. "I'll tell you, but you've got to stop." I knew that once he had what he needed Titus would kill us, but I didn't care. At least it would be over.

Titus broke the spell and faced me, one hand on his hip, the other hanging at his side with his wand pointed at the floor. "Go ahead then."

"Don't, Dusty," Paul whispered through bruised and bloodied lips. "I'm not worth it."

I ignored him. I needed all my focus now. Gargrave was good at mind-magic, and he was paying attention. I needed him to know I was telling the truth. "To access it press the home button three times and then swipe to the left twice."

"Stop!" Paul lurched to his knees, but Gargrave kicked him back down.

"Yes, now we're making progress." Titus flipped the phone around so that everyone could see my instructions had worked.

I exhaled, my heart beating in my throat. "And the pass code is—"

"Don't, please don't," Paul said, his voice a moan now.

"Five-two-one-one-three-eight." The lie came easily. Thank goodness my locker combination was six digits.

Titus beamed as he started to enter the numbers, and I spoke a silent prayer that they'd already tried to open it twice before and that this time the phone would self-destruct.

"Wait," Gargrave said.

Titus's fingertip froze on the screen. "What is it?"

"She's lying."

My heart rate sped up, but I managed not to blink or fidget. "No, I'm not."

Titus frowned, his gaze shifting from Gargrave to me then back again. "I thought she had you blocked out?"

"She did, but he didn't." Gargrave pointed at Paul. "Not this time. I caught it. Just for a second when she said those numbers. His surprise gave him away. They're wrong, and he knows it."

Titus lowered his hand from the phone's screen. He came forward and looked down at his nephew. Then he looked up at me, his expression appraising. "It seems I might've been wrong about the pressure point here. If she won't cave for him, maybe he will cave for her. Kaio-dontia."

I didn't have time to react, not even to flinch. The green flames enveloped me, obscuring my sight and muffling my hearing. But these things only mattered for a second, because in the next there was nothing but pain. I was being burned alive, the flames like a thousand flies eating away at my flesh with teeth made of red-hot needles. I screamed without even being aware of it, the sound an involuntary expulsion of the agony charging through my body.

A blur of movement flashed before my eyes as Eli lunged in front of the spell, trying to block it, trying to absorb it into himself. For a moment, the pain eased, but then Gargrave struck Eli in the temple with the head of his staff. Eli fell and didn't move again.

"Don't hurt her. I'll tell you. Don't hurt her!" Paul's voice barely registered in my ears. It seemed far away, nonexistent.

Titus made a flicking gesture with his wand and the pain increased. I screamed with my whole body, tears pouring from my eyes. *Stop stop stop oh God make it stop. Stop please stop.*

"Three-eight-seven-eight-nine-seven!" Paul shouted.

The spell broke, and I fell back against the chair, trembling. Cold sweat coated my body, but the agony was over. At least physically. I'd never been more relieved in my life, no matter that it lasted only a moment.

Forcing my eyes open, I watched as Titus entered the pass code. The smile that broke across his face a second later told me all I needed to know. He had gotten what he wanted. He held in his hands the power of the Red Warlock—the name of every magickind willing to start a revolution.

Titus put the phone to sleep a second later and slid it into his front pocket. Then he leaned over and patted his nephew on the head. "Thank you, Paul. I'm glad you served a purpose at last. And how ironic it is that love was your downfall. It was your mother's, too."

Paul didn't struggle, but sagged against the floor, defeat like a paralytic drug spreading through his body.

I wanted to scream and jump up and strangle this horrible man with my bare hands, but I couldn't move. I could barely breathe as the aftereffects of the spell lingered on.

"Shall we kill them now?" Gargrave asked as Titus straightened up.

"No, leave them. We shouldn't risk their death being traced back to us. If their bodies are found in the wreckage, there will be questions." Titus engaged the glamour on his wand, turning it back into a watch. He checked the time as he slid it on. "We'll let the sea take care of them." He glanced up at the ceiling. "That is, if the building doesn't do it first."

Gargrave looked like he might argue, but then he nodded.

"Let's go." Titus turned around and headed for the door. He paused just before it and swung back around. "Oh, one last thing." He walked over to Eli, still lying unconscious on the floor. He stooped and pulled Eli's wand ring off his thumb. "I wouldn't want any of you to believe this was going to be your saving grace."

By Selene's quick intake of breath, I guessed she'd been thinking it, at least.

Titus smiled. "If he wakes before the end, be sure to tell him that it wouldn't have worked anyway. This isn't a true wand. I had the power source inside it bound with a spell designed to suppress his dreams. It was the perfect solution to keeping you two off my trail after that useless girl failed to deliver my curse. Well, almost perfect.

At once, I realized the spell on Eli's wand must've been the source of the fog in Eli's dreams. All except for that last one. In his frustration, he'd removed the wand before going to sleep. A lucky break. Not that it mattered now.

"Nevertheless," Titus continued, "it kept him from doing magic, and that is good enough for me. No ordinary should ever be allowed to pretend to be what we are."

With that, Titus shoved the ring into his pocket and turned for the door, Gargrave following after him. I watched them go, dread pounding in my ears. When the door slammed shut, I knew they had won.

And now all that remained was the long wait before dying.

～ 32 ～

The Sinking

No one spoke for several minutes after Titus and Gargrave left, all of us in varying states of shock. I kept my gaze fixed on the door, willing it to open. Willing for *somebody* to come and find us. I even tried closing my eyes and calling for my mom with my mind-magic, but it was pointless. The silver rope of the binding curse created a containment shield around the bound person, blocking in all magic, even mind-magic. The only reason why I'd been able to force Gargrave out of my mind was because he'd had to come inside the shield first.

"I don't suppose anyone has a magical knife stowed in their pockets," Selene said, her voice wry but with a desperate undertone that made tears threaten my eyes.

I shook off the hopelessness and stood, my legs trembling from the effort. Taking a deep breath, I summoned all my strength, and then I walked over to Eli. I bent close and examined the wound on his temple. It looked painful but not deep. His breathing seemed to be growing shallow, and I guessed he would wake up on his own soon. I wanted to touch him, to reassure myself that he was all right, but it was impossible with my hands bound behind me. Instead I leaned even closer to him, brushing my lips against his head in a gentle kiss.

Then I moved past him toward the door. I turned around when I reached it and tried to grab the handle. But after several attempts, I knew it wasn't going to work. I was too short and the handle too large. My fingers kept sliding off it.

"I can't . . . get . . . ahold of it." I let go and straightened up, cursing.

Across from me, Paul struggled to his feet. He looked as weak and uncoordinated as a newborn foal. He staggered over to me. "Let me try."

I stepped aside and held my breath as I watched him turn around and try to grab the handle. He was taller than me. It might work. His fingers grasped the door handle, and he twisted his body to the right, turning it. The distinctive sound of a lock rattling greeted us a moment later.

Paul slumped back against the door and slid to the ground in defeat.

I turned away from him, knowing despair was contagious. I wasn't ready to give up. Not yet.

I walked back to Selene. "Can you stand?"

In answer, she pushed herself up, the gesture awkward with her hands bound. "What now?"

"Turn around," I said. "I'm going to try pulling the ropes off."

Selene frowned. "It won't work, Dusty. You know that."

"She's right," Paul said, his voice faint and hard to hear from across the room.

"I have to try. We have to do something to get out of here."

Selene exhaled then turned around, showing me her back. I did the same, and then scooted until I felt her fingers brush mine. She and I were close enough in height that I was able to reach the ropes around her wrists easily. But the moment I touched them, the skin on my fingers began to burn. I flinched away but only for a second. After the spell Titus had used on me, burnt fingers seemed minor.

I grabbed the rope again and pulled, wincing against the pain as the burning increased. Selene made a choking sound as the rope moved down her wrists just a little, and I knew she was feeling the same burn I was. But she didn't cry out, and I kept at it, pulling with everything I possessed.

It didn't matter. The spell was too strong.

I let go and stumbled forward, panting. My hands felt like I'd held them pressed against a lit stove top. I could feel the blisters forming. I turned and sank to the floor beside Eli, the disease of despair taking over me at last. I hung my head, trying not to cry.

No one spoke for several long minutes. And I knew we were all waiting and wondering when the destruction would begin. It was impossible to tell how late in the day it was. And I had no idea if there would be warning tremors beforehand or if the ground beneath us would just give way all at once.

"He's waking," Selene said sometime later.

I raised my head and watched as Eli stirred on the floor. He groaned and rolled over. "What happened?"

"They're gone, and we're trapped," Selene deadpanned.

Eli scooted and twisted his body until he was able to get into a sitting position, leaning against me for support. "No, we're not. I've got a way out."

I exhaled and shook my head. "Titus took your wand." I paused, then I decided he would be happy to know that his inability to work magic was because he'd been given a defective wand and not because of something lacking in himself. Any happiness, no matter how small, would be welcome right now.

When I finished explaining Eli surprised me with a matter-of-fact nod. "I'd suspected something wasn't right about it for a while now. When I cast that first spell in Miss Norton's class it was so easy. But everything with my wand was like trying to swim through mud. That's why I took Miss Norton's talking stick."

My mouth fell open. "You did?"

"Yes."

Well, I decided, there wasn't much point in being angry now.

"I saw it and had to," Eli went on, getting to his feet. "If we ended up here at the festival, I didn't want to be powerless. And boy, was that the right decision. Now someone come here and take off this bracelet."

Selene stepped forward, and I watched, a welcome surge of adrenaline starting to pump through my system.

"Is that what I think it is?" I said as Selene slid the bracelet off Eli's wrist.

Eli stretched out his fingers, taking the bracelet from Selene. "Yes, it is." Then with an awkward gesture, he managed to disengage the glamour concealing Miss Norton's talking stick. I'd never been so happy to see it.

Eli pointed it as best he could at Selene and said, "Ou-agra."

At once the silver rope binding her vanished. Joy boosted me to my feet as Selene returned the favor for Eli. Then she cast the spell at Paul while Eli freed me. He picked me up in a fierce hug. It hurt a lot, and Eli was unsteady on his feet from the blow to his head, but I welcomed the pain and shakiness, any reminder that we were still alive.

But as he set me on my feet, a loud grumble went through the building, and the floor and walls began to shake.

"It's started." Eli let go of me. "Come on. We've got to get out of here."

Selene was one step ahead of us. She charged to the door and blasted it open with a spell. Then she turned to help Paul, who was struggling to remain upright.

I rushed over to help, too, but then Eli said, "I'll do it. I'm stronger, and you two are better at magic."

I frowned. "What about your head?"

"I'm fine. The dizziness is already passing. Now go."

I hesitated, but only for a moment. I squeezed Paul's hand, then stepped away, making room for Eli, who swung Paul's arm over his shoulder, supporting him.

I led the way out with Selene right behind me. The narrow passageway beyond the door was even darker than the chamber we'd left, and Selene and I both conjured fire in our hands. There was only one way to go, and I headed down it, keeping the flames low. I was afraid I would catch myself on fire as the tremors continued, making it difficult to walk without stumbling. Every few seconds, bits of stone rained down around us from the ceiling.

After walking a little while, the passageway dead-ended.

"That can't be," I said, staring at the stone wall in front of me. My instincts insisted there should be a door or staircase here instead of a wall. I reached out with my free hand and touched the wall, confirming its solidity.

Selene stepped up beside me. "Maybe the way through is hidden." She began to hum a familiar tune, the magical notes of her siren detection spell. Within seconds, the golden outline of a door appeared.

Selene looked at me, and I nodded, the message clear—aim for the center and blast it open.

"One, two, three!" We both hit it with spells at the same time, and the stones exploded outward revealing another passageway beyond as well as a steep staircase leading up. I stepped through and charged up the stairs, but Selene soon called for me to slow down. Eli and Paul were having a rough time. Paul was so exhausted and the stairwell so narrow, Eli could barely help him at all.

Still, we managed it, climbing several stories upward until we reached a passageway on the ground floor leading off to the right. Faint but natural light leaked in through the high windows overhead. The sun must be close to setting.

I extinguished the fire in my hands and headed down the passageway. The first door I came to, I stopped and forced it open, but it only led into an empty room. I moved on, stopping at the next couple of doors only to find more rooms, some empty, some furnished, but none of them providing the escape we needed.

Finally, the last door opened into another narrow passage. I followed it, eventually arriving in a place I recognized—the grand entryway of Senate Hall. Another tremor hit the building, this one stronger than the ones before. One of the pillars on the side of the entryway split at the top and came crashing down, flooding the room with dust.

I coughed and squinted, trying to see a way through. Selene appeared beside me, and she worked some kind of spell that helped to clear the air. It was enough we could see a small side door leading outside. We raced to it, Eli and Paul managing to keep up as the danger of being crushed by the falling debris spurred them on.

Although the entryway had been deserted, the outside lawn of Senate Hall was a mass of people in various states of panic.

Most of them seemed to be trying to flee the giant fissure that had split across the lawn in the place where the first pyres had been in Eli's dream. Fire, pieces of earth, and even water were bursting out from it all at once. I gulped, wondering how many people had been standing there when the ground split. As it was, there were far too many people lying unmoving in the grass, either unconscious or dead.

Guilt pressed down on me as I wondered if we could've prevented this if we'd turned in the cell phone. But right away I understood that if we'd tried, Titus would've stopped us sooner. We'd been trapped from the very beginning. And the scale of his plan was so large and Titus so determined, it seemed impossible that anything could've stood in his way. Even still, the understanding brought no relief.

The stone pavilion, so beautiful inside Eli's dream, had been reduced to rubble, and the four of us had to climb our way through. As I reached the top of a large boulder, I froze, stunned by the sight of a body lying on the other side of it. The man was clearly dead, although I couldn't tell how. There was no blood or sign of trauma. But I knew who he was—Consul Vanholt. It seemed this part of Titus's plan had worked successfully.

Gritting my teeth, I moved on, ignoring the shocked comments from the others. There would be time to process the consul's death later. For now we had to do what we could to stop the rest of Titus's plan from coming to fruition.

Selene turned right when we reached the lawn, heading in the direction most of the people seemed to be running. I moved to follow her, but Eli shouted from behind me.

"That's the wrong way!"

I turned around. "How do you know?"

"The Terra Tribe's practice. They lit the pyres clockwise.

There'll be more fissures that way already." As if his words had been a portent of doom, the ground trembled again followed by the distant sound of an explosion and then the groan of a foundation shifting.

That was all it took to get us moving in the opposite direction. Eli continued to help Paul along, but Paul seemed to be doing better now that we were out in the open. We reached the twelfth pyre moments later after two more explosions. There was panic and chaos here, too, but it was more contained. We could see two of the pyres and both of them were still burning. A group of people surrounded each one, working some kind of collective spell—one intended to stop the Telluric Rods from ripping the final holes through the island, I hoped.

I spotted Lady Elaine among the nearest group and dashed toward her. Her presence bought a rush of relief. She would know what to do to stop this thing.

But then I spotted a couple of men in the familiar red and black tunics of the Will Guard. What were they doing here? Didn't they know that their captain was planning to sink the island? Or maybe they did, and they were here to ensure it happened. They might be working against the spell to stop the rods, even now.

Lady Elaine turned and saw me coming. "What are you doing here, Dusty? You're supposed to be at Arkwell. Go now. That way. They're moving people off the island." She pointed to somewhere off toward the sea in the distance.

I shook my head. "You've got to listen to me right now!" I leaned into her, lowering my voice for fear one of the nearby Will Guards would hear me. "Magistrate Kirkwood is behind this. Captain Gargrave and his men are working for him. They killed Consul Vanholt, and now they're trying to help sink the island."

Disbelief flashed in her eyes.

"It's true. Kirkwood cursed Eli's wand to block our dream-seeing. But we found out anyway and he captured us and brought us here to let the island kill us. How else would we even be on the island?"

The appeal to her logic seemed to work, and she grabbed my arm. "Run that way and find Sheriff Brackenberry. Tell him what you told me." She pointed to the other pyre in the distance. To Selene, Eli, and Paul she said, "You three stay here. We'll need your help." Without a word, I took off at a run, leaving my friends behind. By the time I reached Brackenberry, I was panting so hard I could barely breathe. He gaped at me, completely taken by surprise, but that didn't prevent him from listening as I relayed the story once more, whispering low. I kept glancing at the Will Guard as I spoke, afraid they would know what I was doing and attack.

Brackenberry's expression hardened. He didn't ask me any questions or express any doubt. His faith stunned me as he immediately turned to the deputies next to him and spoke some low instructions to them. The message slid down the line among his men.

"You want to get back," Brackenberry told me. I did, walking backward, too afraid to turn around. Out of the corner of my eye I saw the Will Guards starting to retreat as well. At first I thought it was in response to Brackenberry's men closing in on them, but then I realized the truth.

"It's going to blow!" I screamed.

I turned and started running. A second later a deafening noise rent the air as the ground split in half. The force of it flung me forward. I landed a dozen feet away, arms and face first. I blinked away the stars clouding my vision and struggled to my feet, afraid to turn around and see what was left and what wasn't.

Brackenberry and the nearest of his men had made it, but everyone on the other side of the bonfire had not. All that remained where they'd been was a deep fissure in the earth, like some kind of portal opening up into hell.

The Will Guard had made it as well, but Brackenberry and his men regained their focus quickly. A barrage of spells soared through the air at the three guards, taking them out in seconds. Then Brackenberry shouted at his men to stop the other Will Guard at the last bonfire—the last fail-safe that would keep the island afloat.

I ran with them, wanting to help. But by the time we arrived, the remaining Will Guard had been captured. I slowed down, hope returning at last. Surely, the destruction could be turned back and the damage undone.

As soon as she saw me, Lady Elaine waved me toward her. "Dusty!" Selene, Eli, and Paul were still with her.

I jogged over to her.

Lady Elaine grabbed me by the arms and gave me a shake. "You've got to go back to Senate Hall and climb to the top of the watchtower."

I didn't know what to say, certain for a moment that the pressure of the situation had addled her mind.

She scowled, understanding the look on my face perfectly. "We won't be able to stop the Telluric Rods from sinking the island. The best we can do is delay them long enough for most of us to evacuate."

I gulped. *Most of us.* How many wouldn't make it? I glanced at the pyre and the people surrounding it, holding the explosion at bay with their magic. The moment they stopped fighting it, the last rod would engage and the entire island would go down.

"But *you* can stop it, Dusty," Lady Elaine said. "You can save all of us and the island itself."

I rocked back on my heels. "What? How?"

Lady Elaine leaned toward me, piercing me with her gaze. "The sword. The *Will* sword is on top of the tower, and only you can use it."

"That can't be true," Selene said from my right. "It was supposed to be destroyed."

"It can't be destroyed." Lady Elaine shook her head. "But you can use it to absorb the power of the Telluric Rod and deflect it."

If The Will sword, Excalibur of legend, was still around, it could definitely do what she was saying. But . . . "Why me?"

"Your *dream*," Lady Elaine said through clenched teeth. "The one with the plinth and the tower."

My head spun so hard at this news I almost lost my balance. I turned my gaze toward Senate Hall and the watchtower perched so high above it. The plinth. The tower.

The *name*.

"It's known as Excalibur, although that's not its true name," my mom had told me once.

True name.

BELLANA

It wasn't the ghost of Marrow or Rosemary or Nimue. It was the true name of The Will sword. The name that would give me command over it.

But I didn't know the last letter.

And now, it really was too late.

~ 33 ~

The Naming

"Let's go." Selene grabbed my arm and started pulling me toward the hall. I didn't protest. I was too afraid to admit that I didn't know the sword's name, that I wouldn't be able to command it the way that Marrow had. But I had to try. This was our only chance.

"I'm coming, too," Eli said, falling in step beside us.

I glanced back at Paul, expecting him to say the same, but he looked ready to collapse.

"I won't be any help to you, Dusty."

I turned and touched his hand. "I understand. Do what you can here."

He nodded, swallowing. "I guess it's your turn to promise to stay alive."

I exhaled, my emotions threatening to choke me. "I will."

Then I turned away from him, hoping with all my heart that it was a promise I could keep.

I broke into a run, Eli and Selene keeping pace beside me. The going was hard as the ground continued to tremble beneath our feet, almost rocking back and forth as if the island were nothing but a massive ship in a turbulent sea.

But we made it eventually, at last climbing our way back through the rubble of the pavilion.

"Does anybody know how to get to the tower?" I said, scaling a huge boulder and jumping down on the other side.

Eli blasted a massive chunk of rock away from the nearest door. "There's a main staircase. That's our best bet as long as we can get through."

"We'll manage," Selene said as she squeezed through the door.

I followed after her with Eli coming behind me. Then he led the way to the staircase off to the left of the main doors into the meeting hall. A pile of debris obscured the entrance. I raised my hand, ready to blast it, but Eli stopped me.

"We can't do that in here. You might bring the whole place down."

"Then how do we get past?"

He pointed the talking stick, which already I was beginning to think of as his wand and he as a master magician. "Ana-acro." The top layer of debris rose into the air and then out of the entrance at Eli's command. In seconds, he'd cleared enough for us to crawl through.

"I've got to admit," Selene said as she watched Eli slide through the rubble and mount the stairs. "I'm impressed."

He shrugged. "I've been practicing a long time."

Despite all the destruction around us, I could sense Eli's underlying happiness at finally coming into his power. I just hoped we lived long enough for him to enjoy it.

The journey up the stairs became something close to mountain climbing. We used the hoist spell to clear a path where there was room, but too often we had to claw and scrape and shimmy our way through the wreckage.

By the time we reached the top, my knuckles were bleeding from dozens of nicks, and a thick layer of dust was plastered to every inch of me, outside and in, it seemed. I couldn't draw a full breath without coughing.

The door leading onto the lower roof of the hall wouldn't budge when we pushed against it, forcing us to blast it open with magic. A frightening rumble rose up the stairwell when we did, and we dashed out onto the roof. Right away, I slid to a stop before I tumbled through a hole.

"Everybody walk really easy up here," Eli said.

"No kidding." Selene brushed hair out of her face. It wasn't black anymore but gray with dust.

I bit my lip, my gaze fixed on the watchtower standing more than fifty feet away. An open staircase wrapped around the edge of it, but it looked intact. If I could just reach it.

I glanced at Selene and Eli. "You two stay here. There's no reason for all of us to risk walking over this floor."

Eli shook his head. "No way."

"Yeah, I'm with him." Selene pointed a thumb at Eli.

"But Lady Elaine said only *I* could use the sword. So I don't need you up there."

Eli scoffed. "You don't know that, Dusty. You have no idea what you might find. We're staying with you and that's final. Now stop wasting time."

He turned and started forward, leaving me no choice. We made it a few steps, but then a part of the roof dropped out right in between Eli and me. He jumped forward while I clambered back, both of us just barely avoiding a fall.

Selene grabbed my arm to steady me. "We need to spread out as much as we can to lighten the strain."

"Good idea," Eli said, and he moved off to the right. I stayed in the middle while Selene went left.

Crossing the floor soon became like a trip through the Gauntlet in gym class.

The next hole that opened up in front of me appeared faster than the first, but it was small enough so I jumped over it. Two steps later another hole appeared, this one four times the size of the last. I jumped it anyway, and halfway through the arc, I cast the gliding spell. Magic slid beneath my heels like ice, propelling me forward.

As I landed, a tremor went through the entire island itself, turning the tower into a giant funhouse floor. I staggered forward, fighting to stay upright.

To my left Selene cried out as her entire leg fell through a hole. Eli turned, pointed his wand, and shouted, "Ana-acro."

"Don't!" I screamed, but it was too late.

The spell reached Selene and hoisted her into the air, but only for a second before breaking. It didn't work properly on living flesh.

Selene tumbled, landing hard. I held back a scream as the roof beneath her began to collapse. I reached out with my mind-magic to hold the surface together long enough for her to roll forward, out of danger.

"I'm sorry, Selene," Eli shouted. "Are you okay?"

She made an indistinguishable noise that might've been relief or pain. But then she got to her feet. "I'm okay. Just . . . just don't do that again."

"Right. Never again." Eli wiped sweat from his brow with the back of his shirtsleeve.

We moved on, finally reaching the foot of the steps a short

while later. This time I led. All three of us understood that was the way it should be. As I climbed the first step, my heart thudded against my chest, not quickening, just beating harder as if to steady me for what lay ahead.

The going was easier than it had been on the roof, but far scarier. Every time the ground shook, I had to stop walking and press my back against the side of the tower, praying I didn't tumble over the edge or that the stairs didn't crumble away. It seemed we'd been at this for hours, but I knew it had only been minutes. We were high enough that I could see the entire inner island. Most of the bridges had been destroyed, and the fissures marked the island like giant pockmarks in the earth, still spewing forth rock and fire and water.

As we rounded the other side, climbing higher, I spotted the first hole in the stairs. It wasn't large, only about two feet. I jumped it easily, but the next one was larger by at least a foot. I reared back ready to go for it, but lost my nerve at the last second.

"I'll go first," Eli said. "Then I can help you from the other side." He squeezed past Selene and then me, his hand lingering on my arm for a moment. Then he leaped across, making it look effortless. Selene went next without needing help. Then I went, falling an inch short. My knees struck the edge, and I started to slide. Eli grabbed my wrists, catching me. Then he reared back and hauled me up. For a second as I regained my feet I thought I might pass out from the terror of it. But I shook it off, and we pressed on.

We didn't come across any more gaps as bad as that until we were almost at the very top. I came to a stop and stared out at the open space between me and the last of the staircase. It had to be fifteen feet at least—impossible to jump across. And none of us knew any spells that would get us over it.

I slumped against the wall, defeat overtaking me at last. I was too exhausted to cry. We'd come so close but could go no farther.

Behind me, I heard Eli swearing under his breath, but Selene moved past me, all the way to the edge. She stared at the gap, an odd expression on her face.

"Don't bother," I said, trying to keep the bitterness from my voice. "There's no way any of us can jump that."

"Dusty's right," Eli said. "The best we can do now is head down and try to get off the island before it sinks."

Selene didn't seem to have heard either of us. She stared at the gap a little longer and then tilted her head up, examining the sky.

I touched her shoulder. "What are you doing?"

Selene slowly turned around and faced me, her eyes ablaze with something like excitement. "I can do it."

I exhaled. "No you can't. That would be suicide."

She shook her head. "I can *fly* us across."

It slowly dawned on me—Selene was a siren, and sirens had *wings*. "But how?" I said. "You've never flown before. It was restricted by The Will." No magickind was permitted to fly. It was too easy for ordinaries to spot, too risky.

She nodded. "It *was* restricted by The Will, but not anymore. And I've been practicing, building up strength."

"You've been wh—" I broke off as the answer came to me.

"That's why I've been sneaking out at night," Selene said, knowing my thoughts. "Me and a couple of the other sirens have been teaching ourselves how to fly. It's been hard, and I can't do it for more than a couple of minutes, but I'm a lot better than I was."

It was incredible, and yet it all made sense—her need to be

out at night, to wear dark clothes, even her inexplicable fall into the bushes at Coleville. She hadn't been walking and stumbled at all.

"You've got to understand what it's like, Dusty," Selene went on. "All my life I've been denied this part of myself. It was wrong. So wrong. And when we were fighting Marrow and the Black Phoenix, I could've done so much more if my ability to fly hadn't been stunted. I swore after that night it would never happen again."

"Why are you apologizing?" I said. Selene stuttered, and I reached out and hugged her hard enough she gasped. "It's wonderful. And I'm so jealous and—"

Eli cleared his throat. "Can we save the girl moment for later? Like after we save the world? We're kind of in a hurry here."

Selene and I shared a grin.

"Right," I said. "How do we do this?"

"Hang on a second." Eli touched Selene's arm, drawing her attention. "Are you sure your wings can handle the extra weight?"

Selene exhaled. "No, but I *think* I can. For that short of a distance anyhow."

My heart plummeted into my knees. She didn't know, and if she was wrong, I would fall to my death.

Eli started to say something, but I shushed him, afraid he would insist that we not do it. That wasn't an option. Saving those people was worth the risk. I took Selene's hand and squeezed. "I believe you can do it."

Selene smiled. "Okay, stand back."

I pressed against the side of the tower and waited, my eyes fixed on my best friend. She spread her hands wide, and there was an odd ripping sound, though not of fabric. I watched with my mouth open as wings—as black and shiny as her hair—grew out from her back, narrow at first and then fanning out to their full size. I realized, almost belatedly, that the holes sewn into her jacket were there for this very purpose.

Once her wings were fully expanded, Selene waved me over to her. I did so, trying to keep my limbs from shaking. Her wings were enormous, but I knew that didn't mean they were strong enough to bear my weight. I did my best not to think about it.

"Stand in front of me," Selene said. "And help me hold on." She wrapped her arms beneath mine as I moved before her. "We'll be back, Eli." For a second, the confidence in her voice bolstered my own. But then she pushed me to the edge—and jumped.

We plummeted downward, Selene's wings arching high above us. I bit back a scream, certain this was it, that we would keep falling, at least until Selene let go of me to save herself. But then her wings swooped down hard, beating the air. A rush of wind lifted us up, and we soared forward. She didn't deposit me on the other side of the stairs as I'd expected, but let the momentum of that one stroke carry us all the way to the top of the tower.

The moment we reached it, her wings gave out, and we fell, hitting the stone hard. I sucked in a painful breath and rolled over, glad that Selene had landed to the side of me rather than on top.

Selene pushed herself up with the help of her wings. "You okay?"

"Yeah, I'm fine. But that landing needs work," I said getting to my feet.

She giggled, but my own humor—more of a statement of relief—vanished as I caught sight of the stone plinth set dead center of the tower.

My heart slammed against my breastbone as I stared at it. It looked exactly like the dream, and yet nothing like it at all.

There were no letters engraved on its side, and out of its top rose the hilt of The Will sword, its blade buried a foot deep in the stone of the plinth.

BELLANA

BELLANA

BELLANA

The name sounded over and over inside my head, but it was wrong, incomplete.

Even still, the same pull I felt toward the plinth in my dreams came over me now. Only I realized it had never been the plinth calling to me at all. It had been the sword. Always.

I walked toward it, each step heavy and hard as if some unseen force wanted to keep me from it. But it wouldn't work. That sword was meant for me, and I for it. I knew it as surely as I knew my own name, my own mind.

I stopped in front of it and placed both hands on the bone hilt.

Say my name, a voice that did not belong to my psyche spoke in my mind.

I don't know it.

Say my name.

I don't know it.

Yes, you do. You've always known.

BELLANA

I grabbed the hilt and pulled upward as hard as I could. It wouldn't move.

Say it!

I don't— The thought stopped in my head, giving way to a sudden vision of the dream. I saw the stone plinth again, saw the letters engraved on its surface. *All* the letters. The sword itself was showing it to me straight into my mind as artfully as the most gifted psychic.

BELLANAX

Bellanax.

The moment I thought it, the bone hilt began to warm in my hand. Then a bright light, a mixture of purple and gold, spread down from the hilt, over the runes, and into the stone plinth itself. A second later the stone cracked down the center, and the sword came free.

I held it up, struggling with its weight. But even as I watched, that golden, purplish light enveloped the sword, shrinking it, making it lighter, until the sword was the perfect weight and size for me, an extension of my arm rather than some magical object made of steel.

Bellanax. The true name of Excalibur, the sword of power.

And now it was mine.

Come on, Dusty."

Selene's voice barely registered in my mind. How long had I been standing here? It seemed a thousand years or more, as many years as the sword itself had known. It was ancient, the oldest thing I had ever touched.

Go, a voice said in my mind, and I obeyed, turning toward Selene. She eyed me with open worry, her gaze lingering on the blade. I ignored it and walked to the edge, clutching Bellanax with both hands. Selene stepped behind me and threaded her arms through mine. I couldn't hold on to her this time. But that was all right. With the sword of power in my grasp, we would be fine.

"I should be able to glide us all the way down to the roof," Selene said.

"Okay." I could see Eli below us, and I pointed at him and then down. He nodded and turned to begin his descent.

No fear touched me as Selene pushed me off the edge this time. We glided down as light as feathers, and I landed easily on my feet. I didn't hesitate but started making my way across the roof, leaping the holes effortlessly and with a grace I'd never known before. Somewhere in the far corner of my mind, I knew that I was no longer fully in control, that the sword, that *Bellanax*, had taken control, at least on a physical level. But that was all right. The sword was wise. The sword was powerful. It would see us through.

I was barely aware of the journey down the next set of stairs. Eli and Selene were somewhere behind me, moving much slower than I was. Soon I had reached the ruined pavilion. Then I was across it and running at full speed over the lawn toward the burning pyre in the distance. With the sword in my hand, I felt like I was flying.

But before I reached the pyre, a violent tremble shook the ground, and I stumbled. By the time I regained my footing, the first split had appeared in the earth's surface. Screams broke out as the people standing near the pyre began to flee. The fissure was growing, spreading like a wound. The sight of it terrified me to my core, but fear didn't touch me, not really. All thought fled my mind as instinct took over, and I sped up.

Before me, the fissure was an open, gaping mouth, spewing out flames. I didn't slow, not even for a second. I kept running, and when I reached the edge—I jumped.

The fire enveloped me, flames licking along my skin, leaving behind a trail of pain. But only for a moment. Then something rose up around me, protecting me from the fire. *Magic.* Magic like I'd never known before.

Holding my eyes closed, I fell blind. Something other than gravity pulled me down. It was as if the sword in my hands was drawn to the power flooding out of the Telluric Rod like a magnet of opposite charge. Energy flooded through me, setting my entire body afire. It was coming through my hands from the sword. I needed to let go before it burned me up, but I couldn't. I had to hold on to save those people, to save the island.

So I gripped harder, holding on even as my consciousness slipped away, even as I felt myself dying.

～ 34 ～

The Passing

I dreamed of the tower again. But there was no wind and no plinth. There was only the sword in my hand. It radiated heat like something alive. And I knew on some level it was alive.

Eli was there, on the other side of the tower, watching me with a wary gaze. I beckoned him to me, but he shook his head. "Not while you've got that."

I glanced at the sword, not even aware that I had been holding it in front of me, pointed at Eli. He was afraid. Why was he afraid?

I turned and set the sword on the edge of the tower. The moment it was out of my reach my hand felt empty, my body cold from the inside out. I almost picked it up again, but then Eli was there, wrapping his arms around me.

I gasped, amazed that he could touch me here. "Aren't we dreaming?"

"Yes, but it's your dream, and I'm not really here. You know that, right?"

I nodded.

"And you must wake up, Dusty. You must wake up soon or . . . or you might never wake up."

"What do you mean?"

But Eli didn't answer. He turned to ash in my arms and then disappeared on the wind.

Time passed. I could *feel* it passing around and over me, as if I were a stone set in its river. Eli did not visit my dream again.

Has she said anything?"

"*Not this morning. Not since yesterday.*"

"*Any movement?*"

"*A little. But not enough. Never enough.*"

The voices were familiar, but they were so distorted I couldn't place them. It was as if I were listening to them underwater. *Water,* I remembered the water. A vision of being surrounded by merkind appeared in my mind. I'd fallen—all the way through the earth into the sea. And I would've drowned if not for their help. They'd carried me through the water and then onto dry land.

"*What will happen if she never wakes?*"

I tried to breast the surface of consciousness, but it was too far. And I slipped down, down, down, under again.

~ 35 ~

Aftermath

When I finally did wake, I found myself alone. The room was a familiar one, the bed large and luxurious with a black and white satin comforter. White sheer curtains hung from the single window. Various paintings decorated the blue-gray walls, one depicting a sunset, another an ancient ship caught in a storm.

I knew this place. This was the spare bedroom in my mother's house on Waterfront Lane. Framed pictures of me lined the top of the chest of drawers in one corner. There were too many to count—my whole life captured in still, single moments.

All of this I had taken in without sitting up, and I slowly became aware of how heavy and sluggish my limbs felt, as if they hadn't been used in a long time. I slowly pushed back the bedclothes. When I did, I saw I wasn't as alone as I'd thought. A sword lay in the bed beside me. The blade was sheathed in a leather scabbard, but I recognized the bone hilt.

Bellanax.

At once everything came back to me with startling clarity. The way I had jumped into that burning fissure. The way the sword had known what to do on its own, absorbing the power of the Telluric Rod as it had just begun to explode. It had pulled that power into itself, and then channeled it outward, breaking the spell before it could complete.

And when it ended I had fallen all the way through the hole and into a channel that led me out to sea. The merkind had rescued me, but I couldn't remember anything after that.

Gritting my teeth, I sat up, muscles protesting the movement. The action left me panting and weak as I slumped against the headboard. I was wearing a pair of silk pajamas, the kind with a long-sleeved, button-down front and pants. I ran my hand over my stomach, alarmed at how easily I felt my ribs, my belly a sunken, hollow cave between my hip bones. The sight of my body in such a condition set my head to pounding with fright. How long had I been unconscious?

I peered at the closed door into the bedroom, wishing it would open. I didn't actively engage my mind-magic. I knew I didn't have the energy for it. But after several minutes of this, I gave up the hope, and swung my legs over the side of the bed. The movement was easier, my muscles warming up, but still it left me panting and exhausted.

I slowly slid off the bed and stood, testing my balance. Wobbly, but okay. I glanced at the sword and debated picking it up. I *wanted* it with me, and yet I didn't. It filled me with both awe and terror like a wild beast I wanted to tame but was too afraid to approach.

Turning my back on the sword, I crossed the room to the door. I leaned against it for a moment, catching my breath, and then I pushed it open. I walked down the dim, empty hallway with one arm braced against the wall for support. When I reached the end of it, I looked around the corner and spotted my mother standing in the kitchen across the way, only her head and torso visible over the divider into the living room.

Before I could call out to her, she turned and spotted me. The glass in her fingers slipped and crashed to the floor. She didn't care as she dashed through the kitchen toward me.

"Dusty," she said, pulling me into a hug. I sagged against her, grateful for the support. Mom pushed me back. "You shouldn't be up." She hugged me again. "But I'm so glad you're awake. So, so glad."

The relief in her voice made me feel like crying.

Finally, Mom's grip on me loosened. "I need to call the doctor, let them know you're awake. You go back to bed."

I shook my head. The last thing I wanted was to lie down again. Bright light was streaming in through the back porch window, and I pointed at it. "I want to sit out there."

Moira glanced behind her, debating for a moment. Then she sighed. "All right. For a little while." She ran a hand over my hair tied in a loose braid. "Goodness knows you could use some sun."

A few moments later, I was settled down in a wicker chair on the back porch, staring out at the calm waters of Lake Erie. Despite the warmth of the day, Mom brought me a blanket and wrapped it around my legs. Then she brought me tea and insisted I drink it.

"The doctor should be here soon," my mother said, taking the seat opposite mine.

I took a long drink of the tea, surprised to find I didn't hate it. Finally, I cleared my throat and said, "Is everyone okay? Did the island stay afloat?"

Mom sighed and crossed one leg over the other. "Yes and yes. What you did . . . it was amazing, although if you ever do something so dangerous again, I'll ground you for life."

I smiled, a part of me fully aware that she wasn't joking.

"What do you remember?" Moira said.

I took another sip of tea and then gave her the best summary I could. It was hard talking about it, but only because I was tired and my throat sore from lack of use. "So what happened after the merkind saved me?" I asked when I came to the end of it.

"We took you to Vejovis. You were there a few days while the doctors treated your injuries. There were surprisingly few. Some burns on your arms and legs, mostly healed now and with very little scarring."

I frowned and pulled up my shirtsleeve. The skin there was bright pink, like a newborn baby's. I exhaled in relief. I'd gotten even luckier than I realized. But then I remembered that force that had wrapped around me as I fell—perhaps it wasn't luck at all, but the sword.

"How long have I been unconscious?"

My mother swallowed, and her eyes looked wet. "Ten days."

I sucked in a breath. That long? How was it possible? No wonder she was so relieved to see me up and about.

Mom turned her gaze toward the water. "The doctors worried you might not wake at all. I'm so glad you proved them wrong."

"Me too."

Mom turned back to me, smiling.

"But why am I here?" I motioned to her apartment.

"After that first week, the doctors said there was nothing left to do but wait and see. So I brought you here where I could keep a better eye on you. It's also made it easier for your dad to visit. There are so many restrictions on ordinaries visiting Vejovis."

I sat up. "Dad's been here?"

"Everyone's been here, Dusty. Eli and Selene have come by every day. Even half of the Magi Senate has come to visit you."

I blinked, the mention of the Magi Senate setting my mind to racing. "What about Magistrate Kirkwood? Did they stop him?"

"Oh, yes." A dark look crossed Moira's face. "They arrested him and Gargrave while they were still on Lyonshold. They were on the outer island, along with some of the other senators. Titus pretended to be innocent of everything until he spotted Brackenberry's men coming after him. Then he and Gargrave tried to flee, but they didn't get very far."

For the first time since I'd woken up, I felt good, happy even. I smiled. "Did Brackenberry haul them off to jail?"

Moira stood up. "I think I hear the doctor."

I frowned. "I didn't hear anything."

"I'll be back in a bit." She turned and headed for the door.

"Wait, Mom." I knew instinctively that she was avoiding the question. "What are you not telling me?"

Mom faced me, folding her arms across her chest. "I don't want you to worry about it. Right now all you should be thinking about is getting better."

I glared. "Don't you dare try and do that. I have a right to know what happened."

I could see the debate raging in my mother's expression. Finally, she sighed and came back to her chair. "Gargrave is in jail along with his men."

"And Kirkwood?"

Moira's nostrils flared as she answered. "Titus Kirkwood is dead. He was murdered inside his cell in the jailhouse. And no, they don't know who did it or why, but it's a Magi concern. Not yours or Eli's or Selene's. No matter what you all might think."

I would've laughed if the news hadn't been so terrible. It seemed the Dream Team had been carrying on without me. A sudden powerful desire to see my friends came over me. "Can I use the phone? I want to tell them I'm awake."

Moira looked away from me, her expression impatient again. "I'll do it for you. But no visitors until the doctor clears you. I don't care if Eli and Selene try to break down the door. Understood?"

"Understood."

"Good. Now sit out here and relax while I make you something to eat."

The idea of my mother's cooking filled me with a whole different kind of dread, but as she disappeared inside the house, I did as she asked, resting my head against the back of the chair. I was asleep again in moments.

The next time I woke it was to the sight of a doctor standing over me. The woman seemed nice enough, although her fingers felt like icicles when she had me raise my shirt so she could check my heart rate and breathing. Twenty minutes later she gave me a clean bill of health and a regimen of lots of bed rest and food for the next two weeks, and only approved visitors.

I shot a look at my mom as soon as the doctor had left.

She rolled her eyes. "I told Selene that she and Eli couldn't come over until tomorrow at the earliest. They'll be here as soon as school's out for the day."

I sat up straighter, suddenly remembering my educational duties. "Crap, I have exams coming up."

Mom waved. "Don't get excited. With everything that's happened, you're being given a pass in all your classes with the Magi

Senate's approval. It's the least they could do. I expect sooner or later they'll bestow some award on you, once things have settled down."

I didn't understand at first, but then I remembered Consul Vanholt lying dead among the ruins of the pavilion. No wonder things needed settling down.

"What about Paul? You haven't mentioned him. Is he okay?"

Moira sighed. "He's fine. He's just . . . unavailable. He's been placed in protective custody for his own safety. Word about his uncle has spread despite efforts to contain it. Brackenberry feared Paul might be in danger of retribution. The attack on Lyonshold was the biggest in the island's history. Seventy-two magickind dead."

I swallowed, my throat and eyes burning. So many lives lost. How many were my schoolmates? Even knowing that there could've been a lot more didn't make me feel any better. And poor Paul. It was so unfair. He'd escaped the threat of his uncle only to be put under this new threat.

But maybe there was a light at the end of the tunnel. "And what about my cell phone? Were they able to identify Marrow's supporters?"

Moira huffed, clearly not wanting to talk about it any longer, but I held her with my gaze, insisting she go on. "By the time they caught up with Magistrate Kirkwood the cell phone had been destroyed."

"But that doesn't make sense. Why would he destroy it?"

"He didn't. It was some kind of self-destruct mechanism."

All the air whooshed out of my lungs, making my head spin. *He lied.* Paul had lied. After all of that. Only . . . the pass code had worked. I'd seen it with my own eyes. But then I remembered how he had wanted to make sure the app was hidden again when he first showed us it inside the Kirkwood mauso-leum. Maybe the app had to be shut down properly or it would self-destruct, just another one of Paul's insurance methods.

With an effort I pushed thoughts of Paul from my mind. Maybe there was an explanation for what had happened to the data and maybe not. Either way, it didn't matter now. The list of Marrow supporters was gone.

True to their word, Selene and Eli arrived the next day, both of them eager to see me. Selene hugged me so hard, I didn't breathe for a full twenty seconds.

"I'm so glad you're awake. And if you ever go unconscious for that long again, I'll never forgive you."

Eli hugged me next, far more gently than Selene had. His touch was tender and intimate, full of the longing that still ex-isted between us. But no sooner had he wrapped his arms around me than he pulled away. We were in the living room, and he walked to the farthest sofa and sat down.

I looked at him, sadness squeezing my chest. Nothing had changed. He still believed in the dream-seer curse. I'd known better than to hope things would be different, but it still hurt.

Thank goodness for Selene—she managed to draw my at-tention away from Eli with talk about school and all the things I had missed. She and Eli had attempted to learn more about Titus Kirkwood's death, but they hadn't gotten very far. "But the most surprising thing that's happened," Selene said, "is that Miss Norton gave Eli her talking stick."

"What?" I craned my head at him, noticing the bracelet on his wrist for the first time.

Eli rubbed a thumb over the smooth leather. "Yeah, she says

the wand has formed some kind of connection to me. I guess the magic in it has been mostly dormant for a long time, which is why she used it the way she did in class. But for some reason it's started working again. For me." A slight color rose up in his cheeks. If possible, it made him even more handsome. "But personally I just think she feels guilty about the part her precious Terra Tribe played in the disaster at Lyonshold."

Selene snorted. "I think it's probably a little of both."

I smiled halfheartedly as my thoughts drifted to the sword sitting on the dresser in the spare room. Eli's situation with the wand made me wonder about my own with Bellanax. Had it chosen me? It certainly felt that way.

I glanced at Selene who was watching me with open concern. I pushed hair out of my face. "So speaking of the Terra Tribe, who all—" I paused, swallowing. "Who all made it?"

Eli and Selene both shifted in their seats, neither wanting to go first.

At last Selene drew a heavy breath. "More than you would've expected, mostly thanks to the ritual itself. I guess after they lit the bonfire, they were supposed to walk to the nearest natural water source and extinguish the flames. Melanie was the only one who didn't make it."

I stopped breathing, a terrible pressure wrapped around my entire body. Melanie Remillard was dead? I remembered all too well how we'd fought the last time I'd seen her. And now I would never see her again. I would never have the chance to right that wrong. Tears stung my eyes and I couldn't hold them back this time.

"Who else?" I said, wiping the dampness from my cheeks.

Eli sighed. "Nobody we knew, a couple of seniors and a

freshman. Nine students in all. They're holding a memorial service for them next week at Arkwell before exams start."

Selene nodded, then added in a lighter tone, "Lance is back. They finally broke the curse. Britney's back, too. She's doing so much better. She's still on crutches, but in her mermaid form she's fully recovered, apparently."

"That's great," I said, welcoming any happy news at this point.

"Britney filled in a couple of the blank spots for us," Selene said. "Like how she ended up under Kirkwood's thumb. It seems her mother is a head scientist in a senate-run environmental research lab at Lyonshold. Britney works in the lab with her mom on weekends and stuff. Magistrate Kirkwood was one of the government overseers for the lab, so he'd met Britney a number of times."

Titus Kirkwood had been a horrible man, no doubt, but I could easily picture him being charming and friendly when he wanted to be—a lot like Paul. I bet Titus had an easy time first befriending her. Then later, he'd turned vicious, forcing her to do his vile deeds.

I didn't bother asking if Britney had said what Kirkwood had on her mother to make her do what she did. I knew she hadn't. Britney had been willing to curse and kill to protect her mother. I doubted she would give up that secret now.

I didn't blame her. I would do the same to protect my mother. For some reason the thought made me feel like crying again.

"You okay, Dusty?" Selene said, bringing my attention back to the present.

I nodded. "Just tired still."

She wrinkled her nose. "I don't see how someone who's been asleep as long as you have could still be tired." A smile broke across her face, and she winked. "I'm just kidding. What you did . . . well . . . it was incredible."

I blushed. It didn't feel incredible. It felt like something someone else had done. Once again questions about the sword crowded into my mind. I'd picked it up and held it a hundred times the last two days. And each time I felt that presence. Felt Bellanax. But it seemed less strong than it had on top of the tower. Dormant, perhaps, like Eli's wand had been. Even still, I couldn't forget the way it had seemed to take control of me. Could it do it again? And how far did that control reach? It had already made me jump into a fiery pit.

I shivered and then tried to cover it up with a yawn.

Selene came over and hugged me again. "You get some more sleep. We'll be back tomorrow."

"Yeah," said Eli. "Tomorrow." He stood and turned toward the door, but then he changed his mind and came over to give me a farewell hug. It lasted longer than the first, if only by a couple of seconds. But that was okay. I would take it.

With the way things were changing for the worse around here, I would cling to any good thing I could get.

~ 36 ~

Partings

The following Friday my mom and I climbed into her sports car and headed to an awards ceremony that the Magi Senate was holding to honor Eli, Selene, and me. I didn't want to go, but I was glad it was being held in Vatticut Hall at Arkwell—I'd found myself missing the school these last few weeks. Senate Hall, where such an event normally would've taken place, was a long way from being restored.

The ceremony lasted less than an hour while the newly elected consul, Lisbeth Borgman, formally the darkkind magistrate, gave a speech about the great service we had performed and then presented us each with medals. Selene and Eli received silver lion medals while I received a gold medal emblazoned with a phoenix. The irony of this was not lost on me. Apparently, the phoenix medal was the equivalent of the Medal of Freedom given out by the president of the United States. But all I could think about was Marrow and his black phoenix.

Afterward, there was a small party with drinks and appetizers. Nearly everyone came up to shake my hand and express their gratitude. Within minutes I felt completely overwhelmed and ready to leave. But at least there were a couple of familiar faces, including Sheriff Brackenberry, Lady Elaine, and most of my teachers, of course. I even spotted Mr. Corvus, but I paid him no mind. Eli had put my suspicions about him to rest a few days before.

He had confronted Corvus about the three-ringed symbol in the ancient text and the one in *The Atlantean Chronicle* as well as the stuff in the notebook. Corvus claimed it was a common symbol for unity and the notebook merely a translation of the ancient text. He was a historian, after all. Eli had confirmed the symbol with a bit of research. Its presence in both books was, for once, genuine coincidence.

Sometime later, Lady Elaine asked me for a private word and we headed out to the commons. It was dark, but the full moon overhead made it easy to see.

"How are you adjusting to the sword?" Lady Elaine asked.

At the mention of Bellanax, my hand automatically went to the thick silver band around my left wrist. The day before my mother had walked me through applying the glamour to the sword, the same as I would've to a wand or staff.

"Fine, I guess." I raised my arm. "It's a bit heavy."

Lady Elaine pursed her lips. "I'm sure it is."

"What is the sword, exactly?" I said, all the questions that had been lingering in my mind these last few days coming to the surface again.

"On its most basic level, it's what we call a numen vessel. It contains the ghost of some long-dead magickind."

I shivered, even though her words came as no surprise, given all I'd learned from Deverell. "Is Eli's wand a numen vessel, too?"

Lady Elaine smoothed the front of her black cocktail dress. "Yes. There's a long history of numen vessels bonding with one magickind. The spirits that inhabit them can be very particular about who they want as master."

I turned and sat down on the low stone wall nearby. My energy level still wasn't back to normal. "But this sword belonged to Marrow last. Should I be worried?"

"No, the sword is yours, and will do only your bidding." Lady Elaine sat down on the wall across from me.

I ran my fingers along the silver band, which always warmed to my touch. "But it's so powerful. This was The Will sword. Won't there be people who'll want to take it from me?"

"Only a few of us even know you have it. I suggest you keep it that way. And it's a sword, so I doubt you'll have much reason to go flashing it around."

I snorted, picturing myself standing on a table in the cafeteria as I did my best Xena Warrior Princess impression. "But why didn't the senate just destroy it?"

"Oh, they tried, but nothing worked." She grimaced. "So we bound it to the stone plinth with a spell that only the sword's true master could break."

I crossed my arms over my chest. "But that could've been Marrow. It *should've* been him."

Lady Elaine shook her head. "We don't know much about sword lore in particular, but we do know that physical death breaks the numen bond. Even if the person will be reborn."

I exhaled. "So I'm stuck with this thing until I die?"

"One can only hope." She crossed a leg over the other then said in a gentle voice. "And if you want the truth, I'm relieved it came to you."

I tilted my head. "Why?"

"Because I can think of no one better to have it. There's no denying that it's very powerful and that power can corrupt. But I think you won't be so susceptible."

"Why not?"

"Lots of reasons. Partly because you have such a good heritage. The women in your line have a long history of standing against evil, and sacrificing everything to ensure goodness prevails." A wry smile crossed her face. "I'll admit your mother's methods are a bit unorthodox, but her heart is always in the right place. And look at Nimue. She willingly imprisoned herself in a dream for hundreds of years just to keep the sword hidden from Marrow."

I rubbed my temple. It was a lot to live up to. The band on my wrist felt heavier than ever. "But wouldn't it have been better if Nimue had found a way to kill Marrow and keep him from resurrecting? I mean, *is* there a way?"

Lady Elaine considered the question a moment. "Yes, I imagine there must be some way, but we have a more pressing topic to talk about." I braced myself, guessing what was coming next.

"Eli told me that you know about the dream-seer curse."

I nodded, unable to speak.

"And do you believe him?"

I met her sharp gaze, managing not to flinch. "I don't believe he was lying, if that's what you mean. But that's not the same thing as whether or not I believe in the curse."

Lady Elaine's sigh barely reached my ears. "The curse is very real, Dusty. I can share with you my vision if you would like."

I shook my head, not tempted by her offer even for a second.

"Very well." She stood. "Nevertheless, you should know that we are taking steps to ensure that you two keep an appropriate distance."

Anger heated my face, and I stood up, too. "Oh, I'm aware of it. My mom told me this morning that she booked us on a summer-long tour of Europe." We'd argued about it for nearly an hour, and each time I'd asked if it was because of Eli she'd changed the subject.

"It's for your own good, Dusty." Lady Elaine exhaled. "What reason would I have to lie about this? Do you think I'm a cruel, heartless person out to deny two teenagers the pleasure of true love?"

I wanted to say yes, but I didn't. I knew she wasn't trying to keep us apart because she wanted to. I took a deep breath, struggling to keep the waver out of my voice. "If there's a way to kill Marrow once and forever, then there must be a way to break the dream-seer curse, too."

Lady Elaine's pitying look hit me like a slap. "It doesn't work like that. All magic has a price. Even dream-seeing. And this is it. You and Eli can *never* be together."

I didn't say anything, but turned and walked away, silent tears wetting my cheeks.

All magic has a price.

I knew she was right, but it was a price I didn't want to pay.

The following Sunday my mom and I drove to the airport. I still didn't want to go, but I knew when I was beaten. I was going whether I liked it or not. And it was a trip to Europe. I'd find a way to make the most of it in the end.

A group of people large enough to be called a crowd had come to see us off. Selene was there, of course, along with Lance. They'd been spending lots of time together since his return from Vejovis. Their rekindled relationship didn't exactly fill me with joy, but I figured if Selene liked him then I would make the effort to accept him as well. So far Selene was making it easy as she continued to poke fun at him the same as always, although with definite affection underlying her tone these days.

"Sorry about bringing him along," Selene said, pointing a thumb at Lance and suppressing a smile. "But he insisted."

Lance grinned at me. "Just wanted to say see you and don't hurry back."

Selene stomped on his toe.

"Ouch." He winked at her. "I was just kidding." He thumped me on the shoulder. "Seriously, have a safe trip, and make sure you make it back. I might get bored without our little competition to keep me entertained."

I smirked. "That might be reason enough for me to stay away forever." He only grinned wider. I rolled my eyes at him, and then turned and hugged Selene. "See you soon. Write me lots, okay? I want to hear about your flying practices and stuff."

Selene laughed. "I'll write you entire novels about it. And you better write, too, and send me lots of pictures."

"I will." I pulled back from her and moved on. Lady Elaine stood next to her, and we exchanged a quick and cordial goodbye.

"Be sure to let your mother know if there's anything strange with this." She touched the silver band on my wrist.

I nodded, pulling my wrist away from her instinctively.

Then I walked on, coming to a stop in front of Sheriff Brackenberry. I hadn't expected him to be here at all, but he explained his presence right away.

"Thought you might want this." He handed me a slip of paper.

I opened it and saw an unfamiliar e-mail address. I looked up at the sheriff, waiting for an explanation.

"Don't lose it, and don't share it," Brackenberry said. "But

I'm sure he'd like to hear from you even if he's not allowed to write back."

I swallowed as understanding dawned inside of me. He was talking about Paul. I refolded the paper and slid it into the front pocket of my jeans.

I hugged my dad good-bye next. He kissed me on the top of the head. "I sent your mother an entire list of all the historical sites you *must* visit while you're there. Make sure she follows it."

I smiled at the fierce expression on his freckled face. It would've been more effective minus the glasses and the tweed jacket with patches on the sleeves. There was nothing very frightening about a geeky college professor.

I reached out, and ruffled his hair. "You need a haircut."

He smiled. "So do you."

Then he kissed my head again, and I moved on to the last person in line.

The sight of Eli standing there, waiting to say good-bye to me, made my muscles feel weak. I stopped in front of him, unsure of what to do or say.

"Well, have a good trip," he said. He had his hands buried in his front pockets, making it clear that he had no intention of hugging me good-bye.

I gulped, fighting to keep my voice level. "Thanks. And you have a good summer."

"I will."

I knew I should move on, but I couldn't make my feet move.

"We need to board soon," my mother called from where she stood near the security gate.

I nodded at her, then looked back at Eli. "See you," I said. I turned and started walking toward my mother.

"Dusty," Eli called, that familiar desperate longing in his voice.

The sound of it went right through me, and I slid the strap of my carry-on off my shoulder and let it fall to the ground. Then I spun around and came back to Eli, moving fast before I lost my nerve. I put my hands on the side of his head, even as his slid around my waist. Then I kissed him. Right there in full view of my mother and Lady Elaine. Everyone. I kissed him like it was the last time I ever would. And he kissed me, too, holding me as if he feared I would vanish any second.

Finally, Eli pulled away but only far enough to whisper in my ear, "I'll be here when you get back."

"I'll hurry."

Then I turned and headed toward the security gate, my heart both heavy with the knowledge of the long weeks ahead, but also light with the surety of what waited when I returned.